WHEN I
PICTURE YOU

WHEN I PICTURE YOU

A Novel

Sasha Laurens

AVON
An Imprint of HarperCollins*Publishers*

Without limiting the exclusive rights of any author, contributor or the publisher of this publication, any unauthorized use of this publication to train generative artificial intelligence (AI) technologies is expressly prohibited. HarperCollins also exercise their rights under Article 4(3) of the Digital Single Market Directive 2019/790 and expressly reserve this publication from the text and data mining exception.

This is a work of fiction. Names, characters, places, and incidents are products of the author's imagination or are used fictitiously and are not to be construed as real. Any resemblance to actual events, locales, organizations, or persons, living or dead, is entirely coincidental.

WHEN I PICTURE YOU. Copyright © 2025 by Sasha Laurens. All rights reserved. Printed in the United States of America. No part of this book may be used or reproduced in any manner whatsoever without written permission except in the case of brief quotations embodied in critical articles and reviews. For information, address HarperCollins Publishers, 195 Broadway, New York, NY 10007. In Europe, HarperCollins Publishers, Macken House, 39/40 Mayor Street Upper, Dublin 1, D01 C9W8, Ireland.

HarperCollins books may be purchased for educational, business, or sales promotional use. For information, please email the Special Markets Department at SPsales@harpercollins.com.

Avon, Avon & logo, and Avon Books & logo are registered trademarks of HarperCollins Publishers in the United States of America and other countries.

hc.com

FIRST EDITION

Designed by Diahann Sturge-Campbell

Pride flag © santima.studio/Stock.Adobe.com

Library of Congress Cataloging-in-Publication Data has been applied for.

ISBN 978-0-06-342911-6

25 26 27 28 29 LBC 5 4 3 2 1

For Alissa

WHEN I PICTURE YOU

1

Renee Feldman was not having a good day, and it was barely 3 p.m. She'd overslept and shown up late to open Prince's Coffee, arriving to a gang of impatient early-morning regulars. Then the ice machine went on the fritz—exactly what Renee did not need on this steaming hot July day. She'd done two emergency ice runs to the gas station and come back soaked in sweat, forty pounds of ice dribbling on the floor.

Renee scanned the afternoon crowd as she weighed grounds for cold brew. Prince's had been a major hangout when she was in high school and needed to get out of her house. It was still strange to be behind the counter at twenty-seven, even after nine months there. When she moved back to Fellows, Michigan, from New York City, she'd hoped to find work that made use of her nearly complete MFA in film. She'd applied with every videographer in three counties. The one company that gave her a chance hadn't sent her anything after her edit of a Sweet Sixteen party. It didn't feel fun, they'd said, but Renee hadn't been going for *fun*. She'd been going for *real*, and the birthday girl's parents had fought right in front of her camera. She'd taken the job at Prince's as a stopgap, but now it was her main gig.

Outside Prince's big front window, a pair of teenage girls squealed.

Here we go, Renee thought. The girls were taking selfies, which meant Renee had maximum five minutes before they disturbed the peace inside.

The girls barreled into the coffee shop. One was tall with sharp elbows and shoulders; the other, shorter, had curly hair and a smattering of acne. They both wore the exalted look of pilgrims to a sacred site. The shorter one clutched her phone to her heart, while the taller one filmed her clutching her phone to her heart.

Renee really hoped they wouldn't cry. Girls like this sometimes did.

"Did you know that—there's, like—" The taller girl stumbled over her words.

Her friend took over. "There's this song, by Lola Gray—"

"We really, *really* love her!"

The shorter girl continued, "And she wrote a song, 'My Ever-After,' and she, like, mentions this place?"

The pair waited for Renee's reaction with their jaws slack.

"This is the place from that song," Renee admitted.

At Renee's confirmation, the girls practically began levitating in their white Air Force 1s.

The taller one asked, "Does Lola ever, like . . . come in here?"

Renee shook her head. "Lola Gray probably lives nowhere near here."

"She lives in L.A. Hollywood Hills," the girl corrected, as if it were normal to know where a total stranger lived.

"But, like, has Lola come here *recently*?" the shorter girl pressed.

"Why would she have come here *recently*?"

The girls had a silent conversation using a rapid-fire series of micro-expressions.

"We heard that she's here this weekend because her sister is getting married, and we thought . . ."

Renee gave in. "And you thought she'd get coffee where some boy once promised her a happily ever after?"

The taller girl gasped. "You *do* know the song!"

"We get fans like you all the time," Renee said with an eye roll. "The picture over there is as close as you're getting to Lola Gray." Renee pointed to a sun-bleached photo near the door, of Prince's owner with a fine-boned young woman with tan skin, big eyes, and a cascade of chocolate-brown hair. She was clutching a copy of her first CD and smiling so widely that you could have conducted a full dental exam based on the photo alone. "If you want to hang out here, you need to order something."

Renee had just finished making the girls' iced strawberry matcha lattes when Kadijah walked in. Their long black braids were tied back and the deep brown of their shoulders glistened with sweat under their halter top. In their hands: much-needed bags of ice.

"Kadijah to the rescue!" Kadijah said brightly as they heaved the ice onto the counter.

Renee slid open the freezer, ripped open a bag of ice, and dumped it inside. "Just in time."

Kadijah cocked their head at the girls, who were taking selfies with the picture of Lola.

"More Lo-Lites?" Kadijah said, using the name Lola Gray fans had coined for themselves.

Renee rolled her eyes. "Coming out of the woodwork for the wedding."

"Did you tell them?"

Renee's face puckered, but she didn't dignify the question with an answer.

"They would freak if they knew you were going," Kadijah said. "*I'm* freaking and I'm just a regular adult Lola Gray fan. I'm still mad you didn't get me a plus-one."

"Plus-ones are for dates, not coworkers, even your *favorite* coworker." Kadijah was the hottest polyamorous non-binary person in a twenty-five-mile radius, but Kadijah and Renee were strictly close friends. "I'd rather be there with you than with my mom and her boyfriend. Weddings are just a load of performative sexist traditions, like your father giving you away to another man, or—"

Kadijah cut her off with a dead-eyed stare. "Renee Feldman, you are not going to weaponize feminism to distract me from the fact that you are going to chill with *Lola Gray*. Tonight. Without me."

Renee held her finger to her lips and shot a glance at the Lo-Lites. "I am not going to chill with her. It's been like ten years since we last talked, and even before that, we haven't been friends since eighth grade. She probably doesn't even remember me."

"You *grew up next door to her*," Kadijah said, as if Renee weren't perfectly aware of that fact. "Of course she remembers you."

"Even if she does, it's her sister's wedding. She'll be busy."

Kadijah sighed dramatically. "It's just tragic that you're getting a private concert from Lola Gray when I, an actual fan, have never seen her live. Her last tour sold out in minutes."

"Lola's not performing. I know I'm repeating myself, but *it's her sister's wedding*."

"Exactly! She's going to sing for their first dance. You *have* to Face-Time me." Kadijah swatted at Renee with a rag. "Don't give me that look, Miss *I've Never Been a Fan of Anything*. Lola's the greatest pop star of our generation."

"I don't pay attention to that stuff," Renee said.

"I need you to stop saying things like that if we're going to stay friends. I've been following Lola since *You're Next!* I begged my mom to let me vote for her."

"I barely remember that," said Renee, who remembered it vividly. Lola's run-up to second place on the talent competition show had been all anyone in Fellows could talk about their junior year. Kadijah, who'd still been a middle schooler in Dearborn, had missed the frenzy. "I have better things to do than keep track of Lola's career."

Sure, Lola was a chart-topping recording star who wrote all her own songs. She'd won the Grammy for Best New Artist at eighteen, then been nominated for every album since. *Rolling Stone* had first dubbed her "The Patron Saint of Teenage Girls" and, when her later albums proved she had staying power, elevated her title to "The New Princess of Pop."

In the same twenty-seven years on planet Earth, Renee had only managed to earn a BA from Kalamazoo College and admission to a documentary film MFA program (after a rejection the year before). She was hoping to add the MFA itself to that list, but she'd taken a leave of absence just shy of her thesis project, during which she'd moved back in with her mom. If you stacked up the achievements of the former neighbors against each other, the scales tipped slightly in Lola's favor.

Not that it mattered, because Lola had probably forgotten Renee existed.

Renee slipped her apron over her head and grabbed her tote bag.

"I'll take opening shifts for a week if you promise to tell me everything about tonight!" Kadijah called after her, but Renee was already out the door.

Two hours later, Renee sat in her car outside a brick building that had once operated as a bottle factory, and now operated as a wedding venue called the Bottle Factory. Heat radiated off the asphalt of the parking lot. Under the hot, wet blanket of humidity, everything felt too bright and fuzzed out. Renee could visualize how she'd capture it on film: a touch of overexposure to convey the heat, the pair of men smoking at the edge of the frame, the focus on the older woman in a sequined dress fanning herself on the steps. Maybe she could make her thesis documentary about how wedding venues served as liminal spaces, constructed to create the illusion that love stories were real.

What an insipid concept, the critical voice in her head muttered. Asinine. Plebeian. Anemic. The primary thing Renee had learned in film school was a new vocabulary of fancy insults. Not only did she now know what those words meant, she applied them to herself regularly.

Renee remembered the girls she'd seen at Prince's earlier, the way they'd filmed themselves: smiling easily and crowding their faces into the frame. They'd turned their camera on everything and anything. If they were here now, they'd just be filming, not sitting in a hot car *thinking* about filming.

She slumped forward and set her forehead against the steering wheel. Had it come to this? Was she really *jealous* of teenage girls making content for social media?

Her phone buzzed.

MOM: Are you running late?
We have a seat saved.

Renee wanted a fast-forward button to smash and skip over the wedding altogether. Since her parents divorced when Renee was fourteen, she'd understood that real life wasn't like a Lola Gray song, all drippy romance and happy endings. The tune might be catchy, but the words were ultimately meaningless.

Still, Renee cared enough about Claudia to set aside her doubts for one night. She'd known the Grigorians practically since birth, long before Lola swapped her legal last name for the stage-friendly *Gray*. Lola was Renee's age, and Claudia two years older. When they were young, the Grigorian girls had taken the edge off the loneliness Renee felt as an only child. And there had been times Lola and Claudia practically lived at Renee's, when their dad was away on a trucking job and their mom wasn't quite keeping things together, often in the gaps between young Lola's performances at churches and state fairs.

But as happy as Renee was for Claudia, she could not get over how freaking embarrassing this night was about to be.

Renee had been destined to get out of Fellows. Everyone knew it. She was too smart for her own good, resentful of authority, irritated by Midwestern blandness—and also a lesbian. She dreamed of moving to a city so big she could be whoever she wanted, making art that people connected with, living a life that was exciting and queer. As straightforward as Renee's dreams were, growing up, she didn't know anyone else who shared them—except for Lola, sort of. When Renee left for New York, she was supposed to return as an undeniably cool documentary director. Instead, she'd come crawling back to live in the garage apartment her mom had converted to list on Airbnb. Tonight, she'd have to explain her failure to launch every time someone asked what she'd been up to.

> **MOM:** I can see you sitting in your car.

Renee's head whipped up. Her mother was standing at the entrance to the Bottle Factory with her hands on her hips and her curls frizzing in the humidity.

Shit. Renee checked her red lipstick in the rearview mirror and got out of the car. She was wearing her black jumpsuit. It was her one outfit nice enough to warrant occasional dry cleaning, and it could be trusted to make her look (most importantly) hot and (a close second) too sophisticated for Fellows, Michigan. Then Renee slammed the door of her car directly onto the seat-belt buckle, making the door bounce open and knock her hard in the shin. Renee had driven this same car all through high school and the buckle had gotten caught in the door even then, and she had never gotten used to it. Cursing herself, the car, the heat, and the trauma of human existence, Renee walked into the wedding.

***

Lola was having fun at her big sister's wedding.

She was having *so much fun*.

She'd had fun at the rehearsal dinner, despite being exhausted and having come straight from the plane. She'd smiled graciously whenever one of Josh's family members said, *This must be the famous little sister!* She'd had fun at brunch that morning with her parents and Claudia. She'd done her best to make sure her mom was happy, not slipping into one of her moods. She'd had fun with Claudia and all eight bridesmaids, getting glam done by the professionals Lola had flown in, and posing for pictures in their matching pink robes. She'd ignored the voice in her head that wondered whether she should have taken her team's recommendation to ask everyone to sign NDAs.

Now, she was having fun waiting in the bridal lounge while the guests arrived. By the mirror, Claudia and their mom were doing a final inspection of Claudia's look. Lola hoped this was one of the times Mom's attention felt welcome, and not like the prelude to disaster.

Hanging at the edge of the circle of bridesmaids, Lola timed her laugh perfectly as Claudia's college roommate finished a story about a boozy brunch gone wrong.

Her phone, clutched in her hand, vibrated. She glanced at the screen, then forced herself to decline the call, although she wouldn't have minded an excuse to step out of this room for a moment—even if it was to talk to her manager, Gloriana.

Lola hated that her nerves were so on edge. She'd been looking forward to Claudia's wedding since the moment Josh proposed. She truly liked Claudia's friends. The core group had been close since high school, their relationship welcoming enough to encompass college roommates, new friends, Josh's sister—though never quite Lola herself. That was hardly surprising, since she was never around. Even for the bachelorette in Tulum that Lola had arranged and paid for, she'd only been able to stay for one night.

It was the simple intimacy that wore on Lola. They had an ease with one another as they chatted about fiancés and boyfriends, a promotion, a funny story from spin class. It made Lola's life feel so remote it barely existed, like she was nothing but a song on the radio or an image on a glossy magazine page. She felt either invisible or like the most obvious thing in the room. It was high school all over again: she was still the weird one, tolerated but not accepted, and certainly not understood.

Or maybe she was tense because when Claudia had gotten engaged, a year and a half ago, Lola hadn't expected to be at this wedding alone. Instead, she'd just marked her own anniversary: one year since the worst breakup of her life.

Lola inhaled deeply and forced her smile wider. Her cheeks were starting to get sore.

Her phone vibrated again as the girls broke into peals of laughter at something Lola had missed, and she felt herself give way. Her phone in one hand, she maneuvered toward the door. She'd just step out and re-center herself while she called Gloriana back. But her path took her right by Claudia.

Claudia, lipstick-smudged tissue in hand, said, "Where are you going?"

"I need to make a quick call," Lola answered lightly.

"Seriously?"

"Let your sister do her business!" Their mom snatched the tissue from Claudia, then said to Lola, "Go on, baby, take care of it."

Donna Grigorian never had, and probably never would, stand in the way of Lola working. It wasn't her permission Lola needed.

"I'll be *so* quick, Claudia. Gloriana's calling and it's better that I talk to her now than later, right?" Lola was gripping her phone so hard, she wondered if it was possible for the screen to pop off. "I'm sorry. I asked for no calls today, but—"

"But she ignored you?" Claudia frowned. She had double the normal big sister's allotment of protective instinct, to make up for what their mom lacked. Even after ten years, she didn't quite trust Gloriana. "You let her push you around."

"I do not," Lola said, forcing herself to smile.

"You *do*. You say you're standing up for yourself, then you cave and end up with that look on your face."

"You mean *smiling* because I'm *happy*?"

Claudia gave her a sisterly side-eye that communicated more judgment than the notoriously awful British tabloid industry. "Whatever. Go talk to her."

"Thank you. And stop messing with your lipstick. It's perfect."

Claudia pouted at her. "Really?"

"Red carpet ready." Lola pushed open the door. "I'll be right back. I swear."

In the empty hall, the jittery feeling remained. It wasn't fair that Claudia could make Lola feel bad about working, when Claudia knew exactly how hard Lola had fought for her dream. That dream had bought a house for their parents, and for both sets of grandparents too. It had paid for almost the whole wedding, from Claudia's custom wedding dress to the beautiful florals to the open bar with signature cocktails.

When Lola was starting her singing career, she had imagined that, at some point, she'd reach a level of success and know that she was safe. She'd never gotten there—or hadn't yet. Four albums she'd written herself, seven number ones, world tours, dozens of awards and nominations, and everything still felt like it would slip out from under her with one wrong move. As long as it felt that way, Lola couldn't ignore calls or skip meetings or let herself relax.

Lola FaceTimed her manager. As she waited for Gloriana to answer, Lola watched the video of herself. She was wearing her tried-and-true Lola Gray smile, her eyes crinkled so it looked authentic. The smile was an old habit she'd had since her first meeting with an agent at twelve years old. He'd asked her to smile and she'd given him the enormous grin she'd learned doing pageants. He'd shaken his head and said he wanted her *real* smile. It felt unfamiliar, and a little exciting, to be asked to be herself. But her real smile hadn't satisfied him either. He passed on representing her and recommended that she practice looking convincingly happy in a mirror.

Gloriana appeared, with the signature gray streak in her dark hair. "Hi, honey, how's the wedding?"

Lola swallowed her annoyance that Gloriana knew exactly what she was taking Lola away from. After all, Lola had called *her*.

"It's about to start. I did ask for no calls today."

"I know, but the world doesn't stop for your sister's wedding. Do you want me to tell the team that we've got to pause because you're busy? I'll do it, but I'm not sure how they'll react."

"No, I just mean for next time, no calls means no calls."

Gloriana ran through a list of things Lola needed to approve, emails she'd missed, plans Gloriana needed a yes on—all of it using the pronoun *we*. *We* need an okay; *we're* ready to move ahead. Lola had to remind herself sometimes that she was part of the *we*. The *we* was her team, who worked their asses off for her. The team were the spokes on a wheel that she held the center of, even when she felt more like dead weight dragging behind them.

"We're waiting for your sign-off on the shoot schedule for the documentary," Gloriana said. "We really need to get things moving."

Lola's stomach clenched, the same way it had the first moment her team had pitched the project. It was going on three years since Lola's last album. Fans knew she was taking some time off after churning out four albums by the time she was twenty-four, but to the general public, she was slipping out of the spotlight. It was time to remind the world who Lola Gray was—with a documentary that followed the production of Album 5. Plus, they'd make good money on it. All Lola had to do was let cameras follow her around for a few months. The instant they'd suggested it, Lola's guts had clamped down like the gate of a castle slamming shut. She was generous with her fans and obliged the paparazzi and gave *Vogue* a tour of her renovated place in the Hills before she'd had a chance to sleep there herself. She had almost no privacy already—not only because of her fans and the press, but also because of the vast team of people that kept Lola Gray Inc. a smoothly functioning machine.

But she'd agreed to the film anyway. That was her rule: say yes whenever you can, because you never knew when you'd stop being asked. As much as she was dreading the film, the possibility of her fans forgetting her, of her career slipping away, was worse. Of course, when she'd agreed months ago, she'd had no idea that the next album would still be looming over her as dark and troubled as a thunderhead.

"I'm sure whatever you planned is fine," Lola said. "I don't need to see it."

"Fantastic," Gloriana said.

Just then, the door to the venue swung open and a woman in a black jumpsuit strode through. She had olive skin and a messy, overgrown pixie cut bleached platinum, but dark at the roots. Her lips were painted red and unsmiling, her jawline sharp. Lola's eyes followed as the woman stalked into the hall, noting how the cut of the outfit showed off her strong shoulders, one marked with a collection of tattoos, and how the fabric clung to her curves.

Lola hadn't seen her in years, but she recognized her in an instant.

Renee Feldman.

"Oh no," Lola whispered involuntarily.

"What is it?" Gloriana said.

"Nothing," Lola mumbled. "We're lining up. I have to go."

2

Sitting at table 14 beside her mom, Deborah, and her mom's boyfriend, Dave, Renee regretted not asking for a plus-one. She had no one to invite romantically, but if she'd brought Kadijah, she wouldn't feel like she was third-wheeling a date between people twice her age.

As it was, Renee had been reduced to repeated trips to the bar for refills of the signature cocktail—the Joshinator—to escape her mom's tips for socializing. Deborah could not stop asking Renee: Did she recognize anyone from high school? Was she planning on dancing? Why didn't she try being friendly for once?

Renee didn't want to be friendly. Claudia's friends were a few years older and they absolutely radiated the heterosexuality and basic Midwestern-ness that Renee had constructed her personality around rejecting. Plus, by avoiding them, she could avoid explaining that she was twenty-seven years old, had no money and no prospects, and had become a burden to her parents.

"There's Lola!" Deborah pointed across the room as the entrees were being served. "Go say hi, Ree-Ree!"

Renee did not turn her head. "Mom, you don't just point at a *celebrity*."

"How else am I supposed to tell you where she is? You're not even looking."

"I *can't* look now. She'll know we're talking about her."

Deborah's patience for Renee's etiquette tips was as short as Renee's for hers. "So what? Lola always did like you. Gosh, she looks pretty."

Renee sipped her Joshinator. Claudia's wedding party, including her sister as maid of honor, had been seated during the ceremony, and Renee's spot at table 14 faced the back of the hall. Renee still hadn't gotten a good look at Lola. She had to admit, she was a little curious.

Finally, Deborah excused herself to the ladies', freeing Renee from direct parental supervision. Renee twisted in her chair to search the crowd.

Lola wasn't hard to find.

She was so petite that she should have been swallowed by the chaos of the wedding guests, but Lola drew the light to herself as she floated around the hall. Her dress skimmed her figure, and wisps of chocolate-brown hair escaped her casually romantic updo.

In one slender, manicured hand, Lola held a flute of champagne that remained precisely two-thirds full. She never took a sip. It seemed like every few seconds, someone asked for a picture, and she expertly took their phone and snapped the selfie. Even from this distance, Renee could see that Lola wore the same smile the whole time, whether she was posing or not: a pleasant grin with a crinkle around the eyes.

Renee couldn't figure out that smile: How could it look so real, but feel so fake? But Lola had always been like that: an ex-pageant kid, hungry for approval. She used to blush when she said *the f-word* and go fully red-faced when Renee said *fuck*.

Renee wondered if she still did.

Deborah returned to the table and thrust her phone into Renee's face. On the screen was a blurry photo. "It's Claudia and Josh! Don't they look happy?"

"For now," Renee said, fiddling with her dessert fork. Deborah frowned. Renee didn't understand how her mother could be optimistic about anyone's marriage when her own had dissolved without warning. "What? I'm being realistic."

Dave glanced up from Deborah's phone to say, "Don't worry, Renee. You'll find someone."

Renee gaped at him, horrified that he had unearthed such a traditionalist desire in her exceedingly rational comment. Dave had been her mother's boyfriend for what, four years? He didn't know anything about her!

"I'm not *looking* for anyone," she corrected. "It wouldn't be fair of me to get involved with anyone here. Once I get my thesis in order, I'm moving back to New York."

Dave and Deborah exchanged a look laden with doubt. It was one Renee had seen many times in the last year, and it always made her shoulders curl into her chest.

In a feeble attempt at self-defense, Renee added, "The idea that the one for me might be in *Fellows, Michigan*, is really hetero-centric. Queer people can't just go into any straight space and meet someone because—"

"Oh, stop it," Deborah cut her off. "Dave knows that. He's an ally."

Renee dug the dessert fork into the tablecloth. Dave was an ally, and so was Deborah—even if, when Renee came out, she'd been most concerned that being a lesbian would make Renee's life harder. It took her years to realize that society was the problem, not her daughter. Last summer, Deborah and Dave had gone without Renee to cheer on Fellows's quaint Pride Parade.

"Whatever," Renee said sullenly, as the wedding DJ grabbed the mic.

"Listen up, party people! The sister of the bride requests that you make your way to the dance floor for a once-in-a-lifetime moment!"

Renee groaned. Kadijah was right: Lola was going to perform. Excitement swept through the hall as everyone hurried to the dance floor, where a curtain had been strung up. It pulled back to reveal Lola Gray with her trademark lavender acoustic guitar slung over her shoulder. She looked radiant onstage, like she would have sparkled even without the lights.

That was Renee's cue to hit the bar. She did not need to hear an ode to true love right now, and she'd seen enough Lola Gray performances in high school to last a lifetime.

Lola leaned into the mic. "You were probably expecting a toast, but since I've written a love song or two, I thought I'd play something instead. Claudia and Josh, this is for you."

Renee ordered another Joshinator as the drink's namesake led Claudia onto the dance floor.

Then Lola began to sing.

Renee's gaze drifted past the newlyweds and back to the stage. Goose bumps rose on her skin. This wasn't the Lola she remembered. That girl had always had an awkward eagerness in front of an audience, and her voice had strained at high notes. Now, Lola occupied the stage as if it were her domain, as if her nimble fingers on the frets of her guitar were weaving a spell over the room. Lola's voice was liquid and rich, like warm honey, and it pooled deep in Renee's chest. Renee was transfixed. Lola soared into the song's bridge, the emotion in her voice like a tide pulling Renee out to sea. Lola's eyes were half-closed, lost in the sound. When she lifted them, Renee could have sworn that Lola was looking right at her.

Renee stared back at the woman onstage.

Who had Lola become?

LOLA ONLY PLAYED three songs, but by the time she closed with a cover of "Stand by Me," everyone with a date and the physical capacity to report to the dance floor was having the most romantic moment of their lives—Deborah and Dave included. As Lola left the stage, the DJ transitioned seamlessly to Bruno Mars. Those poor chumps were never getting back to their seats.

Renee would not be joining them. She leaned against a shadowed wall near the bar, hoping the half-drunk Joshinator in her hand made her look less *friendless kid at a middle school dance*, and more *confident bad bitch*.

"Could I please have a sparkling water?" a voice from the bar said.

There was Lola, squeezing a lime into her glass. Alone.

Renee should have said hello. It would have been the polite choice, but it was not the one Renee made.

This was her first close-range opportunity to see Lola since they were eighteen. Her large, dark eyes peering out from under the sweet curl of her lashes, the golden tone of her skin, her heart-shaped face. But there was an air of fragility about her too. The longer Renee looked, the more it seemed that Lola was tired, or a bit sad.

Renee couldn't square the grown woman before her with the girl who'd gone around clutching a velvet-covered journal of lyrics, who did vocal exercises in the middle school bathroom because she claimed it had perfect acoustics, who had once cried at a sleepover because no one wanted to watch *Phantom of the Opera*.

When they were young, Lola and Renee had bonded over being weird, creative kids, but once high school started, they lost the thread of what they'd had in common. Lola doubled down on her dreams of pop stardom, which put her out of step with everyone at Fellows High. It was cool to be a *Billboard* chart–topping star once you'd actually done it, but when you were a teenager telling anyone who'd listen that *one day* you'd top the *Billboard* charts? You were weird. Anyway, Renee had been too busy navigating her own whirlpool of existential depression to think about the girl next door, who was as edgy as a Girl Scout.

Was that why she'd never realized how gorgeous Lola was?

Lola covertly slipped some cash into the tip jar that the caterers had set out despite the open bar. Then she said, "Are you going to say hi, Renee, or just lurk in the shadows?"

Renee straightened up. "I'm not *lurking*, I'm respectfully standing. You and the sparkling water were having a moment. It would have been rude to interrupt."

Lola came over to Renee and set her shoulder against the same patch of wall where Renee had just been leaning.

"I need a moment to find myself again when I get offstage," Lola said.

"Still losing yourself in the music," Renee said. She'd meant it playfully, but Lola's expression stilled. Renee sensed that Lola was on the brink of reverting to the forced, crinkle-eyed smile she'd worn earlier. Renee didn't want to see that smile. She suddenly said, "Your voice sounds better than it used to."

Gratifyingly, Lola didn't smile at that. Instead, her lips quirked to the side and her brows arched. "Wow, a compliment from Renee Feldman."

Renee's cheeks warmed—or maybe that was the cocktail. "Yeah, well. Write that one down in your journal, Lo."

"Oh, I don't need to. I'll remember it forever," Lola said. "I didn't expect to see you here."

Renee shrugged. "We get so few chances to dance the Electric Slide in this short life, and I intend to take each one."

"You're in luck. Josh's family are major Electric Slide people. They do the ties on their heads and everything."

"If only I'd worn a suit," Renee said.

Lola's lashes dipped as her eyes ran down Renee's body. "But I like what you have on."

There was something about how Lola said it, her voice dropping a little low, that made Renee's skin prickle. Platonic compliments women gave each other usually came in higher-pitched, friendly tones. If it had been anyone else—anyone *queer*—Renee would have said this was flirting. But this was *Lola*. It must have been a failed attempt at sarcasm. Where most people had a sense of humor, Lola had a deeply unhealthy work ethic.

None of that explained why heat was blooming through Renee's chest.

Maybe it was an excess of Joshinators, but suddenly Renee felt they could have been in the shadowy corner of a bar, or a house party—someplace actually fun.

Someplace she'd actually flirt.

Not that she'd ever flirt with *Lola*, who had glossed over that comment like it had never happened.

"I'd heard you moved to New York. Film school, right? I'm surprised you came back for this."

Renee tossed back the rest of her drink, nonchalant. "I was here already. I'm taking some time off to get my inspiration back before I start my thesis. You know, refill the creative well."

Lola's lips parted in mock outrage, her eyes sparkling up at Renee. "Did you just say 'refill the creative well'? Fifteen-year-old Renee would be rolling her eyes so hard right now."

"It's an expression!" Renee protested, but she was laughing. She laid her hand on Lola's shoulder. She hadn't meant to do it, not exactly. Just like she hadn't meant to notice how soft Lola's skin was, or to use that touch as a reason to step in closer, before letting her palm skim Lola's arm as it fell.

"But really, that sounds nice. I wish I could take a break for a few weeks." Lola sighed.

Renee didn't correct Lola that her break had lasted a year. "What would fifteen-year-old Lola say to that? Don't tell me you finally learned how to relax."

"Of course I know how to relax. I'm at a party right now."

"And you've had what, one glass of champagne all night?"

Lola's eyes widened, the golden-brown irises edged by a darker ring. "Have you been watching me, Renee?"

"Everyone's been watching you," Renee answered softly.

"Which is why I don't drink with this many people around. I can't do anything too—" Lola made a face, bugging her eyes out. It was shockingly charming.

"If you could, what kind of"—Renee pulled the same buggy-eyed face—"thing would you do?"

Renee must have imagined it. The Joshinators had caused a break with reality. Because it looked like Lola had lowered her lashes, then gently bit her lip.

"I have a bottle of champagne in my room, for later," Lola said. "But what sounds *really* good right now is getting into bed."

Renee's mouth was suddenly dry. She felt herself moving closer to Lola, leaning in as though magnetized. "That sounds good to me too."

"Lola, you better not be on your phone!" Claudia said, running up to them.

Lola spun away from Renee. "I was catching up with Renee. You didn't tell me she'd be here!"

Renee congratulated Claudia, then fended off demands that she follow them to the dance floor. Her eyes kept shifting to Lola, but she was wearing that smile again, the one Renee couldn't tell was genuine or not.

Renee wandered back to her table, shaking her head. Had Lola been flirting with her—and had she flirted back? The very thought was cursed. This was *Lola Gray*, not some hot femme at a queer bar in Brooklyn. Lola was an international pop star. By comparison, Renee was a fingerling potato.

And on top of that, Renee was a *woman*.

Did Lola *like* women? Not as far as Renee knew—and as shallow as her pop culture knowledge was, Renee would have heard if the reigning Princess of Pop had come out.

The idea that Lola was secretly queer was ridiculous.

But until a few minutes ago, it had felt ridiculous to imagine Lola undressing her with her eyes, and Joshinators be damned, Renee was pretty sure that had happened.

Almost as ridiculous as the fact that Renee, who prided herself on never having listened to a Lola Gray album, had been ready to melt for her.

3

Lola had no idea what had come over her.

She had no business flirting with Renee—*Renee Feldman*, whom she hadn't spoken to in years, and who she'd last solidly counted among her friends in eighth grade. But she'd come offstage and she'd felt raw. For weeks, Lola had been worrying about that three-song set: a song from her first album that she'd written after she and Claudia watched *10 Things I Hate About You*; Claudia's favorite of her love songs, "Unwritten Letter" from her second album; and a cover of "Stand by Me," a surprise. Lola considered it one of the most romantic songs ever written, and she'd labored over how best to perform it solo. When the guests stopped watching her and started dancing slow, heads resting on shoulders, she'd known she was pulling it off.

She'd imagined that when she heard "Stand by Me" at a wedding, she'd be slow dancing with someone she loved.

Performing was one of the few things she could do that always felt right. All the different versions of herself that normally took so much effort to balance came together onstage. But tonight, at the end of her set, her heart felt even more than usual like a wound barely patched over in her chest, as if being surrounded by so much love had split her fragile new scars.

Already, Lola had been navigating the reception in an unaccustomed haze of public awkwardness. Her mother, as usual, set Lola on edge. She never knew how Donna would react when her daughters were the object of attention. Thankfully, she seemed to relish the role of Mother of the Bride, so it had been beaming pride, not fiendish jealousy. But that could change in a second, and on Claudia's day, it would be Lola's responsibility to settle her.

On top of that, some of these guests had known her when she was a kid in headgear—literally, her mom had insisted on inviting their orthodontist. They might remember the time she forgot the words to the national anthem at a hockey game. Now, they all wanted their moment with Lola Gray, the star. She didn't want to disappoint them, but she couldn't let her presence detract from Claudia and Josh.

It would have made it all better if she'd had someone at her side, who was there just for her. Someone who could see, even through her smile, that she was spinning out, who would squeeze her hand and tell her she was doing a good job.

But she didn't have that, and she wasn't going to find it here.

What she might find instead was distraction, release.

She hadn't quite gone looking for Renee when she edged around the dance floor to the bar. But she knew Renee would be there. She'd spotted her from the stage: leaning against the wall to show off the tattoos that ran from elbow to shoulder. Renee had this energy as if she'd been born with no fucks to give, and Lola, who cared too much about everyone, always found it magnetic.

As she danced with Claudia, her cheeks flushed as she replayed what she'd said to Renee. Whenever she allowed herself to flirt with a woman, Lola chose her words carefully, to maximize deniability if anything got out. But from the way Renee's eyes had widened, her body canted into Lola's, her meaning had come across.

It was pathetic, getting a rush from a two-minute conversation. She'd probably imagined the sexual tension. Renee had only gotten hotter in the last ten years, and Lola was lonely—lonely and horny.

Which was probably why, while guests were loading into the bus that would take them to the hotel after-party, Lola's thoughts were still caught on Renee.

"You really won't come?" Claudia begged her as Josh's cousins triumphantly emerged from the venue bearing crates of leftover alcohol. "You'd have fun."

Lola gave her an apologetic smile.

"You know I'd love to, but I have an early flight and I'm at a different hotel."

Lola was thankful for the excuse. As much as she wanted to please her sister, Claudia was wrong: Lola would not have fun. She'd feel, as she had all night, like everyone else lived on planet Earth and she was a satellite circling above them.

All night, except that moment with Renee.

Lola waved to her sister as the bus pulled away.

On the other side of it, Renee was standing by her car, looking at her phone.

Suddenly, Lola felt reckless. The guests were gone. Her team had made sure to keep the venue private, and anyway, this was Fellows, not Hollywood. Besides, who knew when—if—she'd see Renee again?

Lola's feet were moving across the parking lot before she realized she'd made up her mind.

"No after-party?" she called.

When Renee looked up and took Lola in, her green eyes seemed to darken. A shiver of excitement traveled down Lola's spine.

"Not my vibe. I don't know why I thought driving myself was a good idea."

"One too many Joshinators?"

"Maybe *one* too many, and now I can't get a car." Renee shook her hair out of her face. "Aren't you going?"

"I already told you what I'd rather be doing," Lola said quietly.

Renee's red-painted lips curved with interest. It made Lola feel bold. "Why don't you come back to my hotel? We can catch up, and I can have that glass of champagne while you sober up."

Renee's brows drew together as she studied Lola. Lola's stomach clenched, steeling for rejection.

But Renee asked, "You sure?"

Lola nodded, then flinched as Renee tossed something toward her. A set of keys hit the pavement at her feet.

"Don't tell me you forgot how to drive, Lo."

Lola's dress pooled on the ground as she bent to grab the keys.

***

Lola's hotel was twenty minutes away in Grand Rapids. The vision of Lola Gray, international pop star, at the wheel of Renee's battered Elantra was absurd and borderline frightening. She was so short she had to move the seat all the way up and adjust every mirror, twice—only to nearly make an illegal left at a red light. Wild honking from her security team, tailing them in a black SUV, had stopped her. Renee hadn't noticed Lola's security at the wedding. Now she wondered if they'd seen that moment at the bar, or the one in the parking lot—if they knew what those moments meant.

If they meant anything.

Safely at the hotel, Lola and Renee were escorted into an elevator by Henry, Lola's head of security, who had thin salt-and-pepper hair and a body like a slab of beef. Lola introduced Renee as a childhood friend.

"We're catching up," Renee said. She didn't want Henry to assume Lola had brought her back here to fuck. Not that Renee was sure that *was* why Lola had brought her back here. Maybe they really would chat about the last few years, and she'd ignore the newfound humming in her blood when she looked at Lola.

"Have a wonderful night," Henry said as he swiped a key card at Lola's door—a standard sign-off or the equivalent of a knowing wink?

Renee peeked around the suite: probably the finest Grand Rapids had to offer, with a separate living room area, a king bed, and a bathroom with a jacuzzi tub. Two gigantic suitcases had puked up their contents onto the carpet.

"Here we are!" Renee turned to see Lola brandishing a bottle of champagne.

Lola peeled the foil off, then twisted free the wire cage and started pushing at the cork. Her forehead wrinkled, glossy lips pursed in effort, but the cork didn't budge.

Renee crossed the room and slid her hands against the neck of the bottle so that the cork was in her fist, although Lola still gripped the body. They were right up against each other, and the space between them seemed to fizz and spark.

"It'll explode if you do it like that," Renee said, conscious of how close her mouth was now to Lola's ear. "You have to be gentle."

One hand tight on the cork, she guided her other to Lola's and twisted the bottle. The cork loosened and pulled free with a sigh. Blue vapor flowed from the mouth of the bottle.

When Renee stepped back, her eyes snagged on the quick, shallow rise and fall of Lola's chest. Then Lola remembered herself, the cold bottle in her hand.

"Can I pour you a glass?"

"I thought I was sobering up," Renee said. "I don't want to overstay my welcome."

"You won't. You can stay as long as you want," Lola said.

"Okay."

Lola went to the table and filled two flutes, her back to Renee. But when she was done, instead of handing one to Renee, Lola took a long look at her from over her shoulder, her eyes dark and her lower lip held between her teeth.

"What is it?" Renee asked.

Lola grabbed something off the table and turned to face her. "It's just—do you mind signing this?" She was holding out a form.

Non-Disclosure Agreement, the document read.

"An NDA?" Renee's eyebrows jumped up. "Worried I'll post an embarrassing picture on Instagram?"

"Sell it to a tabloid, actually, but same idea. Sorry, I know it's awkward, but my team will kill me if I don't . . . and it makes it a little easier for me to relax." Her deep brown eyes flitted between Renee's face and the paper in her hands.

"I don't know, Lo. You've got me all alone in your hotel room, and now you're telling me whatever happens here will be our secret," Renee said slowly, allowing some of that simmering anticipation to enter her voice. "What are you planning to do to me?"

Lola was twisting a pen in her hands and watching Renee intensely. She opened her mouth, closed it again. Renee could tell Lola was fighting the urge to reassure her that there was nothing planned, that Renee had it all wrong.

But by now, Renee was certain she didn't have it all wrong.

"I'll just have to find out." Renee took the pen and scribbled her signature.

As soon as she'd handed the document back to Lola, it was fluttering out of her fingers and to the floor. Lola surged forward. All at once, her lips were against Renee's. Renee startled—she hadn't expected Lola to jump her, nor had she expected the smoothness of Lola's lips, or that she'd taste of spearmint, like she'd snuck a mint without Renee seeing. Renee opened her lips for Lola, leaning down into her eager mouth. There was nothing teasing or subtle about the way Lola kissed her. When she drew Renee's lower lip between hers and sucked, with just a hint of pressure from her teeth, desire surged through Renee's body. If Lola was that hungry for her, Renee was happy to submit.

Lola broke away, just barely, and breathed, "Sorry, is this okay?"

Renee didn't want to think too hard about what this was or wasn't.

"Don't apologize. Don't stop," Renee sighed against her needfully, and Lola didn't.

She notched her body to Renee's like she didn't want any air between them, and kissed her again, her tongue snaking into Renee's mouth. In response, Renee's hands tangled into Lola's hair, pulling a few hairpins loose. Lola moaned against Renee's lips.

Was this really happening? She was making out with Lola—*Lola Gray*—the little weirdo next door who was now adored by millions, who Renee hadn't even suspected was queer. This was the hottest thing she'd experienced in months—no, in *years*. This was better than any of her half-hearted hookups since returning to Fellows. Renee had worried she'd lost the ability to lose herself in lust like this. But now, her knee was bending invitingly between Lola's thighs and her hands were grabbing Lola's hips to tug her closer. A tremor shot through Lola the first time Renee pressed against her, and it set a fire coursing through her. Renee's fingers dug into Lola's ass. She was rewarded by Lola running her hands up the front of her jumpsuit and cupping her breasts through the fabric, her thumbs circling Renee's nipples and sending a ripple of pleasure to her core.

Breathing heavy, Renee cast a glance at that enormous bed. Understanding, Lola pulled Renee over to it, then spun her around, so she faced Renee's back. She fingered the zipper of Renee's jumpsuit.

"Can I?"

"Fuck yes," Renee groaned. As Lola drew the zipper down, Renee could feel Lola's intent gaze on her skin and the clasp of her bra and, as the jumpsuit fell to the ground, the curve of her ass. Then Lola was pushing her up onto the bed and peeling off the straps of her own dress to expose more of that gorgeous skin, almost radiant in its softness.

Renee took in Lola's body: her breasts straining against the lace edge of her bra, the smudge of a birthmark on her ribs, the points of her hips, an ass that would fill Renee's palms perfectly. She was wearing practical, seamless nude-colored underwear—not what you'd wear if you'd been planning to fuck at your sister's wedding—but it clung to her, visibly damp.

As Lola climbed up her body, Renee marveled again that Lola felt totally unlike the squeaky-clean girl she'd known. And she was nothing like the polished entertainer that Kadijah obsessed over. This woman was hungry and messy with need. There was something almost ugly about how her face wore pleasure, like the muscles were unused to moving that way. That look made Renee want to watch Lola come undone completely.

She grabbed Lola's hips and swung her leg over them, so that Lola was on her back, her beautiful dark hair over the white sheets. Renee kissed her jaw, her neck—Lola arched against the bed—then moved down her chest, kissing a trail to her breasts. She took the edge of the lace in her teeth, tugged gently, then cut her eyes up to Lola's face. Her eyes were hazy.

"Can I take this off?" Renee asked.

Lola nodded, and Renee slid her hands beneath her to unclasp the bra. She savored a look at Lola's dark pink areola, already pebbling, before capturing one nipple with her palm, the other with her mouth. Lola's arms were around Renee's head, pressing Renee against her, and she moaned in a way that Renee could feel through Lola's chest. The vibration traveled straight through Renee and right to her clit. But Renee forced herself to ignore her arousal. She wanted to focus on Lola, to coax more of those moans from her.

Renee shifted her mouth to the other side and moved her hand down to Lola's panties, eager to touch her.

But then Lola's hand was over hers, guiding it away, and Lola was pulling her back up into a kiss again.

"Too fast?" Renee breathed against her.

"No, I just want you first," Lola answered. "Is that okay?"

"Of course." It wasn't Renee's plan exactly, but she was flexible. If Lola didn't want to be touched right now, she'd wait.

She lay back against the pillows. Lola had an otherworldly concentration as she pulled Renee's panties off, then slid her hand up Renee's thighs, parting them so that Renee was exposed to her. Renee shivered, ready.

Lola tasted her slowly at first, using her tongue to trace the length of her. Was Lola nervous—inexperienced? Renee moaned encouragingly, just in case. But then Lola drew her tongue up to Renee's clit, closing her lips around it, and—and *fuck*. Renee gasped, her eyes squeezing closed. Lola had barely gotten her mouth on her and already, delicious sensation was building in her. *Not inexperienced, then.* Not at all. God, where had Lola learned to use her mouth like this? She'd always been a perfectionist, but this—

But then Renee wasn't having any more thoughts. Lola slipped one finger inside her, quickly followed by another. Between her hands, strong from curling against the strings of her guitar, and the lips that sang those love songs, Renee's need for release was accelerating. She forced her eyes open and looked down at Lola. Her hair askew and her ass rolling against the bed—not against the bed, against her own hand. Lola was working herself too, Renee realized, touching herself while she sucked Renee's clit.

"That's so fucking hot," Renee ground out as she reached down, weaving her hand into Lola's hair. Lola liked that, Renee could see from how her hips were canting. "Keep doing that. I'm coming—"

And then Lola was taking her over the edge, plunging her into waves of aching pleasure that had her heels digging into the bed. But Lola was coming too, crying out with her mouth still against Renee, her body stiffening in orgasm and then collapsing against Renee's stomach.

Lola came up from between Renee's thighs with her mouth glistening. She looked wild and beautiful, and Renee pulled her in for a long kiss, tasting herself on Lola's tongue.

"That was incredible," Renee gasped as she lay back against the sweat-damp pillows.

Lola nestled against her. "Really?"

Renee gazed down at Lola through half-lidded eyes. Lola's dark eyes were huge and wanting. Renee traced her fingers from Lola's hip up to her shoulder.

"The best head I've ever had. Honestly."

Lola pressed herself closer against Renee and Renee thought she felt a frisson of arousal run through the other woman's body. She tried again.

"You're so good, Lo," Renee murmured. Her fingertips trailed over Lola's skin, raising goose bumps as they went. "Such a good girl."

Lola seemed to stop breathing entirely at that.

"Your turn," Renee said, pushing herself up on her elbows.

"It's okay. I just came." Lola put her hand on Renee's chest and pushed gently. Renee, too spent to resist, fell back.

"So?"

Lola's hand was still on Renee's chest. She had a shadowy, almost forlorn look on her face. "Do you know how rarely I get to be with a woman?"

Renee swallowed hard. International pop stardom be damned, Lola deserved to be with a woman as often as she wanted.

"I want to make sure I remember how you taste," Lola whispered, and Renee's concern, along with every last coherent thought, left her head, as fresh heat flooded her body. If Lola didn't want her to reciprocate, she wasn't going to push it. This was a one-night stand, and Lola knew that.

Plus, it was a crime to interfere with a service top at work.

Renee moaned as Lola's hand trailed lower. "Promise you'll think about me when you touch yourself."

Lola licked her lips, her eyes locked on Renee's. "I promise."

"Good girl."

She'd hardly gotten the words out before Lola was on her.

Can you believe this video from Lola's sister's wedding??? How cute is her cover of Stand by Me? ♡ 8921
Reply

that bridesmaid dress is a slay! lola looks amazing! ♡ 728
Reply

Like this comment if you think Lola should release a cover of Stand by Me ♡ 4273
Reply

↳ If she does I'm playing it at my wedding ♡ 13

Where is this vid from? ♡ 114
Reply

↳ lol I stalked the instagrams of every wedding guest I could find ♡ 62

It's messed up how she made her sister's wedding all about her ♡ 202
Reply

↳ Right??? Came here to say this ♡ 3

4

"Girl, you look wrung out," Kadijah said as Renee pulled herself an espresso and dumped it into an iced coffee at Prince's. Today called for a red eye. "What happened last night?"

"Someone got her back cracked," Zane, one of Kadijah's partners, said from his regular table. His iced oat milk matcha sat atop the stack of poetry chapbooks he lugged to the coffee shop every day.

"Must we?" Renee snapped. "This is a place of business, not Page Six."

Zane clicked his tongue. "Goes to one celebrity wedding, and she's name-checking Page Six."

"Did you at least *talk to her*?" Kadijah hopped up to sit on the counter.

"To who?"

Kadijah glared at Renee.

"Yes, I talked to Lola. Other than the bride, she was the one person I knew under the age of fifty." As she said it, Renee tried really, *really* hard not to think of the way Lola's eyes had traveled down her body at the wedding. *What sounds really good right now is getting into bed.*

"Does Lola Gray party? She comes off like such a good girl," Zane said.

Thankfully he didn't notice Renee inhaling her coffee. Memories flashed through her mind: Lola's body hovering over her, that divot of concentration in her brow as she ground the heel of her hand against Renee's clit at precisely the right moment. Lola's face slick and her breathing heavy as she looked up from between Renee's legs.

"I want to know if Nash was there!" Kadijah said.

"Who?" Renee asked.

"Nash Walker, Lola's *boyfriend*?" Zane sputtered.

Renee's stomach lurched. Lola hadn't acted like someone with a boyfriend last night, not that Lola's infidelity was Renee's business. Maybe it was casual with this Nash Whoever, or they had one of those misogynistic rules where women didn't count as cheating.

Though the way Lola had asked, *Do you know how rarely I get to be with a woman?* made Renee think that wasn't the case.

"She didn't have a boyfriend with her," Renee said.

"What about Ava Andreesen?" Kadijah asked.

To Renee's horror, Zane and Kadijah, with perfect coordination, flung their right hands in the air, the left over their hearts, and cried, "*LavaTruther Till I Die!*"

Renee's nose scrunched in annoyance. "This is one of those moments when our age gap feels really significant."

"Don't tell me you're not a LavaTruther!" Kadijah cried. "Lava-Trutherism is the theory—backed by highly convincing evidence collected by a dedicated online community—that Lola Gray and Ava Andreesen were *secretly involved*."

"Like, romantically?" Renee hoped they didn't catch the hitch in her voice. Not that her voice had any reason to hitch.

Kadijah rolled their eyes. "Yes, Renee. Romantically—and *sexually*."

"Okay," Renee said.

"As girlfriends."

"Right."

"Lesbian girlfriends."

"I get it."

Kadijah spun their braids into a work-ready bun. "Just spelling it out, since you're the last queer woman on the planet who didn't know about this."

Ava Andreesen was a Swedish socialite who'd parlayed a stint on a short-lived reality show about Upper East Side rich kids into a career of hosting red carpets, playing herself in movies, occasionally modeling, occasionally DJing in Ibiza, and doing whatever else the nonworking wealthy did to fill their days. Normally such a person would not be on Renee's radar, but Ava Andreesen was also famously bisexual. With her blonde bombshell looks and a stylish gap between her front teeth, she radiated a reckless girl's girl energy. She was a divisive figure in the queer community. Some people loved that Ava seemed like the kind of chick who'd take you out for margaritas then talk you into a threesome. For the same reason, others felt Ava embodied a straight man's fantasy of a bisexual woman. Renee didn't know if the feeling in her gut was jealousy, or if she was kind of turned on. She *had* wondered where Lola had learned such an expert way around a woman. It was hot that Lola might have practiced on Ava what she'd used on Renee.

"No way Ava was there," Zane said. "She and Lola don't even talk anymore. Which is the best evidence ever that #Lava was real."

Renee took a long pull of her red eye. "Thank you for this fascinating info, but neither of those people were there."

"One more question," Kadijah said. "Was Lola giving off queer vibes?"

"Seriously?" Renee tried not to blush. "I'm not going to gossip about her with you."

"It should be illegal to be this un-fun," Zane whined.

"Hold up, we've got to suspend judgment," Kadijah said. "Did you actually get some last night?"

Renee made a face that hopefully approximated her regular scowl.

"You got me." Renee's voice was thick. "I connected with one of Claudia's friends, and we totally fucked all night."

Zane frowned. "You *can* just say no."

But Kadijah narrowed their eyes. "Renee's sarcasm is the lie that helps us understand the truth. You *did* go home with someone."

Renee's cheeks heated as she cursed herself for having friends who understood her.

"Ooh, who?" Zane cried. "Are you going to see her again?"

"Of course not." Kadijah laughed. "Walk Away Renee doesn't do relationships."

"I hate it when you call me that," Renee said, maneuvering past Kadijah to walk away. "I'm going to make the schedule for next week, so I hope you're happy with this exchange."

"You know I'm not!" Kadijah yelled, as Renee slammed the office door.

Squirreled away inside the office, Renee did not work on the schedule. Instead, she spun slowly in the stained desk chair and let her mind drift to last night. Well, *letting* her mind drift wasn't exactly right. Her mind had been solidly shipwrecked since she'd woken up to the sound of Lola showering and snuck out of the hotel room.

She should have said goodbye, thank you, something, *anything* instead of slinking away. Renee had her fair share of experience with casual hookups and one-night stands—a little more than her fair share, actually. She was perfectly capable of handling the morning after. But Lola was different. Renee had realized whose bed she was in and *panicked*. In the moment, it seemed right to spare them any awkward small talk about how the evidently closeted, Spotify-sweetheart

Lola Gray had just spent the night absolutely railing her burnout ex-neighbor. They had the NDA, after all.

An early-morning drive home and hot shower later, Renee realized that maybe leaving *hadn't* been especially kind. Lola had treated her to an amazing night, gotten her off so many times that Renee had lost track. Now Renee couldn't even thank her, because they hadn't exchanged numbers.

Renee was struck all over again that Lola liked to top. Liked it *a lot*. Femmes could always surprise you, but most women Renee had been with took turns giving and receiving. Maybe Lola needed time to feel comfortable enough to receive—or maybe she didn't like to receive at all. Renee's skin warmed as she contemplated what made Lola moan, exploring with her fingers all the places Lola liked to be touched. What her face looked like as she came. Next time—

Renee scrubbed a hand over her face. There was no *next time*. They hadn't exchanged numbers because there was no need to. Anyway, Renee didn't do *next times*, and Lola lived in a different world, practically on another planet.

Which was for the best. Lola's career and their history aside, Renee wouldn't have broken her no-second-dates streak for someone so romantic, so worried about what others thought. Kadijah and Zane might make fun of Renee for being single, but at least she didn't waste her time.

Plus, how was she supposed to get her thesis project together if she let herself get hung up on girls?

Renee, a little dizzy now, stopped spinning. When her shift ended, she'd get to work on her thesis. She was not going to look up pictures of Lola, and definitely not masturbate to those pictures—not that she had had a specific plan to do that, but it wasn't going to happen. No, she was going to go through her meager list of shitty ideas and pick one to move forward with.

It was time to refocus. She wasn't going to let Lola Gray be the only success story from Fellows High School's class of 2015.

Thus resolved, she pulled up her email on her phone—and her stomach dropped straight to the floor.

> Renee—
>
> The registration deadline for the next semester is upon us, and with it, the official end of your leave. To remain enrolled, you must register for next semester. Your final graduation requirement is the thesis project, for which you must complete a two-semester independent study with a faculty mentor. If you have not registered and paid tuition and fees by August 1, you will be terminated from the program.
>
> Let's avoid that. The paperwork will be a nightmare.
>
> Be in touch if questions
> - D
>
> Dragan Kapić
> Professor of Documentary Filmmaking
> Dean, Documentary Film Program, New York Institute of Film

Buzzy white noise flooded Renee's ears—as if her hearing had paused to allow her body to focus on the prospect of throwing up. Renee strongly felt that no email should be more powerful than her esophageal sphincter, but she barely managed to make it out of the office and to the trash can before yakking.

"Are you *that* hungover?" Kadijah thrust a roll of paper towels at Renee. "I can handle things here if you want to bounce."

"It's not a hangover," Renee managed, although physically, she was hung over the trash can. "I got an email from the program. It's my last chance to go back and . . . and that's it. I can't do it."

"Come on," Kadijah said. "If it's the money, you'll figure something out."

Renee blew her nose and was rewarded with a coffee-flavored burning.

Kadijah was right to assume money was the problem. The MFA was the most expensive gamble Renee had ever taken. The first two years of tuition ran over $150,000—and that didn't cover the cost of living in New York. While other students had scholarships or trust funds, Renee had relied on loans that she'd probably never manage to repay and, in emergencies, her mother's generosity. Tuition in the final thesis year was significantly cheaper, but Renee was already in so much debt it barely mattered.

All that debt, just to discover that she couldn't hack it.

Directing documentaries had been Renee's dream. She'd started in high school, filming on her phone, then scrimped and saved to buy her own camera. She'd been the star of her small college's film studies program. A prestigious MFA program like the one at the New York Institute of Film was a long shot—especially after her first application was rejected—but she wanted to learn to make films from the best. When she got in, she'd been elated, but that joy had dimmed only a few hours into orientation. Her cohort of seven students included a woman who'd already won an international prize for her short documentary on survivors of the Darfur conflict, and a guy whose grandmother was an Old Hollywood actress. They'd gone to schools like USC and NYU, and kept asking her where Kalamazoo College was, even though Kalamazoo was in the name.

Renee tried to prove herself. The first year, they spent more time critiquing films and digesting film theory than making anything.

Renee quickly learned that vicious criticism was both rewarded and came easily to her, but her classmates didn't hold back in tearing into Renee's proposed projects any more than she did theirs.

And it wasn't just the students—the professors gave feedback like they were hunting for sport, and nothing satisfied like a kill shot. While the other students easily connected with the faculty, Renee was never able to tell which professors wanted her to push back against their words and which expected her to thank them for their brutal insights.

As they said in the program, "Everyone *wants* to make films. Not everyone *can*." The words swam in Renee's head like her own personal hymn, the evil lullaby that whispered her to sleep, the alarm that woke her in the morning. She found herself tearing apart every idea she had before it was even fully formed, all of her work conducted in a panicked, last-minute frenzy, her stomach on fire at every screening.

It was after her fifth panic attack, at the end of her second year, that Renee realized she needed a break. Just as everyone else was developing their thesis plans and choosing mentors, Renee announced she was going back to Michigan to find a thesis topic by connecting with "regular people."

Her mom and Dave met her at the airport with a bundle of balloons. They meant well, but it made Renee feel like a failure, an Icarus who'd tried to soar but, instead of dying elegantly, had come home to live in her mother's remodeled garage unit.

That first night sleeping on the Ikea bed meant for Deborah's Airbnb guests, Renee promised herself she wouldn't get stuck. She'd follow Instagram accounts about curing burnout. She'd meditate. She'd do morning pages. She'd return to New York to make the most brilliant and thought-provoking thesis her program had ever seen.

All she had to show for it now was a mostly empty notebook and a box of film stuff, including her old camera, gathering dust under her bed. Also, insomnia, which might not be unrelated.

"You can't give up on your passion, Renee," Kadijah said. "I know you're really talented."

A boil of self-hatred burst in Renee's gut.

"No, you *don't* know that," Renee said more viciously than she'd meant. "You're obsessed with *Summer House*, which is the stupidest of all the Bravo franchises, and true crime podcasts, and—and *Lola Gray*! The kind of films I want to make would put you to sleep."

Kadijah's kohl-lined eyes were stony. "Let me get this straight: my taste is so trash that it's an insult for me to say you're talented. Because if you were actually talented, I'd think your stuff was shit."

Renee swallowed hard. She was ashamed of herself for lashing out at Kadijah when they were nowhere near the right target. "That was mean. I'm sorry," she mumbled.

Kadijah turned away. "All right, Walk Away Renee, why don't you make that schedule at home? Like I said, I can handle things here."

5

Lola was leaving LaGuardia in the back of a black SUV. Her phone lit up with a text from Claudia: a photo of her and Josh sipping cocktails with little umbrellas under a cabana. Lola grinned. Nothing made her happier than Claudia's happiness, and her sister's smile hadn't dimmed in the week since the wedding.

The wedding—the night of the wedding.

Lola's face heated.

She kicked herself again for giving in to her desire to take Renee to bed. She didn't feel ashamed, not at all. The NDA she'd picked up off the floor of the hotel that morning was ironclad—though it had been punctured by Lola's heel in her rush to kiss Renee. Lola just worried that for the rest of her life, whenever she thought of her sister's wedding, she'd think of how intoxicating it was to finally get the taste of Renee on her tongue, the feeling of Renee's fingers snaking into her hair, how Renee had called her *Lo*, which no one ever did. How could Lola let her memories of her sister's day be overwhelmed by a one-night stand?

Lola massaged her temple as the New York skyline came into view.

Perhaps *how* wasn't entirely a mystery.

All the years since she'd last seen Renee had made no difference. Lola's body hadn't forgotten what it felt like to look at Renee and course with longing.

When she was a teenager, her feelings for Renee had come out of nowhere, like thunder from an unseen storm. Their childhood friendship had faded with the start of high school, as Lola's commitment to her dream began to consume all her time and attention. Then sophomore year, she had come back from a disappointing trip to L.A. and gone to pick up the missed assignments Renee had collected for her. When Renee had opened the door, Lola saw that she'd hacked off her hair, in retaliation, Renee said, for her mom forcing her to remove the eyebrow piercing she'd done herself. There on the Feldmans' stoop, Lola had felt like she was seeing Renee for the first time—not as a childhood playmate, but as her own person, rebellious and tough and unbearably cool. Renee was angry at everything, because of course she was—Lola knew what her dad had done. Lola had wanted to pull Renee against her, soothe her pain, and taste a little of that wildness.

Back then, it was just a massive unrequited crush, the kind sixteen-year-olds wrote a million songs about and then got over. But in all the years since, Lola had never been able to move on.

She still had to sing about it every night.

Half the tracks on her debut album, *Seventeen Candles*, were about Renee, including her breakout hit, "Jean Jacket." Or, not *about* Renee, but not *not* about her either. Lola's early songs were about the romance of teenage longing: lust, pining, heartbreak, and hoping that the cool girl next door in her jean jacket would finally, truly see you.

Renee hadn't. Neither had anyone else. Lola had spent high school obsessing over her career, not going on summer-night drives with the top down and her hair streaming in the wind, like she sang about. That first album was so rich with yearning because it was about how badly she wanted things that never happened: dances she'd had to skip, dates she was never asked on, kisses no one gave her. Falling hard into the kind of love that changed everything, when she'd never fallen into any kind of love at all.

It was easy to hide the gender of whomever she was singing about, when she wanted to: use *you* and *we* and the listener filled in the rest. She'd known even then, before she was truly in the business, that being bisexual wouldn't help her get where she wanted to go.

Lola was still so careful, discreet. It wasn't like her to hit on a woman surrounded by wedding guests, when only a tiny handful of people—her parents and Claudia, select members of her team, a few of her closest friends—knew she liked women at all. But when she saw Renee waiting in the parking lot, she knew it was her last chance to live out that teenage dream.

The SUV hit a pothole, jolting Lola back to reality.

She'd had her fun. That night was an ending, closure for the past—not the beginning of something new.

Lola forced her mind to the writing session she had calendared for the afternoon. Maybe she could channel all of this into a song. "Jean Jacket, Part 2"—the fulfillment of that unrequited crush from the original, coming full circle. She opened a note on her phone and typed,

> it's ten years later but we're better older

> the way you looked at me tonight
> made me want to be bolder

Lola could feel it coming together—snapshots of moments, the beginning of a chord progression.

Something about your soft skin, legs tangled in the sheets—

No, that was obviously feminine: a man's legs didn't tangle in the sheets.

She edited it to we're tangled in the sheets.

A chill washed over Lola.

It didn't matter how she changed it: everyone would say it was about Ava.

Lola Gray lyrics were famously diaristic, the kind of songs that made listeners feel like confidants. Lo-Lites spent hours picking apart her words, trying to connect them to Lola's life. Lola had enjoyed it once as a special bond with her fans. But the breakup with Ava changed things. She couldn't bear the thought of her fans plundering her lyrics for evidence of her secret love, her secret heartbreak. Already, in the two songs she'd released about Ava, they'd been alarmingly good at finding it.

Lola deleted the line. The vision of the song crumbled.

Lola rubbed her eyes. She hadn't realized that writer's block felt like a physical block: any way she turned, her mind hit another dead end.

She hadn't realized because she'd never had writer's block before.

Lola didn't have jaw-dropping vocal range. She couldn't dance her way out of a wet paper bag. She was pretty, but sex appeal wasn't her major selling point. An exec had once told her that she had a likable sweetness, but wasn't "100% charismatic," like his other top artists were.

What Lola had was *songwriting*, a gift for finding the right words and pairing them with a melody that kept them dancing in your head for days.

At least, that was what she *used* to have.

She hadn't finished a song in months.

In more than a year.

An incoming call from Gloriana saved her from staring at the empty space she knew she'd never fill with a song.

"Good news! We've got a director ready to go and we just need your sign-off. Once that's done, things will start moving quickly, since we're already behind."

Lola suppressed a groan. She couldn't even remember why finding a director had taken so long.

It was grossly unfair that ignoring the documentary couldn't stop it from happening, especially given that Lola was not just the star, but had formed a production company, on her team's recommendation, for this project. She and Gloriana were executive producers, which meant they handled big-picture things like securing a director, while a producer named Micah ran the day-to-day. Streamy was already signed on to distribute the finished product to its 75 million subscribers and had posted most of the film's budget.

"Great," Lola said. "Who is it?"

"Chess Waterston."

The seat belt tightened against Lola's chest as she lurched forward. "*Chess Waterston?* No. Absolutely not."

"Lola—"

"I'm not working with Chess Waterston."

"He did the film about Tatiana Jones that got tons of eyeballs. *Super* viral."

"Because it was all about rehab and her second marriage. It barely mentioned her music." Lola squeezed her eyes shut.

"If this is about keeping private things private, do not worry. We'll get tons of days with Nash on the calendar. Chess will never know. It will be a totally safe space."

Now Lola's eyes flew open in a burst of frustration. Gloriana knew she was bisexual. After all, Gloriana kept track of the NDAs. She had managed things with Ava, kept the label off her back, and—in the wake of the secret breakup—found Lola the perfect PR boyfriend. Currently she and Nash Walker were a year into a love affair manufactured to grab headlines. The issue wasn't whether Lola's sexuality was off-limits for the documentary; Gloriana knew it was off-limits everywhere.

"That's not what I'm talking about," Lola said. "Haven't you heard the rumors about him?"

"Those are rumors."

"Rumors always come from somewhere." Lola forced herself to pause. She had to put this in a language Gloriana understood. "The optics will be terrible. It's only a matter of time before those rumors hit the press and lawyers—or *the police*—get involved. Look up his blind items. I don't want my name mentioned in them."

"I hear you," Gloriana allowed. "But we need to start filming ASAP. We've committed to a timeline for Streamy—they want to see a full cut three months before the album comes out. That puts us at March."

"But I'm *still writing* the album." Technically, true. "It doesn't have a release date yet."

"We were planning for June. You know that, Lola."

"We *discussed* June. I said it felt fast." Lola fought to keep the anxious pitch from her voice.

"You did express that, but as I recall, you also said you could make it work. So let's do that, okay? We're obligated to Streamy now for March. We're lucky Chess can hop on board. Directors aren't usually available on such short notice."

"We need to find someone else who is."

Gloriana clicked her tongue. "I'm not saying that you're being difficult, Lola, but others could see this as difficult."

I've earned the right to be a little difficult, Lola wanted to say, but she clenched her teeth. She didn't want to be that person, who got famous and lost perspective. She was the executive producer. This was her problem to solve.

"What if I can find an alternative?"

"This isn't the time for fun and games. If we miss this deadline, we're liable. You could end up owing Streamy a lot of money."

"Give me until the end of the week," Lola said. "If I can't find another director, we'll go with Chess."

* * *

"You want me to *what*?" Renee bolted upright in bed and almost dropped her phone. The room was dim, the shades down against the noon sun.

Renee had spent the week since receiving Dragan's email simultaneously marathoning *Gilmore Girls* on her laptop and playing a match-three game on her phone. She'd completed six seasons and 187 levels so far. She was about to connect four sapphires for another win when she accidentally answered a call from an unknown number. She had not expected Lola on the other end—how did she even get Renee's number?—asking something completely absurd.

"I'm FaceTiming you," Lola said.

"No, I'm—" Renee slapped her laptop closed and yanked up the shades just in time to see Lola's heart-shaped face appear, curtain bangs framing those huge eyes.

"Were you asleep?" Lola asked.

"No! I—I just got back from the gym." Renee ran a hand through her hair, which only made it stick up at odd angles. "Say again what you're asking me to do."

"We're making a documentary to tie in with my next album. Interviews, some backstage footage, following me around—that kind of thing. The financing is set and Streamy is distributing it, but we need a director."

"You want suggestions? Look, if you miss me that much, you don't need a reason to call."

Lola's eyes flashed. "I didn't—no, Renee, I want you to do it."

"Very funny," said Renee, who did not actually find it very funny. Her face stiffened into an expression halfway between a dismissive laugh and something alarmingly like fear.

Lola remained serious. "I need a director; you're a director. You said you went to film school for documentaries."

"I'm *still in* film school." For now. "That doesn't mean I'm a director."

"Is there some certification process, like you have to get a license to be a real director?" Lola asked. "Or can you just, you know, direct this film?"

Lola was right. On a technical level, Renee could do it—probably, with a life-threatening amount of stress. But she couldn't *actually do it*.

Could she?

Renee's heart lurched. For an instant, she saw it all clearly: the title card showcased on the Streamy app, *The Real Lola Gray—Directed by Renee Feldman.* Her work and name beamed out to millions of viewers around the world. It was the kind of project that directors worked their whole careers for. But just as quick, acid was eating away at the edges of that vision. Millions of viewers meant millions of critics, reviewers digging into her, plummeting Rotten Tomatoes ratings, her classmates and MFA faculty and everyone on earth judging every frame. She'd barely managed to piece together her term projects before she'd taken leave. There was no way she could handle this.

"I'm not the person you're looking for," she said around the lump in her throat.

"This is a huge opportunity. I thought you'd be excited."

"I don't need any favors from you, Lo."

"I'm not trying to do you any." Lola's eyebrows tightened. "Don't take this the wrong way, but you weren't my first choice. I've been calling people for days."

Renee intended to hang up—to have *already* hung up—but curiosity got the best of her. "Why?"

Lola huffed out a breath. "My team hired a director who's totally off base. I just found out, but production's down to the wire. If I can't find someone else, I'll have to work with him."

"Who?"

"Chess Waterston."

Renee's mouth dropped open. "But he sucks! My friend Kadijah made me watch that documentary he did about Tatiana What's-Her-Name, and it was just so . . . uncomfortable."

"I know!" Lola brightened as she leaned closer to the camera. Renee was suddenly glad that Lola had insisted on a video call. "Of course, we'll take care of the equipment and crew, and you'll get paid."

A paycheck that would make a real dent in her debt.

"The only thing is," Lola added, "shooting starts next week."

"*Lo!*"

"Streamy wants a cut by March."

"March? It's almost August!"

"That's why I'm desperate! You are literally my last hope."

"Wow, thanks for keeping me humble."

"Don't roll your eyes. This could launch your career."

"I'll think about it," Renee said.

"Thank you." Lola sighed with relief. "Don't think too long. I need an answer by tomorrow. And Renee? This is strictly professional. It's not—"

"Right, no, yeah!" Renee hurried to agree. "Exclusively professional."

RENEE WALKED INTO Zumba to find her mother running through her stretches. Deborah went to classes at the Fellows Community Center religiously. Renee preferred almost any other activity to cardio-dance set to a reggaeton beat, but Deborah paid for a monthly gym membership for Renee specifically so they could attend this class together. She hadn't made a secret of the fact that she hoped Renee would spin that membership into her own gym-going routine, which would ultimately turn her whole life around.

Deborah knew something about turning her life around. Renee had always admired the way that her mother, abruptly thrust into single-parenthood, had worked her way up to principal of a local elementary school. But Deborah had never understood why Renee couldn't just *make films*, if that's what she wanted to do. A few months off from school was one thing, in Deborah's mind, but a year of waffling was something else.

Also, Deborah loved the Grigorian girls, so when Renee told her about Lola's offer, her reaction was predictable.

"How sweet! Lola's helping you get back on track," Deborah said.

Renee yanked the knot in her shoelace tight. "Actually, I'd be doing her a favor. She said that. She needs a director, and I'm a director."

"Okay, sweetie," Deborah said, in a tone that meant she didn't believe that any more than Renee did. "It's wonderful that you're going to help Lola."

"I don't think I'm going to do it," Renee said, getting to her feet. "It's not the right move for me."

"Oh, Renee, really? At some point, you have to push yourself forward. If you keep waiting for everything to come together perfectly, you'll end up stuck."

"I'm not stuck," said Renee, who was stuck. "I'm just not ready for a job like this."

"Well, life's like that sometimes, isn't it? We're not always ready for what it throws at us, but there we are." Deborah pulled one arm across her body to stretch her shoulder. "You girls always had a connection. That's got to count for something when you're making a movie about someone."

Renee hadn't considered that. She knew Lola better than any other director would—certainly better than Chess Waterston. But on the other hand, Renee *didn't* know Lola, not anymore. She still couldn't square that smiling, stage-ready version of Lola with the woman who'd brought her back to her hotel room and kissed her like her life depended on it. Renee was beginning to understand why Kadijah and Zane were obsessed with Lola Gray. There was the squeaky-clean girl photographed on the red carpet beside her equally squeaky-clean actor-boyfriend, and then there was the woman caught sneaking out of Ava Andreesen's house with what looked like a hickey, if you zoomed in and squinted. Which was the real Lola Gray?

"What did your dean say?" Deborah asked.

"I can't tell him about this!" Renee scoffed. "Dragan Kapić has shown his work at *Cannes*. He was almost nominated for *an Oscar*. I'm not going to impress him with a movie about the teen queen of Michigan."

This had no impact on Deborah whatsoever. "You should ask if you could use this as your thesis project. The timeline is perfect, isn't it?"

"The timeline is *ridiculous*! My thesis only has to be thirty minutes, and I'm stressed enough about finishing that by May. This is *a full-length feature due in March*. That's only eight months!"

Deborah's hands were on her hips. "But wouldn't it be nice to be *done*? Dave and I want to take a trip to New York for your graduation."

The instructor took her place at the front of the class, so Deborah and Renee moved to their spots. Renee was in no mood for a fitness dance party, but at least it would end this conversation. Because unfortunately, Deborah's idea made some sense.

"I'll talk to Dragan," Renee conceded as a reggaeton beat filled the air. "But this is so far below his taste level, he'll never approve it."

"Phenomenal!" Dragan said over Zoom. He was wearing a Western shirt embroidered with blue roses, and glasses with matching blue frames. "I love it!"

"You do?" Renee said. "But it's so *commercial*."

"Film is an expensive art. A true filmmaker finds a way to put his artistic stamp on any project."

Renee was shocked. Dragan could discourse indefinitely about nonfiction film as the art of knowledge, or interleaving visual story with conceptual purpose, or cinepoetics, but she had never heard him admit that films had budgets.

"To stand as your thesis project, this film must go beyond simply showing this Lola person singing songs. It must have real cinematic value. A story, with purpose, yes?"

"Yes," Renee said.

"You'll check in with me every few weeks."

"*You'll* be my advisor? For real? I mean, thanks—I mean, I'm not sure I'm doing it."

Dragan squinted at her. Renee felt like a bug caught under a magnifying glass. "Why wouldn't you?"

Renee wanted to explain that it was terrifying, that she couldn't conceive of a scenario where this didn't end disastrously.

But she couldn't say that. Dragan had only ever treated her as a problem to get off his desk, and now he wanted to take her under his wing. Renee recognized a last chance when she saw it.

Spending a few months with Lola might not be that bad.

It might even be kind of nice.

6

Lola anxiously sipped an iced turmeric latte in the glass-enclosed conference room at Gloriana's Hollywood office. Gloriana herself sat at the head of the large table. The stylish ribbon of silver running through her black hair was the only visible sign that she was, in fact, the same age as Lola's mother. Despite her assiduously wrinkle-free fair skin, to Lola, Gloriana had the reassuring presence of an older woman, full of wisdom and experience and, when necessary, tough love.

Ringing the table were core members of Lola's team. There was Veronika, her longtime publicist, whose wardrobe of stylish neutrals belied the fact that she was an absolute bulldog, professionally speaking. A representative from the comms group that did social media sat beside her, as well as someone from marketing and brand relations. Lola's creative director was there, and the label had someone on speakerphone. Micah, the man-bunned producer, was there too. He kept checking the time on a Rolex that he'd once explained to Lola, against her will, was durable enough to wear surfing.

Several assistants were also present. Lola's assistant, Cassidy, always looked like the most highly strung person in the room. Her milky complexion mottled red when she got nervous, which was often. A lot of stars worked with friends as personal assistants, but Lola had hired Cassidy as a favor to Cassidy's uncle, a top exec at her label.

On her first day, Cassidy had arrived with a perfect coffee order and a stammering speech about how she wasn't there to spy for the label, but to do the best job she could. Lola had appreciated the honesty, but she knew that no matter how many NDAs Cassidy signed, if Lola ever tried to enforce them, she'd jeopardize her relationship with her label. Lola did come to trust Cassidy when the secrecy with Ava made it unavoidable, but she'd always kept Cassidy a little at arm's length.

They'd gathered to meet the documentary's director. At least, that's what they would have been doing, if Renee had been there.

Gloriana's assistant looked up from her phone. "She's almost here. Traffic out of LAX."

"Who doesn't expect traffic out of LAX?" Gloriana muttered.

"It must be unusually bad today," Lola offered. She'd really had to make a case for Renee. Once the team had gotten past their surprise that Lola was seriously putting her foot down about Chess Waterston, they had not been happy. They'd been even less pleased when the replacement Lola found didn't have an IMDb page. Lola showed them the student films Renee had sent over, which were great—but at under ten minutes, hardly evidence that Renee could handle a feature.

Lola had pivoted. Renee had lived next door while Lola was writing *Seventeen Candles*. They'd gone trick-or-treating together as kids, done extra credit projects for physics class together. The Feldmans' house had been like a second home. That history would set the film apart. Veronika got on board, but Micah had worried that Renee simply lacked the experience for this kind of job. "Then you can help her!" Lola had suggested, a little desperately. "Isn't that what producers do?"

Gloriana had relented. They'd go with Renee, under Micah's supervision. After all, Gloriana had added, delivering the film on time was more important than producing something good.

Now, as the seconds ticked by, Lola felt less and less ready to see Renee again. She'd spent much of the week reminding herself that working with Renee would be completely fine. Better than fine—really good! Lola had told Renee that things would be purely professional, and Renee had cut her off in her rush to agree. Not that it took a psychic to figure out Renee's feelings: you didn't slip out after sex without saying goodbye if you liked someone.

The problem was, Lola caught herself thinking about Renee, and not just reliving memories of their hookup. Over lunch, she'd find herself wondering if Renee would scoff at the idea of salad for every meal, and soon she'd be imagining Renee skimming a menu, her gaze flitting to Lola's at a tucked-away table. She'd lay awake, alone in bed, wondering if Renee slept naked and whether she liked to be the big or little spoon, and how it might feel for Renee to push her down into the mattress.

Just then, a receptionist led Renee, with her suitcase and backpack, up to the conference room. Her platinum hair was the only point of light in her all-black outfit: unzipped hoodie over a clingy racerback tank, work pants, thick-soled boots. The outfit was as poorly suited to August in Los Angeles as it was to a professional meeting—but it was incredibly well-suited to Renee.

Lola's breathing went shallow as self-consciousness crowded into her body. What her face was doing, how she was holding herself, did she look normal? It was not only that Renee would see her, but also that Gloriana would see her see Renee—Gloriana, who'd asked why the director Lola had suggested sounded familiar. She'd found Renee's name on the signed NDA and demanded, in the delicate way that Gloriana made demands, an explanation. It was too late for second thoughts. Renee walked through the glass door—and hooked the wheel of her suitcase on its edge.

Renee's bag fell to the floor with a tremendous *smack*, as she stumbled, breaking her fall across the nearest thing to her, which was Lola's lap. Below her, Renee was on her knees, her fingers splayed over the skirt that was taut across Lola's thighs, her breasts pressing into Lola's bare legs. The green eyes that met Lola's were rounded with shock, the mouth just slightly open, the full lower lip pushing forward. Lola could simply reach down, run her thumb across that lip. Maybe Renee would take it into her mouth—

Gloriana cleared her throat like the overseer at a girls' reform school.

Renee scrambled up.

"Are you all right?" Lola asked. Her heart was beating everywhere, down to the tips of her fingers.

"Completely." Renee didn't look at Lola as she took the seat beside her, but her cheeks were pink. "Sorry I'm late. The traffic was wild."

"A classic L.A. welcome!" Gloriana said. "Renee, we're incredibly excited to have you on board."

They did introductions, with each team member echoing how truly incredible that excitement was, even as they eyed Renee warily.

"Welcome to Team Lola!" Gloriana said. "Let's talk goals for this project. After four enormously successful albums, Lola has taken some time away from the spotlight."

Lola fixed her eyes on the eco-friendly straw biodegrading into her latte. Lola knew how it sounded when someone in her position "took time away." At best, it was ungrateful: her dad had worked hard his whole life, and until Lola started making real money, he'd never been able to *take time away* from long-haul trucking. At worst, it made people think she'd needed rehab or had some kind of breakdown; addiction and mental health issues were legitimate medical problems for normal people, but for celebrities, they were juicy scandals.

Although, Lola supposed, she hadn't been *that* far from a mental breakdown, after Ava. If things had gone differently, Album 5 would have already come out, full of the perfect, honest love songs she'd written.

Lola herself would have already come out, with a girlfriend beside her.

But without Ava, there had been no reason for any of it: not to come out, or record those songs, or even force herself out of bed.

Which was how she ended up here, listening to Gloriana tell Renee that the world needed to be reminded that Lola Gray existed and that they loved her. Sitting through a meeting like that was a very effective way to make yourself feel unloved.

"We—and Streamy—want something accessible and authentic, but fun. Nothing controversial," Gloriana was saying. "Fans should feel like we're peeling back the skin on their favorite pop star, and letting them see that, underneath, she's a regular girl, just like them."

"*Peel Lola's skin back*," Renee echoed as she scribbled in her notebook. "I wasn't expecting the horror angle, but it could be really fresh."

Lola nearly choked on the last sip of her latte.

"That's funny." Gloriana gave Renee a tolerant smile. "We want viewers to feel that closeness you have with a sister or a best friend."

"Which is why it is so phenomenal to have you on board," Veronika chimed in. "Lola's childhood best friend behind the camera is a storyline in itself. *So much* we can do from a publicity perspective."

"Before we get ahead of ourselves," Gloriana said, "Renee, you'll be working very, very closely with Micah. We know this shoot is a big lift for you—a little beyond your previous experience, I'm sure you'd agree—so Micah's here to take the pressure off. From technical questions, to pulling together a product that Streamy will be happy with, and hitting that deadline—he's your guy."

Renee shot a wary glance at Micah. "My guy?"

"Exactly!" Gloriana said. "Micah, the floor is yours."

"This is the shooting schedule." Micah passed a folder across the table to Renee.

"You already prepped this?" she asked.

Micah's man-bun bobbed as he nodded. "We need to hit the ground running."

Renee scanned the document. "How closely are you expecting me to stick to this?"

"*Very* closely," Micah said. "With all the schedules involved, there's no margin for error. But we've calendared out a nice balance of bigger events and intimate moments that will showcase everything fans love about Lola."

"I should have been involved in drafting this," Renee said with the kind of bluntness Lola was incapable of.

"As I'm sure you know, Renee, films are highly collaborative." Gloriana's smile, familiar to Lola, gently conveyed conversation-ending finality. "We all collaborated on this schedule so you can, as Micah said, hit the ground running."

"Right," Micah continued, ignoring the unease scrawled across Renee's face. "Shooting starts tomorrow. The crew can't wait to meet you."

Renee sighed, nodding unhappily. Then she turned to Lola. "If shooting starts tomorrow, when are we meeting? Dinner tonight?"

An awkward silence settled over the conference room. No one ever asked Lola about her schedule. In most meetings like this, only Gloriana addressed her directly.

Cassidy spoke up from the corner. "Lola has a dinner at eight and before that—"

"Before that, please clear my afternoon," Lola said.

"But you have—" Pink rose on Cassidy's cheeks.

"Whatever I have isn't more important than this. The Streamy deadline and all that," Lola said. "If we want this film done right, I can carve out a few hours to meet with the director."

THE MEETING ENDED. As everyone filtered out of the conference room, Lola took a moment to study Renee. She was sorting through the various documents she'd been given. Her brows were drawn, and she was chewing the inside of her cheek. There was something comforting in the fact that Renee looked a little out of place in the glossy setting of Lola's life.

"Are you going to say hi, or just stare at me like a weirdo?" Renee said without raising her eyes.

An easy grin spread across Lola's face. "Stare at you like a weirdo."

"That'll make filming hard," Renee said wryly. But then Renee did look up. Her gaze shifted slowly down to Lola's mouth and lingered. "I take it back. If you keep smiling like that, it'll be a breeze."

"Smiling like what?" Lola asked.

Cassidy interrupted before Renee could answer. "Your car's here."

As Lola and Renee headed for the elevators, Gloriana popped out of her office. "Renee, *so* nice to meet you. Lola, let me steal you briefly."

Lola stepped inside and Gloriana pulled the door closed after her.

"We can still pull Chess back in," Gloriana said.

"I don't want Chess. That was the point of hiring Renee."

Gloriana peered at Lola through the bottommost edge of her glasses. In flats, Gloriana was several inches taller than Lola, and she never wore flats. The height difference made Lola feel like a child.

"I'll only say this once, Lola: don't let this get messy."

Lola opened her mouth to protest, then closed it again.

Her first impulse was denial: she had no idea what might be getting messy or why. But that was a lie for everyone else, not for Gloriana, the keeper of the NDAs.

"I won't," Lola said. "There's nothing going on between me and Renee."

"I'm glad to hear that," Gloriana said. "You can see how that would be really undesirable from our perspective, right?"

"Absolutely," Lola agreed.

Lola had confided in Gloriana that she was bisexual when her career was just beginning. Gloriana had thanked her for her bravery, then explained, "In this industry, details about your life are currency. You need to manage your wealth, just like you do at the bank." They'd both felt Lola's sexual orientation wasn't information the public needed to know. With Lola always tied to men, it had never mattered.

Then came Ava.

Gloriana had cautioned Lola not to lose her head then too. But Lola hadn't listened, so Gloriana spent a year protecting her, making sure the world—including most members of Lola's team—believed the women were just super close friends. Together with Veronika, she killed any story that said otherwise. When Lola had wanted to include a song she'd written about Ava as a bonus track on *Wild Heart*, then decided to release another as a stand-alone single, Gloriana had made sure the lyrics were sufficiently obscure and agreed. The songs did well, but now Lola wished Gloriana had put her foot down. Those songs—along with her indiscretions with Ava—had spawned a community of fans. The #LavaTruthers obsessively analyzed Lola's songs, photos, posts, and who knew what else for signs that she was into women, generally, and one woman, specifically.

At least she had Gloriana to thank for stopping her from putting everything on the line for Ava, like she'd wanted to.

"And if anything does happen, we've got Chess in our back pocket," Gloriana said, giving Lola's shoulder a reassuring squeeze, as if Lola had raised the concern herself.

But as Lola joined Renee in the hall, she found herself wondering why it had felt like a threat.

7

At a table in the corner of a farm-to-table restaurant, Renee scoffed at salad-for-lunch exactly as Lola had expected. Renee attacked a plate of steak and eggs as she perused her slightly crumpled copy of the shooting schedule.

"*Flutter by Lola Gray, perfume scent consultation,*" Renee read, then crammed a forkful into her mouth. Around her food, she said, "*Swimwear collaboration design meeting.* What's with this corporate stuff?"

"They're other ventures I'm involved with," Lola explained as she assembled a perfect bite of her macrobiotic salad. "This is a great opportunity for cross-promotion."

"Perfect. I've always wanted to make a film about swimwear design." Scanning farther down the page, she read, "*Make-A-Wish meeting, schedule TBD.*"

"What do you have against Make-A-Wish?" She didn't expect Renee to love everything the team had planned, but that was how the business worked: Renee had been hired to do a job, not reinvent it.

"I have something against putting kids with cancer on camera for clout."

"They don't all have cancer," Lola said. "I've done Make-A-Wish six times."

"And now they want it in your movie." Renee dropped the paper on the table and stabbed it with a finger. "I'm already falling asleep watching this thing and we haven't even shot it yet. We need to say something real here."

Lola shifted uncomfortably. The point of the documentary was to make people forget she'd stepped into a dimmer part of the spotlight and bridge the gap in income between albums. *Saying something real* wasn't necessary.

"Do they always talk around you like that?" Renee crossed her arms. She'd taken off her hoodie, and the tattooed muscles of her arms and shoulders bulged distractingly. Lola forced herself not to look. "At that meeting, it was like you weren't sitting right there."

Lola's grip on her fork tightened. She'd learned years ago that any meeting with more than two people wasn't a place for her voice to be heard. She was used to it now—maybe *too* used to it, because hearing Renee say it like that made her feel seen. But as the spotlight sometimes did, it also made her feel horribly small.

"It's business. That's how it works."

"Is that how you want *this* to work? You really want to shoot—" Renee grabbed the paper again and read: "Stylist meeting, *Fit to Live*. Glam session, *Fit to Live*. Red carpet premiere, *Fit to Live*. What even *is Fit to Live*?"

Lola blinked at her. Did Renee live under a rock? "*Fit to Live* is going to be the biggest movie of the fall. Nash is the star, so I'm committed to the premiere."

"Right, your *boyfriend*, Nash Walter."

"Nash *Walker*." Maybe Renee really did live under a rock. She and Nash had been in constant circulation in the tabloids, thanks to their PR teams working overtime. "Do you have a problem with him?"

"It would have been nice to know you had a boyfriend before we—"

Lola silenced Renee with a raised hand. The neighboring tables were empty, but they were still in public.

Renee corrected course. "I mean, before I could have met him at the wedding. But I didn't even know I should have been looking for a boyfriend."

"I assumed you knew. We've been all over the tabloids for months," Lola said, conscious of the fluttering in her belly at the thought of Renee being jealous. It hadn't occurred to her to mention Nash to Renee, since she didn't think of him as her actual boyfriend. "Anyway, the relationship is almost over."

Renee pulled an exaggerated frown. "No, babe, you can work it out!"

"Check page three."

"*Break up with Nash Walker,*" Renee read dubiously.

"It's a PR relationship," Lola said in a hushed voice. "Management sets it up. Everyone does it when you get to a certain level. Nash needed a girlfriend for a few press cycles, and I—well, I haven't dated anyone publicly in a while, but my fans love thinking they know exactly who my albums are about. Don't feel bad if you believed it. You're supposed to think we're really together."

"I didn't think anything. Someone asked if he was at the wedding, so I googled him, saw he looked like an overgrown sea monkey in gray sweatpants, and forgot all about him."

"The sea monkey and I are pretty close friends." Nash and Lola's platonic chemistry was what made the PR relationship believable. Their fans didn't need to know that their bond was less *young lovers* and more *human sacrifices commiserating on the altar*. "You should interview him."

"An interview with your fake boyfriend is already on the list." Renee flipped back to the first page of the schedule. "Or should I say, your *current* fake boyfriend? What about that guy from *You're Next!*? Didn't you date for like five years?"

Lola bit back her exasperation at Renee's tone. If Renee was truly curious about Lola's love life, she would have hung around the morning after instead of bolting during the five minutes Lola spent in the shower.

"Three years, and his name is Kyte," Lola corrected. She and Kyte had met as contestants on *You're Next!* Her second album was all about falling in love with him, and her third processed their breakup. "That was real. He still gets death threats from fans who think he cheated on me. The truth is, we both realized we wanted other things."

Renee leaned in across the table, eyes narrowing. "You mean you realized you wanted p—"

"*Renee!*" Lola blushed so fast and intensely, it was as if her cheeks had caught fire. She pressed her lips together, deciding, then said cautiously, "Actually, I'd known since high school that I was interested in . . . what you're asking about."

Saying it out loud had her heart racing hard enough to make her a little dizzy. Lola could count on her fingers how many times she'd explicitly come out to someone—certainly never in a public restaurant.

"You did?" Renee said, her eyebrows popping up.

"Yes. Not that it's relevant, because that's not going in the film. Gloriana would never in a million years approve it."

The mention of an authority figure reactivated Renee's teenage sensibilities. Her expression rumpled. "Why would she need to?"

"Because she's the executive producer, and my manager."

As she said it, Lola's ribs tightened with embarrassment. She didn't want to explain how the industry worked to Renee, who had only barely grasped the situation with Nash. Lola's life wasn't like Renee's. Lola couldn't just be whoever she wanted—well, be whoever she truly was. *Lola Gray* was a business as much as a person. There were optics to consider, sales, her image, the reaction on social media, the fans, her label, and the impact on the dozens of people who depended on her for their livelihoods.

"I know what you're thinking," Lola said.

Renee's eyes were fixed on her. In this light, Lola could see gold threaded in the green. "You do?"

"I have a"—Lola checked the room and hushed her voice further—"fake boyfriend and I'm not, you know, *honest* about who I am. Don't try to tell me you like my music, because I know you never have, and you're already regretting that you're making a movie about my life when it's so—so *stupid*."

When Lola finished speaking, her napkin was twisted in her hands, below the table where Renee couldn't see it.

Renee scoffed instead. "Your life's not stupid, Lo." She brushed the schedule to the edge of the table. "*That* is not your life."

Lola went still.

"These are setups, and you didn't come up with them. You're right that I don't really want to film you trying on clothes or smelling swimsuits or whatever. Because that's not who you *are*."

Lola's throat felt thick. She longed to ask who Renee thought she was instead.

"What I want to know is what story *you*—the real you, Lo Grigorian, not Lola Gray—want to tell," Renee said.

Lola wanted to laugh. The irony was that fundamentally, she wanted to tell the same story that everyone else on her team did: the writing and recording of Album 5. Unless she started writing songs in the next few weeks, the film crew would be watching her career implode instead.

Gloriana already suspected something was wrong. A month ago, she'd mentioned there were people she could bring in if Lola needed help. Everyone used ghostwriters, Gloriana said, and she had someone who could write in the Lola Gray style so seamlessly, Lola would forget she hadn't written the songs herself. Then, it had taken all of Lola's overdeveloped sense of self-control to simply say, *No, thank you. I promise things are moving along.*

The truth was, she'd rather never perform again than pretend she'd written someone else's words. It wasn't just her integrity. Lola's music was at her core. Writing and performing her songs was the only thing that made her feel truly like herself, without any compromises. Free. Without that, there was no Lola Gray. There was barely a Lo Grigorian.

"I guess I'm not sure what I want," Lola finally said.

"That's okay." Renee set her forearms on the table. "We can find the story together. Right?"

That *we* seemed to mean something different from when Gloriana said it, and for a moment Lola allowed herself to hope. Even if this ended in disaster, at least she had Renee on her side.

"Right."

8

The first day of shooting, Renee pulled her rental car up to the gate of Lola's house in the Hollywood Hills. She was so exhausted that she almost couldn't feel the anxiety thrumming in her chest, her stomach, the palms of her hands.

Almost.

She had spent the previous night sleepless, too hot, and snarled in the sheets of her hotel bed, thinking of all the reasons she should back out before she totally humiliated herself.

She wasn't qualified to direct *anything*, let alone a feature-length film, a monthslong shoot, under the eye of Lola's team—who clearly didn't want her here, since they'd assigned Micah to babysit her. Renee nearly longed for the toxic atmosphere of her MFA program. At least there, like a toddler tripping over her own feet, she didn't have very far to fall before hitting the ground. Here, she risked plummeting from much greater heights.

In the dim hotel room, Renee had mentally composed a dozen panicked emails to Dragan, and actually looked up the deadline to withdraw for a tuition refund. She'd begun accepting that when Kadijah called her Walk Away Renee, it would no longer refer to her abysmal dating record. It probably wasn't too late to get her job back at Prince's, if she begged. She had steeled herself for the look on her mother's face: disappointed, not surprised.

But then, as the sun was lightening the sky, Renee thought about Lola.

Or more accurately, thought about Lola *again*. This time, it was an image of her that wouldn't leave Renee's mind—and not the image of Lola's mouth falling open as Renee's lips tightened over her nipple, which Renee barely thought about anymore. No, it was of Lola sitting in that production meeting like a silent piece of set dressing, while the real players talked around her, *about* her. But she *had* put her foot down about working with Chess Waterston.

Lola said she didn't know what she wanted out of a film about her life. What Renee heard was an unspoken *yet*. She was putting her story in Renee's hands until she figured out how she wanted it told.

When it came down to it, Lola needed her.

That felt big. It felt important.

Now, the gate swung open and Renee drove up to a generous, Spanish-style home in white stucco with a terra-cotta roof. A burbling fountain stood in the middle of the circular drive, ringed with mature palm trees. Renee whistled through her teeth. Lola had come a long way from Fellows. The crew had congregated near the craft services van serving coffee, surrounded by hard-sided cases of gear.

Micah loped over to meet Renee as she parked. His tan glowed in the bright morning sun, a fitted chambray shirt hinting at the taut physique beneath. He looked fresh in a way that felt personally offensive to Renee, who felt as fresh as the crumpled wrapper of a fast-food breakfast sandwich. She frowned down at her dingy black polo. She'd chosen it after agonizing over whether to wear a normal T-shirt or something nicer to signal she wasn't just another crew member. She had settled on the worst possible compromise.

"There she is, our woman in charge!" Micah said. "Let me introduce you."

Renee met the sound operator and his assistant, the gaffer and best boy, an additional camera operator, two production assistants, a makeup artist and her assistant, a hairstylist, a still photographer for behind-the-scenes shots, and Micah's assistant. Renee's mouth went dry. Outside of professional shoots where she'd been a production assistant, the largest crew Renee had worked with was three people. Once.

After Renee greeted everyone, she pulled Micah aside as she poured herself a much-needed coffee. The acidic first sip turned her stomach. She chased it with another swallow.

"Big crew," she observed.

"It's a big production."

"Sure, but we're not going to be able to get that *authentic* feeling with twenty-five people behind the camera. Do we really need *two* makeup artists?"

Micah was looking at her like she'd proposed they shoot the film on first-gen iPhones. "We want everyone looking their best."

Renee sighed. "Then let's get one of them inside with Lola."

"No, no, Lola's in hair and makeup with her own people," Micah said as his phone rang. "Check in later!" he mouthed, then clapped Renee on the shoulder—at the exact moment she'd raised her cup for a sip. The black coffee sloshed straight down the front of her polo. Cursing, she pulled the soaked fabric away from her body. At least the coffee wasn't hot enough to burn. Micah, already mid-conversation, hadn't even noticed what he'd done. Renee grabbed a stack of paper napkins and began to rub at the stain. The napkins instantly disintegrated, leaving wet white nubbins clinging to the black material.

"You gotta blot, not rub," someone said.

Renee looked up. This was Alejandro, the sound operator. He looked to be in his mid-thirties, with light brown skin and a mop of black curls under a Dodgers cap.

"It's fine," Renee huffed. "This shirt isn't exactly a family heirloom."

Although Renee had to admit that the first day of shooting, when they were filming with Lola's stylist, manager, and publicist as they chose a look for the premiere of Lola's fake boyfriend's blockbuster, was not an ideal time to be wearing napkin crumbles.

An anxious strawberry blonde, flicking at the screen of an iPad, approached Renee.

"Can I show you where you'll be filming?" she asked.

"That would be great. Remind me, you're . . ."

"Cassidy. Lola's assistant," she said.

Cassidy led Renee through a gigantic front door that looked hewn from a hundred-year-old oak and a marble entryway, to a spacious sitting room with a fireplace and huge cream-colored couches.

"Jason St. Jude will be here in an hour, and Gloriana and Veronika will be here in thirty," Cassidy said.

Perfect. That meant she had about thirty seconds to decide where to set up the cameras. Renee pulled at the now-cold, wet fabric of her polo as she took stock of the space and tried to focus. There were so many people waiting for her, so many choices to make. She felt like she'd forgotten where she was supposed to begin.

Cassidy must have read the panic on Renee's face. "Um, maybe I could tell you how these things usually go?"

"Yes, please," Renee said.

"So Lola tries on the dresses in her office, so we'll need that off-limits for the crew."

"Absolutely."

"And then she comes out to model them. I think in front of the fireplace is a nice spot for that, because Gloriana and Veronika can sit on that couch there. And when Jason arrives, he usually wheels in a garment rack with all the dresses right in the front door. It's so glamorous."

"Okay, right," Renee said, then took a deep breath and turned to the crew. "Let's get Camera B on a tripod focused on the couch. We're going to be getting the manager's reaction there. And I'll handle Camera A on a gimbal. The first shot's going to be Jason St. Jude coming through the front door with the garment rack full of dresses. Let's get moving!" she said with as much authority as she could muster.

The crew got to work. Renee gave Cassidy an appreciative nod. "Thank you."

Cassidy responded with a slight smile. "No problem. Lola asked me to make sure you got your bearings."

"Oh. Well, I appreciate it. Where is Lola?"

Cassidy pointed at the massive staircase with a fancy wrought-iron railing. "Upstairs. Turn right, the door at the end of the hall."

Moments later, Renee was poised to knock when Lola's bedroom door swung open.

"Cassidy, can you—oh, Renee!"

"Hi!" Renee's eyes went wide. Lola was wrapped in a robe, her hair up in rollers, her legs bare.

"Hi—I wasn't expecting you! I mean, not up here." Lola leaned against the jamb. "Nervous for your first day of filming?"

"I'm not nervous," said Renee, whose stomach was a Gordian knot of nerves.

Lola smirked at her. "You wouldn't be, Renee Feldman."

"What's that supposed to mean?"

"Just that you're always so confident. Nothing intimidates you." Lola's expression clouded as she took in Renee's outfit. "What happened to your shirt?"

Renee tugged at her polo, which did not make the trail of napkin particles less visible. "Oh, that—craft services coffee was a bit of a jump scare."

"Oh my god, I'll get Cassidy to make you a cappuccino." Then she grabbed Renee's hand and pulled her into her bedroom.

Lola led her past the bed, which Renee absolutely did not look at with any curiosity, and into a truly massive closet. Lola knelt, her robe riding up to reveal a smooth swath of thigh, and pawed through a lower rack of hangers.

"What are you doing?" Renee asked.

"Finding you something clean to wear. You can't go out there like that."

"It's no big deal." Renee crossed her arms. "As a PA, my stuff got ruined all the time."

Lola shot her a scolding look.

"Fine, yes, a clean shirt would be good. Thanks."

"Here." Lola stood, holding up an oversize white button-up.

Renee looked at the label and started. "This has got to cost a thousand dollars!"

"Do you want it or not?"

Without thinking, Renee gripped the hem of her polo. She pulled it up high enough to expose the band of her sports bra when Lola let out a faint gasp, the button-up bunched in her hands. Renee paused and waited for Lola to turn around.

But she didn't.

Renee didn't either.

The cool, climate-controlled air swept over her skin as Renee pulled the polo over her head. Part of her still expected Lola to be looking away when Renee saw her face again—but she was doing the opposite. Her dark doe eyes widened as they took in Renee's body, flicking from her sports bra to the black lines of her tattoos to her stomach. Wherever Lola's gaze traveled, Renee's skin prickled at the attention. First her nipples tightened, then the feeling gathered between her thighs.

Renee reached for the shirt that Lola was clutching. "Can I have that?"

"Oh! Sorry!" Lola thrust it toward her. Her cheeks were rosy, her breathing a little quick, Renee noticed with satisfaction.

As Renee buttoned the clean shirt—thanks to the oversize cut, it fit—Lola grabbed the dirty polo from the floor. "I'll take care of this," she said, brushing by Renee as she walked out of the room. "I should get dressed."

DOWNSTAIRS, GLORIANA AND Veronika had arrived and were having additional makeup applied on top of the full faces they were already wearing.

Alejandro eyed Renee's fresh shirt.

"It's Lola's," Renee explained.

Alejandro's brows furrowed in confusion. "It is?"

Renee kicked herself. He hadn't needed to know that.

"Yeah, we're, um, old friends," Renee said. Although the way Lola had just eye-fucked her hadn't felt *friendly*. "Now where's that gimbal?"

They had just finished testing light levels when Lola Gray descended the grand staircase and officially arrived on set. Her hair was out of the rollers, looking gorgeously tousled, the curtain bangs brushing her cheeks. She was dressed simply in jeans and a striped boatneck shirt, her feet bare. Renee bit her lip, watching Lola introduce herself to the whole crew. It was frankly bizarre how perfect Lola looked, like she'd wandered out of a Godard film.

Lola turned to Renee, those big eyes peering up at her through thick lashes. "Where do you want me?"

Renee's mouth went dry.

Shit, no, she had to concentrate. This was the most important day of her professional career. It wasn't the time to fantasize.

"Let's get you answering the door."

Renee tailed Lola to the front hall. When Lola opened the door, she threw her arms around Jason as if he were her closest friend, then slapped on an awestruck look as she saw the garment rack full of sparkles. "All this, for me? Gosh, I feel like a princess!"

Renee winced. It was campy, but that was okay. Lola would relax once she got used to filming.

"How do you think this is going?" Alejandro whispered to Renee two hours into the shoot. Lola was off with Jason getting into a new dress.

Renee rubbed her temple. "First day jitters."

Lola had tried on seven dresses, none of which satisfied Gloriana, Veronika, and Jason. Some would upstage Nash—Renee had to suppress a groan at the idea of Lola dimming her light for that sea monkey. Once, to Renee's horror, Veronika had said a crystal-encrusted number made Lola's diminutive frame look bulky. Despite their negative comments, Lola's smile had not left her face for one moment. She had squealed at each new dress, repeated the princess comment, and several times announced how excited she was for Nash's big premiere. With each look, instead of giving a real opinion, she'd made a comment about how lucky she was to have the chance to wear such a pretty dress by this big-name designer—obviously, they had an arrangement with the brand. Renee was fairly certain that Lola hadn't liked any of the looks at all.

Jason emerged and presented Lola in a clingy black dress with cutouts exposing the side of her stomach and hip and much of her back, strung together by bits of glittery rope. The dress had so many parts missing that Renee couldn't figure out how it was staying on.

"What do we say?" Jason cooed. "I say, *fabulous.*"

"Oh, *yessss*," Gloriana purred, as she snapped pictures to send to Nash's people. "That's it."

Renee glared at the dress, trying to see what they saw.

"Completely agree. It's grown and sexy," Veronika said. "Mature, but in the *right* way, you know?"

Renee's jaw tightened. All the cutouts and sparkles were as mature as a twenty-one-year-old on her first trip to Vegas. And no one had bothered to ask Lola's opinion. She was smiling stiffly, her hand hovering over the bare skin of her stomach.

"Yes!" Jason chimed in. "Mature but still very, very young and fun."

Renee moved closer with the camera. "Lo, how do you like this one? We need your reaction."

Lola's eyes darted to her and Renee knew she was right: Lola *hated* this dress.

"I do *really* like it," Lola said diplomatically. "But I want to try a few more. Jason brought so many pretty things."

Finally, Lola came out in a dress that she wasn't smiling in—at least, not the smile she'd been wearing all day. This dress was bias-cut emerald-green silk, draped from a halter neckline. The color lit her warm brown eyes so that they were almost gold. The low back showed plenty of skin, but unlike the other dresses, it would not have been at home at a nightclub. She looked sophisticated, elegant—and *definitely* sexy, Renee thought as she watched the silk dance over Lola's curves.

As Gloriana took her pictures, Lola's shoulders were relaxed, her fingers creating ripples through the skirt. She was calmer and more confident than she had been all day.

"You don't look happy," Jason said.

"I don't? I think this one's so pretty," Lola said.

"This isn't it," Gloriana said, like she hadn't heard Lola at all.

Veronika *hmm*'ed emphatically. "I agree, it's the black one."

The Lola Gray smile was back.

"Oh, seriously?" Renee groaned before she could stop herself.

Gloriana's attention snapped to Renee, her mouth tight. "All right, Renee, since you insist on contributing from behind the camera, what do you think she should wear?"

Renee focused on the camera, not on returning Gloriana's glare. "It's clearly this one. It's the only dress she's looked a little bit like herself in. You feel good in this one, don't you, Lo?"

Lola cast her eyes up at Renee. She looked a little taken aback, but a little pleased too. "I do."

"Which you would know, if you made an effort to get her opinion, instead of telling her what to do," Renee said.

"Renee, Lola has us here for our professional expertise." Gloriana would have used the same tone to talk to an eight-year-old. "We don't tell her what to do and she's perfectly able to give us her opinions—as she often does. Now, I think we're done. Everyone agrees it's the black one? Cassidy, send this over to Nash's people to confirm."

Cassidy nodded, but her eyes were tracing a nervous triangle between Lola, Renee, and Gloriana.

"Let's send this one too," Lola said. "I do really like it. And it's always good to have options."

Gloriana opened her mouth, closed it again. "Whatever you say, Lola."

9

That evening, Lola sat at the piano bench in her home studio. The white baby grand had been a gift to herself after her first Grammy. Lola trailed her hands over the ivory keys, experimentally pressing down on a B-flat.

The space was full of throw blankets and cushy pillows. It held her favorite acoustic guitar, as well as the one she'd learned to play on, an electric keyboard, and a few percussion instruments, along with an electronic drum pad. A desk had everything she needed to rough cut demos—unused now for months. A glass-fronted cabinet stored every journal and notebook she'd written lyrics in, from middle school to the present. Through the enormous windows overlooking Los Angeles, dusk had turned the sky deep indigo.

It had been her favorite room in the house, but the peace she'd felt here eluded her now.

Once they'd stopped rolling, Lola couldn't wait for Jason to pack up his dresses and for Gloriana, Veronika, and the crew to clear out. She'd been annoyed at how much energy it took to be on camera in her own home and the effort to hide her dislike of the uncomfortable, revealing looks the team wanted for the premiere—though somehow, Renee had seen it anyway.

She had promised herself that once they left, she'd get to songwriting in earnest. She'd renewed that vow every time she'd looked at

Gloriana, who had worked so hard for Lola, who had stewarded her career, and imagined the disappointment on her face when she realized that Lola hadn't been honest about the next album.

Lola had a session with her longtime producer scheduled for next week, to be documented by Renee's cameras, and she could *not* show up with nothing written. She just needed one song.

Lola played a C-minor chord, then let the melancholy sound fade.

In her phone's notes app, she scrolled through lyrical phrases and ideas. In the past, songs would spark in her mind, a whole story kindled by the few lines she'd saved, the arc of a melody catching, until everything flared together. Now, thumbing through her notes, she felt none of that combustive creativity. She felt instead like she was stumbling through some horrible funhouse of warped mirrors.

She came to what she'd scribbled after Ava left her.

Most of it didn't rise to the level of a lyric, just wild declarations she never got the chance to make aloud.

I'll never stop loving you.
Tell me what you want and I'll do it. I always have.
How could you do this to me?

Lola squeezed her eyes shut and pressed her palms to her face. When would it stop hurting? It had been a year. A year and three weeks.

SHE'D FIRST SEEN Ava onstage at a movie awards show, presenting the award for, of all things, Best Kiss. Her blonde hair was huge and wild, and a fishhook grin exposed the famous gap in her front teeth. Lola was transfixed. Somehow, even from so far away, Ava had known. Her gaze lingered on Lola with the ghost of an invitation. Moments later, Lola won for Best Movie Song, and Ava was waiting backstage. It set off a year of secret dating: stealing weekends to spend in each other's arms, wearing the same perfume so they'd smell like each other, walking red carpets knowing that later their gowns would be puddled on the floor.

Lola had never been infatuated with anyone like she was with Ava. It was like being plunged underwater—unexpected and completely engulfing. Just thinking of her made Lola feel electric—and she thought of Ava constantly, especially in the long weeks they spent apart when Lola channeled her fixation into her music. She wrote Ava dozens of songs. Some were tales of lust and Ava's ice-blue eyes and all the things Lola wanted to do to her, but others told the story of a whirlwind romance, of being swept away in a secret love affair.

Lola had truly believed they were falling in love.

After all, Lola had always been a romantic. When she was young and things were chaotic at home, she escaped into stories where love was powerful enough to change the world. Love was supposed to be grand and demanding and even painful. Maybe that was why she missed all the red flags.

Like how when they were apart, Ava could be so bad at keeping in touch that Lola sometimes wondered if she missed her at all. Or how, when they were in bed, Ava was always the focus of attention, and never Lola.

Or how when Lola pressed that she wanted to spend more time together, Ava would invite her to a DJ gig or to come as her date to an awards show—things she knew Lola couldn't do. Lola tried not to be hurt by it, to convince herself that Ava wanted to go public because she loved her, even if she'd never said so. Already, Ava pushed her boundaries, tugged her into the bathroom at an event, gave her a "friendly" kiss on a red carpet.

Real love required sacrifices. And if Lola wanted this to be forever-love, the kind that lasted a lifetime, she would have to make some.

She'd sat down with Gloriana and told her she was ready to go public with everything: her sexuality, her relationship, and an album of songs about Ava that she was ready to take to her producer. Gloriana had slowly adjusted the thick frames of her glasses, then said, "Let's talk it through."

Gloriana had sketched out a full media plan, tell-all interviews, a couples photoshoot in a major magazine, a color story for her Instagram in the colors of the bisexual flag, a special line of merch. And more serious issues—the business impact of losing part of her fan base: conservatives, outraged parents of eight-year-old Lo-Lites, and fans who lived in countries where same-sex relationships were illegal. Then Gloriana had put her hand on Lola's knee and told her, "Just do one thing for me before we move forward. We can spin you coming out because you're in love, but if things fall apart, the narrative gets more challenging. We don't want to handle a breakup on top of all this. Just make sure Ava's committed."

"Don't worry," Lola had said.

It felt so stupid now to remember how excited she'd been to tell Ava her new plan.

"I know you want more from me, from our relationship," Lola had begun.

"Oh, Lolly, I—" Ava interrupted.

Afterward, Lola would always wish she'd just let Ava say her piece. Instead, Lola grabbed her hands and squeezed. "No, I want that too! What we have is just—it's so special, it feels almost like magic, you know? I don't want to hide it anymore."

"Lolly—"

"Gloriana is already on board. My team will know the best way to debut the relationship—and there's going to be so much to deal with me coming out. But we can get through it. I'm going to record those songs so my whole next album can be about you! Wouldn't that be perfect?

"There's just this one thing—Gloriana wants me to make sure we're really committed to each other, just because there's going to be so much attention on our relationship. We are, right? I know I am. Honestly, I'm in love with you, Ava."

It was the first time she'd said that.

"*Lola.*"

Lola could never describe how it felt when Ava said her name like that. The sensation of pins and needles, half numbness, half pain. The sudden lightheadedness, like the world slipping out from under her. Ava was wearing this horrible, pitying look, and Lola was the object of that pity.

"God, this is really awkward." Ava extricated her hands from Lola's grasp. "I totally support you coming out and releasing those songs and all that, but when it comes to our relationship, I'm not in the same place."

Lola closed the piano's key lid and cast her eyes to the cabinet of her old journals, full of words that came straight from her heart. Writing was so easy when love was an adventure that lay ahead, heartbreak seemed glamorous, and just thinking about the girl next door could pull a song out of her. Would she ever find that ease again?

Lola drafted a text to Cassidy:

> Let's reschedule the producer session for after the festival next month. I want to focus on that performance.

She hesitated. Normally she'd run that by Gloriana, and there was filming to consider. But the thought of showing up to her producer's studio with nothing made Lola genuinely feel like she might puke.

She hit send and headed to the kitchen. She needed tea. Tea would help.

Someone had hung Renee's laundered shirt in the hall, enormous coffee stain gone.

Lola worried her lip, remembering that morning. She'd just wanted to make sure Renee felt her best for her first day, but she'd ended up gawking like a thirteen-year-old who'd never seen a pair of tits before.

Not that Renee seemed to mind.

They were *really* nice tits. Her nipples had hardened right before Lola's eyes. And the straps of her black sports bra had framed her strong, tattooed shoulders, her stomach taut as she pulled the polo over her head.

Lola had to get a hold of herself. Thinking about Renee's boobs was a victimless crime, but it opened the door to doing more than *thinking*. Maybe Gloriana's warning wasn't so unnecessary after all.

Lola put the kettle on.

She wasn't going to let things get messy. She was the consummate professional. Which was why, while she waited for the water to boil, she texted Renee in a very professional capacity.

> Congrats on the first day of shooting! 🥂

There. She set her phone down on the counter. It lit up immediately.

> I wish that was real booze

> To celebrate?

> First day kinks, that's all

> I hope it wasn't anything I did.

No, no you were so good.

I shouldn't have said anything about the
dresses. You're supposed to be able
to ignore me behind the camera.

> You've always been hard to ignore

Lola's face immediately warmed. The blue bubble of words was undeniably flirty, without even an *lol* or *haha* to dilute it.

> But you were right. The green
> one was my favorite.

Lola normally held her tongue while Jason and her team gave their opinions. Like Gloriana had said, their job was to craft her image. They weren't just excellent at it; they had the best interest of her career at heart. That was far more important than which dress Lola liked most. Still, the emerald silk had made her feel, somehow, more like herself. Renee had seen it too.

I know. It was the only one you
didn't do that smile for.

Lola stilled.
Renee was typing, then not typing, then typing again.

For what it's worth, it was my favorite too.

10

As Micah had promised, the schedule had them hitting the ground running, but the gait wasn't exactly elegant, given the clunky staged shoots and enormous crew. Renee dedicated her second coffee each day to summoning the energy for Micah's "quick chats" about adhering to the schedule and making every shot count. She was starting to believe in telepathy, given how often she could feel him second-guessing her every choice.

He had a lot of chances to do so.

Managing a crew required making a zillion decisions and delegating responsibility, something Renee had never done in her life. The multitasking of working solo, like Renee was used to, was taxing enough, but now she was operating Camera One while hoping Camera Two was getting good B-roll, parsing entertainment industry jargon, listening for helicopters overhead that would ruin the sound, and worrying Lola was too tired to film—all with an audience.

Fortunately, Renee had fallen into a good vibe with the crew. She thanked her lucky stars for Alejandro especially. He'd started in the industry straight out of college and had a ton of experience. Alejandro navigated the set and all the equipment with such professionalism and ease that Renee questioned whether an MFA was actually better than industry experience. He had saved her from at least a dozen amateur mistakes.

Despite all that, Renee's inexperience wasn't the shoot's biggest issue.

The problem was Lola.

It was nearly September now, two weeks into filming, and Lola still had an effortfulness that fizzed over everything with a bland positivity. When they shot a smell test for her next perfume, Lola said with a straight face that she'd always been passionate about scents. Filming some yogilates workout, Lola explained that as a performer, her body was her instrument. Everything she said felt calibrated to project the image of America's Sweetheart. She never mumbled or said *um* or *uh*. If she didn't answer in a complete sentence, she politely asked, *Could I go again?* Renee had been hoping the sessions with her producer would unlock something—and yield footage of actual music making—but the first two had been rescheduled.

It was too much Lola Gray and not enough *Lo*.

Today, they were filming in Lola's spacious kitchen as Lola "casually" made lunch for friends. The friends in question were seated at the large marble island: her former assistant and another fellow contestant from Lola's season of *You're Next!* Renee had questioned this set of alleged friends, since Lola appeared not to have spoken to them in some time, but Lola hadn't wanted to bother her higher-profile connections.

Renee glanced at Micah and Gloriana watching from behind the crew. Gloriana sometimes popped by the set unannounced. That was her right as executive producer, but Renee felt a stomach ulcer developing whenever it happened. She needed to cut back on those caustic craft services coffees.

Before them, Lola looked incredible in a white tank top, with her chocolate-brown bangs drifting into her face. She was meant to be chatting with her friends while chopping parsley for tabbouleh salad, but she was doing it in a way that suggested no more than a passing familiarity with parsley, knives, her kitchen, and, possibly, human interaction.

As Lola laughed too loudly at something her ex-assistant said, Alejandro muttered to Renee, "She better stick to music. Can't act her way out of a paper bag."

"She's not supposed to be *acting* at all," Renee said through her teeth.

"Then *direct her*, director," Alejandro said.

Renee cleared her throat. "Let's pause." She stepped around the camera tripod and approached Lola. "Hey, Lo, you know there's no reason to be so tense, right?"

Lola set the knife down—parsley clung to her hands—and she looked up at Renee with a wounded look in her warm brown eyes. "You think I'm tense?"

Renee's gaze slid over the clenched muscles of Lola's jaw and the tendons standing out in her neck. "It's reading that way on camera a tiny bit. Try to act natural."

"You have a whole film crew crammed into my kitchen. It's kind of hard to act natural." Lola's shoulders had crept up to her ears.

Without hesitating, Renee faced the crew. "Okay, if you're not doing something important, get off my set." *My set.* She'd never said that before, but if Lola needed a smaller set, Renee was going to give it to her. "And while we're at it, let's cut Camera B."

As the crew reacted, Renee set her hands on Lola's shoulders. Shit, her muscles were tight—but her skin was so soft. Renee kept her voice low. "Lo, you need to get your head in the game. Having lunch. With friends. We had lunch two weeks ago, so I know you can do it. I've seen it happen."

Somehow, she'd started gently kneading Lola's muscles. Lola didn't seem to mind. She rolled her shoulder into Renee's touch. "That was different. It's awkward to just stand around talking about myself."

"Sure, it's a weird situation. But hey, remember the time you forgot the words to the national anthem? Freshman year, I think."

Lola's eyebrows leapt up. "What?"

"At the hockey state regionals. You got to *And the rockets*, and you blanked."

"I'll never forget that," Lola grumbled. "You were there?"

Renee nodded, her hands still working. "My cousin was playing. Why don't you tell them that story?"

Lola gave her a playful glare. "I wouldn't have hired you if I'd known you were just going to embarrass me."

"I thought you hired me for my killer insight into your past," Renee replied.

"Same thing."

"Good gi—I mean good. Jokes are good. Now go make them for your friends." Renee drew her hands away and Lola went back to her parsley.

From behind the camera, Alejandro was staring at Renee.

"What?" she hissed as she joined him.

He just shook his head and adjusted his grip on the microphone. But behind him, Gloriana—who, Renee noted, had ignored her instructions about leaving the set if you weren't doing something important—was watching Renee with a thin frown.

Renee shook it off. She was allowed to kick people off the set, to pull a camera, to give the subject of her film a pep talk. And a shoulder rub. Lola had just looked so *tense*. And now—

And now, Lola was sweeping parsley into a bowl and smiling to herself. "Did I ever tell you guys about the time I forgot the words to the national anthem?"

"That's more like it," Alejandro whispered.

Lola laughed—her real laugh—at something her friend said, then she raised a hand to one shoulder, right where Renee had been massaging. It must have been the lighting, but Renee thought she saw her blush.

IN HER HOTEL room that night, Renee's eyeballs were withering like old grapes as she entered hour three of reviewing the dailies on her computer. Long shoot days could generate a dozen hours of footage that might be distilled into a minute-long clip in the final cut of the film. Staying on top of the dailies was essential. It also meant that even after they wrapped each day, Renee spent hours looking at Lola.

Renee played back the bit where she'd rubbed Lola's shoulders. She hadn't meant to film it, but she'd forgotten to cut. She should delete it—it was *not* making the film—but then she watched Lola's eyes slip closed, the subtle way she'd leaned into Renee. Her cursor hovered over the trash icon, then drifted back to play. It was a bad idea to delete *any* footage at this point, wasn't it? You never knew what you'd need. She made a copy of the clip, moved it onto her personal hard drive, and deleted it from the files she archived on the production company's server. Then she set all the files to backup, flopped down on the bed, settled her headphones over her ears, and played Lola's first album.

It was surreal now to hear Lola's voice without Lola herself there. Since this job tied Renee's art to Lola's, Renee had been listening to Lola's music whenever she needed to get into Lola's head—in other words, every day.

Renee had never truly listened to Lola's songs. As a teenager, she'd liked music with screaming in it, because she'd always felt like screaming herself. Pop was too upbeat, too aggressively straight. Where were the songs about crying in your room after coming out to your mom went worse than you'd expected, or about the moment you realized your dad really wasn't coming home again? Pop music was meant to be for everybody, but it made Renee feel like an afterthought.

As a teenager, Renee believed true artists—like herself, hopefully—labored in obscurity, attaining perfection before showing anyone their work. She'd told her friends that she wanted to be a director, but never confessed how deep that desire ran. Meanwhile, Lola was earnest and unashamed about her ambition, playing her original songs at every school talent show for the same kids who made fun of her, and at the county fair for total strangers. Instead of finding it admirable, Renee had cringed at the sincerity, embarrassed that Lola was brave enough to take herself seriously.

Even though reactions like Renee's were the reason that she required bravery in the first place.

When Kadijah talked about why they loved Lola Gray, they spoke about getting swept away in the world of Lola's stories. Renee was beginning to understand that—though not quite how Kadijah had meant.

It was impossible to listen to one of Lola's songs and think of anything but Lo. Renee could almost see Lola's thin, skilled fingers picking out the notes on her guitar, how her eyes crinkled when she laughed, how she sat with her knees pulled to her chest when she was tired. How that smile of hers was sometimes a mask, sometimes armor, but when it was genuine, it felt like a blessing.

Most of all, Renee wondered who Lola's songs were about.

Renee had done her research, under the supervision of Kadijah, who was still sending her old interviews and YouTube explainers. The cultish Lo-Lites were devoted to analyzing Lola's lyrics for revelatory details and easter eggs about her life. Lo-Lites were consumed with matching names to songs. A lyric mentioned flannel, and they'd find a photo of some indie musician wearing plaid while holding Lola's hand. She'd sing about a Mendocino sunset, and they'd unearth an Instagram post geotagged at Sea Ranch, when she was briefly linked to some comedian.

Renee consumed this information academically. It didn't make her jealous to think of these men with Lola, who was obviously too good for them. She didn't wonder how Lola behaved in their presence, if she was Lola Gray or Renee's Lo. She didn't contemplate what other NDAs might be floating around, whose names were hastily scribbled on those contracts, or what gender of people those names were attached to. If any of these thoughts arose in Renee's mind, it was in some dusty and easily ignored back corner.

While Renee avoided any curiosity on that final point—the gender of Lola's lovers—some Lo-Lites were consumed with it: the #LavaTruthers. Lyrics like *I'm the cat that got the cream*, from "Just Between Us," a non-album single released after *Wild Heart*, were canonized as crystal clear evidence of a relationship with a woman—specifically Ava Andreesen. Any time Lola sported an outfit short of full femme glamour, or was photographed in blue-and-pink bisexual lighting, or wore her nails short, the LavaTruthers entered it into their catalog of evidence.

Lola had not mentioned Ava to Renee. She *had* mentioned that she had known she was bisexual in high school, which was extremely interesting. That meant that the songs on Lola's first album—written when Lola was still living next door to Renee and before her first boyfriend, Kyte—could have been about girls.

Which girls, was the question. Lola had probably crushed on a straight cheerleader, or someone from the child-pageant circuit, or that hot forward from the Fellows High girls' soccer team. Renee wished she had her junior yearbook. It would be more helpful than any gossip site.

Renee's favorite song from that first album, "Star Sign," began to play.

I want to be closer to you,
But what else is new?

Renee rolled over and pressed her face into a pillow. The fact that she *adored* this song was among the biggest surprises of the last few very surprise-filled weeks.

The melody was compulsively listenable, but the lyrics felt visceral and real. "Star Sign" was about waiting for a signal that your crush liked you back. The lyrics alluded to the night sky and waiting for a falling star. The song always stirred an emotion that Renee couldn't quite name—longing? Nostalgia? It made her think of one of the last times she and Lola had spent together, just before Lola left for *You're Next!* Their physics teacher offered extra credit to anyone who watched a mid-February meteor shower. She and Lola had stayed up until 2 a.m. drinking Red Bull and hot chocolate in Renee's living room, then huddled together against the cold, their boots squeaking on the snow, as stars fell to earth like confetti.

It was unreal that a seventeen-year-old had written a song that unearthed memories that Renee hadn't realized she'd forgotten. Memories Lola had probably forgotten too.

"Star Sign" built to a cathartic bridge that was nearly impossible not to sing along to. When Lola's voice loosed all that pent-up desire into the line *You were watching the stars, but I was watching you*, Renee got chills. After the bridge, true to Lola's romantic bent, her crush saw the sign they needed and realized they wanted Lola all along.

It made Renee wish that she had really been part of Lola's life back then, instead of being such a self-obsessed dick. While Lola had been sitting in her bedroom—the same bedroom that Renee had in her own identical house—writing lyrics with a wisdom beyond her years, Renee had probably been getting into a fight with her mom and punching the wall so hard she pockmarked the plaster. Not that she'd done that *so* often, but she had lost her temper a lot as a teenager.

If she'd been closer to Lola back then, Renee would already know who "Star Sign" was about.

Maybe that was the problem: Renee didn't know Lola well enough anymore for her to open up on camera. Today, reminding her of that story about the national anthem had gotten her laughing at herself. If Renee wanted more of that, relying on their shared past wouldn't be enough. She needed to get closer to Lola *now*.

Renee reached for her phone.

11

Renee slid into a red leather booth at the Formosa Cafe. She looked delighted as she took in the vintage black-and-white headshots lining the walls, the crimson Chinese lanterns, dragons, and knot patterns woven into the decor. In one corner, there was a full-size trolley car, retrofitted to hold tables.

"This place is awesome," she said.

"I thought you'd like it," Lola said. "Clark Gable and James Dean used to hang out at the bar. There's a studio lot across the street."

When Renee had texted that evening asking to grab a drink, Lola had been surprised. Her schedule and security concerns, along with the schedules and security concerns of her friends, seldom allowed for spur-of-the-moment plans. But Lola jumped at the chance. A drink with Renee would be so much more fun than finding convincing replies to Gloriana's requests for progress on new music.

A waitress took their order: crab rangoon to split, a Mai Tai for Lola. Still making her final decision, Renee studied the cocktail menu. As she did, she absently ran her fingers past her ear and into the short, dark roots at the nape of her neck. Suddenly, Lola was imagining her own hand there, her lips pressed to the delicate skin. Lola swallowed hard as Renee chose a drink called Passion and Paradox.

Lola's Mai Tai arrived in a tall glass, sunset-colored, with pineapple leaves and a cocktail umbrella sticking out of pebbled ice.

"Oh, gimme a taste," Renee said, then winced. "Was that out of line? I keep forgetting you're super famous now, not just Lo from next door."

"Hey! I'm still Lo from next door." Lola passed her drink to Renee. Renee's red lipstick marked the straw. "Let me try yours."

Renee's coupe glass was full to the brim. As she edged it across the table, the orange liquid threatened to spill over the side. Lola dipped her head to the glass and slurped a taste.

Renee clicked her tongue. "They let you out of the house with manners like that?"

"Barely," Lola said solemnly. She cut her eyes to Henry at the bar. "I have to be supervised at all times."

Renee laughed and inched her drink back to her side of the table. "How do you think filming's going?"

Several thoughts collided in Lola's head: that the shoot was a disastrous distraction from songwriting; that without the distraction, she might have already given in to her demons and posted a screenshot note announcing her retirement; that sometimes, when the cameras were rolling, she felt like she was watching herself from behind them, rather than living in her own head; that the words *It's going great* needed to come out of her mouth.

She'd hesitated too long. Renee's expression shifted subtly in understanding. There was no point in lying to her now.

"I can't say I'm enjoying it, but don't worry about me! I'll manage," Lola added with a bright smile.

"I'll worry about you if I want." Renee's green eyes were so serious under furrowed brows.

Lola stopped smiling.

"You deserve to be comfortable on set—and it makes for better footage. Today went better, after some of the crew left, didn't it? I'm going to keep things more minimal moving forward, especially when we're in your space."

"I'd appreciate that. Thank you." The knot of tension in her chest felt a little looser.

"I always take care of my star," Renee said with a wink.

"I thought I was your first star."

"Well, at school I made a very moving short about a bodega cat in my neighborhood and I made sure she had tasty treats and pets."

"Nice to know what I have to look forward to." Lola had expected Renee to laugh, but instead her face had fallen. "Don't tell me it ended badly for the cat."

"No, the cat's fine, as far as I know. I just get kind of down when I think about my work from grad school."

"Why? The cat movie sounds adorable."

Renee's mouth pulled into a grimace. It took her a second to answer. "My brain just goes straight to all the feedback I got. The negative stuff—I don't remember the positive comments at all."

Lola leaned forward. "Hey, criticism can be really hard. It hurts. Especially at the beginning. Everyone says you need a thick skin but no one tells you how to get one."

Renee softened a little. "Do you have any tips?"

"I mean, try writing four albums of hyper-personal songs about your love life and letting the public tear them apart."

Renee snorted. "Hardly enough content there in my case."

"Come on, I'm sure girls are all over you." Lola fiddled with the tiny paper umbrella from her Mai Tai.

"Not to sound overconfident, but that's not really the issue. It's more that I'm not much of a relationship girl."

"Maybe you haven't met the right person."

"I've met plenty of people. Sex doesn't always have to mean something. But the sapphics, right? They get so attached. You must know how it is."

Lola didn't know what to say. There was a deep-buried part of her that ached to hear Renee talk so casually about sex. It basically confirmed that their night together meant nothing. But far more urgent was an electric thrill of recognition. Lola couldn't remember the last time she had a conversation with a woman like this, where liking women felt normal, not a challenge to outfox, or a very brave choice, or worse, a fatal vulnerability. Renee simply knew Lola liked women and treated her accordingly. It probably meant nothing to Renee, but to Lola it felt miraculous.

"Yeah, for sure," Lola said. "I'm, uh, usually the one getting too attached."

Renee perked up at that. "Oh yeah?"

Lola's throat felt tight, but this was *Renee*. If she couldn't talk to Renee about this, how would she ever talk to anyone? "That's what happened with my last . . . girlfriend."

"Was that . . . ?"

"Ava." Her voice was thin. Thankfully, Renee had leaned in, her shoulders hunched up like they were having a top-secret conference. Which, Lola supposed, they kind of were. "You probably saw the rumors."

"I happened across them, yes," Renee said. "So, you guys were for real?"

"I thought so." Lola took a sharp breath, then said, "I thought I was in love with her, but I guess I got too attached, like you said. Actually, I wanted to go public."

"You did? Like, with everything?"

Lola nodded, her eyes on the tablecloth. She'd torn the cocktail umbrella entirely to shreds. "I thought that would make her happy. Because we could really be together. I had a whole album I wanted to record about her. And then she left me."

"Damn. I'm sorry, Lo. That's awful."

"It's okay. It was a while ago now. But I had to shelve the album and that's why it's been so long since I've released anything."

"Which is why you're doing the doc."

"Right."

"Which means, in a weird way, that your breakup is really responsible for our whole friend-reunion film-collaboration thing."

Lola laughed in spite of herself. "I guess it does."

"And what about coming out? Do you want to talk about it?" Renee asked.

Lola didn't have it in her to explain. She just shook her head.

Renee's hand was creeping across the table toward Lola's, with her eyebrows rumpled sympathetically. Suddenly Lola knew that Renee would listen to her talk about Ava all night, if Lola needed her to. Or take her dancing, or sit through an ice cream–fueled *Sex and the City* marathon, or whatever else Lola asked. Privately grieving all that she'd lost with the relationship had been so hard, so isolating—but now that she had someone to share it with, she wasn't sure she needed it anymore.

"I just want to forget it ever happened," Lola said.

"I got you, my star." Renee looked around for the waitress. "Where's that cocktail menu?"

12

Lola pushed her voice for the last bar of "Part of Me" as her guitar reverberated with the final chord. She was perched on a stool, one heel on the crossbar. As she let her voice soar through the song's end, she set her guitar down in a waiting stand and grabbed the bedazzled mic. She reminded herself not to break eye contact with the audience, to keep that connection. Her backing band shifted into a different key for the opening of "Wish I Never Met You" as Lola strutted over to the piano. She began the first verse on time, but shoving the mic into the stand took a fraction of a second too long. By the time her fingers were on the keys, she missed her cue.

She cut the song off. The band went quiet.

"I was late. I'm sorry," she called out. Lola balled her hands into fists, then released the tension before shoving herself off the piano bench.

"*Barely*," called Simone, Lola's performance coach, from the middle of the soundstage where they'd been rehearsing for the Denver Corkscrew Fest. "Come take a look at the video."

"Late is late," Lola said flatly, adjusting the white patent go-go boots she'd wear for the performance. On top, she wore shorts and a crop top. "This transition has to be right or we're cutting it."

"We're not cutting it; the fans are going to love it," Simone said. "They go crazy for 'Wish.'"

Lola settled her guitar over her shoulder again. "That's why it has to be perfect. Let's take it from the last chorus."

As the drummer counted them in, Lola's focus narrowed to this song, this performance. For now, her audience was small: Simone, plus Gloriana, who'd stopped by unexpectedly, Cassidy, Micah, and Renee with the crew. But in a few days, it would be thousands of fans at the festival. Lo-Lites paid hundreds of dollars to see her live, some of them driving for hours to get there. She wasn't going to disappoint them with shoddy transitions.

This set was shorter than what Lola had played on her last tour, which ended more than a year and a half ago. They'd done seventy-five dates on four continents, over five months. She'd booked the headlining slot at Corkscrew around the same time, when "Just Between Us," a song about the thrill of a secret relationship, was shooting up the charts and Album 5 was still on schedule. She was meant to be playing that album at the festival. Now, she was hacking apart her old tour set and hoping her fans would stay interested.

It took three more attempts to get the transition smooth enough to look effortless, and tight enough that the key change between the songs felt like a ratcheting up of energy, not an accident. Then Lola had them run it twice more, to lock it in. As usual with rehearsals, everyone else was satisfied long before Lola.

She hadn't loved the idea of getting this rehearsal on film. Or she hadn't until Renee had greeted her that morning by playfully shoving her shoulder and saying, "Okay, Miss Teen Queen, ready to show me what you got?" It was uncharacteristically goofy, as if they were at some kind of basketball scrimmage, not an eight-hour rehearsal. Lola had asked what she was talking about, but Renee had puffed up her chest and said, "See you out there," before going to check the cameras.

For hours, Lola had been giving this rehearsal her all. More often than not, she found herself spotting Renee from the stage. She hadn't intended to keep locking eyes with her, but she had to look *somewhere*. Besides, Renee was always staring right back at her from behind the camera, her lip curled halfway to a smile. Lola found herself trying to coax that smile out fully, tossing her hair or arching an eyebrow at a clever lyric or letting her voice really go. Rehearsals could be such a slog, but with Renee watching, this one was flying by.

Lola took her place center stage, her lavender guitar over her shoulder, for the first song of the encore. "Star Sign" was a fan favorite from *Seventeen Candles*. Lola picked out the opening notes, her head bowed. The opening of "Star Sign" had always been a major moment for the fans: she whispered the first line into the mic like a secret, then raised her head as fans joined in for the second. It always gave her chills to hear thousands of them singing it with her.

I want to be closer to you.

But what else is new?

This time, she lifted her eyes and saw Renee.

It was only muscle memory that kept her from fumbling the chords.

When she had written this song, she'd never imagined that she'd sing it for Renee.

It was about Renee, after all, the night they'd stayed up to watch a meteor shower together for an extra credit assignment. It had been a kind of torture to spend those hours with Renee—the comforting familiarity of Renee's living room, where Lola had always felt safe, and the aching romance of watching the sky together amid the bright white snow. Lola had wanted nothing more than to kiss her. But she couldn't. She wasn't brave enough. She was terrified that Renee would reject her, or, somehow worse, that her love would add to Renee's pain, instead of making it better. In the end, they'd just watched the stars fall together in silence and Lola had channeled her feelings into another song about what could have been.

Lola let her voice swell.

You were watching the stars, but I was watching you.

But Renee was here now, and she was listening. The story in "Star Sign" ended differently than it had in real life. Lola sang that if she was lucky enough to see falling stars, she might be lucky enough for her crush to kiss her—and her crush does. But the song could be a little melancholy: Lola spent the first two verses about to give up the torch she'd been carrying for an unrequited love. But singing it now, for Renee, it didn't feel that way.

It felt like a promise.

As the final note faded, the audience broke into applause.

"That's what I'm talking about!" Simone cried.

"Wow, Lola, just wow!" Gloriana said.

They paused for a break. Lola sat on the edge of the stage, a little breathless, and accepted a mug of tea from Cassidy. She felt alive, sharpened in the way that only a good performance could do.

Renee approached with her camera, Alejandro and his mic in tow.

Lola smirked down at Renee from the stage. She had a perfect view of Renee's shoulder muscles tensing under the weight of the camera.

"So did I bring it?" Lola asked, one eyebrow arched.

Renee sucked on her lip, considering. "Oh yeah, it's been broughten. I can't wait to see the actual show."

"Look who's becoming a Lo-Lite," Lola said, pleased with herself. "What was your favorite song?"

Renee wasn't even pretending to look at the camera. The gold in her green eyes caught the light. Lola liked Renee looking up at her like this. She wanted to slide her fingers into Renee's messy bleached hair.

"That one at the end. 'Star Sign.' It's my favorite of all your songs."

"It is?"

My favorite of all your songs.

Renee's head bobbed. "It sounded different than it does on the album."

"I tried something new," Lola said, the corners of her mouth lifting, pleased that Renee heard the difference.

Alejandro cleared his throat. "Guys?"

"Right!" Renee checked the viewfinder. "Okay, Lo. Can you explain what you're rehearsing for?"

Lola still had a faint grin on her lips when she answered, "The set at Corkscrew Fest is going to be the very last show for *Wild Heart*."

"So this is a goodbye," Renee said.

"Or a good riddance," Lola said without thinking. *Shoot.* She shouldn't have said that on camera. "What I meant was, I love the songs on *Wild Heart*, and I'm so grateful my fans love them too. But when you have a big album like that, you can't let yourself get stuck. I'm ready to move on."

Lola paused. In her mind, *Wild Heart* had become just as associated with the tragedy of Ava as the canceled album: if she'd gotten to release that, no one would be talking about *Wild Heart* anymore. That was what she'd actually meant by *good riddance*.

"Move on to what?" Renee asked.

For once, this question didn't trigger an avalanche of anxiety. Lola just said, "Wouldn't you like to know?"

They started another run-through. As Lola waited offstage for her cue, she felt good. Maybe if this kept up, she could ride the feeling into a productive writing session. What she'd said to Renee had given her hope: maybe the next big thing for her was already there, waiting for her to uncover it.

Lola strutted onstage. The first number went perfectly, but they were halfway through the second when something went wrong. Someone pushed in through the side door, letting in a wide beam of sunlight that silhouetted the figure. Lola kept singing, but when she heard someone ask about security, she faltered.

Lola couldn't make out who the stranger was, but no one was stopping him from heading confidently toward the stage—not even the camera tracking him. Lola's pulse ratcheted higher until it throbbed in her ears. The intruder had to be someone she knew, to be allowed into her rehearsal—but obsessive fans sometimes managed impossible things.

Just as she was about to panic, the man came into focus, and though her heart was still racing, Lola knew what she had to do.

"Nash!" she cried.

She shoved the microphone into its stand, hopped down from the stage, and flung herself into his arms. With her face pressed into his neck, she smiled, genuinely, at the familiar scent of his Black Orchid cologne. Nash lifted her off the ground and spun her in a circle, then pulled her into a kiss—or what looked like one. He held her face in his hands, then she put her hands over his, forming a wall to block what their mouths were or were not doing.

Nash released her but kept her in his moony-eyed gaze. His wavy blond locks were swept back, his lips cherubically pink. Nash was a professional actor, but even still, his ability to gaze at her like he was head over heels was impressive.

"Hello, beautiful," he said, weaving his fingers into hers.

"What are you doing here?" Lola said. "You're supposed to be in Montana."

"I had a break in filming, so I decided to surprise my girl." Nash winked at her. No matter how many times Lola had explained to Nash that he didn't need to act like some Old Hollywood cowboy to convincingly date a woman—and in fact, doing that was kind of gay—he would not stop winking at her. Probably because it always made her giggle.

"I've missed you so much!" Lola said. "I wish our schedules matched up better."

This scheduling problem had been pre-identified as the fracture point for their relationship. With their breakup two months away, and Nash filming *Horsebreaker* in Montana while also promoting *Fit to Live*, they were supposed to mention their busy lives whenever possible.

"I never get to see my baby," he said, tucking a loose tendril of hair behind her ear.

Lola clicked her tongue at him. She'd told Nash that *baby* as a term of endearment gave her the ick, so naturally Nash had turned that into an inside joke. He pulled her against him again and whispered into her ear, "My itty-bitty baby."

"*Nash!*" Lola threw her head back and slid her arms around his waist. They were used to ensuring their relationship read as romantic on camera—not the cameras of a film set like Nash was used to, or photoshoots like Lola was, but to the cameras of paparazzi and cellphone stalkers.

But there was another set of cameras here.

Micah and Gloriana were watching with smug satisfaction, but at the back of the space was Renee, her arms crossed and shoulders bunched up. Even from this distance, Lola could tell she was grinding her jaw. Renee hadn't been in on the surprise, Lola realized—even though it must have taken a lot of coordinating to get Nash here at the right moment. Renee stalked over to Micah, pointed at the side door, then followed him out into the parking lot.

As Lola watched her go, Nash slipped behind her, his arms over her shoulders, and leaned down so their faces were side by side.

"Baby, you're *staring*," he said into her ear. "Who is she?"

***

In the parking lot, Renee shaded her eyes with her hand. "Want to tell me what's happening here, Micah?"

Micah slid on his Ray-Bans. "Nash reached out to Gloriana about surprising Lola, and we thought it would be a perfect moment."

"And you didn't want to tell me about it?"

"It's a surprise, Renee. You ruin it by telling too many people."

"I'm not people, I'm *the director*!"

Micah raised his hands innocently. "Hey, I thought you wanted these natural-feeling moments. Surprise is great for that."

"You think *that's* Lola being natural?" Renee flung her hand toward the door.

"I said natural-*feeling*. There's a difference," Micah said. "If that's all, I'm going back inside."

The door swung shut behind him.

Renee seethed at Micah and Gloriana. Hadn't they realized they were watching a master at work? All day, Lo had commanded the room. In her shiny white boots and little shorts, she took uncompromising control of the rehearsal, then delivered a performance of "Star Sign" so incredible it had given Renee chills. At the break, Lola had been herself without any prodding or coaching. She'd *complained about something*, like a regular person with regular emotions.

It was actually pretty sexy.

Now, she'd been reduced to pretending to make out with a guy who looked like he thought yogurt was too spicy.

Lola deserved better than a fake romance, better than Micah's dumb setups and distracting surprises. Renee didn't want her film to be a part of that.

Documentaries were supposed to tell the truth.

If she couldn't do that, how would Dragan ever pass her thesis? He'd emailed the other day, requesting an update. She'd thought she'd have something positive to report, but now, all over again, it felt like the project was slipping away from her—not that she'd ever had it squarely in her grasp.

Renee squatted on the ground and put her head in her hands, trying to get her breathing steady. Someone waved a cold bottle of water in front of her face. When she looked up to accept it, Cassidy was standing over her.

"Thanks," Renee mumbled before taking a swig.

"You should move or you'll be in the shots," she said, then waved to someone parked in an innocuous gray car.

A bald-headed man in a wrinkled button-up got out. He was holding a camera.

"Seriously?" Renee muttered. A few moments later, Nash and Lola strode into the parking lot. Immediately the rapid-fire clicking of the camera's shutter began. They were holding hands, and even though they clearly saw the photographer, they didn't quicken their pace. Lola's hair was thrown up into a claw clip and she'd changed into jeans.

Those *jeans*.

Renee tried not to let her eyes linger on how the denim clung to Lola's ass because she wasn't a creep, but Lola was literally walking away from her.

The pair hopped into Nash's massive, shiny truck and pulled away. Once they were gone, Gloriana emerged wearing a gigantic pair of sunglasses.

"What the hell was that?" Renee flung a hand at the man. "Why didn't security deal with him?"

Gloriana waved to the paparazzo, who saluted her in response. "Honey, *we* called *him*."

Renee's mouth fell open.

Gloriana smirked. "You really don't understand how any of this works, do you? There's no point in getting Lola and Nash together if no one sees it. That's what a relationship *is* in this town."

***

"You went to high school with her?" Nash said with a salacious gasp.

Lola nodded. "We grew up together. Next-door neighbors."

"And now you have a huge fat crush on her."

"Keep your voice down!"

Lola was glad to spend the evening with Nash. Having gone through the effort to get him to L.A., they needed to be seen in public. The couple had gone to a juice place, where they'd pretended not to notice the dozen people with their phones out, then they'd changed their outfits and gone to dinner—giving the paparazzi stationed outside plenty of time to snap photos.

"In a straight way, obv," Nash added. "What do they call it? A girl crush!"

"I did have a tiny thing for her in high school, so I might have some . . . feelings left over."

"The feelings I saw looked piping hot."

Lola let out a huff, but she couldn't deny it.

"Well, I'm happy for you," Nash said. "It's been forever since things ended with you-know-who." They had an agreement not to say Ava's name aloud—though now that she'd talked to Renee about her, maybe they didn't need it anymore. "It's time you got back out there. Who knows what could happen? She's the director, you're the muse—you're practically scissoring already."

Lola choked on her spritz and Nash's eyes went wide.

"Lola! You did not! When?"

Lola blushed furiously. "It was before we were working together, at my sister's wedding."

"What did Claudia say?" Nash asked.

"She didn't say anything because it wasn't worth telling her. It was supposed to be a one-time thing. I mean, it *was* a one-time thing, and now we're keeping it professional."

Nash nodded solemnly. "Which is why she was staring at your ass in the parking lot."

Lola threw the sprig of rosemary garnishing her drink at him.

"Hey! This is a nice restaurant!" he cried.

"What about you? How are you surviving in Montana?" Two months ago, Nash's boyfriend had decided that a closeted actor's lifestyle—even an actor as hot and up-and-coming as Nash—wasn't for him. They broke up just before Nash left for Butte.

Nash frowned down into his beef tartare. "Not to be dramatic, but it's literally the worst thing ever. Some days, I'm okay, and then some days, I'm just completely *not*. It's lonely, you know? The cast and crew are great, and we hang out, but then at the end of the day, I still want to call him."

"You can always call me."

"It's not the same," Nash said. "Anyway, I'm planning to fuck so much while I'm in town that when I get back to the middle of nowhere, I'll be completely over him. Grindr is so hit or miss up there."

"You are *not* on the apps!" Lola hissed at him.

"Relax! I'm just enjoying the dick pics, not meeting up with anyone. It's *Montana*. I'd probably get hate-crimed."

"Just be careful." Lola regretted the words the second they were out of her mouth. Nash didn't need her to warn him what was at stake, any more than she'd needed Gloriana to tell her not to let things get messy with Renee.

"I'm phenomenal at being careful," Nash said. "Been doing it all my life."

New photos of Lola and Nash dropped ♥♥♥   ♡ 1267
Reply

↳ I am literally so obsessed with them. How he's holding her hand??? 👀   ♡ 1386

↳ Tag yourself I'm the chick staring at Lola's ass   ♡ 876

  ↳ same   ♡ 48

  ↳ me too lol   ♡ 5

  ↳ I'm the girl watching the chick stare at Lola's ass.   ♡ 306

    ↳ That's Lola's assistant Cassidy!   ♡ 157

13

Corkscrew Fest was a blur.

The skeleton crew of Renee and Alejandro rode with Lola from the hotel to the festival site. The moment their SUV pulled into view of the back gates, the horde of Lo-Lites gathered there burst into screams. As they slowly rolled past the fans, who had clearly been waiting for hours in the unseasonable Labor Day heat, and through the security gate, Lola asked Cassidy to find someone to hand out water. Then she asked the driver to stop and, to Renee's surprise, hopped out of the car. For the next thirty minutes, Lola stuck her hand through the chain-link fence to sign autographs and squeeze hands, and once, to touch the head of a baby. Renee was transfixed: she kept expecting Lola's fake smile to appear, but it never did. Lola gave every fan her undivided attention. She listened to their stories and teared up or laughed along with them.

From there, they tailed Lola: to a meet and greet where she met more fans with the same care, to interviews with local radio and recording promos for Corkscrew's sponsors, to a Zoom conference meeting about the swimwear line. Lola was in constant motion, the sole exception being the ten minutes in which Cassidy forced her to sit down and eat something, but as night fell, everything narrowed to the moment when she'd take the stage. Her obligations gave way to mugs of tea and hair and makeup and stretching and vocal warm-ups. Lola stopped acknowledging the camera. And then, seemingly all at once, the band, backup dancers, and Lola were joining hands backstage to visualize a successful show, over the growing roar of the crowd.

Renee took her position at the side of the stage, alone with her camera. They'd license the performance footage from the festival, but Renee wanted to capture these hidden, backstage moments. Alejandro was out enjoying the show. Even with the nicest mic the production had, he wouldn't be able to pick up anything over the roar of the speakers.

A shiver of anticipation ran down Renee's spine as she filmed Lola in her final moment in the wings: her small body, clad in a sparkly minidress, was taut with concentration, her expression hard as she listened to a legion of fans call her name. Then she got her cue, and she was *on,* strutting onto the stage. A wave of screams, of cheering, of sheer *energy* rolled off the crowd like a solar flare—and into it, Lola began to sing.

Renee had watched Lola rehearse. She had heard at Claudia's wedding how Lola's voice took on another quality in front of an audience. Renee had imagined she knew Lola in her element. She hadn't fully understood that Lola was a *star*.

Lola navigated the stage like she owned it. She was in perfect synchronicity with the band, backup singers, and dancers, like the fluid parts of a single creature. At the chorus of her opener, Lola tossed her hair and held out the mic and the audience burst into sound, singing her lyrics back so loudly they must have been heard for miles around. All these fans knew every word to every song. And Lola had written them all, deliberately chosen each syllable that formed their connection.

That connection was the power of Lola's music. Renee couldn't believe she hadn't realized it before. Yes, it was romantic and a little dramatic and earnest. But it meant something important to her fans. Hell, it meant something important to Renee.

Renee didn't know if she could render this feeling on film. But she wanted to try. It had been a long time since she had felt a spark like that, and it raced through her like a sugar rush.

The main set ended, and Lola ran offstage opposite where Renee stood. Renee zoomed in on Lola catching her breath, with her hands on her hips and her head tipped back. She looked so small—so human—when just a few moments before she'd been a supernova.

Just then, Lola looked across the stage and met Renee's gaze. In the middle of everything, Lola smiled—her real smile. Renee grinned back so widely she bit her lip to avoid looking silly.

Then the band came back on, and someone handed Lola the lavender guitar. Lola strode to the center of the stage, slipped it over her shoulder, and strummed one single note . . .

The crowd went crazy, cheering louder than they had all night. Renee's heart went to her throat. As Lola stepped up to the mic, her gaze slid stage left—and she locked eyes with Renee.

"*I want to be closer to you,*" Lola sang. A smile teased her lips. "*But what else is new?*"

* * *

Lola's trailer was dim, lit only by the ambient glow of the floodlights outside. She was alone. She needed it after the rush of a big stage. It was exhausting to tap into the emotions behind every song and let them read on her face, in her voice, through the strings and keys. It was what made her live performances so special. Her fans loved that Lola felt the same things they did, that she traveled with them through trouble and joy and hope. But tonight, there was one person in particular that Lola hoped had felt that connection.

Lola allowed herself a small, relieved sigh. No matter what her label and Gloriana and even Lola herself feared, her fans hadn't forgotten what they loved about Lola Gray.

Her phone lit up, aggressively bright in the trailer's dimness. As if she'd heard Lola thinking, Gloriana was calling.

"Hi, honey! How'd it go?"

"You know me, nothing's perfect. But I think it went well," Lola said.

"Listen, I wanted to chat as soon as possible." Lola froze, bracing herself for something she wouldn't want to hear. "You've canceled your last two sessions with your producer. You were prepping for this show, and I love that, but it's time to get to work. We need progress on demos."

"I *am* making progress, okay? I don't want to rush the material."

"I don't want you to either, but I'm the messenger here. The *label* needs reassuring. They were understanding about the delay, but now it's time to prove we were worth it."

Lola's bottom lip was so tightly pinched between her teeth, the skin was breaking. Even if the gap since her last album had cut into their profits, she'd still made her label hundreds of millions of dollars. Now she felt like she'd been scolded for putting off her homework.

"Maybe it's time to explore bringing someone in. Artists do it all the time, completely discreetly. There's no shame in asking for help."

"I don't need help!" Lola cried, panic flaring through her. "I need time and space to focus. I have so much going on, and then this movie too—how can I write when cameras are following me everywhere?"

Gloriana sighed. "A show of good faith would help, so stop canceling on Ackerlund. We still pay for those sessions. You have time booked with him next week, so show up, put some work in, and everyone will be happy."

"Of course," Lola agreed, her voice small. "No problem."

By the time Lola emerged from her trailer, any satisfaction from the show had been swept away by a simmering anxiety. Henry sat outside, but Cassidy had already left to meet up with friends. Renee, Alejandro, and a few members of Lola's band were chatting at a picnic table nearby.

Renee sprung up the moment she saw Lola.

"Lo, you were *amazing*!" Renee said. "Guys, wasn't I literally just saying how amazing she was tonight?"

"You've got a new number one fan," Lola's bassist said before taking a swig of his beer. "We're sticking around. Some of the other acts are chilling till loadout's done."

"Are we invited?" Renee said, linking her arm with Lola's.

"For sure," he said. "Lola doesn't usually hang, but you can definitely join."

Renee shot Lola a look of mock outrage. "Lola doesn't usually hang?"

"I just played a show, and I stink, and—"

"I was under the impression that everyone at this hangout just played a show. And you don't stink. Actually, you smell weirdly good."

"Renee!" Lola said, which only encouraged her. Renee twisted so they were facing each other, then took Lola by the shoulders and shook her. Lola couldn't help but giggle.

"*Come on*, Lo. You just played a *massive* show, and you worked *so* hard, and you were *stupidly* good, so now you get to relax and celebrate! Come for fifteen minutes. If you're not having fun, we'll leave."

Lola glanced at Henry. "He has to stay as long as I do, and he's probably tired."

"Me, I'm a night owl," Henry said. "Go have a little fun."

"Please?" Renee squeezed Lola tighter. "I've never been to a music festival after-party, and I don't want to go without you."

Lola's reluctance was no match for Renee's shining, eager gaze. "I can't say no to that."

What she meant was *I can't say no to you.*

THE FESTIVAL ORGANIZERS had set up an area for the artists, and two dozen people were gathered there now. Under trees strung with cafe lights, there was a fire pit ringed with Adirondack chairs where some lounged, picnic tables where others were eating a late dinner, even a hammock. Lola took quick stock of the faces present, trying to figure out whom she should meet, which people her attention would mean something to. She tried to put her smile on as they got closer, but it felt too heavy to stick. A few feet away, Lola stopped.

"You good?" Renee asked.

"I'm not sure I have the energy for this. For you, this is a party, but for me, I have to make sure I'm being friendly and saying the right things—it's exhausting."

"Has it ever occurred to you that people don't just like you because you're nice?" Renee said. "You have, like, a really good personality."

"I do?"

"Yes. So just relax. I will get you a drink if that's what you need to get properly lubricated."

"Do you have to say things like that?" Lola said, blushing.

"Clearly I do," Renee said, noticing her cheeks. "Look, you don't even have to talk to anyone. You can just hang out with me. It's up to you. Okay?"

"Okay," Lola conceded.

TO LOLA'S SURPRISE, she did have fun, and not just with Renee, but with everyone. She tried not to apologize too much for missing everyone's sets and let herself float along the fringes of conversations with no pressure to participate. Renee took care of the socializing, so Lola didn't have to. Renee chatted easily with everyone, telling them how she and Lola were childhood friends, and asking about everyone's favorite films about the music industry. It was easy—nice—feeling like she and Renee were a pair.

Eventually Lola contented herself with sitting on the edge of a wide, flat hammock, sipping her second hard seltzer, and lazily taking in the scene around her. Her eyes kept wandering to the most buzzed-about act, an edgy Korean girl with a long black ponytail, who performed as Saint Satin. Her name was Chloe, and she was just twenty-one years old. Earlier, she'd approached Lola—a bit starry-eyed but playing it cool—and confessed that *Seventeen Candles* had inspired her to start writing songs as a twelve-year-old.

Now, Chloe was chasing a gorgeous young woman through the party. She had plastic butterfly clips hidden through her short afro and pink glitter on her round cheeks and she wasn't very hard to catch. Chloe trapped her in her arms, and Butterfly Clips pressed her laughing mouth to the underside of Chloe's jaw. As Lola watched, Chloe raised her vape pen to Butterfly Clips's lips. Pinned happily against Chloe's chest, she took a hit, then slowly exhaled it into Chloe's mouth, before the pair broke apart giggling amid pale tendrils of smoke.

It was a little exhausting, but Lola couldn't stop watching Chloe. She floated among the picnic tables, swigging a beer, careening into the arms of her friends then belting out a random song line, and every so often, finding Butterfly Clips for an instant of reassuring affection. It sent a strange ache through Lola's chest. Chloe looked radiantly young—younger than Lola had ever been. When she was Chloe's age, she'd already released her second album.

Renee walked up and handed Lola a fresh seltzer. Her eyes followed the line of Lola's gaze. "Someone's having a great time."

"Her first album comes out in a few weeks. This is probably the biggest show she's ever played."

"*That's* why she's so happy." Renee settled into the hammock beside Lola, setting it swinging wildly. "I thought it was the weed."

It stuck in Lola's throat. Renee was right. Chloe *did* look happy—that's what Lola had missed. The singer straddled Butterfly Clips on a picnic bench and leaned down to kiss her deeply, as someone yelled, "Your trailer's right there!"

"I wonder if anyone ever said anything to her," Lola said.

It wasn't just that Chloe was queer. Saint Satin's whole image was queer. Her songs were unapologetically queer, and her fans were even queerer. She got called a "queer breakout artist," a "queer rising star." It was that pigeonholing that Lola had been taught was dangerous: that if she strayed too far from the path of straightness, she'd get covered in the muck of her bisexuality and no one would see anything else.

But Chloe didn't seem trapped.

Lola felt Renee watching her. "Did anyone ever say anything to you?"

Lola pressed the tab of her seltzer can against her thumbnail. "They didn't have to. I got into the industry ten years ago. Things are probably different for her than they were for me."

"Why can't they be different for you too?"

Lola shrugged. "Success makes things more complicated. The stakes keep getting higher. But that's a good thing, isn't it? It means I'm lucky, right?"

There was a soft, sad look in Renee's eyes. Suddenly, Lola needed Renee to agree with her, because otherwise—she wasn't sure, but her chest had gotten tight, her pulse ticking higher as she waited for Renee to recognize that what she'd said was true.

But Renee just said, "I have an idea."

She heaved herself off the hammock and went over to Chloe, whose side of the exchange was hyper-enthusiastic nodding. Renee came back brandishing the vape.

"*Renee!*" Lola cried as she dug her feet into the ground to steady the hammock for her.

Renee fell back and set them swinging again. "We're in Colorado. It's legal. Wait—don't tell me you've never smoked weed before."

"Of course I have. I'm not a nun."

Renee narrowed her eyes. "Are you sure? Sometimes I get nun vibes."

"Because God sent you here to test me?" Renee broke into a delighted smile, and Lola grinned back. "I take a gummy now and then to sleep. It's just . . . we're in public."

"We're surrounded by security, inside a chain-link fence, which is also surrounded by security, and we're fifty feet from your personal bodyguard. That's not what I call being in public."

"There's an entire industry set up to catch people like me in the wrong moment."

"Lo, the only person here, other than me, who gives a fuck if you smoke weed is Saint Satin. I think she's going to frame this vape when I give it back to her."

Lola groaned. "She's a fan. I'll have Cassidy send over a gift to thank her."

Renee took a deep pull from the vape. A froth of vapor flowed from her lips as she said, "Let no good deed go unpunished, right?"

"What's that supposed to mean?"

"That girl could not have been happier to share this with you. You don't need to send her an Edible Arrangement with a thank-you note." Renee took another hit. "Anyway, if someone did leak a photo of you smoking, it would probably help your image."

"And what image is that?"

"Uptight. No fun. Good girl." Renee winked. "Now stop sulking, and hit this."

THEY ROCKED IN the hammock.

The night felt crusted in sugar, the cafe lights twinkling, the woodsmoke from the fire, little bugs zipping happily through the air.

Against her, Renee was a solid weight. The hammock pressed their bodies together no matter how they lay. For stability's sake, they'd settled on Renee on her back, with Lola curled against her side—"You're a koala," Renee had said. "And I'm your tree"—making them both laugh so hard they nearly flipped the thing over. One of Lola's legs had hooked itself over Renee's and her face was pressed against her shoulder. Renee smelled intoxicatingly like men's deodorant and musk and salt from the long, hot day, and the sleeve of her T-shirt was rucked up.

Those arms that Lola couldn't stop herself from staring at.

Lola slipped her hand around Renee's bicep. Her knuckles grazed the side of Renee's breast. She should move them.

She didn't.

"Feeling good?" Renee asked.

Lola felt warm and loose. She tried to say something clever, but all that came out was "Yeah," and a giggle, as she buried her face in Renee's shoulder. She wasn't really high enough to be acting like this, was she? But thinking about it only made her tremble with laughter. It didn't matter, because Renee was there. Renee wouldn't let anything bad happen.

Lola lifted her head and peered at Renee.

Renee was grinning.

Lola wanted to run her tongue over those teeth.

"God, you're adorable." Renee's voice was syrupy as Lola's head fell back against her shoulder. "I want to make a movie about you."

"You *are* making a movie about me."

"Am I?" Renee sighed. "Sometimes it feels like there's none of you in it."

"What d'you mean?"

"Who you were onstage, who you are right now—that girl vanishes when the cameras are on. I want to see you on film the way you are when we're alone."

Lola angled her head to see Renee better. Her green eyes were heavy-lidded, her lashes barely curled, but her brows were low.

"Then film me when we're alone," Lola said.

Renee gave her a faintly devious look, then twisted her body against Lola's to pull her phone from her pocket. The motion set the hammock swinging again, rolling Lola into her, and Renee's arm slipped under her, holding Lola against her chest. They were too close together for a good angle, so Renee filmed them both with the front-facing camera.

"Not what I meant," Lola whined, although the grainy, half-lit image of the two of them was transfixing. "I'm a mess!"

"You're gorgeous. You're perfect," Renee said. "You always are."

Lola watched herself smile in the camera. It wasn't her normal smile. It was a little silly and off-kilter—and Renee was beaming at her like she'd never seen anything so glorious.

"Introduce yourself for the audience," Renee said.

Lola tried to force herself into a straight face, and failed, then finally managed to say, "I'm Lo. I'm a songwriter, and a singer."

Their eyes met through the camera and Renee let out a slow breath.

"Yeah, I want you like this," she said in a low voice.

Then have me—kiss me, right now. The thought was clear and sky blue and felt like the ring of a bell, loud enough that Renee must have heard it. Lola's gaze glided away from the camera as her knuckle traced along the line of Renee's jaw.

Someone coughed.

"Sorry to—interrupt or whatever. Can I get my vape back? We're heading out." Chloe was bashfully scratching the back of her head. Butterfly Clips stood a few feet behind, knotting her fingers with impatience at their separation. Renee shifted on the hammock to hand the vape back. Cool air flowed like creek water into the new gaps between them.

Lola's mouth went dry as her head came back together. What had she been *thinking*? To kiss Renee in front of all these people?

"We should go too," Lola said. She stood as gracefully as possible when one was a little high, a little drunk, and lying in a hammock.

Renee headed back to the trailer for her stuff, while Lola said her goodbyes. As Butterfly Clips pulled Chloe away, Lola heard her say, "They make a hot couple."

Were they talking about her and Renee?

Did she want them to be?

Lola played her first show in a year and did all her hits, except what? Just Between Us. Her last single!!! Which is ABOUT AVA ♡ 428

Reply

↳ She didn't play the #Lava tracks from WH either ♡ 52

↳ I am so convinced #Lava was real. ♡ 21

↳ The math is mathing! ♡ 4

↳ I would die to know what happened between them. Literally I don't think my body could take it. ♡ 78

Am I seeing things or is Lola singing to someone off-stage at Star Sign? ♡ 64

Reply

↳ Was Nash there? ♡ 13

I was at this show it was incredible. Lola is a queen!! ♡ 307

Reply

↳ Same I cried through the whole thing, I love her so much ♡ 2

14

Renee hoisted the bag of gear up her shoulder, where it was fighting with the strap of her backpack, and rang Lola's doorbell.

As soon as they'd gotten back from Denver, Renee had called Micah for a meeting.

"I'm cutting what's on the schedule for Tuesday," she'd said.

"Why? The dog rescue will be a great humanizing moment."

"Because as much as Lola loves dogs, she doesn't volunteer at dog rescues, Micah," Renee said. "And I think you know that. I'm going to be working with her one-on-one."

"Doing what exactly?"

"Humanizing her another way."

"I suppose the dog rescue isn't critical," he granted. "Send me the details so I can tell hair and makeup. You'll need some lights and we'll get Alejandro on audio."

"No hair and makeup, no crew. Trust me, I'm great at shooting solo. And hey—we're keeping costs down, right?"

"Gloriana won't love this," he said.

"Then don't tell her." She'd added some Lola Gray–worthy positivity into her tone. "Come on, Micah, be a team player on this one."

Now, the door swung open to reveal Lola, not an assistant or housekeeper or any of the staff she'd promised would be out of the house. Lola wore an oversize cardigan, leggings, and glasses.

"You wear glasses?" Renee said.

"Hello to you too," Lola said as she led Renee into the kitchen. "I'm supposed to take a break from my contacts when I can. I was up late last night. Album stuff. You want a coffee?"

"'Course."

Lola grabbed a mug. Renee watched her, not even bothering to set her stuff down. She couldn't get over how Lola's doe eyes looked even larger than usual behind the lenses. Her hair loose and long, the unconscious way she swept it out of her face, and how the sleeves of her sweater bunched up at her wrists. She looked like Saturday morning. Renee was overwhelmed with a vision of Lola tucked into the corner of a couch, her glasses slipping down her nose as she filled in the crossword puzzle, the two of them playing footsie.

Lola pressed a few buttons and the smell of coffee filled the kitchen. "I don't think it's fair to hold someone to promises they made after you pressured them into using drugs."

"For the record, you were fully sober when we set this up. If you want to back out, that's cool. But I do think this is what the film needs. If it doesn't work, I'll cut it. Worst-case scenario, you spend the day with me."

Lola handed her a mug and leaned against the counter beside Renee. She scrunched up her nose. "Gross."

"Come on, you know you love me," Renee said.

Lola let out a laugh and her eyes darted away. Suddenly Renee was acutely aware of how close they were standing and how empty the house was.

Lola cleared her throat. "I need to put my contacts in."

"Keep the glasses," Renee said. "The fans will think they're adorable."

Now, AS RENEE followed Lola into her studio, anticipation fluttered in her belly. She and Lola had planned on focusing on Lola's music: her process, the stories behind her songs—the artistic, personal things she might not want the whole crew around for. Renee felt as if she were being admitted to an inner sanctum.

The studio was so much cozier than Renee had imagined. Sun streamed through huge windows onto a pillow-packed couch and a fluffy sheepskin rug. The room was full of the stuff of Lola's music: a white piano, the rack of guitars, a shelf of shiny gold and cut-crystal awards, a computer hooked up to a mic, a keyboard, and some additional gear.

Lola flopped down on the couch while Renee set up the camera, then triple-checked the SD card, batteries, and backup batteries. She attached a mic to the camera, then set another recorder on the coffee table as fail-safe. She cracked her knuckles, then her neck. If this worked how she was hoping, she'd finally have something of quality to show Dragan. She might even be able to drop the staged shoots entirely.

Lola yawned, then rubbed her temple under the arm of her glasses.

Yes, *this* was what Renee needed: Lo, playing with her phone and her cheek smushed against the couch cushion, a little tired and undone. If Renee could keep Lo in that place, away from the show-pony version of herself, this could work.

Renee hit record. "Lo, can you explain where we are?"

Lola lifted her eyes, the wrist holding her phone going slack. Renee braced herself for Lola Gray to return and present the room like an overeager Realtor.

But instead, Lola arched an eyebrow and said, "This is where the magic happens."

Renee *blushed*.

"Just kidding," Lola said, pushing herself off the couch. "Most of the time I use it for songwriting."

"I—um—you know I'm recording, right?"

Lola burst into giggles. "You should see your face."

"I don't need to, because I know it looks entirely professional."

"I'll go again." Lola straightened up, but to Renee's relief she didn't bring out that high-gloss sheen. "This is my home studio, where I write most of my songs."

Lola gave a tour. As she did, she sounded—normal. Like she was talking to Renee, not a reporter or her management. She explained that the awards displayed in here were only the ones she'd won for songwriting, with the one exception of the prize she'd taken at the Fellows High School talent show their freshman year. After the pageants her mom had put her in, it felt like the first thing she'd won for herself. She showed off a letter she'd received from Elton John after her second album, dried roses preserved from a bouquet from Stevie Nicks.

Lola stopped at a glass-fronted cabinet full of notebooks. She had one hand clasped behind her neck, the other hidden in the sleeve of her sweater. "These are my journals."

"Like where you do the actual writing?"

Lola grinned. "Yes, the actual writing. I use the notes app on my phone too, but there's nothing like working the song out on paper."

"There must be a hundred notebooks in there," Renee said, staring at the cabinet.

"I haven't counted, but they go back before *Seventeen Candles*."

"You always had a journal with you back then."

Lola's dark eyes darted to Renee. "I got made fun of enough for it."

Renee shifted uncomfortably. She hadn't made fun of Lola herself—at least not to Lola's face—but she'd never stopped anyone else from doing it either. "I'm sorry. I kind of hoped you'd forgotten about that."

Lola's hand slipped from her neck and she looked directly into the camera. "It might shock you, dear viewer, but I was not terribly cool in high school. Right, Renee?"

"I wouldn't say *terribly* cool," Renee said carefully. "You had other priorities."

"Come on, you can admit it. I was different. Even you didn't like me in high school."

Renee flushed. "You probably don't remember, but back then I didn't like *anyone*."

"I remember," Lola said quietly.

Renee wished she wasn't holding the camera. "I really am sorry. If I'd known better, we could have been real friends. I was too busy being an idiot."

"It's fine. I was halfway out of Fellows anyway, and you had a lot going on."

"So did you. That's not an excuse." Renee's ribs were suddenly too tight. "Anyway, I like you now, enough to make up for it."

Lola was looking at her with her lips parted, her eyes round. Renee hastily angled the camera at the journals. "Can we look at them?"

"At my journals?"

"No, no—I mean, let's film you looking at them."

"They're sort of private." Lola hesitated, her fingertips light on the latch of the cabinet door. "But . . . all right. Why not?"

HALF AN HOUR later, Lola sat on the floor, her old journals fanned around her.

Renee couldn't believe Lola had allowed her this. She understood exactly how personal an artist's notebooks were, that they carried the unrefined contents of your heart and mind. The other artists Renee knew were devoted to a singular style of notebook, imported from places like Japan or Germany, and could not create without them.

Renee herself preferred a specific Finnish brand with dotted pages that she imagined would fit in at a film archive.

But Lola, whose notebooks probably *would* end up in an archive, had begun writing songs before she knew how artists were supposed to behave. Her notebooks were in all shapes, colors, and sizes: floppy college-ruled things with stickers on the cover, fancy leather-bound sketchbooks, staticky black-and-white composition books, girlish diaries with tiny locks. The spines were cracked and bindings bent, corners battered and covers peeling. Renee thought of her own notebooks, stored under her bed in Fellows; even the used ones looked nearly as pristine as the day she'd unwrapped them.

Lola got to her knees and pulled out a thick accordion file folder. "This is where I keep most of the scraps."

"The scraps?"

Lola fluttered her hand as if everyone knew this term. "When you have an idea, so you just grab an old envelope or whatever? It's excessive, but I like to save everything I can."

"You're saying you can write a whole song on an old envelope."

"Sometimes you have to." She rummaged through the file and pulled out a subscription card from a magazine. It was covered in cramped writing, some of it crossed out, other parts circled. "That's 'On a Dime.'"

Renee was gawking at Lo, but she couldn't help it. "On a Dime" was from the last album. It hadn't been a single but charted anyway after a sped-up bit of the chorus, where Lola almost growled—*you wanna see me turn on a dime?*—went viral. It became her first dance number one.

And Lola had written it on a literal piece of trash.

She held the card up for the camera and explained, "I was on a plane somewhere and we were held on the tarmac, and it came to me."

"The *whole song*?"

Lola smiled sheepishly. "In that case, yes. I recorded the demo on my phone before we even landed. But that's not how it usually works."

"Tell me how it usually works."

Renee sat across from Lola on the floor, the camera in her lap, as Lola flipped through notebooks. Some were filled when her handwriting was still big, childlike loops, others with a bubbly high schooler's hand. She'd pause, and say something like, "This page is literally tear-stained" or "Don't tell anyone, but this song is actually about *The Bachelor*." Sometimes she simply pressed her lips together, a furrow in her forehead, and didn't say anything at all.

It was like having the corners of Lola's mind turned out before her, but Renee still felt ravenously curious. She knew Lola well, but at the same time, she'd never know enough. Everywhere there was intimacy and absence.

That same intimacy and absence marked all of Lola's songs: precise details, but when you pulled back, the picture felt universal.

"I've never written more in my life than in high school. Most of these songs I never played for anybody."

"How does it feel looking at them now?" Renee asked.

Lola watched the notebook she'd been examining fall closed. "It's a little hard. Songwriting was an escape. When things were bad at home and things were bad at school, I kept my brain busy with stories. I was writing songs about a different life than what I had."

Renee's eyes flicked to the camera, wondering, for a moment, if Lola had meant to say that on film. She rarely spoke publicly about her family. When Lola had first become famous, her mother practically had the tabloids on speed dial, telling stories about all the sacrifices she'd made for her baby. That was bullshit: even as a kid, Renee understood that Lola only held her mother's attention when she was in the spotlight—in a pageant, performing for a crowd, on TV. When Lola wasn't, her mother's interest in, well, mothering was unpredictable, and her father was gone a lot on his trucking routes. That was why Deborah had often sent Renee next door to ask if the Grigorian girls wanted to come over for dinner, or to do their homework or watch a movie. Lola—and Claudia too—had succeeded in spite of her mother, not because of her.

"Anyway, a lot of these songs are fantasies," Lola said.

"Fantasies?"

Lola arched an eyebrow. "You knew me in high school, Renee. Did you think everything on *Seventeen Candles* really happened?"

"You could have been getting up to stuff on the weekends."

"I was working on the weekends. Anyway, it wasn't only the songs that were fantasies. *Music* was a fantasy. I thought I'd be swept away into this brilliant career, and everything would change." She shook her head with a self-effacing laugh. "What kind of kid daydreams about a job? No wonder I didn't have friends. Of course, now that I have everything I wished for, I realize I didn't know how good I had it before."

"What do you mean?"

Lola leaned back against the couch, clutching the journal in her lap like a security blanket. "There was no one watching. No deadlines, no pressure, no producers or managers or label, no fans. I didn't have to worry about what they'd read into the lyrics, who they'd think I was singing about, if it'd go viral. The only person I truly risked letting down was myself. At the time, I *hated* that no one else cared. Now sometimes I wish I was back there, when nothing I did mattered to anyone." She frowned, then added, "It's arrogant, isn't it? I spend so much time thinking about myself, my feelings, my stories, so I can turn them into songs that strangers can listen to. Now I'm doing this documentary. What if I'm not that interesting?"

"I think you're interesting," Renee pointed out. "This is interesting."

Lola balled her hands into the sleeves of the cardigan. She didn't look at Renee when she spoke. "You're not worried that America's Pop Princess has run out of things to say?"

"There are a lot of things you don't say."

Lola raised her eyes. "That's not the same thing," she said quietly.

Renee wasn't sure how to respond. As a director, she should keep Lola talking. But as someone who cared about her, she really just wanted to give Lola a hug.

She settled for changing the subject. "Tell me about the first song you learned on the guitar."

"The first?" Lola thought for a moment, then her face transformed with a mischievous grin. "You're going to love this. It was 'What's Up?' by 4 Non Blondes."

"It was *not*," Renee gasped.

"It was."

"That's a fucking dyke power move."

"Renee!"

"Sorry, I meant fucking bisexual power move."

"*Renee!*" Lola cried again, but even as she glared at the camera, she was laughing.

"I'll cut it, relax. You can't expect me *not* to react when you tell me you learned to play guitar on *one of the gayest songs of all time*."

"It wasn't intentional. I was teaching myself and it's super easy to play. It's only five chords."

"How did I not know that for our whole childhood you were holding solo sing-alongs to queer classics next door? Okay, okay, okay." Renee crossed the room, set the camera on the piano, and grabbed a guitar.

"For the film?" Lola asked.

"Forget about the film." Renee's lip quirked into a crooked grin. "I want to hear you scream that chorus."

Her eyes sparkling, Lola got to her feet and slung the guitar over her shoulder. "It's actually illegal to sing this song sitting down."

So they danced, belting out the words together and wailing at the chorus, flinging themselves around Lola's studio until they collapsed in a heap on the couch, their cheeks flushed. Lola's eyes were glimmering—that sadness that Renee had seen but not understood faded.

Renee shook her hair out of her face and said, "Next you'll tell me you know all the words to 'Fast Car.'"

"Of course I know all the words to 'Fast Car'!"

Inside Renee, something was zinging, singing, pitched with delight. "Prove it."

15

Renee arrived at the home of Ackerlund, Lola's longtime, single-named producer, feeling excellent.

The footage from Lola's studio had taken her breath away. Golden light illuminated Lola, among the splayed-open journals, like a fairy ringed by white roses. That shot had magic, beyond any doubt or criticism. She cut together a short clip to send to Dragan. He responded with a single-word message: "Intriguing." It was the most positive feedback she'd ever gotten from him.

Since then, she'd filmed solo with Lola twice more. First, they drove around to all the places Lola had lived in L.A., starting with her tiny first apartment. The second time, they'd hiked up to the Griffith Observatory. That had ended up as more of a hangout, since filming while hiking was a lot harder than Renee had expected.

It felt like an ace up Renee's sleeve—proof she could make the kind of film she wanted, one where Lo acted like herself. She was funny, kind, and fundamentally optimistic in a way that felt fascinating and foreign to Renee. But at the same time, there was a melancholy air about her. One moment she'd be laughing about a story from her last tour, and the next, a dark cloud would drift over her. If Renee asked her what was wrong, she'd brush it off. Still, it was progress.

The session with Ackerlund was in a converted pool house in his enormous backyard. In the back was a recording studio for demos, but they'd be shooting Lola and Ackerlund running through new songs in the lounge area.

The prospect of hearing Lola's latest work put a spring in Renee's step even as she tracked down Micah. He was frowning into his phone by the sapphire pool. She clapped him on the shoulder.

"Nice place, huh?" Renee said.

Micah didn't raise his eyes. "For sure. My wife hired the same landscaper."

Not even this extremely Micah-y response could dent Renee's mood. "Where's our girl? She was due on set five minutes ago."

"That's what I'm trying to figure out," Micah said, then moved away to answer a call.

Renee frowned. Lola was never late. Micah's body language on the call wasn't reassuring either: hunched, his phoneless hand shoved in his armpit, chin jutted out.

Micah came back with his report. "She's running late, but she's coming."

"Was that Cassidy?"

"Gloriana. She promised Lola will be here." It had never occurred to Renee that she might not be. Why would Gloriana be talking to Micah about Lola's schedule? That was Cassidy's job. Before Renee could ask, Micah said, "I'll grab Ackerlund so we can get going on his interview."

By the time cameras and lighting were rearranged and Ackerlund was getting dusted with anti-shine powder, Lola still wasn't there.

Renee texted, Everything ok?

Yes! Held up at home. So sorry!

Renee frowned. Lola should have been there thirty—no, forty-five minutes ago, and she was only leaving home now?

"So Ackerlund, what three words would you pick to describe Lola?" Micah asked. Renee rolled her eyes. Yes, Ackerlund was wearing sunglasses with yellow lenses and had clusters of prayer beads looped on his wrists and neck, but he had been one of the top-performing pop producers for the last five years. He was behind fifteen Hot 100 number ones, five of them with Lola. Surely, there were more interesting things to discuss.

Ackerlund didn't appreciate the question either. "Lola's a pop genius. The best I've ever seen," he said evenly. "Most artists come in with the lyrics, or an unfinished idea, and we build from the ground up. Lola brings me demos that are already pure ear candy, and I'm just putting polish on."

Renee's chest swelled. Lo was so good that Ackerlund, one of the defining producers of the era, was gushing about her.

He went on, "Lola's got an amazing gift. She's able to tap into emotion that feels honest and personal in the context of a hyper-relatable pop song. The first session I did with her, I knew this girl wasn't making songs for ten thousand people, or a hundred thousand people. She was making music for a million people that feels like it was made just for *you*."

Still, as the interview went on, Renee began to wonder how well Ackerlund knew Lola. Making art together was personal, vulnerable. But as Ackerlund said, Lola was an expert at creating the feeling of intimacy, while giving as little of herself away as possible. Did Ackerlund know Lola sometimes wrote love songs about women, or that the relationship with Nash was staged? Did he know what it meant when she wore that crinkle-eyed smile, when she looked desperate to please?

Did he know the girl who looked down at her old notebooks and wondered if she'd run out of things to say?

Where *was* Lola, anyway?

Renee's phone buzzed. It was a text from Cassidy.

Lola had a migraine. She needed to rest up before the premiere tomorrow. She wouldn't be coming.

16

"Eyes down."

A brush swept across Lola's eyelids. Her hands were in the custody of two manicurists, and a hairstylist was attaching extra extensions to the back of her head.

"So, this is how the Lola Gray sausage gets made," Renee said.

Lola wedged one eye open to look at Renee. The hotel room was crowded with her glam squad in red-carpet-prep mode. Renee, trying to stay out of the way with her camera, had ended up leaning her hips against the windowsill in front of Lola. She was wearing that jumpsuit again, the one from the wedding, with the same heels and the same red lip. The soft light coming in through the sheers lit up the curves of her body. Lola, sitting below Renee, with her legs crossed under her and dressed only in a loose button-up and boxer shorts, felt nearly naked staring up at her.

"This isn't even my final form," Lola said lightly, as the makeup artist waited for the glue on a strip of false lashes to get tacky. "Could I please have a sip of my iced coffee?"

The coffee was on a nearby table, but Lola's job for the moment was to move as little as possible.

"I got it," Renee said. She set the camera down, as the makeup artist applied lashes to Lola's half-closed lids. The makeup artist moved away, and Renee raised the straw to Lola's lips. As she took a long sip, a cold bead of condensation dripped onto the bare skin of her thigh.

Dozens of different people had held Lola's drink during glam, maybe even hundreds, and the only sensation she'd ever experienced was a spike of awkwardness. Yet, there were three other people touching Lola in that second, and Lola could feel Renee more keenly than any of them—Renee's closeness, her scent, her attention. Lola's body responded with a wave of heat that gathered between her legs.

Lola's tongue ran over her lips, trying to put the thoughts out of her mind.

But when she raised her eyes, Renee was still above her, her red lips slightly open and her own eyes hazy as she gazed down at Lola. No—not at Lola, at Lola's *mouth*. Suddenly, Lola was remembering the last time they'd been in a hotel room together, when Lola had drawn down the zipper of this same jumpsuit, revealing the muscles that made a valley of Renee's spine, the lace edge of her panties, the gorgeous fullness of her ass, and how—

No, she had to stop this. Why was Renee wearing the jumpsuit again anyway? Didn't she own another outfit?

Lola cleared her throat. "Thanks."

"My pleasure." Renee put the coffee down and grabbed the camera, which had, of course, been pointed right at them. "Caffeine's good for headaches, right?"

"Right," Lola said. "But I'm feeling much better today."

God, she hated the slimy feeling of lying, but what choice had she had? Before the session with Ackerlund, she'd spent every night sleepless, racking her brain for the kernel of a song that might work, but Ava was like salt plowed into the earth of her creativity: nothing could take root. Anything new she wrote, the LavaTruthers would spin for their theories. Anything romantic—from longing and lust, to love and heartbreak—was radioactive. What was she supposed to do, transition to a career of female empowerment anthems and dance club hits? Lola Gray wrote love songs. She wouldn't be herself if she left that behind.

She'd tried to make herself meet with Ackerlund anyway. Well, she tried, then panicked, wept a little hysterically, iced her face to calm down, only to lose it again. She'd promised Gloriana, who had promised the label, that she'd have something to show for herself and she simply *did not*. Finally, Cassidy had called Gloriana, and Lola had babbled out something about not being ready, needing more time, *just a little more time*. Gloriana had told her to make it work. That seeing Ackerlund would help. That a little songwriting assistance was one phone call away. Lola had promised to go, but once she'd hung up, she couldn't stop thinking of the cameras, not only Renee, but all her fans witnessing her downfall.

On some technical level, it wasn't a lie. She hadn't had a migraine, but her brain felt like it was on fire.

And now Renee was here, looking sexy as hell and tending to her, and Lola wanted nothing more than to crawl into her arms.

"Anything you need, just tell me," Renee said.

Lola swallowed hard. She wondered what Renee would have done if Lola had let her take the lead during their night together after the wedding. At the time, she'd wanted Renee to remember that night like a reverie. With Ava, she had taken satisfaction in doing exactly what Ava liked, and what Ava liked most was being the center of attention.

Renee would be different; Lola was certain. She wished she'd allowed herself to discover exactly how.

"Let's get you dressed," Jason St. Jude said as the glam squad wrapped up.

Lola unfolded herself from the chair and followed her stylist into the bathroom.

"Isn't she gorgeous?" Jason brushed a hand over the dress, setting the emerald silk shimmering. It had taken some legwork, and a whole lot of emails, to convince Gloriana and Veronika that she should wear the emerald halter, not the black cutout minidress they preferred. They'd caved when Lola suggested that the more provocative outfit could read as desperate once she and Nash broke up. Nash's premiere was their final big appearance as a couple: these photos had to count. The emerald dress was more romantic, like she was trying to make the relationship work, not attract a new man. The narrative was a little misogynistic, but Gloriana and Veronika valued optics above all else. She was still a little embarrassed that, had Renee not spoken up about the dress, Lola wouldn't have either.

Now, anticipation fluttered in Lola's belly. She couldn't wait to see what Renee would say when she saw it.

Jason helped her dress and made sure everything was secured, taped, and covered, then buckled her into the sky-high heels.

"Can you see if Renee's ready?" Lola asked as he gave her a final check. "She wanted to film the reveal."

Jason slipped out, and Lola heard him say, "Another Jason St. Jude masterpiece is complete!"

By force of habit, Lola faced the mirror and practiced her smile, the corners of her eyes crinkling. It looked off. This dress didn't belong to someone who would wear that smile. It was for someone a little more alluring, more withholding. Harder to please.

When Lola walked back into the room, Renee was ready with her camera. Lola posed like she would on the carpet. Twisting her shoulders to bring out the angles of her collarbones, pouting her lips, turning to highlight the open back.

"Yes, girl!" Jason cried, snapping his fingers amid the *ooh*s of the glam squad.

Renee didn't say anything at all. As the hairstylist gave her bangs a last adjustment, Lola asked, "So?"

Renee blinked at her, her gaze moving from the dress—Lola's body—to her face and down again. "That's the dress," Renee said, her voice a little low, a little awed.

Lola's whole body heated at the way Renee was looking at her—almost like she was imagining how the green silk would look falling from Lola's body and pooling on the floor.

"Ready?" Cassidy said, clutching her phone. Her pale eyes flitted between them. Cassidy had witnessed the dress debate, had encouraged Lola to insist. That was probably why she looked so delighted.

THEY MET NASH in the hotel's parking garage and carefully loaded into the SUV, mindful of everyone's easily creased red carpet attire. Renee took the back, Nash and Lola in the first row of seats.

Nash twisted around and stuck out his hand to Renee. "We haven't officially met. I'm Nash. You're the documentarian I've been hearing so much about from our girl here."

"You can ignore him," Lola said.

Nash rolled his eyes. "Cute dress, baby. Very Keira Knightley in *Atonement* of you."

Lola rolled her eyes in return. "I know you hate it."

"Sorry, what?" Renee said.

"Oh, it's just not his taste," Lola explained. "Nash likes shiny things."

"That doesn't give him the right to—" Renee began, but thankfully Nash tossed his head and talked right over her.

"I never understand why you don't just cover yourself in crystals and rhinestones whenever you get the chance. If I were a girl, that's what I'd do."

Lola glanced at Renee. She'd only ever told Renee why *she* needed a PR boyfriend. Nash's reason for a PR girlfriend was his to reveal—and Renee certainly hadn't learned it when Nash showed up to her rehearsal in full hetero cosplay. But now, in the privacy of the SUV, he was being himself. Renee, never that good at hiding her feelings, wore her newfound realization on her face.

Lola said, "If you were a girl, you'd learn fast that rhinestones are crazy uncomfortable when you're sitting in a movie theater for three hours." She paused a beat. It was something Nash had mentioned before, what he would wear if he were a girl, not only on the red carpet, but to parties, to the beach, to brunch. Lola didn't know what he meant by it—she wasn't sure if *Nash* knew what he meant by it—so usually she let the comments slip by. But now, wearing the dress Renee had inspired her to fight for, she wondered if she shouldn't take them more seriously. "Your stylist could put you in less masculine looks. More feminine, or androgynous. Tons of designers would love to dress you."

Nash dismissed that with a chuckle. "Maybe if I make it to Cannes one day, my management would let me wear a shirt with the teeniest, tiniest ruffle. But they'd make me burn it before I left Europe."

Lola changed the subject. "Are you feeling good about the premiere?"

Anxiety flashed over Nash's face before he schooled it back to sunshine. "Completely. I can't wait for everyone to see it."

Lola looked back at Renee. "Nash did his own stunts."

"I did! Well, except the ones the insurance company wouldn't sign off on. I got to do a lot of really cool fight scenes too. At least, I think they'll be cool," he said, deflating a little.

Lola reached for his hand.

"I did the best I could, but with action movies, you never know. When they put it all together, they might pick my worst take because it works with some CGI explosion. And then I'll be upstaged by a stupid fireball."

"Speaking as a director, I don't think a fireball could upstage you," Renee said. "You have a lot of charisma."

Lola watched Renee, a glowy feeling spreading inside her to see two of her favorite people, together.

"Really?" Nash asked, his golden retriever energy surging again. "You have to tell me what you think. Promise to find me at the after-party?"

"I'm only authorized to film parts of the red carpet, not the after-party," Renee said.

"Oh, stop it," Lola said. "She'll be there."

* * *

They pulled up to the theater on Hollywood Boulevard. Lola prepared mentally for the noise that would burst over them once they hit the carpet. She and Nash shared a reassuring glance and then they were on. Flashes flashing, photographers yelling. Nash moved down the carpet first, then Lola, each posing solo, then as a couple. When they came together, Lola angled her body into his and he set his hand on the small of her back.

"Give her a kiss, Nash!" one photographer yelled, and he leaned down and kissed her cheek.

Lola's attention kept straying to Renee, following a few feet behind with her camera. Her face was set, her focus on her work amid the red carpet chaos. As she and Nash arranged themselves again, he leaned into her ear. "Distracted by your girlfriend?"

Lola shot him a cutting look, then remembered herself and relaxed her face.

"I will step on your foot in these heels and make it look like an accident," she said under her breath.

After the photo call, she and Nash separated for press. Lola delivered sound bites about the film and her dress, and evaded questions about new music. Nash would be tied up until the screening began. She could have headed into the theater, but she lingered at the end of the red carpet for Renee.

"I have to run this camera back to the car," Renee said, although she didn't move to do so. "You didn't have to invite me to the afterparty."

"Nash wants you there—and I do too. I kind of hate these things, but . . . maybe I'd hate it less with you."

"Oh. Okay then, yeah." There was nothing left for her to do but walk away—Renee's seat was in some balcony level nowhere near Lola's—but she hesitated. "I forgot to say this earlier, but you look truly incredible. The dress is even better than I remember." A flush bloomed over Renee's cheeks. "Right, so. I'll see you later."

"Yeah, later. I mean—thank you," Lola said, her cheeks warming too.

As Renee headed off, Lola cast a final look down the red carpet. The stream of people had dwindled, so Lola could see the street. One SUV was still waiting, its passenger's toes reaching for the ground: ankle boots, leather pants, an expanse of flat stomach—

Lola's body reacted before her brain understood: her heart beat too slow and too fast at once, her insides crumpling like a fist. She knew those slim hips, the arc of bone protruding from the waist of the pants, the smooth skin of that midriff. She recognized the exact bra that was entirely visible under a cropped mesh top: Ava had scolded her once for pulling too hard on the lace.

Ava.

A bright flash of frustration burst through Lola. It wasn't *fair*. This was Lola's boyfriend's premiere—Lola's space, not Ava's. No one from

Nash's team had warned Lola—although why would they, when the two women were nothing but ex-BFFs? And Ava had shown up in old lingerie and leather pants—when Lola had suffered through weeks of negotiation just to wear a dress she liked—and of course, Ava looked completely, horribly amazing, exactly like she always did.

Lola bit the inside of her cheek hard and used the burst of pain to center herself. Her brain was collapsing into a vortex of toxic thoughts. She had to get off the red carpet.

Lola forced herself to head into the theater. Her seat would be up front with Nash, and far from Ava's. She passed under an enormous poster of Nash and his female costar surfing the hood of a car as it sailed away from an explosion. Ava's presence behind her felt like exactly that kind of devouring fireball.

Would Ava speak to her at the after-party? Ava wouldn't bring up all the pathetic, pleading texts Lola had sent, would she? Or should Lola initiate a conversation, in a bid for the upper hand? No, that was ridiculous; she'd never controlled a single thing in their relationship.

She'd done everything in her power to keep Ava, and it hadn't been enough.

Lola hadn't been enough.

When Lola reached her seat, she felt a wave of relief that made it difficult not to cry. She wished she had someone there who understood, but she was completely alone.

Ava is here no one told me she'd be here, Lola texted Gloriana.

Really? We were told she rsvp'd no.

Can I leave, Lola texted, her eyes stinging. I can't be here I don't want to be in the same room as her

It took Gloriana an eon to respond.

> It's best to stay. Leaving will fuel more
> rumors. You'll look like you're running away.
> And we have an obligation to Nash.

Lola's eyes burned with unshed tears. There was no way she could sit through the movie knowing that Ava was somewhere behind her. Gloriana was right about the rumors and her obligations but—but that didn't mean Lola had to do what she asked.

Lola texted Renee, then hurried up the aisle, deliberately ignoring the eyes following her as she left. She pushed open the door to the mostly empty lobby as the lights were dimming.

Before her, like something out of a ghastly dream, stood Ava: snacking on popcorn, statuesque and beautiful, blonde mane tousled like she'd styled it with a romp in the sheets.

Time slowed down, in the hellish, drippy way it did in nightmares where you needed to run but your legs were Jell-O. Ava's icy blue eyes caught Lola in their beam, then widened, like she'd spotted something shiny she wanted to tear to shreds.

Lola was entirely, completely fucked.

"Lolly, babe!" Ava strutted toward her while waving off the usher asking them to take their seats. "I thought I might see you here."

Lola's brain was broken. She couldn't even attempt to say something cutting or dismissive; she just wanted there not to be silence, not to have Ava's eyes on her. "Nash is my boyfriend," she said stupidly.

"Right." Ava scrunched up her face like she was promising not to tell Lola's secrets. "But you two aren't, you know . . . are you?"

Lola was too stunned to speak, but Ava sailed past the silence as if it were an answer. She popped a piece of popcorn in her mouth, then let a considering gaze drip down Lola's body as she chewed. "You're looking gorgeous though. This dress is something else. So, what happened to all those songs you wrote for me?"

"I—I went in another direction," she choked out, because she'd heard Gloriana explain it that way. If only she'd listened to Gloriana and stayed in her seat, this wouldn't be happening.

Ava's smile faded a touch. "Well, I hope you didn't change your plans on my account. I wanted to hear you sing about me on the radio."

Lola's chest was too tight, her throat too narrow, her breath too shallow. *Of course* she'd changed her plans on Ava's account! Ava knew that without their relationship, Lola couldn't release an album of sapphic love songs. Ava understood the careful construction of a public image perfectly well when it came to herself, but when Lola had explained, repeatedly, how delicate coming out would be for her, Ava had acted like she was making excuses.

Lola didn't know what to say. There weren't even words in her head anymore—they'd melted away, just like her ability to write.

The thought was the final crack in the fragile defenses that had been restraining sheer panic. The building swell of tears was hot and stinging, her lower lip trembling, her breath speedy, and Lola *knew*: she was going to break down in public, right in front of Ava Andreesen.

17

When Renee got Lola's text—meet me in lob y noe—it was alarming. Spelling errors like that could only happen when you'd really ambushed autocorrect. Renee stepped on the toes of a dozen of Hollywood's petty nobility to get out of her seat. Then it was down two flights of carpeted stairs. *What was wrong? What had happened?* She didn't know, but Lola needed her and that was enough.

Neither woman noticed as Renee approached: Lola, because she couldn't take her eyes off Ava, and Ava, because she seemed like the kind of person who found noticing other people distasteful.

Normally, Renee might have been turned on to see two stunning women locked in a gaze like MMA fighters who couldn't decide if they were about to kiss or kill each other. The sapphic energy was off the charts. This time, a feeling bitter and entirely unlike arousal surged inside her. She wanted to snap Ava Andreesen in two like a pretzel stick.

Then she heard Ava say, "I wanted to hear you sing about me on the radio."

Renee flinched. How dare Ava say something like that in public? How dare she speak to Lola at all?

Renee announced herself with subtlety: "Hello, ladies!"

"Yes, we know the movie's starting." Ava waved her off, then said to Lola, "These ushers are so rude."

Lola's panicked gaze flashed at Renee. There were tears standing in her eyes. *Shit.* Renee needed to get moving.

"Actually, I don't work here," Renee said. "I'm with Lola, and I need to steal her... because... her Covid test results came back and it's not looking good."

"Oh my god, Lolly, gross." Ava recoiled several feet. "Drinks when you're negative! I have a new number so message me on Instagram."

Renee didn't wait for Ava to enter the theater before putting her hand on the warm skin between Lola's shoulder blades and steering her toward the women's restroom. Lola's heart was beating so hard her small body seemed to shake, her breaths shortening even further into quick, wet wheezes.

"I got you, almost there," Renee murmured. She hauled open the restroom door, shoved Lola inside, then dashed down the line of toilets, checking for feet. Five minutes into the first screening of the biggest expected blockbuster of the year, the stalls were blessedly empty.

Then she looked at Lola and said, "Okay, go."

Lola's face crumpled as the tears surged free.

How could anyone look this beautiful as they cried? Renee circled her arms around Lola. She collapsed against Renee's chest. She fit against her perfectly, her tears wetting Renee's collarbone.

"I'm sorry," Lola gasped. "This is so embarrassing. It's the first time I've seen her since..."

"Shh, it's fine. I got you." Renee moved her hand in slow circles on Lola's back. "I got you. Seriously, who even is this chick? What's she known for other than making the best of a bad orthodontic situation and not brushing her hair? Those pants are probably giving her a yeast infection as we speak." Lola huffed something like a laugh into Renee's chest. Renee pulled back. "But you? You're a real-life musical genius. You're literally adored by millions. Your next album is going to break every record in existence."

Okay, that was overkill. Her pep talk only made Lola's hyperventilating worse. Lola buried her face in her own hands.

"The next album is—it's—" Lola's voice cracked.

Renee eased Lola's hands down. Mascara was smeared over her cheeks. "It's going to be even better than whatever you wrote about her. It's going to be incredible, like a hundred number one hits."

But Lola's doe eyes went huge and clouded with fear.

"*Shit*," Renee whispered as it clicked into place. The canceled sessions with her producer, the delayed album, the way Lola had wondered if she had anything left to say. "You have writer's block."

A fresh tear streamed down Lola's cheeks. The confession raced out of her with desperate urgency. "I haven't written anything in a year. The label needs the album—everyone needs the album. *You're supposed to be filming me recording the album.* And I have nothing. Absolutely *nothing*."

"Okay, okay. Just breathe. You still have loads of time until it's due, right?"

"It's supposed to be released in June. That's nine months. It sounds like a lot but I'm so behind, it's almost hopeless. Gloriana can tell something's wrong. If I can't fix this, she'll make me use a ghostwriter."

"Absolutely not. Lola Gray writes her own songs," Renee said.

"Maybe Lola Gray doesn't exist anymore," Lola said in a thin, exhausted voice.

Renee pulled Lola against her again, but this time slid a knuckle under Lola's chin, tilting her head up to meet her gaze. "Fuck Lola Gray. I'm looking at Lo Grigorian. You are kind and funny and empathetic and talented and brave enough to take yourself seriously. Your work ethic is off the charts—actually excessive, to be honest, and really fucking inspiring. You care so much about making everyone around you feel valued. And not to get superficial about it, but you're the hottest person I've ever seen in real life, and I'm saying that in a building packed with celebrities." Renee swept a tear from Lola's cheek. "Maybe your one flaw is that you have bad taste in girls, but who isn't guilty of that now and then?"

Just then, someone pushed open the bathroom door. Instantly, Renee broke away and threw her bodyweight against it. "Closed for cleaning, go upstairs!" she shouted, then pulled out her phone. "I'm calling the driver."

"Gloriana said I have to stay."

"And why did Mommy say that?"

"I committed to Nash," Lola sniffed.

"Nash will forgive you. The sea monkey isn't so bad."

"We don't want it to look like I'm running away from Ava."

"Why not?"

Lola's mouth fell open. "Because people will *talk*."

"I'd rather them talk than put you through this torture."

Lola hugged herself, uncertain. Renee hated seeing her like this, pulled in two so hard she was splitting at the seams—especially when one direction was so transparently what Lola truly wanted.

"You don't understand," Lola said. "There's all this pressure I'm under."

Renee put her arms around Lola again. Maybe it was too much, but she only wanted to comfort her. As gorgeous as Lola was in that dress, she also looked small, and cold, and Renee wanted to hold her close and make sure she was safe and warm forever.

"I can see the pressure you're under. I can see that it's tearing you apart. It's okay to leave. If you need permission, I'm giving it to you." An idea-shaped bubble rose to the surface of Renee's brain. She gave Lola one last squeeze. "Let me take you away from this, Lo."

You are not going to look at this picture from the Fit to Live red carpet and tell me these two are a happy couple.
♡ 17.9K
Reply

↳ She's fixing to bite Nash's head off
♡ 3087

↳ Yeah I wonder why 🏳️‍🌈 🏳️‍🌈 🏳️‍🌈
♡ 524

Ava was there too! #LavaForever
♡ 32
Reply

Lola and Nash are soooo cute like literal goals and you all are making this gay stuff up! Get a life haters!
♡ 14.4K
Reply

↳ #LolaGBTQ #LavaGBTQ
♡ 45

↳ I have a life and this is what I choose to do with it
♡ 1034

Someone tag that girl that does the lip reading videos I wanna know what they're saying
♡ 1844
Reply

↳ I think it's "make it look like an accident"
♡ 73

↳ omg what
♡ 3

Slay queen! That dress!
♡ 40.3K
Reply

↳ She ate and left no crumbs
♡ 4698

There's a blind item saying Lola ran out of the premiere before the movie even started ♡ 629

Reply

↳ I saw that too ♡ 2

↳ bc she had covid ♡ 85

Any pics of her and Ava? ♡ 1

Reply

The way Nash looks at her you can tell he loves her so much ♡ 348

Reply

18

"I can't believe we're doing this," Lola said.

Renee let her eyes stray from the highway that curved around Lake Michigan, to steal a look at her passenger. Lola was staring out the window, an easy smile on her face as she watched the indigo sky darken.

"People take vacations, Lo. Happens all the time," Renee said, though she felt like they were getting away with something too. Driving a rental car down US-131 with Lola in the passenger seat shouldn't have been so thrilling, but knowing that it was just the two of them—no crew, no security detail, and soon, once they got to Deborah's cabin, barely even cell reception—had her feeling a little giddy.

It hadn't felt real until she and Lola were at the Van Nuys Airport that morning. When Renee had told Lola she wanted to take her to the cabin up north for a few days, they weren't yet a full block away from the *Fit to Live* premiere. She'd expected Lola to balk at the idea, but she'd asked when.

"As soon as we can," Renee had said.

"Tomorrow?"

"I'll buy tickets on my phone, right now."

"No, wait—let me make a call first."

Lola was dialing before Renee could protest. She was probably calling Gloriana or Cassidy, derailing their secret getaway into a snarl of permissions. "Hey, Tati. How are you? . . . Honestly, not great. I need a favor. Can I use your jet? Normally I use the label's but I don't want to ask—ha, I know, you get it . . . Flying out tomorrow and then back in"—Lola's eyes cut to Renee—"five days?"

Five days.

Less than twenty-four hours after Lola was hyperventilating in a movie theater bathroom, they landed at Cherry Capital Airport outside Traverse City, Michigan, in Tatiana Jones's private jet.

Night had fallen by the time they'd collected the groceries Renee had ordered on her phone and turned onto a gravel drive fringed with trees. Winter came quick up north. Though it was early October, the leaves were already yellow, or blanketing the ground. Soon the muted green of pine needles would be the only source of color. Renee's blood thrummed with anticipation as they pulled up to the house. She killed the engine and flung open her door. Crisp air welcomed them in a chilly embrace. "I want to show you something."

"Shouldn't we put the groceries away first?"

"The groceries will be fine, it's like forty degrees."

As soon as Lola was out of the car, Renee grabbed her hand and tugged her around to the back deck.

"Wait, it's so dark, I'm going to trip—*oh*."

Before them, Lake Michigan stretched to the dark horizon, a rich blue-black that sparkled quicksilver where it caught the moonlight. The moon hung half-full in a sky that was clear of clouds, but freckled with uncountable stars. They could hear the waves pulsing steadily at the beach below, and above, the wind whispering through the trees a hushed sound like *yes*.

All Renee's excitement resolved into something still and certain.

Lola was staring at the sky. Pale moonlight washed over her face and caught brightly in her eyes. Then she let out a small, delighted gasp. "A shooting star! Did you see it?"

Renee had a lifetime to watch shooting stars. Lola, in this moment, was more precious.

"No," Renee said. Her voice was already a little ragged.

As soon as Lola met Renee's gaze, the space between them charged with electricity—Renee reached for Lola and in the same instant, Lola moved into her arms, as if she belonged there, as if she'd always been there. Her hands went to Renee's waist, her head tilted up, waiting. Renee drew her closer, and kissed her.

For all the times Renee had wanted to kiss Lola in the last weeks, she tried not to rush now. It was so gentle at first. Lola's lips were smooth, her skin cold and breath steaming in the night, Renee's eyelashes brushing hers. Renee cupped her cheek, her fingers finding their way into her soft hair. It wasn't anything like how they'd kissed in that hotel room, brash and a little frantic. This was precious—a delicate thing built of every moment of these last weeks—every casual touch that meant more, every private laugh, every vulnerable moment they'd shared. And more than that—of ten years apart, and all the shit they'd borne witness to for each other before that.

Renee couldn't believe that all of that had brought them to this moment. She tugged Lola harder against her and parted her lips with her tongue, so she could take Lola's lower lip into her mouth and suck. She tasted like sweet relief and hunger all at once.

Lola moaned, pressing her nose into Renee's cheek as she deepened the kiss. Her hands snaked into Renee's coat, then under the back of her shirt, her touch deliciously cool against Renee's hot skin. Her fingertips bit into the flesh of Renee's back, pulling her closer, closer. They couldn't be touching any more than they were with their coats on, but Lola wanted more.

Wanted this.

Wanted her.

The thought threatened to overwhelm Renee, as Lola rose up on her toes to slide her tongue into Renee's mouth.

A gust of wind rolled off the lake, buffeting them with freezing air. Lola seized up. Renee broke away, resting her forehead against Lola's. They were both panting, lips swollen, and Renee would have bet money that Lola was on fire, exactly like she was, even if her skin was freezing.

"Inside?" Renee asked.

"Yeah." Lola's voice sounded raw.

But Lola didn't move. With Lola's breath warm against her mouth, Renee didn't want to move either.

"Fuck," Renee breathed.

"Yeah," Lola said again.

RENEE FUMBLED WITH the house key, so jittery was she from Lola's nearness. Finally inside, Renee rambled, excusing her mom's cheesy lake house decor and apologizing that the heat wasn't on and warning of the ladybug infestation. For all the girls she'd been with, Renee wasn't used to being nervous.

It was hot as hell.

Lola hardly said anything at all. Her quiet wasn't awkward or avoidant. It felt more like an agreement: the moment on the deck was banked like a fire, to allow them to do all the little things that needed doing in the empty house.

Then all at once, the two of them were facing each other in the harsh light of the kitchen.

"I—"

"Are you—"

Lola reached for Renee's hands and ran her thumbs over her knuckles. The rich darkness of her eyes, an abyss Renee could vanish into. Maybe she already had. Her heartbeat fluttered as Lola's gaze shifted from her lips to her eyes, and back again.

Suddenly Lola let out a laugh. "How are *you* the nervous one?"

Renee wet her lips. "I think you like it when I'm nervous."

Lola closed the distance between them, slid her hand to Renee's neck, and kissed her.

Renee yielded to the smell of her perfume and the way her thick hair tangled around them like spiderwebs. Renee forgot her nerves, forgot anything but the hungry pressure of Lola's mouth, the *need* that simmered from her fingertips to her belly to her clit.

They stumbled down the hall to the bedroom. Renee kicked off one of her sneakers as Lola tugged her in for another kiss, and she lost her balance, sending the picture on the wall swinging. Steadying them, Renee seized Lola's waist. She guided her backward toward the bed, until Lola's legs hit the mattress and she fell against the duvet. Renee climbed up over her, so their thighs were interlocked. Lola hissed out a breath as Renee's body pressed against her. Renee let Lola take the lead. Her deft fingers worked through the buttons of Renee's flannel. Lola arched off the bed as she flung Renee's shirt to the floor and brought her mouth to her chest. Renee fell into the sensation of Lola's teeth against her nipple through the fabric of her sports bra, of Lola's strong hands sliding down the back of her jeans to grip her flesh, to the whisper of a moan that caught at the back of Lola's throat with every breath.

"Fuck, Lo—" Renee pushed herself back to unfasten and shuck off her jeans. She searched for the words for what she wanted and how badly, but she was messy and desperate and all she could manage was "Lo, *please*."

Lola pulled Renee back down with one hand. The other, she slipped into Renee's underwear.

Renee cried out as Lola's fingers brushed against her. Below her,

her arms framed Lola's face, those hungry eyes watching Renee with greedy attention. Lola's fingers teased Renee's folds, so tantalizingly near what Renee needed that it was almost painful. Renee's breaths hung ragged around Lola's name, her hips rolling with need. Then all at once, Lola sank two fingers in, bringing the heel of her hand to Renee's clit. Renee cried out, her arms trembling. But Lola's hand kept up that perfect rhythm, and Renee bore herself down against her—until she began to clench around Lola's fingers. At that precise moment, Lola changed the angle of her wrist, increasing the pressure against Renee's core. It was exactly what Renee loved, and, *fuck, Lola remembered.* She'd—but then Renee was plummeting over the edge of pleasure, her body and mind lost to this moment, to sensation, to *Lo.*

Renee panted into the duvet, her body half flung over Lola's. Their legs hung over the side of the bed—they hadn't even made it anywhere near the pillows.

"I've never come that fast for anyone," Renee whispered.

"I'll make you wait next time."

Renee brushed back a lock of hair that was stuck to Lola's forehead. The night after the wedding, she'd tried to please Lola and been denied. She still didn't know if Lola was a top or simply nervous with new partners. She could have asked what Lola wanted, what she liked. But the moment between them felt fragile, precious. She didn't want to interrupt it with a discussion that Lola might not be prepared for.

Renee sat up. Lola pushed herself up too, then ran her palms up Renee's back, grazing the straps of her sports bra between her shoulder blades, her touch drifting over Renee's traps and over the swell of her shoulders.

"You're still wearing your shoes," Renee said.

Lola looked down. She was still fully clothed, while Renee was in her underwear. "I'm sorry, I forgot . . . Oh." Lola trailed off as Renee slid off the end of the bed and sank to her knees in front of her. Renee took Lola's right ankle in her grasp. Lola was wearing some kind of designer hiking boot, and tomorrow, Renee would tease her about that, verbally. Now, she was going to tease her in an entirely different way. Slowly, keeping her eyes on Lola's as much as she could, Renee worked open the knot of her shoelace.

"I can take off my own shoes." Lola's voice carried the hint of a nervous laugh, but her gaze was skimming over Renee's kneeling form.

"I know," Renee said. "But can you let me do it for you?"

Renee slipped her fingers a few inches up the opening of Lola's jeans to caress the skin there. Lola's nervous smile was gone. She held her lip between her teeth. Her hair spilled over her shoulder, and her eyes fixed on Renee, darkly curious.

Lola nodded.

"Thank you." Renee's voice was so low, it rasped against her throat. She pulled Lola's boot free, then her sock. She kept her palm against the top of Lola's foot, fingertips teasing her ankle, as she moved to the other side. Once that boot was on the floor, Renee slid her hands up Lola's denim-clad shins, to her knees. She spread them with gentle pressure and settled herself in the space between them.

"That shouldn't have been as hot as it was," Lola murmured, her chest rising and falling.

Renee eased her palms up to Lola's thighs, until her fingers twisted into the belt loops of her jeans. "Can I?"

"Yes," Lola breathed.

Renee opened the button and zipper. Lola lifted her hips. Renee slid the jeans down. She tossed them away, then took her time trailing her fingers and palms along Lola's soft skin. Still kneeling, she brushed the crease of Lola's thighs, then swept her hands back to the firm globes of her ass.

Lola's hands fisted in the duvet.

Renee pressed her body against Lola's legs, letting Lola's skin touch hers wherever she could. She bowed down to kiss the inside of her knee, then the rounded tops of her thighs, stopping to rest her cheek a mere inch from where Lola's panties covered her. Wetness had soaked them through.

Renee's eyes fluttered closed, and she drew a long, deep breath. Lola's scent hit her like the rush of blood to her head, intoxicating and thick and sweet. Renee cursed with pleasure as her body arched involuntarily into Lola's. Her grip on Lola's ass was so firm, Renee felt it when the muscles flexed to meet her.

Renee wanted to bury her face in Lola. She wanted to haul Lola off this bed, rip her panties off, and feel Lola's thighs straddling her cheeks, then work her until she was shaking and boneless. Renee wanted it so badly, her jaw was quivering.

But this wasn't about what Renee wanted. Renee would have spent the rest of the night with her face in Lola's pussy, but she was afraid that if she suggested it, Lola might agree just to please her. She could feel that Lola had tensed a little, even as she was obviously enjoying the attention. Renee didn't want Lola to agree. She wanted Lola to *want*.

They had time to figure it out. Lola was a perfectionist, but Renee was just as dedicated to her craft.

Renee inhaled a final pull of Lola's scent, then raised her head and stood—taking the hem of Lola's shirt with her. Though still in her bralette and panties, Lola looked up at Renee as undone as she had the night after the wedding. She held her lip in her teeth, her breathing short. Her nipples strained against the black lace. Renee grazed the back of her knuckles over them. Lola's breath caught in her throat as she surged forward into Renee's light touch.

Renee grinned. "You liked that?"

Lola answered by tearing the bralette over her head and pulling

Renee's hands to her breasts. Renee rolled Lola's nipples between her fingers. Lola's face crumpled as she whined with pleasure. Lower, Lola's thighs pressed together, seeking friction.

"Do you remember our first night together, how you were touching yourself while you went down on me?"

Lola nodded.

Renee kept her fingers toying with Lola's nipples, firing sparks of pleasure through her.

"Can you do that now?"

Lola's hand shot to her pussy. Her hips canted off the bed as she rubbed at her clit. As she got closer, her breathing went ragged, and she pressed her face into Renee's stomach.

"That's it," Renee breathed. "Just like that."

Lola snaked her free hand around and sank it into Renee's ass, pulling her against her. Fuck, that was hot. She couldn't see Lola's face but could feel her hot breath—could hear how completely wet she was. She was still teasing Lola's nipples, and they were rock hard.

"You're doing so good. I can tell you're close."

Lola's body rocked. "I am," she choked out.

"Tell me how close."

"I'm so—I'm almost—"

Renee wove a hand into Lola's hair. She wanted to see Lola's face as she orgasmed—it would probably push Renee over the edge again herself—but she wasn't sure if Lola would want that.

"Then come for me."

Lola jerked, gasped, then whimpered. Her body went rigid, arching into Renee's. Renee bit into her own cheek as Lola cried out once, then again, and with a final shiver, went limp against her.

WHEN RENEE CAME back from the kitchen with two glasses of water, Lola's hair was splayed across the pillow. Her eyes were closed, her expression relaxed. A sheen of sweat glistened over her chest. Renee's heart stuttered to see her like that—not only gorgeous and half-naked, but languid and easy, all the rigid scaffolding of Lola Gray cast off and scattered across the bedroom floor or left back in Los Angeles. Just Lo.

Renee knew she'd do anything to keep her feeling like that.

Then Lola opened her eyes. Her gaze slid over Renee, still standing in the doorway.

"What's wrong?" Lola asked.

"Nothing. Everything's perfect."

"Then stop staring at me and come here." Lola licked her lips. "I'll go slower this time. If you're ready again."

Renee absolutely was.

19

Lola woke with her face buried in Renee's neck. She was curled against Renee's body like a melted big spoon, her stomach pressed into the mattress but her arm and leg splayed over the woman breathing evenly next to her.

Stars shot through her chest as she remembered last night. The kiss she'd waited for since she'd written "Star Sign"—a kiss that felt like finally being seen, without having to hide or pretend or impress. Like getting exactly what you wanted, without having to ask for it at all.

Then afterward . . . Lola had imagined having sex with Renee many times. Hell, she'd actually done it before. And last night still managed to be better than any of that. Never had she imagined Renee begging for her touch, or the vulnerable way Renee cried out as she came. And then, what she did next—Lola had never fantasized about anything like that at all. It had been as if Renee wanted to serve her, and it had made her feel safe and wildly desperate at the same time. No one had ever made her feel that way—none of the men she'd dated, including Kyte, and certainly not Ava.

Lola grinned as she tried to extricate her limbs from Renee's without waking her.

"Where're you going?"

"Getting up."

"No," Renee groaned. "Why?"

"It's late, almost ten."

"So?"

Renee turned on her side so she was facing Lola and snuggled down into the bed, so her head was nestled below Lola's chin, their breasts pressed together, their bellies, their legs, and all of it so lovely and soft.

"Don't make me miss you," Renee mumbled.

"Okay." Lola smiled into the crown of Renee's head.

Her answer was a contented sigh.

IT WAS AFTERNOON before they made it out of bed, after sex, sleepy and slow, hands moving over skin under the down duvet.

"I cannot believe you wanted to get up so early," Renee said as she laid out the ingredients for an epic breakfast. "We have nowhere to be, plus there's a three-hour time change."

"I'm not used to lying around." Lola passed Renee a mug of coffee. They'd quickly established that Lola was not suited to food prep duty. "And I didn't expect you'd be so into snuggling."

"I'm usually not," Renee admitted.

Lola bit her lip, pleased. "Well, usually I have a hard time sleeping with someone else in the bed."

Renee looked up from the onion she was chopping. "Shit, I'm sorry—do you want one of the other beds?"

"*No*," Lola said. "Absolutely not. I slept great. I feel incredible, honestly."

Renee's grin was crooked, satisfied but still hungry, and Lola knew she was wearing the same expression. She slid in behind Renee and ran her hands up her back.

"Stop that, or we're never going to have anything to eat," Renee said, even as she pressed her hips against Lola's.

Because Lola was also hungry for food, she dropped a kiss between Renee's shoulder blades, then gave her space in the kitchen. She explored the living room, looking at family photos, a TV with an old DVD player, shelves stuffed with worn paperbacks and board games. In the corner, an acoustic guitar leaned against the wall.

She brushed her thumb experimentally across the strings. It was a battered thing, the varnish worn and one of the pegs chipped.

"That's Dave's," Renee said. "I'm sure he'd love it if you played it."

"Maybe I'll go tune it on the deck while you finish cooking?" Lola said tentatively.

"I'll bring everything out when it's ready."

Lola pulled on a fleece and, outside, settled into an Adirondack chair in full sunlight. She tuned the guitar, then let her fingers wander over the strings as she watched the lake. The water was a thousand shades of blue, the quiet punctuated only by her playing and the warble of birds.

When Renee had suggested they escape L.A., Lola hadn't really believed it would achieve much. She'd been so overwhelmed, she'd have agreed to go anywhere. She'd never done anything remotely like this before—running off without even her security, asking Cassidy to cancel her obligations, texting Gloriana that she'd be unreachable for a few days at Renee's family lake house. Once they were on the plane, she'd imagined it might be a nice break, before she finally confessed to Gloriana that the songwriting part of her brain was broken. As for her and Renee, she hadn't dared to hope for anything.

Lola had not once considered that she might actually feel peaceful here—that that was what Renee had wanted to give her. One day and, already, the sharp mid-autumn sunlight and quiet rustling of the trees, stirred by the breeze from the lake, made the demands of her career and the people who issued them feel so distant. Renee had threatened not to give her the Wi-Fi password, but Lola didn't even want it now. Her phone was somewhere inside—wherever they'd dropped their things last night.

No deadlines, no publicity, no fans, no record labels, no manager, no team. Just her and Renee.

Her and Renee.

Four more days of this. Already she wanted more.

Lola was picking out a melody when Renee appeared with plates of scrambled eggs and potatoes with onions and bacon, a bottle of ketchup under her arm, and set them on the weathered table.

"What are you playing?" she asked.

"Nothing, just messing around," Lola said as she set the guitar aside.

They ate in easy silence, watching the water.

Renee cleared her throat. "We need to talk."

"About us?"

Renee was digging her thumbnail into the grooved wood of the table. It made Lola nervous. "Yeah, I—when I invited you here, I didn't think last night would happen. I didn't plan that."

"I liked last night. And this morning."

Renee's hand stilled. "I did too. I really liked it, Lo."

"So what's wrong?"

"Nothing. I mean, um—usually, when it's just sex, I'm chill. Like I know how to keep it uncomplicated. But this is . . . It's more than just sex to me. And we're not only friends either. I mean, it's been amazing to reconnect and find our old friendship again, but if I'm being honest, I don't see you like a friend anymore." Renee scrubbed a hand through her hair. "God, why is this so difficult? What I'm trying to say is, I like you, Lo."

Lola bit her lip. "You were really onto something when you said I like it when you're nervous."

"Lo! I'm being vulnerable here."

"I know, I'm sorry." She reached over and stilled Renee's hand. She had flaked off long splinters of weathered wood. "I like you too."

"You do?" Renee's eyes widened.

"Come on! Why do you think I took you back to my hotel at the wedding?"

"Because you were horny, and I was there?"

"You were more than just *there*," Lola said. Her head was buzzing. "To be honest, I had a huge crush on you in high school, Renee. That night was meant to get it out of my system."

Renee laughed. "Jeez, Lo, I already admitted I like you. You don't need to make up some love story."

"I'm not making it up. You're the first girl I ever fell for."

"But I can't be," Renee said softly. "I was a raging mess back then."

"I know. It was kind of hot. I spent every waking minute trying to make other people happy, and you just didn't give a damn."

"At least I impressed someone." Renee grimaced. "Come here."

She tugged Lola into her lap, her arm easily fitting around the small of Lola's back. Lola clung to Renee's shoulder and kissed her, slow and deep. Renee's lashes fluttered against her cheek and Lola promised herself she'd remember that featherlight touch as long as she lived.

Renee broke away. "Wait, Lo—have you ever written a song about me?"

Lola froze, which lit Renee's face with delight.

"*Seriously?* On *Seventeen Candles*? Which one?"

"Yes, on *Seventeen Candles*." Her face was hot. "More than one song. It's like . . . half the album."

Renee blinked at her.

"Actually, maybe a little more than half?" she squeaked. She couldn't believe she was admitting this. "You have to understand, that crush was *severe*. I thought I'd never get over it. I guess I kind of never did? Sorry, I hope that's not too much—it was so long ago and you were never supposed to find out."

"It's not too much. You could never be too much." Renee wove her fingers into Lola's, then set a kiss on her knuckles. "Do you remember the night we watched the meteor shower?"

"Of course." Lola's heart was suddenly too big for her chest. "I sing about it all the time."

The way Renee was gazing back at her was nothing short of luminous.

"That's my favorite song." Renee kissed her. "It's my favorite song in the history of songs."

They left the dishes on the deck for the birds to pick at.

THEY SPENT THE rest of the day snuggled on the couch under blankets and took turns picking old DVDs from the collection: *Notting Hill*, which Lola could recite lines from, and *Wild Things*, which Renee said was "not supposed to be here." The movies didn't hold their attention. Once Lola was in Renee's lap, it was a guarantee that later, they'd spend ten minutes searching for the last scene they remembered.

Renee refused to lift Lola's ban from the kitchen. She was assigned drinks duty instead, so at night they drank the two cocktails Lola could make: Manhattans and chilled white wine. She simply let herself enjoy watching Renee move around the kitchen, and how her forearms rippled as she handled a knife or flicked her wrist to toss ingredients in a pan.

Afterward, Lola queued up songs that she loved over the speaker. She tried very hard to be nonchalant about Renee's opinion of them, but it was like introducing old friends you desperately wanted to get along. Renee asked Lola what she liked about each. Lola would begin explaining the structure of the bridge or semantic fields of the lyrics, but always ended up yelping, "It's the greatest love song of all time!"

"They can't all be the greatest love song of all time," Renee protested.

"Why not?" Lola asked, pulling her in for a kiss.

THE NEXT DAY, they took the stairs down to the beach and walked the damp, windblown shoreline. The sky was spotted with clouds that split the day between sharp light and shadow. Lola hadn't bothered to put her contacts in, or any makeup on, and her hair was hastily pulled back. Before they left, Renee had dug out an old jacket for her. It crinkled whenever she moved, and the sleeves hung past her hands, but Renee insisted that the wool coat she'd brought was too fashionable for northern Michigan.

Lola's hand was on the door when Renee said, "Maybe I'll take my camera—I brought my old one. Not for the film," she added. "For me. For us."

Down at the beach, Renee filmed the wind whipping Lola's hair around her face, and their conversations about nothing in particular, and how the reflection of the sun on the water made Lola squint. Lola scoured the ground for leopard-spotted Petoskey stones, and though she didn't find any, she found a dozen other special shells or rocks. Each time she let out a gleeful little cackle, then rinsed her new treasure in the lake and showed it to Renee.

Renee zoomed in on a red stone in Lola's palm that she declared was definitely an agate.

"How do you know what an agate is?" she asked.

"I've worked with several crystal dealers," Lola answered seriously. "Why are you laughing?"

But Renee couldn't stop giggling even after Lola added the definite agate to her pocket collection.

Lola asked, "Can I hold the camera?"

Renee handed it over, then stood behind Lola, stooping a little so their eyes were level. "Hold it here," she said, maneuvering Lola's arms, then her fingers. "That's the zoom. The autofocus is on—"

"Can I hold it like this?" Lola asked. She turned the camera around in her hands, so it pointed toward them. In the eye of the lens, they could see the reflection of their faces, Renee's nestled over Lola's shoulder. A lock of hair escaped from Lola's ponytail and caught on the knit of Renee's beanie.

Renee slid her arms around Lola's waist. "You can hold it like that."

"Look at us," Lola said, grinning at the image of them.

Lola kissed Renee's cheek, and watched her smile grow.

BACK AT THE house, Renee fiddled with the camera.

"You can't put that thing down," Lola said.

"I like filming you."

"You like *filming*. That's the awful thing about being an artist. You can't stop doing it."

"Then play something for me." Renee cocked her head toward Dave's guitar.

Lola grabbed it and stroked her thumb over the strings. "*You are my sunshine...*"

"Not that—what was the song you were playing before? I liked that."

"That wasn't a song, it was nothing. I don't know if I even remember it."

But her fingers found the melody again, as Renee began to film.

LOLA COULD NOT get enough of Renee. She was obsessed with her body: her breasts, full enough to overflow Lola's hands, her ass cheeks peeking out from the bottom of the shorts she wore in the morning, the dimples on her thighs and the dark hair between her legs. She was robust and solid and alive to Lola's touch. Lola felt like she'd never tire of hearing Renee draw out the sound of her name, long and slow, as she came.

But as much as Lola had her fill of Renee, she was holding something back. She still hadn't let Renee fully reciprocate. It wasn't that she didn't want Renee to touch her—she did, and Lola loved it—but when her attention turned to Lola's orgasm, Lola tensed and found a way to redirect things.

Renee seemed like the kind of person who would mention it, but Lola almost didn't want her to. It was crushingly embarrassing to admit that she was uncomfortable receiving pleasure. It had always been so much easier to worry about making sure her partner was happy, and taking pleasure in that. It meant that Lola's partners didn't often make her come.

But now, with Renee, she wanted to.

THEY WERE SITTING on the deck watching the sunset on the third day. Their conversation had drifted off when Renee said, a little abruptly, "I think you worry too much about making other people happy."

"Yes, I'm a people pleaser." Lola laughed. "But you seem to be enjoying it."

Lola had meant it as a sexy joke, but Renee's expression was earnest.

"You know I am. I love it that you like giving. It's so hot how much it turns you on. And you're really fucking good at it. But I'm wondering if that's the *only* thing you like. I'm not sure how much you want me to touch you."

"You *do* touch me."

"But I could touch you *more*. Like, I could get you off, if you wanted. Or not, if you don't."

Lola chewed the inside of her cheek, unsure what to say. She wished that being honest didn't have to be so embarrassing.

Renee was watching her without judgment. "We're just talking, okay?"

"I'm just not always sure what I want," Lola finally managed. "It's easier to think about the other person first."

"Okay," Renee said. "But the other person should be thinking of you too."

"I know, but they don't always, do they?"

"Did Ava?"

"With Ava, we never had a lot of time together. I wanted to make sure she was happy, so we didn't waste it."

Renee darkened. "She said getting you off was a waste of time?"

"No, she didn't!" Lola didn't know why she was defending Ava. It was worse that she had thought that about herself. Shame shivered in her belly. "We both liked it when things were about her. When it came to me, I would get so anxious. I'd ask her to stop or—or I'd fake it."

"Why were you anxious?" Renee asked gently.

Lola's cheeks were burning but she made herself answer. "At the beginning, she was always talking about how she had such amazing oral skills, she could make any girl come like that, and I felt all this pressure, like if I didn't—you know, and do it fast, then she'd be disappointed. I guess I thought I'd relax about it eventually, but I never really did."

The muscles in Renee's jaw flickered as she ground her teeth.

"You look mad," Lola said.

"I am—at Ava. You were uncomfortable and the person who's supposed to make you feel good didn't care. She got what she wanted and did nothing in return." Suddenly Renee went pale. "Is that what you think *I* want?"

"No," Lola said forcefully. "Look, that relationship had a lot of problems. But I *wanted* to make her feel good, like I want to make you feel good."

"I don't understand," Renee said. "That night at the wedding, I hadn't seen you in years. You had no reason to care how I felt."

"You know I did." Lola's gaze flickered to Renee's eyes, then back to the lake. She didn't want to look at her while she explained this. "And at the wedding, I was spinning out. I felt like my career was slipping away, and I'd always imagined myself there with Ava. Sometimes, when the pressure's that high, sex feels like this one perfect thing I have control over. That feels *right*. I wanted to lose myself in you for a few hours."

"Fuck."

When Lola looked over, Renee was shaking her head.

"What's wrong with that?" Lola's whole body was hot, despite the cold air.

"Nothing's wrong with that. What I meant is, you are so fucking hot. And I appreciate you telling me that." Renee pulled Lola's hand toward her mouth and kissed her knuckles, then her palm. "But what if you thought about sex as more about *feeling* good, than *being* good? Because you *are* good, Lo. I'll tell you that a million times, in bed and anywhere else you need to hear it. But you deserve to feel it too, don't you think?"

There was a lump in Lola's throat. Somehow it felt like the conversation had become about more than orgasms, and she couldn't express why. "I guess so," she managed to say.

"I know you do," Renee said. "And you trust me, don't you?"

"Yes."

"Then trust me with this. Let's try some new things together. Maybe you'll find something you like, or maybe you won't, but we always have fun in bed, right?"

"We do." Lola felt herself smile. "Okay. I think I'd like that. But I don't want to make any promises, like if I can't—"

"The only promise I need is that you'll tell me what feels good and let yourself feel it. We can stop whenever you say—if you come or if you don't." Renee paused to lick her lips. "But I have to warn you, I can be very, very patient."

Lola's gaze snared on that mouth. There had been so many moments in the last few months when Renee had known just what Lola needed. Even on their first night here, she'd found a way to satisfy Lola without bringing any of this up—hell, they'd both come without even taking all their clothes off. Lola trusted Renee. And she wanted this. "Should we . . . start now?"

20

Lola's heart was a mess of anticipation and nerves as she led Renee back to the bedroom. She knew she wanted this, and she trusted Renee—she just didn't entirely trust herself. She felt naked and vulnerable even before Renee laid her back against the bed and thumbed the edge of her shirt, asking, "Can I take this off?"

Lola nodded and Renee eased it over her head. Lola hadn't been wearing a bra and her nipples tightened instantly. Renee dropped the shirt to the floor, soon joined by Lola's sweatpants and Renee's clothes. Renee moved between Lola's hips. Her hands went right to Lola's breasts, her mouth to Lola's lips, then her neck as she worked her way down.

Lola allowed herself to relax a little. This was familiar territory, and it felt good. Renee always felt good—the weight of her body, the brush of her short hair against Lola's skin, the cup of her palm against Lola's breast. She swept her thumb over her nipple, then added more pressure. Lola felt herself light up. Renee knew that Lola liked this, that her breasts were achingly sensitive.

Renee captured a nipple in her mouth, sucking and teasing until it was almost painfully taut. Lola whimpered. Each caress of Renee's tongue sent pleasure racing through her, but there was still a small yet insistent voice in Lola's head asking if she was behaving like Renee wanted.

Renee raised her head and met Lola's eyes. "Breathe, Lo."

"I am," Lola said lightly, but her breaths were tight and fast.

Renee placed her palm against Lola's sternum. Lola stilled.

"Breathe for real."

Lola took a deep breath into her diaphragm, then her lungs, and watched Renee's hand rise with her chest. Then another, encouraged by Renee's steady gaze. She let the muscles of her back and shoulders loosen, then her hips, allowing her thighs to spread wider against the bed. Renee nestled her body between them, warm and heavy against Lola, and tantalizingly close to her clit.

"That's my girl," Renee said, and pinched Lola's nipple.

The praise paired with the sensation flooded Lola with unexpected heat and her hips rolled suddenly beneath Renee. Renee's eyes flashed and she rocked against Lola in response. Lola pressed back, seeking more contact. Renee slowly—too slowly—trailed her hand down Lola's stomach, then lower to the crease of her hip. Renee's hand dipped, skimming her but still not touching her enough, and Lola's hips moved again. A mewling sound escaped her lips. Lola couldn't remember making a noise like that before, but then again, no one had ever teased her like this.

"Not yet," Renee breathed, then dragged her hand away. As she did, she allowed one finger to part Lola's slit and graze her clit, and this time Lola gasped for real.

Renee shifted so her thigh was notched against Lola and, at the same time, took Lola's hands and pinned them to the pillow beside her head. Renee's weight lay against the length of her, pressing her into the mattress. That thigh rocked against Lola, kindling a heat that was so good, but not near enough.

Renee's breath brushed against Lola's ear.

"This okay?"

"Yes," Lola gasped. It was more than okay. Somehow Renee's

weight on top of her was making Lola forget herself entirely. Her body had vanished and all that was left was pure feeling—the sensation building from her clit, the sparking in her nipples as they ground against Renee. Renee's mouth was hot and wet on her ear, her teeth grazing the tender flesh of her earlobe. Lola cried out and hooked her leg over Renee's for added pressure, but Renee kept her attentions on her ear until Lola was writhing against her, sweat sticking their bodies together, and Lola choked out, "Can you—"

Renee released her hand from Lola's and used it to turn Lola's head, giving her access to the other ear. Shivers racked Lola's body as her now-free hand grasped Renee's back.

"Can I what, Lo?"

"Can you touch me?"

"Where?"

Lola bit her lip, then said, "You know where."

Renee took Lola's mouth in a deep kiss, pressing her lips hard against her. As she did, Renee let out a deep, appreciative moan. That sound flooded Lola with renewed heat, even before Renee pulled back and said, "I'll do whatever you want."

Renee pushed herself off Lola and sat back. But with her weight gone, Lola felt incredibly naked, overexposed, and her earlier fears of being the focus of attention came storming back. She grabbed Renee's waist.

"No," she said. Renee held still, her lips parted in anticipation as she waited for Lola to say more. Suddenly Lola became aware of another feeling, beneath that familiar anxiety and even her churning arousal. A sense of calm at her core—the knowledge that Renee would take care of her, no matter how unrestrained she allowed herself to feel. "Stay here with me."

"Okay," Renee murmured. She laid herself against Lola again, that full-body sensation settling over her. "Like this?"

"Like that. I want to feel you on top of me."

Renee kissed her mouth again, and her neck, and slipped her hand between them. She lingered at Lola's breasts, but once she had her whimpering again, her touch trailed lower. Lola's hips canted up against Renee's fingers as they traced her slit.

"You're dripping."

"I know," Lola said raggedly.

"Exactly how I want you."

A swell of satisfaction swept over Lola again. She would never get tired of seeing Renee's green eyes cloud and her cheeks flush with lust for her. She was still teasing Lola's entrance and it wasn't enough. Lola wanted her closer.

Lola bent her knees to clutch Renee's waist, pressing herself against Renee's fingers.

"I want you inside," she whispered.

At once, Renee's face shifted into something almost devilish, eyes glinting. Lola felt like she might come just from looking at it.

"Say that again."

"I want you inside me, Renee," Lola said, grinning.

When Renee entered her, the fullness she'd been craving swept over her. Lola's eyes snagged on how the muscles of Renee's shoulder worked, how her arm disappeared between them. She went slowly at first but then Lola moaned *faster* and Renee's thrusts came harder, juddering through their bodies. Lola's knees gripped Renee, her hips bucking desperately as Renee grazed her clit again and again. Pleasure was building hot and fast inside her, and she screwed her eyes closed.

"That's it," Renee panted against her. "Let yourself feel good for me."

Then Renee crooked her fingers inside, brushing against Lola's G-spot. Lola cried out. It sounded so vulgar, but she didn't care. She let go of any sense of control or reserve and gave herself over to the building intensity. Lola was almost thrashing against Renee's pistoning hand now, frantic and desperate.

Renee groaned. "God, I love to hear you."

"Don't stop," Lola gasped. "I'm close—"

"Will you look at me, Lo?" Her voice sounded different—raw.

Lola did. As she met Renee's eyes—tender and riveted on her—she felt herself bear down against her fingers, and the wave of her orgasm crashed against her. Lola's back arched, her hands grappling against Renee, as a brutal wave of pleasure lit up her every nerve—and then a second wave, and then a third, and Lola let herself be swept away, untethered save for the way Renee's eyes never left hers, the anchor in a storm they'd brewed together.

It was minutes before either of them could speak.

Renee rolled off her and onto the bed. Her hair was stuck to her forehead. Both of their bodies were tacky with sweat.

Lola felt limp, liquid. Renee met her eyes with a questioning look.

"I want . . . I want you to do that again," Lola said.

Hours later, Lola lingered at the kitchen counter as Renee prepared dinner. Even the other side of the room felt too far away, but dinner was already late enough, so they'd pledged to keep their hands to themselves. Lola busied herself examining the family photos on the wall.

"This is a cute picture of you and your mom," she said, pointing at one. "I forgot you dyed your hair green. Eighth grade, right?"

"Summer before." Renee glanced at the picture and huffed a laugh. "My dad called it pond scum. He was actually in that picture, but my mom cut him out."

"She did?" Lola looked closer. She hadn't noticed the edge of a man's shoulder at the border of the photo.

"She cut him out of all our pictures. I came home one day and she'd pried all the frames open and was going at the photos with scissors. Then she hung them back up like they'd always been that way."

"That's awful," Lola said.

Renee shrugged. "Yeah, the pictures looked ridiculous. They were all too small for their frames."

"That's not what I meant."

When Renee didn't say anything, Lola added, "I can't imagine anyone leaving you like that."

Renee scratched at her eyebrow. "We don't need to imagine it."

"Do you ever talk to him?"

"He texts on my birthday." Lola gave Renee space to continue, and after a moment she did. "He wanted everything to be fine between us, right away, but I was so mad at him. At first, he'd call me and ask how school was, and I'd say he would know if he hadn't abandoned us. He was all, *This is about me and your mom,* and *I'll always be your dad.* Like he didn't realize he'd left me too. Eventually he had enough of *my attitude,* and then it was *I don't know what you want me to do.*" Renee laughed dryly. "As if it wasn't fucking obvious, right? He decided to give me some space to cool off. I guess we're both still waiting on that."

"I can't believe he put you through that."

"I think it's part of why I really connect with documentaries. They cut through the bullshit to find what's real and true. That's what I want to do with film—say something honest. Tell a story, with a purpose." Renee shook her head.

"What is it?"

Renee hesitated for a moment, then said, "Before you called me about this job, I was about to drop out. I wasn't going back after my leave."

"Oh, Renee." Lola leaned against the counter beside her and rubbed her arm. Renee leaned into her touch. "Why?"

"I just . . . couldn't do it. I couldn't *make films*. It's the one thing I dreamed of my whole life and then when I got the chance, I froze. I thought it was the program, but when I was on leave, I was still talking myself out of every idea I had for my thesis. None of them were good enough."

"I don't believe that."

"Which part—that my ideas were bad or that I talked myself out of them? Because both are highly believable to me."

"The first part," Lola said. "I've seen your work, Renee. I know you have great ideas. You should have more faith in yourself."

"Are you kidding? I had everything I'd dreamed of at that program, and I went running back to my mom's house."

"And you tried again. You're making your thesis, and it's going to be so much bigger and better than anything you could have done before." Lola stilled. "And if it isn't, at least you'll know for certain that it isn't your fault."

Renee frowned at her. "How's that?"

She hated to say this, but she had to make Renee understand. "I don't know what will happen to the film once everyone realizes I don't have anything for the next album. You think the staged shoots were bad, wait until you're watching me sing ghostwritten songs at gunpoint."

"Hey, let's not get ahead of ourselves." Renee slipped her arms around Lola's waist. "I'm making this film, and you're making this album. You're Lola fucking Gray. You'd written what, a thousand songs before you even met Ava? Plus, now you have your original muse back. I'm like catnip for your creativity."

Lola laughed, and Renee, satisfied, pulled away to fill the pot for pasta.

"Thank you for blessing me with your presence," Lola said, watching her muse's muscles flex as she set the pot on the stove. "It's not only Ava, though. The LavaTruthers are going to pick apart anything I write and connect it to her, no matter how careful I am."

"So?"

"So, then the rumors that I'm bi will explode, and it'll be a huge mess."

"Lo, your fingers probably still smell like my pussy."

"*Renee!*"

"I'm just saying that you *are* bi. Nothing's wrong with that."

"I know nothing's *wrong* with it. I'm happy with who I am. It's complicated professionally. I can't simply announce I'm bi for no reason, especially when the whole world knows my history with men. With Ava, Gloriana wanted to hard launch the relationship at the same time, so everything would make sense, for the public."

"I think the public would have gotten the idea without her."

"My team didn't think so. And they were the ones who'd be spending months crafting a narrative, to make sure the announcement is really worth it." Seeing how low Renee's brows had fallen as she spoke, Lola added, "You have to understand, I'm a whole industry."

"But you're also just a person, who deserves to be herself."

Lola felt suddenly that she might cry. "It's not that simple for someone in my position."

"Okay, I get that." Renee searched her face. "But it doesn't seem like this is making you very happy."

"That's not always the most important thing," Lola managed.

Renee pulled Lola to her chest. Lola felt the words vibrate when Renee said, "It's important to me."

"Let's go into Petoskey today," Lola said. It was their last day.

They were naked in bed. Renee lay on top of Lola, her body deliciously solid.

"Might be nice," Renee mumbled. "There's a farmers' market. Antiques."

Lola's fingers wandered through Renee's hair. "If I wear my glasses and a beanie and that weird jacket, no one will recognize me, right?"

"No one's expecting a celebrity up here." Renee squirmed contentedly against Lola's chest. "But can we lie here a little longer first?"

"Okay. A little longer."

Petoskey was charming. They walked down the beach to check for Petoskey stones—with no luck—before heading up the hill to the town. Views of the bay peeked out between brick buildings with quaint striped awnings and streets with old-style gas lamps. They stopped at antique stores, where Lola picked up and put down a hundred different knickknacks, from crystal figurines to matchbooks to old-fashioned cheese graters, and Renee challenged herself to find the most over-the-top vintage gown. Lola had never had a real pasty, so they found a bakery and bought the last ones in the case, biting into the flaky crust while the white-haired woman behind the counter explained that she still made them in the traditional style, with rutabaga, potato, and beef filling and suet in the dough. They wandered into a used bookstore where dust floated through the air, and in a narrow aisle, Renee reached for Lola's hand.

Lola pulled back when their hands brushed, bumping against a shelf about polar exploration. "Sorry," they both said at once.

"It's just—" Lola said.

"No, yeah, I get it."

"No, I—" Lola glanced around the empty store. It seemed safe enough. Praying this wasn't a mistake, she slipped her hand into Renee's. "I want to."

Renee beamed back at her.

They grabbed dinner at a craft brewery that had a heated outdoor area with a food truck serving kimchi poutine and laksa carbonara.

Lola swallowed a bite of gochujang-covered cheese curd and washed it down with a guava sour. "I have to admit, this is better than I expected for rural Michigan."

"This isn't rural Michigan. We're adjacent to the Traverse City micropolitan area." Renee was sitting beside her on the picnic bench. Below, their feet tangled together.

"Makes sense. It feels very micropolitan here."

Lola glanced around the other tables. No one was paying attention to them. They were chatting around the fire pit, or playing cornhole. Lola suspected that the bachelorette party at the table in front was full of Lo-Lites, but they hadn't spotted her.

Renee saw her checking and squeezed her hand. "You're fine, okay? With those glasses, you're like the lead in a nineties teen movie, before the makeover reveals that you're devastatingly hot."

"You're such a flirt." Lola grinned. "You know, this is my first real date with a girl."

"How does it feel?"

How *did* it feel? It felt so normal, it was almost unreal. They were out at a bar, sharing fries and having beers, like regular people did. They weren't sneaking around, because hiding was the best they could do, or scheduling sleepovers weeks in advance. It wasn't hard to imagine some alternative timeline where she and Renee had grown together instead of apart. Maybe they would've moved to Grand Rapids or Royal Oak, and had a queer circle of friends that teased them about being high school sweethearts. A life where they had their own house on the lake.

"It feels good. I wish we could stay here forever."

"We can come back. Whenever you want. Well, we need Deborah's permission, but you know she loves you."

As they walked back to the car, Lola felt bold. She didn't want to forget this moment. She felt better than she had in months, in a whole year—maybe longer.

She pulled Renee into a kiss, right there on the street.

Lola's beanie slipped back as she tipped her head up. Her dark hair tumbled free.

"Should you get that?" Renee murmured.

She should, but she loved the way Renee was looking at her. Lola put her fingers lightly to Renee's jaw, rose up on her toes, and kissed her again.

She didn't think, at the time, that it had been so obvious.

21

As Lola drove away from Renee's hotel, her lips were a little swollen from their goodbye. They'd restrained themselves in front of Lola's driver, because NDA or not, no one should have to sit through excessive PDA. Alone now in the back of the SUV, Lola pulled her legs up to her chest. She waited for that familiar ache to announce itself—the feeling that she'd been ripped away from something warm and wonderful and might be left cold forever. That was how she'd felt after her weekends with Ava: still famished for affection, fearful that she'd never have it again, ashamed at being so needy.

But as they glided off the highway, the ache hadn't come. She felt hungry for Renee, still, but there was none of that fear that this would be the last time. She knew it wouldn't be.

The driver navigated the tight turns that led up the hill to Lola's home, and Lola realized that she felt something else, something she hadn't felt in a long time.

Lola left her bags by the door. The house felt big and empty—she'd asked Cassidy to make sure no one was there when she returned. She went directly to her studio, grabbed a notebook, and began to write.

HOURS LATER, LOLA'S brain felt wrung out, and her body sore from sitting so long. Dazed, she was surprised to see that it was already dark. She could not remember when she had last eaten. She should have been exhausted from traveling, from writing so much, so fast—one song ready for Ackerlund, and the foundations of two more. But she wasn't tired. She would crash soon—but not yet.

Come over? she texted.

Thought you'd never ask, Renee replied.

"WE CAN'T HAVE you taking off like that. You had everyone scrambling. Poor Cassidy nearly had a panic attack, Micah's hysterical about getting off schedule, and I don't know where to start with the fallout from the premiere." Gloriana's face glowed on Lola's phone.

Lola groaned internally. "The premiere was a week ago. I'm sure no one's talking about it anymore."

"They are, Lola. They're saying that you saw Ava, so you abandoned your boyfriend on the most important night of his career."

"The premiere of *Fit to Live* was *not* the most important night of Nash's career."

"*That's* what you choose to respond to?"

Lola imagined the #LavaTruthers filming their TikToks, gleefully pinning new evidence to their conspiracy theory boards. Usually, such thoughts made her feel like her insides had been scooped out with a melon baller and plopped in wet red orbs on the floor. But now, she reached for that feeling, and it wasn't there. The story the #LavaTruthers were weaving was none of her business anymore. Maybe it never had been.

"What do you want me to say?" Lola countered. "I did see Ava, and I did get upset. You should have warned me that she'd be there."

"It was an oversight, and I apologize for that. But you have a job to do. You can't run off like a scared little girl whenever you see her."

Lola ignored how the accuracy of Gloriana's description stung. Instead, she remembered how liberating it had felt when Renee gave her permission to leave the premiere. Renee and Claudia were right;

Lola needed to push back on Gloriana more. She tried to borrow a bit of Renee's self-assurance.

"I needed a break, and I took one. The press thinks I had Covid, and Cassidy knew where I was the whole time. It's not like I was on some kind of drug spree. I was watching movies with Renee."

Gloriana's eyes narrowed ever so slightly at Renee's name. "So busy watching movies with Renee that you ignored your calls and texts for five days."

"There was no reception."

"Or internet? People send emails from the top of Mount Everest, Lola. I'm sure that technology has made it to Michigan. You've taken plenty of time off in the last year, and you've always stayed available."

Lola pressed her lips into a flat line. Gloriana knew that Lola hadn't spent her recent time off doing anything that might have counted as rest and relaxation. She'd spent it crying on the couch or staring at the ceiling over her bed.

"I'm sorry you're mad," she said, in a self-assured tone that Lola imagined Renee would use.

"I'm not mad, Lola." Gloriana shook her head. "What I am is disappointed."

The words curled sickly in Lola's gut. It had always been easy to see Gloriana as the figure that Lola's real mother had never managed to be. When Gloriana had signed Lola as a client at the age of sixteen, Lola's mother had been pushing her into any opportunity with a paycheck attached. It was Gloriana who introduced the concept of making choices that prioritized career longevity, who'd given Lola the strength to stand up to her mother's self-serving demands to be part of her fame. Her whole career, Gloriana had been her bedrock. Lola had always been grateful for that, even if now, she felt like a child about to be sent to her room.

"We checked in with Nash's people," Gloriana went on. "We want to get the two of you together again to smooth this over. This week, before he goes back to Montana."

The idea of pretending to be in love with Nash now sent a shiver of revulsion through Lola's body. Nash knew why she'd ditched the premiere—she'd texted him while they were still driving away. He'd be ecstatic about her and Renee. But Lola had bigger concerns than holding hands with him in public.

"No," she said.

"No? What do you mean, no?"

"I mean, I'm not going to do any more appearances with Nash." Part of Lola was frightened of Gloriana's reaction, but another, unexpected part felt righteous. Maybe she should say no more often. "I need my calendar cleared for the next few weeks. Cancel anything that's not essential. I've asked Renee to update the shooting schedule."

"*What?*"

"I'm focusing on the album. I already booked time with Ackerlund."

"Oh. Well. Fantastic." Gloriana added a congenial smile, as if they'd never disagreed at all.

As Gloriana agreed to her demands, Lola felt like a superhero transforming into her most elite form, power coursing through her veins. When the call ended, Lola found Renee in the kitchen. She pushed her up against the cabinets and kissed her, hard. Then she pulled Renee's shorts off, hooked her thigh over her shoulder, and tasted her until she came.

"What do you want now?" Renee asked, catching her breath. Lola wiped her lips against the back of her hand.

"I want to work," she said.

"Can I watch?"

Lola went to her studio and picked up her guitar.

Renee picked up her camera.

*　*　*

Renee stood beside Alejandro, recording Lola and Ackerlund working out a bridge. "More, *ah-nuh, uh-huh*," Ackerlund said. Renee had no idea what he meant but Lola sang something different. Renee wasn't sure how, but it sounded better.

"Then drums," she said, snapping her fingers.

Ackerlund tapped something out on an electronic pad. Lola bobbed her head to the new beat, then grunted her approval.

Renee grinned behind the camera.

It was mid-October. In the two weeks since Michigan, Lola had been on a tear. Her writer's block had crumbled to reveal a trove of all the creative energy that she hadn't accessed for more than a year. It was inspiring to see how fast things could change—and how Lola had changed with it. She was more assertive than Renee had ever seen her, as if she'd redirected the energy she usually put into being Lola Gray to the part of her brain that churned out pop hits. She was writing all the time, scribbling on scraps for her scrap folder, muttering into her voice memos. She would mentally disappear in the middle of a conversation over dinner, or crawl out of bed as Renee was drifting off. Renee would wake late at night to drag Lola out of the studio, lecturing her about the value of sleep.

Renee hadn't slept at the hotel since Michigan.

The original shoot schedule was history. Renee had pared down the crew to just herself and Alejandro on sound whenever possible. They'd left the biggest points—the breakup with Nash, a trip to New York, the sponsored placements that couldn't be cut—but dropped everything staged. Gloriana hadn't been pleased, but Lola had stood up to her, insisting that they follow Renee's schedule, which accommodated her creative process, or they could pause filming until the album was done.

The new arrangement made the relationship simple to hide. As Lola's documentarian, Renee was entitled to access, so she followed Lola everywhere.

Privately, it felt like they were locked in feverish competition for who could want the other more. Coming home from the studio, there were days they barely made it to the bedroom, leaving a trail of shed clothes on the stairs and through the hallway.

The relationship was far more serious than anything Renee had experienced before. To Renee's surprise, that felt *good*. Lola would say something like, *What if we went back to the lake house every year?* And Renee, who had kicked girls out of bed for suggesting brunch the morning after, found herself answering, *But for our first anniversary, maybe somewhere special, like Iceland?*

Renee had always assumed she'd never fall in love. She had never bothered to learn the signs.

She missed the *falling* part entirely.

Now, Lola and Ackerlund went through the lyrics again.

"Too busy watching the stars, I didn't see you watching me."

Renee bit her cheek to keep from smiling. This song, "Starcrossed," was about trying so hard to resist your feelings that you couldn't see what was right in front of you—until suddenly, you did. The lyrics were a collection of the traces Renee had left on Lola's life in the last few months, built around the melody she'd made up at the lake house. The song was different from Lola's past work—more mature, unafraid, less romantic fairy tale, and more grounded. It also sounded, to Renee's ear at least, unmistakably queer. She knew the lyrics were about a woman, but there was something in the tone of the song—the uncertainty that Lola could have what she wanted, the effort to resign herself to a crush—that felt distinctively sapphic. She kept stealing glances at Ackerlund, wearing those tinted sunglasses, wondering if he understood.

Ackerlund's head bobbed. "I like that little riff on the 'Star Sign' bridge. What was the original?"

"*You were watching the stars, but I was watching you.*" Lola's cheeks pinked as her eyes darted to Renee's.

"Then we go," Ackerlund said, humming a little, "*Why did I wait so long to feel your arms around me? How long have we been in the middle of our love story?* Let's develop that more. You've been waiting for him, you've got him, what's next?"

The male pronouns were a fishhook in Renee's guts. Renee would have thought she was incapable of being shocked by heteronormativity, but it was outrageous that Ackerlund could be so oblivious to what was right in front of him. Could Ackerlund really believe that Lola had pined over Nash like this?

Lola wasn't going to correct the pronoun Ackerlund had used, Renee knew that. There was no reason to announce that the song was actually about a woman right now. Even if that woman was standing right there.

But she couldn't stop herself from hoping.

A crease appeared between Lola's brows. She rubbed her palm against her forehead, scrubbing it away. "What about, *This is so much better than my fantasy?*"

22

Renee Zoomed with Dragan in early November in her office in Lola's house. Technically it was a guest room that Cassidy—Lola had never attempted to conceal their relationship from her assistant—had suggested designating as Renee's workspace.

"Before we discuss the material you sent, you received the invitation for the reception, yes?" Dragan asked. "We have no RSVP from you and it's less than two weeks away."

The New York Institute of Film's Fall Reception was an orgy of networking and fundraising where alumni and patrons of the arts got to meet the brightest lights of NYIF's programs. If you were one of those stars, you could make career-defining connections. If you weren't, you were still expected to attend.

"I don't know if I can make it. We're shooting in L.A.," Renee said. Renee didn't mention that by a stroke of bad luck, Lola was scheduled to be in New York for a gala to combat childhood hunger that same week, with Renee in tow.

"Make an effort, Renee. I want to see you there," Dragan said.

Renee sat up straighter. "You do?"

"One of our third years, directing a major feature? Friends of the institute will be very impressed. Now, let's discuss your work."

Renee's stomach lurched as Dragan flipped through his notes. The two-minute clip she sent him was meant to set the tone for the broader film. She'd worked hard on it, which meant that she was simultaneously fiercely proud of it and terrified that it was in fact total shit.

Set to a voice-over of Lola speaking about making music, a short montage played:

Lola taking a deep breath before going onstage at Corkscrew, then a wide shot of the massive crowd.

Lola as a little girl, singing in the Grigorians' living room, then as a teenager on *You're Next!*, followed by the clip of Lola with her high school journals.

Lola smiling and posing on the *Fit to Live* red carpet, then alone, working a song out on her guitar with her glasses on and her face tensed in concentration.

Renee had tried to juxtapose Lola Gray, high-gloss America's Sweetheart, with the Lo she knew, who was hardworking and earnest and talented beyond belief. The contrast was meant to emphasize the tension between the public and private, the persona and the person behind it.

"Aesthetically, it's strong. Your footage has a lovely quality," Dragan said. Renee's heart fluttered at the positive feedback. "However, what I'm seeing here is a pretty girl in pretty dresses, singing pretty songs."

Her heart crashed back down to earth.

"But she's not just a pretty girl," Renee objected. "That's what I'm trying to say. The public sees this polished image, but behind it there's a woman working her ass off."

Dragan made a face as if she'd served him wine that had gone sour. "That is true for many famous people. Festivals now are overrun with celebrities making these films about themselves."

"Lola's different. She's more of a songwriter than a performer." It didn't come out the way Renee had hoped. She sounded like a fangirl, not a director.

"Documentary filmmakers tell a story to serve a purpose. Where purpose and story meet is where our magic happens. Without purpose, the story is meaningless. It leaves no trace on the viewer. Without story, the purpose is an academic exercise, and the film becomes tedious."

Renee nodded. Dragan had written an entire book on this point, which she had read so many times she could recite sections from memory.

"You're saying that your purpose is to demonstrate that your subject is different than people think because she works hard."

"That was a little reductive. I meant—"

"I don't need an explanation, Renee; the work speaks for itself. Where is the spark? The originality? If I am not a fan of this person, I have no reason to watch."

"But this is already a lot better than what they hired me for," Renee said feebly. "They wanted something entertaining about her next album."

This visibly repulsed Dragan. "Do not insult your vision by comparing it to that of these *businessmen*. They are not artists. They work with *numbers*. You, Renee, are a *storyteller*. You go deeper. You push. You do not define success on their insipid terms. That is your responsibility to yourself, to the medium—to the *truth*."

This was the most dramatic speech Renee had ever heard over Zoom, and it set nausea pulsing through her stomach. Even with all Lola's faith in her, Renee was still at square one.

Dragan removed his glasses and glared at Renee through the screen. "As we say, everyone wants to make films, but not everyone can. This is not always a question of talent. It never has been with you, Renee."

Renee was dumbfounded. What question *was* there besides talent? You were good enough, or you weren't. Your education and career were just a series of elaborate tests to measure that goodness, and Renee had stalled out at a critical cutoff.

"Talent is helpful, but talent is like potential. Easily wasted. You must be *committed*. To be willing to do what needs to be done to serve your art. That commitment is where you have always been weak. Take risks and stand by them!" Dragan sighed heavily. "If this Lola Gray is as good as you say, maybe you can learn something from her."

* * *

Lola was on the couch, laptop on her thighs. She was eager to hear what Renee's thesis advisor thought of her work, but she needed to concentrate. It was less than eight months until the planned release date and her creative director wanted to finalize a direction for visuals, based on some unfinished tracks. The visuals would dictate not just the album cover, but the atmosphere of her music videos, merchandise, the live show aesthetic, even her red carpet looks. The color story he proposed was all jewel tones with burning pops of color. After-dusk indigo with electric red. Ferny green with aquamarine. Scarlet with white. It was a far cry from the pastels and bright colors that themed her past albums.

It was amazing to Lola how fast her work was evolving. The songs she'd written since Michigan felt different. They were still the radio-friendly love songs that Lola Gray was known for, but they were more authentic than the romanticizations of her life she'd written in the past. This album would feel more luscious, like the cherry in a Manhattan, like rumpled bedsheets in the dark. A little messier, a little hungrier, a little more free.

She heard Renee's footfalls on the stairs and closed her laptop.

"Did he love it?" she called. "*Oh no*, darling, come here."

The corners of Renee's mouth were pulled down, her chin wrinkled and eyebrows drawn. She fell onto the couch, then slumped to lay her head in Lola's lap. Lola immediately slid an arm over her stomach. Renee clutched it to her, as Lola's other hand petted Renee's messy hair.

"He says I don't have a vision." Renee's voice was weak and gravelly. "The film needs purpose."

Lola scowled with resentment for this man she'd never met. "Then he doesn't know what he's talking about. You have tons of vision. This film is so much better for you being part of it."

"He's right, Lo," Renee groaned. "Dragan didn't tell me this to tear me down—actually, I think, he called me talented."

"You *are* talented."

"Talent doesn't matter! What matters is telling *a story with a purpose*." Renee pushed herself off Lola's lap and hunched over with her hands buried in her hair. "The problem is *me. I* can't make it happen."

Lola's heart hurt for her. The only thing she could think to do was rub circles on Renee's back.

"When will I finally accept that I can't do this?" Renee said with a burst of pained frustration. "I've been on the brink of failure for so long. Why can't I let it go?"

"Because you're closer to your dream than you've ever been. You're making a feature film—exactly what you've always wanted. I know how terrifying it is when you're waiting for all the pieces to come together." Lola leaned against her and set a kiss on her shoulder. "I wish there was something I could do. But I have faith that you'll figure it out, just like you had faith in me. I'm writing some of my best work ever, and you've unlocked that in me. If it wasn't for this film, I don't know if I would ever have resolved my writer's block. That's some kind of purpose, right?"

Renee straightened. "What?"

"Maybe not the kind of purpose Dragan wants, but it means something to me."

"Your writer's block," Renee whispered. "That creative struggle. Maintaining your artistic integrity in a commercial industry. The burden of success—"

"Are you free-associating?"

Renee faced Lola, a light in her eyes. "What if *that's* the story we tell? Your team wants a movie about happy little Lola Gray making her happy little album, but the truth is, it's been hard. You've had to fight for it. You're still struggling to tell your story."

The rightness of it hummed like a struck tuning fork. The film Renee was proposing would show her as the artist she understood herself to be, not the glossily packaged Lola Gray that fans had always seen. Her team said the film should show the authentic, human side of Lola Gray, but they actually wanted the same old girl. Lola didn't feel like that girl anymore.

But still, there was an undeniable safety in Lola Gray's image. The messy parts of Lola's life didn't exist for Lola Gray, or for the public. Her writer's block had been so painful, had gnawed away at Lola's sense of herself for so long, that she still hadn't confided in anyone but Renee.

Renee was watching her expectantly. "What do you think?"

"I like it—but it sounds pretty personal."

"It would be. But it would be honest, too."

"I'm not sure how I feel about people watching me struggle."

"Even if it's a struggle you *win*?" Renee said.

Lola pressed her lips together. She was proud of having dragged herself back from the brink, and of the music she was making. But what Renee seemed to have forgotten, which Lola never could, was that this story was inextricably tied up with her sexuality. Ava and the heartbreak, the shelved album, then Renee and the future.

She said, gently, "I don't think you can tell that story without explaining why I had writer's block in the first place."

"Oh, right." Deflated, Renee fell back against the couch, that grim look returning to her face. "That's okay—really, it is. I'll come up with something."

Lola's face fell too. Compared to Renee's idea, the current concept for the film felt even duller and emptier than it already had. All those weeks ago, Renee had offered her the opportunity to say something with this film. It had scared Lola then. It still did, but this time, the lurch of fear was the kind she felt when she'd just started working on an ambitious new song.

"God, I wish we could do it though," Lola said with sudden passion. "You're right, it would make a phenomenal film. We could express what songwriting really means to me and show people who I am now. It's just—" Lola balled up her hands and pressed them to her eyes. "If only I'd come out already. If I'd gone through with it after Ava left me. It feels like there's never going to be the perfect time to do it, and I'm so sick of worrying about it."

Renee eased Lola's hands away from her face and held them.

"What if this is the time?" Renee said. "Why not tell that part of the story, too?"

Lola blew out a breath. "To even have a conversation about it, we'd have to go through fifteen meetings. It's a massive operation. We'll probably have turned the film in to Streamy before everything's ready."

"Dude, I know the parade planners can be a handful. When I came out, I had the local news, a marching band, and a chili cook-off. It was a lot to coordinate, and I was only a fifteen-year-old in Fellows." Lola smiled at the sarcasm as Renee slid an arm around her and pulled her into her chest. "The perfect time to come out is when you're ready. That's it."

"I *am* out, to everyone that matters," Lola said, looking up at her.

"Maybe everyone who matters is more people than you think. You told me you were on the brink of giving up songwriting, the thing you care the most about in the world. What are you going to do when this album comes out? Are you going to tell the world that it's about Nash? What happens when Gloriana sets you up with your next boyfriend?"

Bile rose in Lola's throat, but she swallowed it down and said, "In this industry, you have to make compromises."

"In a compromise, both sides give something up. Do you want to come out, Lo?"

"Yes," she said without hesitation. "I've wanted to for years. It just feels impossible."

"I promise it's not. I'll be right there beside you. We have the film and the album. What do you say?"

Lola's mind raced, cycling through the catalog of anxieties she'd been maintaining for years. But then she looked at Renee, hardly breathing as she waited for Lola's answer. Renee, who was solid, who stood up for her. Who imagined a future that Lola couldn't believe in on her own.

"Okay."

"Okay?" Elation broke over Renee's face. "Seriously? You're being serious?"

"Yes, I'm being serious," Lola said, laughing. "You're right. This is what I need."

Renee pulled Lola close for a long kiss. "This is going to be *amazing*," she mumbled against her mouth.

Lola pulled back. "I just need to tell Gloriana."

"*Telling* her, not asking her, right?"

"Right."

Lola and Nash are over??? ♡ 34.8K
Reply

↳ I'm crying rn ♡ 1017

↳ It's so messed up. I hate that Lola gets her heart broken again and again. ♡ 21.5K

Normalize context. Someone tell me what happened. ♡ 891
Reply

↳ They were too busy. He's filming Horsebreaker in Montana and she's not in Montana ♡ 241

↳ They said it was amicable ♡ 164

↳ Ya right after she amicably ran out of his movie premiere with Ava? ♡ 72

↳ She did what??? ♡ 1

Who else is mega excited for the breakup songs we are getting out of this ♡ 20.7K
Reply

↳ reading my mind ♡ 306

↳ She's writing the next album now!! ♡ 1146

↳ Finally ♡ 82

↳ She;s going to rip him a new one. Nash better watch out ♡ 11

↳ Yall are terrible people like this is so dark ♡ 48

#Lava is back—if you believed these two were together, I don't know what to tell you! Like, gay people exist!
Reply

♡ 3810

↳ #LavaGBTQ

♡ 1127

↳ #LolaGBTQ

♡ 839

If Nash hurt her, the Lo-Lites are coming for him
Reply

♡ 33.1K

↳ fr does he know who he's messing with?

♡ 2897

↳ Can we all chill. Remember you do not know these people in real life.

♡ 34

I am literally shaking they made me believe in love what am I supposed to do now
Reply

♡ 2868

23

A few days after Lola and Nash's breakup went public, the full film crew convened at Lola's house. It was the first time they'd shot with everyone in weeks. Lola found herself trying harder than usual to ignore Gloriana, who was observing from beside Renee. They'd be meeting later that afternoon, and Lola intended to make the conversation about coming out, for real.

But for the moment, Lola was curled under a cashmere blanket on her living room sofa, wearing her glasses and a crushed expression. She delivered her best heartsick sigh as Cassidy told her, apparently for the first time, that news of the split had broken.

Cassidy had been looking forward to her first big moment in the documentary as Lola's confidante while she navigated the sadly familiar waters of heartbreak. It felt a little ironic. More than anyone, Cassidy had seen Lola truly heartbroken: the unwashed hair, the weight she'd lost, the bouts of tears. Now, Cassidy was the only person who knew that Lola was truly moving on. Lola hadn't told her sister or Gloriana about Renee, but Cassidy ran Lola's life. It wasn't her first rodeo when it came to managing the logistics of Lola's secret relationships, and she'd treated the whole thing with encouraging but polite discretion.

So, when Cassidy's brows tented and she asked, "How are you doing?" it was almost hard for Lola to remember that she was meant to be sad.

"I'm okay. Tired," Lola answered, which was true. She and Renee had been up late, talking about their plans for the film and experimenting with the vibrator they'd ordered. This morning, when the makeup artist had commented on the purplish circles under Lola's eyes, Renee had suggested they let them show.

"Nash and I tried to make it work." Lola sighed. "We just couldn't invest the time the relationship deserved. Nash's career is taking off, and I'm focusing on my next album. In this industry, it's so hard to put your relationship first."

Cassidy tilted her head empathetically. "You make a lot of sacrifices for your career."

"No one gets where I am without sacrifices."

"Do you ever wonder if it's worth it?"

Lola blinked at her. Cassidy's expression was open but serious. This was a genuine question, Lola realized, not from the script she'd been given.

"I'm blessed that you can even ask me that. It's hard to find love—for everyone, not just me. But I have to keep believing that there's someone out there for me."

"Cassidy, ask if she's writing songs about Nash," Gloriana called out, arms crossed. She did not look entertained by Cassidy's digression.

Cassidy did as she was told.

Lola was meant to say that her fans could look forward to a Nash-themed break-up album, even if she'd never written a single thing about him. Instead, she said, "I always try to be honest about what I'm feeling, and to put that into my music. Nash will always have a place in my heart."

WHILE THE CREW packed up, Lola led Gloriana into her office. Lola used this room so seldom that it looked exactly as it had in its

Architectural Digest shoot years before. She hated how it felt like a room in a dollhouse, with herself the doll, playing at business.

She and Gloriana sat in a pair of armchairs as they ran through details related to the breakup. Gloriana summarized the reaction in the tabloids and on social media, reviewed upcoming plans for Lola to step out looking fabulously single, and reminded her that the comms team would be scheduling times for her to respond to select fans' comments on her post announcing the split. As Gloriana neared the end of her agenda, Lola started to sweat. The words stuck in her head like a song: *telling, not asking.*

"Just two more points, of a more personal nature," Gloriana said, her tone losing its businesslike edge. "Now that you're publicly single, I need to check in about your relationship with our esteemed director."

Lola's breath hitched. "With Renee?"

As if Gloriana could have meant anyone else.

"I'm aware that you two have been spending significant time together, and of course we have the Michigan incident." Gloriana inclined her head. "Is something going on there?"

Lola swallowed hard. She hadn't been expecting this. It wasn't that she'd specifically hidden the relationship with Renee from Gloriana—she would, of course, find out eventually. It was just that what she and Renee had was so new, so precious. She'd hoped for more time before Gloriana dragged her into discussions about the optics and deflecting scrutiny and a contingency plan for their eventual breakup. Part of her, optimistic, recalled how Gloriana had insisted that Lola could only come out if her relationship with Ava was serious. Things with Renee felt serious already, so that might ease things along. But Lola's gut was telling her that as much as Gloriana had resisted things with Ava, she seemed to like Renee even less.

And that, Lola had to admit, might have been a teeny tiny part of why she hadn't told her manager about the relationship already.

"Well, yes. Something is going on," she said. "We've really, you know, reconnected. I know you didn't want things to get messy, but I promise they're not, and they won't be. Everything's been really great, actually."

Gloriana knew how long Lola had been alone, how bleak she'd felt after things with Ava ended. Now, Lola hoped for something like congratulations.

Instead, Gloriana said, "You know, I wish you'd come to me with this, instead of making me ask. I can't protect you from things you don't share with me."

"I don't think I need protection right now," Lola said with an apologetic smile.

"I'll have an updated NDA sent to her."

This was the perfect time. Lola could segue right into the coming-out conversation, explaining how she wouldn't have quite so many secrets to keep once the film was done. *Telling, not asking.*

Before she could get the words out, Gloriana grimaced and said soberly, "Trust is a delicate thing. I need to make you aware of a situation. Nash's people informed us that there has been an incident regarding an exchange of photographs."

Lola went cold all over. She had warned Nash that something like this could happen. He'd promised he was being careful, but how careful could you be exchanging nudes as a public figure? She knew how isolated Nash was feeling on the monthslong shoot. The *Horsebreaker* set was in the middle of nowhere.

Still, there were some risks you just couldn't take. Nash knew that.

Then again, Lola knew it too, and it hadn't always stopped her.

"His blackmailer took advantage of the two of you being in the news," Gloriana said. "It's been handled. The photos are deleted, and his payoff has been transferred. Nash's manager floated the idea of extending your relationship, but with our plans for the album, we declined."

Lola could barely follow Gloriana's words. As much as she sometimes strained against her team's management of her image, having that control ripped away was terrifying. People like Lola and Nash had to justify their right to a private life, again and again, even if they weren't gay and closeted. Everyone at their level had learned to be stingy with their trust. Letting someone in meant handing over a weapon they could use to destroy your career, your business, your life.

"Our concern now is keeping you in the clear if Nash's indiscretions do come out. Veronika's worked up a few angles."

"What kind of angles?"

"Just what you'd expect: he deceived and betrayed you; this explains why he never had time for you. And of course, he hid this dark secret from you."

Her stomach clenched. She loved Nash. She couldn't imagine dragging him in the press to protect herself, especially when she was guilty of the same crime he was. Which wasn't a crime at all.

"Dark secret? That feels kind of homophobic."

"Lola!" Gloriana blanched. "Let's be careful throwing that word around."

"I'd rather say that I support him on his journey or something. Since I do."

"I'm not seeing how that approach would help us, but for now, this is only a contingency plan. Hopefully it will stay that way." Gloriana stood and settled her Birkin in the crook of her arm. "Don't look so upset, honey. I only mentioned this because I know you care for Nash. I thought you'd want to know."

"Of course I want to know! I feel terrible for him."

"So do I. Can you imagine being so cavalier? He got lucky this time, but one slipup like this can annihilate a career in a hot second."

THE INSTANT THE front door closed behind Gloriana, Lola grabbed her phone and ran to her bedroom. She shut the door, then went to the bathroom and shut and locked that door too, and only then did she allow her tears to fall.

Can we talk? she texted Nash.

Instead of a reply, she got a FaceTime call.

"If you're going to beg me to take you back—honestly, I'd consider it," he said through a broken smile. He was in his trailer, wearing a denim shirt and bolo tie. Outside the window, a dusky mountain range was visible. When he saw she was crying, his face fell. "I guess they told you."

"Oh, Nash, I'm so sorry."

"Hey, I'm okay. It's taken care of. You don't have to cry."

"I do have to cry, because I love you, even though you're an idiot."

"Everyone agrees with you there," he said. "Me included."

Lola wiped a tear from her cheek. "Fuck whoever did this."

"Is that Miss Lola Gray using the f-word?"

"I save it for times I need it to count," she sniffed. "Tell me what happened?"

Nash told her the whole story: a moment of weakness for someone who wasn't even special, then the demand to pay to stop the photos from leaking, and the humiliation of confessing his transgression to his manager.

"You know, when he threatened to leak those photos, I almost told him to do it. Make it look like an accident."

"*Nash—*"

"I'm kidding! Forget I said that. I'm tired, is all. The days are so long on this shoot."

"No, I know what you mean. Lately I've been thinking of coming out."

"Really?"

She told him everything that had happened in Michigan, and the idea for the film.

"What do you think?" she asked.

He sighed. "Part of me wishes I could do something like that. And part of me already has the anxiety shits from hearing you talk about it. But I'm proud of you. It's cute that you're in love with her enough to come out."

"I didn't say I'm in love with her!"

Nash rolled his eyes.

There was a knock at the door. Renee's voice: "Lo, are you okay? The crew's gone."

"Go," Nash said. "I'm good, baby. Honest."

"Okay. Call me anytime."

"You're my favorite ex-girlfriend." Nash winked, then ended the call.

When Lola opened the bathroom door, Renee had an arm braced against the jamb. Her face was wrought with concern.

"What happened with Gloriana? You ran up here so fast. Don't tell me she said no, because I will—"

"I didn't get to bring it up. Something important came up, and I can't tell you what it was. I'm sorry."

"That's okay." Renee took in her tear-streaked face. "Come here."

Lola buried her face in Renee's warm shoulder. Renee's arms were steady and strong around her. A final tear spilled from Lola's eyes as the panic she felt about Nash drained away. She was okay. She was safe. She was in control.

"I'll tell Gloriana soon, I promise," she said into Renee's chest.

Who's this woman? She's in the background of at least five different photos of Lola ♡ 338
Reply

↳ Renee Feldman she's directing the documentary ♡ 271

↳ For real? Her imdb has almost nothing on it ♡ 9

↳ She's an MFA student at the New York Institute of Film. She's listed on their website ♡ 19

↳ She went to Claudia's wedding you can see her in the background of this pic ♡ 82

↳ They went to high school together!!!! There's a photo from their yearbook junior year pinned on my page ♡ 136

↳ How do you have Lola's high school yearbook ♡ 18

↳ ebay! I know I'm crazy . . . ♡ 7

↳ Omg so cute Lola's high school friend is making her documentary ♡ 34

↳ I love it. That's so Lola ♡ 2

↳ We're getting a Lola movie????? ♡ 0

24

Renee frowned into her suitcase. She'd stopped by her hotel room to pack for New York. Her bed, covered in clothes, looked like the site of the recent vaporization of several goth teenagers. The problem with a mostly black wardrobe was that visually, it made packing confusing.

Renee was dreading this trip. She hadn't been back to New York since she left with her tail between her legs. Her RSVP to the Fall Reception was still unsent. Twice she'd filled out the form to decline, only to have Dragan's voice in her head saying *I want to see you there* stop her from hitting submit. She'd decided to decide later. She already had to bring her black jumpsuit, her only nice outfit, to wear to Lola's gala—she could rewear it if necessary.

When her phone buzzed, Renee snatched it up, eager for distraction.

Kadijah texted, Deborah came into Prince's and she said you'd been out here and didn't tell me?

Renee groaned. She hadn't talked to Kadijah in weeks.

> I wasn't in Fellows, I went up north to the lake house.

> I thought you were too busy working to return
> my texts, but you got time for a whole vacation.
>
> Wait
>
> Renee
>
> Did you go up there with her?

And *this* was the problem with secretly dating a closeted celebrity: you had to evade the legitimate questions of people you were only ever honest with.

> If I had, that would be a good
> reason not to tell you.

> 😲
>
> You took LOLA GRAY to your
> mom's lake house?

Renee's heart was bursting with feelings for Lola, her head filled with thoughts of her, and she didn't have a single person to talk to about it. Even still, she wasn't sure she would have been ready to tell Kadijah if she could have. Kadijah, with all their polyamory and ethical non-monogamy, fancied themself a relationship guru, and Renee, a delinquent. Renee didn't want Kadijah's teasing about Walk Away Renee's avoidant attachment style.

Instead of responding, Renee counted out twice the pairs of underwear she'd realistically need for a five-day trip. The screen lit up several times before Renee looked again.

👻

Wait but why

For the movie? I thought she had covid

Renee bit down on a cuticle, wishing sharply, all of a sudden, that Kadijah would just leave her alone.

> It wasn't for the film. Just a last-minute weekend trip thing.

Then why? bc of the breakup with Nash?

Not because . . . you know?

> Not because I know what?

The blinking dots showed Kadijah typing. Renee could practically hear the click of their acrylics on the phone screen.

If you're gonna be in the entertainment industry you need to get on social media. I am literally begging you to download tiktok.

> Micro-video offends my artistic sensibilities

See if this offends your sensibilities

The link Kadijah sent took a second to load on the website, since Renee didn't have TikTok downloaded, but the video's tags hinted at the content: #LolaGBTQ #LavaTruther #lesbiansoftiktok #wlw. The creator's username—QueerforJeanJacket—referenced the track from Lola's first album. Renee used to think "Jean Jacket," which was about secretly pining after a jean-jacket-clad crush, had a classic teenage Americana feel. Renee's brain still hadn't fully integrated the reality that she herself had bought the jean jacket in question at Target, and it was hanging in her childhood closet.

The video played. The face of QueerforJeanJacket hovered in front of a paparazzi shot of Lola and Renee, like a green screen. Renee was startled to see it: she hadn't realized she and Lola had been photographed leaving that restaurant, where they'd grabbed dinner after a long day at Ackerlund's studio.

"If you, like me, believe with every molecule of your being that this woman"—QueerforJeanJacket pointed to Lola in the image behind her—"is queer, then you have probably noticed that she's been seen a lot with this woman." She pointed to Renee. "Who is she? Let's talk about it."

A lump grew in Renee's throat as QueerforJeanJacket cycled through photos of Lola that included Renee, going back all the way to Claudia's wedding. QueerforJeanJacket theorized that Renee was not only Lola's documentarian and childhood friend—as demonstrated with pictures from their literal high school yearbook—but also Lola's lesbian rebound from Ava. (A separate video was coming on the theory that Nash was a beard.)

The penetrating unease caught her off guard. The photos would have felt violating in any case—Renee wasn't used to seeing high-resolution photos of herself from such a variety of angles—but these specific photos seemed to chart the course of how she'd fallen for Lola, even before she realized it was happening. That was still so private; Renee hadn't told a soul. Here, the evidence was laid out in a three-minute video, like a cracked case.

"I, for one, would love Lola to come out," QueerforJeanJacket concluded. "Renee's so hot, I'm about to start a stan account—let me know in the comments if you're into that. But honestly, I hope Renee is the one for Lola. I just think it would be so cool to see Lola marry a woman."

Whoa, how did they jump from rebound to *marriage*?

Renee sat down on the floor, in the middle of the room. Her heart was suddenly racing. No one in their right mind would mention her name in the same sentence as marriage. She hadn't even had a proper long-term—or short-term—relationship. She'd burnt so many romantic bridges, she might as well be traveling with matches and kerosene.

She called me hot, she wrote to Kadijah.

Don't read the comments.

What's in the comments? They're saying I'm not hot?

Never read the comments! And the point is, is something going on with you two?

Yeah, I'm filming her documentary.

Be for fucking real.

Renee fell back so that her spine was flush to the carpet. Even if she wanted to tell the truth, she'd signed an NDA. Using *that* as an answer was an answer on its own.

Maybe she didn't need to say anything at all. Kadijah could believe what they wanted for now, and it was only a matter of time before they took the relationship public, wasn't it?

Renee heaved herself off the floor and finished packing.

She left Kadijah on read.

Despite Renee's fears, traveling to New York with Lola was nothing like returning to the city that had teased her with a good time, then chewed her up and spit her out. They stayed in Lola's apartment near Gramercy Park, a rich-person neighborhood unfamiliar to Renee. Lola's packed schedule allowed for none of the things Renee would have wanted to show her in the city: no tour of Flushing's dumpling houses, excursion to Green-Wood Cemetery, or night out at a sapphic party at the Woods on Wednesdays.

Not that they could have done the last one anyway.

Lola had warned Renee that with news of her breakup with Nash, the paparazzi and fan attention would be intense. Renee dismissed her concerns: New York wasn't like celeb-crazed L.A. The first time they rode the elevator down from Lola's penthouse to slip into a waiting car—Lola mentioned wanting to upgrade to a place with a garage—Lola wore a large pair of sunglasses and clutched her coat closed like a security blanket. She looked so uncomfortable that Renee wondered if maybe Lola really didn't like the city. Then the elevator doors opened and Renee heard the screams.

The police had erected a barricade on the sidewalk to keep the fans and photographers back. Flashes popped in Renee's vision as the paps demanded that Lola pose for them or comment on the breakup. Above their cries, Renee could hear the higher-pitched squeals of "Lola! I love you so much!" or "I drove from Vermont to see you!" Renee wished she had her own suit of armor to match Lola's.

Then someone yelled, "Renee! Ohmigod, that's Renee!"

Renee's head snapped up reflexively.

"Renee, put us in the movie!" the girls cried over the whirr of clicking shutters. Renee's vision was blotted with the bluish afterburn of flashes.

"Renee, are you and Lola dating?" someone yelled.

Then Cassidy was yanking Renee into the car.

NIGHT ONE WAS a dinner with some of Lola's famous girlfriends. It was a stunt to show Lola thriving post-breakup, but Lola said she was genuinely looking forward to it. Lola had an hour to rest at her apartment before the glam squad arrived. She spent it in bed with Renee.

Renee's leg was nestled between Lola's thighs and her arm was splayed across Lola's chest. Lola ran a lazy palm down the curve of Renee's waist and settled it on the globe of her ass.

"Do you want to come to dinner?" Lola asked.

Renee nuzzled against her neck. "I can't shoot four people with one camera. And the sound would be terrible."

Lola inched back to peer at Renee, whose face was smushed half against the pillow and half against Lola's shoulder. "Not to film. I want you to meet some of my friends."

Suddenly, Renee felt more alert. She'd never actually agreed to meet anyone's friends before—part of keeping it casual—although some girls had sprung it on her anyway. It never went well.

Renee did a quick review in her head to confirm that she hadn't done to Lola any of the messed-up shit she normally did, like deliberately ignoring her (impossible, they worked together) or flirting with someone else in front of her (also impossible, Renee could barely look away from her). Lola's friends had no reason to dislike her—unless, of course, she messed up at dinner and gave them one.

She wriggled her body against Lola's. "What have you told them about me?"

She'd meant it playfully, but Lola winced.

Oh.

"I mean, are you out to any of them?" she asked instead.

"I am to Tatiana. I should warn you; she might give you a hard time. She thinks I have terrible taste in partners."

"You do. With one exception," Renee said.

"But I'll have to introduce you to the others as a friend." Renee could feel Lola's body tensing up beneath her. "I'm sorry. I understand if you don't want to come—"

"Stop it. Of course I want to meet your friends." Renee kissed the worried line of Lola's mouth. "I just hope they don't get jealous of all our slumber parties."

As SHE AND Lola strode past a photographer and into the glitzy Tribeca restaurant, Renee was a bundle of nerves. The restaurant was in a former bank, with towering Corinthian columns, dark green marble, and shiny gold accents everywhere. Following Lola's security through the space, Renee felt insufficiently stylish in her trusty jumpsuit, which she'd have to wear to the gala tomorrow night too. At least no one was noticing her: Lola was wearing a figure-hugging dress that made her look like an angel sent from heaven to make Earth sexier, and heads turned as she passed by.

They were shown through a vault-like door two feet thick and into the former deposit box room. It had been converted into a private dining space, with part of the restaurant's wine collection on display. Fancy, but a little claustrophobic. Lola's friends were already seated: Carolina de Jong, a willowy half-Dutch, half-Chinese model with bright white hair slicked into a bun; Rosalie Thomas, a gorgeous actress who'd gotten her break as a Bond Girl then pivoted to producing to advocate for better roles for Latina actresses like herself; and Tatiana Jones, the mega-huge pop star positioned as the bad girl counterpoint to Lola's squeaky-clean image.

Renee started to sweat. It was like being admitted to a secret meeting of the High Council of Hot Girls. Lola didn't notice that Renee was out of place. She beamed as she explained how they'd grown up next door to each other and reconnected exactly when Lola needed an up-and-coming director. Working with someone who'd known her for so long had unlocked her creative process and allowed her to be so much more in tune with herself. Lola was looking at Renee with stars in her eyes, and Renee blushed at the praise. If Lola had stopped talking for more than a few seconds, Renee would have kissed her.

Well, not actually. But she damn sure wanted to.

The waiter took their orders—Renee chose a frilly little salad because she wasn't sure who was paying and wanted to avoid financial ruin—and excused herself to the restroom. Outside the vault, the air felt looser. She took a deep breath while someone's bodyguard pointed her in the direction of the private restroom. Before the bathroom door had swung closed, it was shoved back open and Tatiana Jones pushed her way in.

Renee stepped back. "Um—I think this one's single occupancy?"

Tatiana trapped Renee with a hard stare. "I want to have a talk with you. About Lola."

"Sure," Renee said nervously. A lot of things had gone wrong in her meet-the-friends history, but she'd never been cornered in a bathroom.

Tatiana was not a large person, but with her mane of wavy blonde hair and the double-breasted blazer she was wearing as a minidress, she had more than enough attitude to crowd the small space. It was obvious that Tatiana did not smile unnecessarily—the kind of person who has a bad side. She leaned against the sink, leaving Renee standing in the middle of the marble floor.

"Lola's a very special person," Tatiana said flatly. "She's very special to me."

"To me too," Renee said.

"She's sensitive. She doesn't guard her heart like someone in her position should. So when I see her falling for someone, I take it as my responsibility to ask the questions I know she won't."

Renee's own heart swelled at the thought of Lola falling for her. "Ask me anything."

"When did you find out about Lola's documentary?"

"When she called and offered it to me. I was in grad school. Well, I was on leave."

"Meaning, this is your big break."

"Meaning, I wasn't looking for a big break. I was trying to make a thirty-minute thesis film and I couldn't even manage that."

Tatiana arched an extremely well-defined brow. Beneath it, her gray eyes were unforgiving. "You expect me to believe that?"

"Obviously," Renee said tightly, then pressed her teeth closed against any further ill-considered comments. As much as she didn't appreciate an international superstar's judgment of her stunted professional life, Renee could not lash out at Tatiana Jones. This was one of Lola's closest friends, the person Lola had really invited her here tonight to meet. And Tatiana was trying to protect Lola. That was something Renee more than understood. She sucked in a breath through her nose and steadied herself.

"But I see why you might not believe it. This is a huge opportunity, whether or not I was looking for it. To be honest, it's completely terrifying knowing that millions of people are going to see my first film. I'm trying not to think about that too much, because I'll start having panic attacks and I really don't have time for that. Instead, I'm just trying to focus on making something Lola can be proud of."

Tatiana tilted her head. "Okay. Lola said you hadn't spoken in years. Not since before her first album, and yet now"—she raised those sharp eyebrows again—"you have quite a personal interest in her. Explain that."

"How could I not have an interest in her?" Despite the interrogation, Renee found herself smiling. "I saw her over the summer at Claudia's wedding and she was just magnetic. I truly never expected to fall for her. I mean, that's like right out of a Lola Gray song, if you think about it."

"I did think about it." Tatiana folded her arms.

"Well, I didn't. You can ask my friend Kadijah; I'm basically allergic to relationships."

"And a relationship with a massively successful, kindhearted woman is the exception?"

Shit, this is not going well. The FBI could probably learn a thing or two from Tatiana's interrogation techniques.

"To be honest, I sort of wish she was less massively successful?" Renee said in a last-ditch defense. "Lola's basically a normal person—well, an unbelievably talented normal person. It sucks that she can't have a normal life." Renee swallowed hard. "Look, if you're worried that I'm pretending to be into her so I can get something out of the relationship, don't be. First, no one in their right mind would have to *pretend* to be into Lola. She's fucking incredible. And second, I'm fundamentally incapable of pretending to like anyone, even when I should. Just ask Gloriana—or anyone else on Lola's team."

"Gloriana doesn't like you?"

Renee rolled her eyes. "I was on thin ice from the start, with the *having no experience directing films* thing. Then I kidnapped Lola and took her to Michigan instead of torturing her with her ex like Gloriana wanted—thanks for your help with that, by the way—and since we've been back, Lola's been standing up to her left and right. So yeah, I'm not her favorite."

The sliver of a grin inched across Tatiana's face.

"Anything else you want to know?" Renee asked. Now that she'd found her footing, she almost wanted the interrogation to continue.

She *liked* proving herself worthy of Lola. She was glad that Lola had a friend like this—who could not be more unlike her—who felt a responsibility to look out for her.

"That's all, for now," Tatiana said, and Renee knew she'd passed.

Renee glanced at the toilet. "I actually do have to pee."

"Go find the other restroom," Tatiana said, opening the door for her.

BACK IN THE vault, the conversation found an easy rhythm. Carolina and Rosalie were generous with making sure that Renee understood whatever industry development they were discussing, and Tatiana had somehow signaled her approval to Lola, who was practically making heart eyes at Renee across the table.

So this is how meeting the friends is supposed to be.

At least, *sort of.* In the ideal scenario, all the friends knew you were dating.

Toward dessert, the conversation circled back to the documentary.

"I did one of those docs a few years back," Tatiana said, then sipped her soda water with bitters.

"I've seen it." Renee fumbled for something complimentary. "It was very . . . affecting."

"Please," Tatiana snorted. "It was trash."

"Maybe a little," Renee agreed. "Chess Waterston directed it, right? He was almost signed on for Lola's, but she wouldn't work with him."

"Lola's a smart girl. Smarter than me. I knew Chess was skeezy. But my management loved him, and I had just gotten out of rehab. Have you been to rehab?"

Renee shook her head.

"It's therapy seven days a week for months. When I got out and my management said a film would let me tell my own story, I thought, Perfect! My story was all I'd been thinking about." She pointed a long, spiky nail in Renee's direction. "Do not agree to do *anything* your first week out of rehab. I gave Chess a lot more access than I should have."

"It sounds exploitative," Carolina said, in her Dutch accent. "I know that upsets you, but it's important to say. In my industry, young women get taken advantage of all the time."

"Carolina's started an organization for model's rights," Lola said as an aside to Renee.

"The young women in your industry are literally children, Carolina." Tatiana rolled her eyes. "I was twenty-six. And I'm the one making money off the doc. Was I exploiting myself?"

"You were made to do something you weren't comfortable with." Carolina's eyes were enormous on her fine-boned face. "That is not right."

"I own my bad decisions," Tatiana said testily.

"This is why women need to fight to tell our own stories," Rosalie interjected. "Your film should have been an empowering experience, Tatiana. But women still aren't allowed to be the complicated, messy, authentic people we are. It's why I always wanted to produce."

"That's what Renee and I are trying to do," Lola said. "Tell my story *my* way."

"You have an incredible platform," Rosalie said. "What are you planning to say?"

Lola adjusted her bangs and glanced at Renee.

Just tell them.

She was cut through with a sudden, piercing desire for Lola to be honest. These women wouldn't care if she was bi. Rosalie was practically asking her directly.

Just tell them—fuck it. Tell them.

"We're keeping that under wraps for now," Lola said.

25

The next morning, Renee woke to Lola dropping a kiss on the back of her neck. The room was dark. She mumbled good morning but Lola had already crawled out of bed for her shower. The time change was killer. It felt like 5 a.m.

"Go back to sleep," Lola said.

Renee rolled into the warm spot where Lola had been lying and mushed her face into the pillow. Lola's day was packed with appointments—a meeting with the swimwear people, then shopping with her stylist before the charity gala. Renee was off until the evening.

White noise from the shower filled the room, but Renee couldn't fall back asleep. She curled her legs up to her chest, so her body was a compact ball in the center of the bed.

She couldn't stop thinking about last night. Leaving the restaurant, Rosalie led the way, then the newly single Lola, her arms linked with Tatiana and Carolina. Renee brought up the rear—which made sense, because the paparazzi needed their shots of the girl gang, not Lola's documentary director. It wasn't fair to be bothered that she hadn't been able to hold Lola's hand. Just like it wasn't fair to be disappointed that Lola hadn't told Carolina and Rosalie who Renee truly was to her.

After all, Renee had never really been in the closet like Lola was: she'd stormed out at fourteen and never looked back. She didn't truly understand what it was like for Lola. But it still seemed to Renee that confiding in her friends would have been a reassuring first step on this journey.

Lola returned wrapped in a robe and immediately stubbed her toe on a suitcase.

"You can turn the light on," Renee said.

"You sure? I don't want to bother you." Lola's voice was hushed, though Renee was clearly awake.

Renee reached for the bedside light herself.

"Maybe I want to watch you get dressed."

The bathrobe swallowed Lola's frame, and her hair hung loose and wet. Renee held out her hand. When Lola came closer, Renee pulled at the robe's belt. It fell open, revealing a strip of her still-damp body. Renee slid a hand inside the robe and cupped the jut of her hip. "Get back in bed with me?"

Lola wetted her lips as the robe slipped from her shoulders. "Just for a minute."

Renee held up the duvet for Lola to slip in. She nestled into Renee's arms. Water bled from the dark ropes of Lola's hair into the pillowcase. Renee sighed with deep satisfaction. Lola kissed her, slow and sensual, a long good morning. The kind of enveloping kiss Renee wanted to spend the whole morning getting lost in, just the two of them under the blankets in the half-dark room and the taste of mint lingering on Lola's lips.

"I don't have time for—for more," Lola said. Renee loved that Lola still hesitated to refer directly to fucking.

"I know. I just wanted to hold you. I'm going to miss you today."

Renee traced a line of kisses along her jaw, up to her ear, then stopped. They both knew what would happen if she kept going. "Maybe I can come meet you, for the shopping stuff?"

"I'd love that, but it's your day off."

"I know. But you do rely on my fashion advice."

Somehow, Renee had imagined strolling with Lola from store to store, where she'd sit patiently like the world's best boyfriend, telling Lola she looked smoking hot in everything she tried on. In reality, she'd signed on to a multi-hour, tightly managed affair. They waited in the black SUV while the showroom was cleared, or they were ushered to a private room, where the stylists' or brand's pulls were waiting. Lola deferred to their recommendations almost every time.

While they waited for the next set of picks, Renee browsed a rack of women's suiting in a rainbow of jewel tones. She thumbed the sleeve of a rust-colored set.

"Why don't you wear something like this, Lo?" Renee said.

"It's not really my style. But these are gorgeous."

Renee hadn't moved past the rust-red suit. "They are."

"Why don't you try it?" Lola said.

"It doesn't come in black," Renee said. She did like that wearing black made her look tough, but it was also practical, cheap, and, most of all, safe—even if it could be a little boring.

"You seem to like the red."

Renee turned away from the rack and shoved a hand through her hair. "It's nice, I guess, but it wouldn't fit anyway."

Cassidy lurked up beside them, phone in hand. "Lola, Chloe confirmed for dinner tomorrow."

"What dinner?" Renee asked. "I thought we were free tomorrow."

"Remember Saint Satin? It's hard being new in the business, so I reached out to her. More established artists did that for me, when I was starting out, and it really meant a lot to me. I like to pay it forward."

"You're only saying that because Chloe's a massive Lo-Lite."

Lola bumped her shoulder against Renee. "I've already got a fangirl following me around everywhere."

Renee's heart swelled happily at Lola's teasing. "I don't want to be replaced! Am I invited?"

"Not this time. Why don't you get dinner with a friend?"

Renee chewed her lip for a moment. "Actually, tomorrow night there's this annual party that my MFA program throws. The Fall Reception. All the faculty and students go, and a bunch of industry people and alumni come."

"You never mentioned that."

"I can't go anyway. I didn't RSVP," Renee said.

"At least come up with an excuse that makes sense," Lola said flatly.

"Fine. I can't go because I don't want to."

"Then why bring it up?" Lola said with a raise of her eyebrow.

Renee winced. "Because I like to keep you informed about what's going on in my life?"

"*Renee.*"

Renee folded her arms. "Maybe a tiny, little part of me wants to go. Dragan said he wanted me there. And it would be nice to go to this party without feeling like a fucked-up little gremlin."

"So, what's the problem?"

"To everyone I went to school with, I *am* a fucked-up little gremlin. Dragan's been nagging me for updates and I can't even tell him that I found a meaningful direction for the film. Sorry—I didn't say that to pressure you. It's just *true*. I can't tell Dragan until you tell Gloriana."

Lola's fingers drifted toward Renee's hand, but she caught herself. "I'm sorry. I meant to talk to her before this trip, but things got busy. I'll do it first thing when we get back, I promise. But you should go. You can't tell me it doesn't turn you on a little to think about walking into that party knowing they're all wrong about you."

Even if it didn't match her reality, Renee liked the image of her that Lola had in mind: confident, unbothered, striding into that party like she was out of fucks to give. But more than that, she knew *Lola* loved that image.

"Let Dragan show you off, and we can meet up after at the Saint Satin show."

THE FOLLOWING AFTERNOON, Renee walked alone through the brisk November chill back to Lola's apartment. They'd just wrapped the final shoot of the trip—a photoshoot—and professionally, the visit had been a success. She was happy with the footage she'd gotten, especially at last night's gala. In the film, it would be a moment to reflect that all of Lola's sacrifices had been worth it, to allow her to reach people like this.

But as Renee's feet carried her closer to her destination, the satisfied glow from a job well done dimmed: the Fall Reception was beginning in an hour.

Lola wanted her to go, but Lola didn't understand what it would feel like for Renee to be there. Lola was massively successful, a powerhouse who had climbed to the top of her industry. When Lola Gray walked into a room, eyes were on her because she *impressed*. When Renee walked into the reception—*if* she walked into the reception— eyes would be on her in the way they'd be on a dog that walked in on its hind legs: the near-dropout who'd stumbled onto the opportunity of a lifetime.

Renee hoisted her backpack up her shoulders as Lola's doorman called the elevator for her.

She'd skip the gala. She'd nap, then take herself out for dinner before the Saint Satin show. She'd tell Lola she didn't have anything to wear, which was true: her black jumpsuit was dependable, but wearing it three nights in a row was a little excessive. It was starting to smell.

In the apartment, she waved to Cassidy, who had taken off on an earlier errand and was now on the couch with her iPad, then headed to Lola's room.

When she got there, she found a garment bag laid across the bed with a white envelope inscribed with her name. Renee slid her thumbnail under the seal and pulled out the card.

If I can't be there with you, at least I can make sure you look good—Lo

Renee pulled down the zipper of the garment bag and gasped with delight. Inside was the rust-red suit she'd admired the day before. How had Lola known? Renee hadn't been able to stop thinking about this outfit, even though it was nothing like what she usually wore, and cost far beyond what she'd ever spend on clothes. But more than that—Lola had known that Renee would lose her resolve, that she didn't have anything to wear other than that jumpsuit, that she would need the extra confidence that Lola always managed to give her.

She hoped it would fit. There were three reasons Renee avoided tailored pants: the first two were her hips and ass, and the third was a lack of funds for alterations. Up top, her chest was full enough she didn't usually mess with button-ups or suit jackets, as much as she wanted to. But even if the suit didn't fit, the gesture meant a lot.

There was a knock on the door. Renee opened it to see Cassidy, looking rather proud of herself. Beside her stood Lola's hairstylist, her makeup artist, and a third woman, who introduced herself as a tailor.

"We heard you've got a party to go to," Cassidy said.

RENEE'S STOMACH WAS in knots as she walked into the reception at the NYIF's faculty club. She could not beeline for the bar: that stank of desperation, evidenced by the first-years clustered beside it. Their frightened eyes darted around the room, afraid to recognize anyone, but also afraid not to.

Renee remembered that feeling. She had only been able to get through forty-five minutes of her last Fall Reception, most of which she spent slamming plastic cups of red wine, until she spilled one down the front of her favorite sweater. She'd fled with several mini chocolate eclairs wrapped in a napkin in her jacket pocket.

But today she was wearing a designer suit, the pockets of which would never be sullied by miniature pastries. When she saw Lola later, Renee wanted to say that she hadn't let herself be intimidated.

"Do I spy Renee Feldman, my star student?" Dragan said. His face was ruddy from the rakija he always insisted everyone sample at the party. "You made it!"

Renee accepted his cheek kisses. "Last-minute change of plans. We're shooting in the city this week."

Dragan took her by the arm. "I have some friends of the institute to introduce you to, but while I have you, I am expecting an update before the end of the month. Resolving some of those issues we talked about—finding the purpose, making sure you're creating something with meaning, yes? Remember, it's not only your reputation attached to this film. It's the program's and *mine*."

"You can trust me," Renee said. "We're sorting out final details with Lola's management. I'll have news soon."

"Wonderful! Now, there are a few agents here..."

DRAGAN INTRODUCED RENEE as one of the up-and-coming stars of the program. Renee wished she'd been able to take notes on all the names, which adopted a leave no trace policy during their brief time inside her brain. Whenever Dragan dropped that Renee was making a film about the pop star Lola Gray, someone would recall that their daughter or niece was an enormous fan, as were all of the daughter's or niece's friends—actually, they were all rather obsessed with her! When they asked for more details, Renee hedged: *exciting new ideas* this, *reinvention of the subgenre* that. It felt bizarre to talk about her *unvarnished approach to biographical filmmaking*, when the film's new direction wasn't greenlit, but everyone took Renee's bullshit at face value. An hour later, her pockets were packed—not with mini eclairs, but with business cards; she had never thought to make her own. She vowed to update her website, assuming she hadn't let the domain name expire.

Eventually, the editor whom Renee had been chatting with stepped away and she had a moment alone to refocus. She should have been feeling good. She *wanted* to be feeling good. She'd been celebrated, bragged about, introduced to the most prestigious friends of the institute. Instead, her stomach was sickly clenched, and it wasn't from Dragan's rakija. Everyone seemed to be expecting her work to be great—for *Renee* to be great. But the truth was, Renee didn't really have a film yet.

Everything was riding on Lola.

"Renee? Hi!"

Renee turned to see two members of her old cohort, Meredith Shay and Steven Lombardi. They awkwardly hugged hello. They'd graduated the previous May. Renee hadn't spoken to either of them in a year and a half.

"We were so happy to hear you were back in the program," Steven said.

Before Renee's surprise at that could fully sink in—neither of them had been big Renee Feldman fans—Meredith said, "Tell us about this huge thesis project you're working on. Some celebrity documentary?"

Renee steadied herself. Yes, these people had eviscerated her work before, but maybe that was water under the bridge.

"It's a documentary about the singer Lola Gray, as she records her next album," Renee said. The phrase was now well-rehearsed.

"Wow, that's *huge*," Meredith said, then chased her words with a sip of her martini. "How did you even get in the room for a job like that?"

"Good luck, mainly," Renee said with a self-deprecating laugh. "Lola and I grew up together."

Meredith and Steven exchanged a look clearly signaling that furious activity in the cohort group text was in the near future. Already, Renee could practically hear them bitching about her unearned opportunity while wishing they had the same connections.

"I can't wait to see what you do," Meredith said. "It's always so *interesting* when one of these big celebs tries to show some depth."

Renee bristled, thinking back to the dinner with Lola's friends. All of those women had plenty of depth. But she didn't snap at Meredith. Instead, she summoned some of Lola's poise. "Exactly. It's so challenging for women in the public eye. Their stories get misrepresented all the time. Lola wants to take back the narrative."

"I thought Lola Gray wrote all her own songs," Steven countered. "Who's she taking the narrative back from?"

"You'll see in the film," Renee said evenly. "Even famous women are embedded in power dynamics. Just because you don't understand them, doesn't mean they don't exist."

Meredith finished off her martini. "I'm glad we're finally getting a film explaining how hot, cis, straight white girls are the true victims of a system that celebrates hot, cis, straight white girls, because you're right, I *don't* understand it."

"Oh my god, stop!" Steven swatted Meredith on the shoulder. "We're all dying to see what you do, Renee. This is a once-in-a-lifetime opportunity, right?"

"Right." Renee swallowed hard.

"It could totally make your career."

"I know."

"And I thought *my* thesis was stressful! But, like, no pressure!"

Steven and Meredith laughed. Once, their needling would have sent Renee directly into an anxiety spiral. Even now, she felt the rattle starting in her chest. But she willed herself above it and thought of Lola, her story and her faith in Renee. Steven and Meredith were jealous, and that wasn't Renee's problem. After all, it would only get worse once they saw her work.

"It's been great catching up," Renee said. "But I have another engagement to get to."

26

Lola waited for Chloe in a private booth at the back of a trendy Italian restaurant. Her phone vibrated.

I can't believe you did this! And a tailor too?

You like it?

It's perfect. I'm in love.

Lola felt all her blood rush to her head.

🐼

I'll send you a pic as soon as I have it on.

No, don't! Surprise me at the show.

😈

"Lola?"

She looked up, still grinning, to see Chloe standing before her in baggy jeans and a vintage Chicago Bulls jacket. Almost hidden by the large sleeves, her fists were clenched anxiously. Lola jumped up to give her a reassuring hug.

Though Lola had missed Saint Satin's set at Corkscrew, that memory of Chloe at the after-party had inspired her to request an early copy of the album. It was packed with pop songs structured around dynamite hooks and lyrics that were a little clever, a little dirty, and very fun. Chloe shared writing credits on all of them, and Ackerlund had produced the album. Saint Satin could be huge—if Chloe worked hard, if the right people liked her, and if she had a gigantic stroke of luck. Lola remembered her own moment, before it all blew up. She'd had a fan base and industry experience from *You're Next!* She'd thought she understood what she was getting into. She hadn't realized the roller coaster she'd strapped herself into had barely begun to move.

In person, Chloe was much like Lola remembered her: full lips, straight brows, and long, shining black hair, but she didn't seem to care overmuch about being pretty. Chloe was a few years older than Lola had been when her first album came out. Twenty-one was an age where you wanted the whole world to look at you, and Chloe had that *it* factor that would make the world stare. If Lola hadn't noticed how Chloe kept cracking her knuckles, she would have bought the younger woman's aura of perfect self-assurance.

"Congratulations on your album! It's good, Chloe. It's really good."

"Thank you," Chloe said earnestly. "I'm trying not to get too invested in praise and all that, but it does mean a lot coming from you. You were a huge influence on me."

"Really?" Lola said with an encouraging smile. "I don't think our sounds are very similar."

"Not anymore!" Chloe laughed. "I've worked hard to find my own sound. But my earliest stuff? It was all Lola Gray–coded. But, like, queer."

Lola's smile froze on her face.

Chloe continued, "Little Chloe really saw herself in you. Your first album fucking ate and left no crumbs, and you were only seventeen! Knowing you wrote all your own songs and you were killing it meant *a lot*."

"And it means a lot to me that I inspired an artist like you," Lola said. "I know how hard this business can be. The pressure can be overwhelming, and you don't always have good people to talk to. I want you to know that I'm here for you."

"See, I always knew you were fucking cool," Chloe said in a way that forced Lola to think about everyone Chloe might have had to defend her to.

They talked over antipasti and arancini about Chloe's break.

"A lot of people say I got discovered on TikTok, like that's easy to do," Chloe said. Where other artists might have been cowed by some of the hate Chloe had already received, even at this point in her career, she'd responded to it with a fiery faith in herself. "I was working my ass off. That song charted in the Hot 100, and I wrote, recorded, and produced it *in my bedroom*."

"It's a huge achievement," Lola said.

"Especially for a queer woman," Chloe said proudly.

Lola sipped her water. She'd never thought to frame her own accomplishments that way. "Has your label been supportive of your, um, identifying as queer?"

Chloe puffed out a laugh. "They didn't have a choice."

Lola dug her teeth into her cheek. There was something about Chloe's confidence that made Lola feel insufficient. Renee had the same self-assurance, and Lola had always envied it. She wanted so much to be liked—to be loved—that despite all her success, the idea of simply not trying to win others over made her skin crawl. Maybe it was a queer thing—not to care so much what others thought.

"I meant, when you came out to them, they reacted positively?"

"I didn't really have to come out. I was never hiding. I can't create if I can't be myself, and I'm never going to be that shiny, happy, girly pop star. No offense—we love a high femme queen—but I'm not her."

"That's great," Lola said, trying not to think about why she hadn't been strong enough to do the same. "I hope it stays that way. Sometimes the label will say one thing, then do another."

"I'm not worried about that. My label's like, *The market's ripe for an edgy sapphic pop star.*" Chloe popped a piece of soppressata into her mouth, chewed, then said, "I have a rule that anyone I work with has to hold space for me to be authentically myself. If they can't, they're out."

Sudden sympathy washed out Lola's envy. Chloe was so young, so green. The idea that anyone in the public eye could be their authentic selves was painfully naive. Celebrity flattened everything. It made you into a product with a target market and a sales pitch. When Chloe heard her label call her an *edgy sapphic pop star*, she saw an opportunity to be herself. She didn't yet realize that she'd been assigned a role, an image, a narrative.

"You're not concerned about being pigeonholed?" she asked.

"Oh, I definitely don't want that," Chloe said, as if some artists *did* want to be pigeonholed. She slung an arm across the banquette. "I'm not going to fit into their little box. If they think I'm too much, fuck them. I *want* to be too much, because for too long we've been forced to be too little. I want to be the first woman to have a number one hit about sucking clit."

Lola sucked in a sharp breath at Chloe's crassness. The truth was, Lola had already achieved that milestone with the post–*Wild Heart* single, "Just Between Us," though she'd chosen more oblique language. She didn't mention that to Chloe. She'd never mentioned it to anyone.

"Queer women have always been here, but we've been marginalized for so long. I have a duty to be the role model I didn't have when I was younger," Chloe went on, impassioned.

"You really think that still matters, now?" Lola asked. "There are so many queer people in the public eye."

Chloe's expression puckered with outrage. "*Yes*, representation still matters. It would have meant the world to me to see someone like me, a Korean lesbian, making music. If I didn't get to have that, I want to make sure every other little Korean girl does. Queer people in the public eye have that responsibility."

"That sounds sort of political," Lola said. She sounded so timid.

"Being queer *is* political."

Queer was a term Lola had never tried to apply to herself. It described the kind of person you chose to be, not just who you lusted after. What Chloe was talking about was more than simply coming out. It was obligation to community beyond oneself.

Tentatively, in her head, Lola tried the label on. *I'm queer.* But before she could sit with it, she was envisioning Gloriana's reaction. The closest Lola Gray got to politics was events like last night's gala against childhood hunger, which was about as uncontroversial as an issue could get.

Lola's bodyguard interrupted them. A woman claiming to be Chloe's girlfriend wanted to be let back. Chloe jumped out of her seat and introduced her. Vivy—the woman Lola had thought of as Butterfly Clips—wore a big, fannish smile.

"It's lovely to see you again," Lola said.

Vivy's eyes went wide, but she turned them on Chloe. "Babe, did you hear that? *Lola Gray remembered me.*"

"Course she did, pretty girl," Chloe said, her voice full of affection.

Right there, in view of the whole restaurant, Chloe pulled her girlfriend in for a kiss.

LATER, LOLA SIPPED a vodka soda alone on the VIP mezzanine at Irving Plaza. Her drink was half-gone but it hadn't quieted the nagging guilt that she'd put off talking to Gloriana. She could practically hear Gloriana asking why now, if bisexuality was an important addition to Lola's public image or more of a private concern, what would happen when things fell apart with Renee and Lola moved on with a man. Lola had promised Renee that she would stand her ground, but already she felt like a little kid, begging to be listened to.

Coming out was already overwhelming, and she hadn't even officially started it yet.

Lola's gaze drifted over the crowd below. They hadn't spotted her yet, but with hundreds of people on the floor, it was only a matter of time. The venue was packed with young women and non-binary people buzzing with excitement. It was obvious that these fans were obsessed with not just Saint Satin, but each other. They were checking each other out, taking selfies, stealing kisses from strangers who might be lovers by the night's end. Lola wondered what it would feel like to be down there—to lose herself in the hot press of bodies.

There was a unique pain in witnessing someone else's euphoria: rib-scraping loneliness and jealousy of watching the specific kind of joy that you longed for, and being unable to join in. It was the same feeling Lola had had watching Chloe at the Corkscrew after-party, like sparklers had been set off in her heart, but all they'd done was reveal how huge and lonesome the darkness there truly was.

Lola bit her lip. She would talk to Gloriana. She'd do it soon. She could text her right now, to schedule a meeting.

But even when Lola did come out, she'd never have what these

Saint Satin fans did. She'd never get lost in a crowd or kiss a stranger. This moment, tonight, was the closest Lola had come—might *ever* come—to going to a gay bar. These same people might hate her for having dated too many men or having stayed closeted too long or simply because she was bisexual. She'd happily lose any homophobic fans, but she wasn't under the illusion the queer community would simply embrace her. Everyone would have an expectation for how she was supposed to be. She'd inevitably disappoint some of them. And that felt perilously close to failure.

Would it all be worth it?

Renee's arrival interrupted her thoughts.

Relief bled through Lola as Renee came forward, her churning thoughts already quieting. Renee looked insanely hot in the suit. It walked the scintillating line between feminine and masculine, as Renee often did, which always sent a rush of heat through Lola's body. Lola wanted to pull Renee close and kiss her, because she looked incredible, because Lola was proud of her for braving the reception, because Renee's touch would ground her—but also because kissing Renee would prove that she belonged in this room full of queer people.

But she couldn't kiss Renee—not yet. After an awkward hesitation, they hugged, though Lola dared to slip her hands inside the jacket to cup Renee's hips.

"That suit," Lola said, pulling back to better rake her eyes up Renee's body. "If it weren't for all these people . . ."

Renee flashed her a crooked grin. "Won't matter soon."

She'd been thinking almost the same thing, but hearing it from Renee, she felt a pinch of anxiety. Renee's gaze was drifting over the crowd below, but she wasn't looking at them like Lola had. Being here was nothing special for Renee, who had been out for half her life. She knew she fit in already.

"How was the party?" Lola asked.

"It was weird. Well, no, it was good, but that was weird. Dragan wasn't kidding about showing me off." She pulled a handful of business cards from her pocket. "Agents, producers, I don't even remember who else."

"That's incredible!"

"It is, isn't it? I even talked to two people from my cohort and I felt myself starting to spiral, but I was like, no. They're going to be eating their words eventually. Or I hope they will."

"They *will*," Lola said. Renee's words were optimistic, but she was gripping the mezzanine railing so tight that the velvet was pulling at her shoulders. "Then what's wrong?"

"I'm just thinking about how badly I need this film to be *good*. Everything's riding on this. I'm not going to get a second chance. I didn't deserve *this* chance—"

"Renee—"

"It's a fact, Lo: I got this job because you were desperate, and I was there. That's not going to happen again." Renee closed her eyes and took a big breath. As she blew it out, she straightened up and pulled her shoulders back. "But you know what? That's okay. We have an amazing story to tell. It's going to make a phenomenal film. I have nothing to worry about. Right?"

"Right," Lola assured her. Her heart raced to see Renee like this—sure of herself. Hopeful.

Renee slipped her arm around Lola's waist, drawing them together. Renee's green eyes looked dark gray in the low light, solemn and searching. "This is what you want, isn't it?"

What Lola wanted most of all right then was to feel Renee against her.

"This is what I want," Lola said.

"It's okay if you're not ready. I can figure something else out for the film. But I need to know."

Lola looked up at her and pressed her hips forward. "I'm ready."

"And that's the truth, not what you think I want to hear?"

Lola laughed. "I wouldn't lie to you. I'm not changing my mind."

But her words sounded more certain than she felt.

A relieved smile crossed Renee's face, but rapidly melted into something darker and wanting. Her hand skimmed from Lola's waist to her ass, sending an electric shiver in its wake. Her fingers tightened against Lola's flesh, as she leaned into Lola's ear. "That's my girl," Renee whispered.

Lola gasped, as heat gathered between her legs. Lola's body bent reflexively into Renee's, her face upturned to beg for a kiss. But just as quickly, Renee let her go and jutted her chin toward the stage. The crowd cheered as Saint Satin's band grabbed their instruments. Lola's body went to ice. There were a thousand people down there.

"No one saw that, right?" she said.

"Relax, Lo. They're not looking at us," Renee said, as Saint Satin took the stage.

Lola wanted to believe her, although it sounded too good to be true.

My queer heart is EXPLODING, Lola and Renee at the Saint Satin show??? ♡ 17.5K
Reply

↳ 🔥🔥🔥 ♡ 828

↳ 〰️〰️〰️ ♡ 584

↳ Lola looks like she wants to climb her like a tree ♡ 13.0K

↳ Can't blame her tbh ♡ 1807

No one can convince me these two are not a thing ♡ 6493
Reply

↳ girlfriends for sure ♡ 1018

↳ 100% ♡ 26

Yall are freaking out about nothing. Everyone knows they're old friends ♡ 1224
Reply

↳ Seriously Lola can't even go to a concert with a friend without you saying it's a date ♡ 827

↳ What about that body language says *friends*? ♡ 921

↳ #morethanfriends ♡ 12

100% of St Satin fans are queer, so if Lola's a fan . . . ♡ 927
Reply

It's low-key pathetic that you are so invested in a total stranger's life

♡ 87

Reply

↳ Lola's not a stranger!

♡ 2

Fanfic incoming!

♡ 107

Reply

↳ Drop the link!

♡ 8

27

"Here's my favorite client!" Gloriana cheek-kissed Lola as she welcomed her into her office. "That girls dinner got exactly the reaction we were hoping for. Although I was surprised to see you dragged Renee along."

Gloriana gestured for Lola to sit on the couch. The velvet upholstery stuck to the material of Lola's skirt. As Gloriana settled into a chair across from her, her assistant followed with a laptop.

"Actually could we talk, just us two?" Lola said. Her hands were already clammy.

"Oh—certainly." Gloriana waved off her assistant. As the glass door shut behind her, Gloriana said, "What's going on, honey?"

Lola felt a rush of affection for Gloriana. Gloriana was the first person who understood the blood, sweat, and tears that Lola dedicated to her dream, and the extent of the sacrifices she was willing to make. She'd promised young Lola that she'd make it all worth it, and she'd never steered her wrong.

But on the heels of that love came a clawing fear: the prospect of disappointing Gloriana made Lola almost physically sick. But coming out wasn't disappointing, she reminded herself. She was just anxious. She was losing her nerve.

"I've been thinking," Lola began. "With the new songs coming along, we're at a turning point. I wanted to revisit the idea of my coming out."

"Oh! Yes, certainly we can have that conversation."

That wasn't so hard. "Great! I was thinking that the film is the perfect opportunity. We can control the narrative, instead of leaving it to a journalist. And it would give the film a purpose—not just *Remember who Lola Gray is?* But like, *This is who she is.*"

Lola trailed off. It sounded so much better when Renee said it.

"And who Lola Gray is, is what, a gay person?" Gloriana said.

Lola winced. "Bisexual—or maybe queer. So, that, but also an artist, a songwriter, someone who cares about her fans. I can do all of those things better if I'm honest about who I am."

"It's an interesting idea." Gloriana pursed her lips thoughtfully. "Let's set the movie aside for the moment. If we decide to do this, we can discuss how to make the announcement later. Help me understand why *now*."

Lola tried not to let her expression fall. Gloriana's job was to ask these questions, but that didn't change the fact that Lola had wanted Gloriana to simply say yes without running through every pro and con. That was a childish, unprofessional thought. No one got to Lola's level, or into the stratosphere beyond it, by doing exactly what they wanted.

"With the breakup with Nash, my fans think I'm single. We'd have to give it some time, so I don't look like a greedy bisexual." Lola giggled nervously to dismiss the stereotype. Gloriana didn't. "Um, the media attention would be good for the album. The music I'm making now feels more mature anyway, so it could be an opportunity to debut a new image. And—and what's the big deal, right? It's not like I'd be the first bisexual pop star."

Gloriana clicked her tongue. "It'd be better if you were! *That*, we could really capitalize on."

"I just meant, Lady Gaga is out and no one ever talks about it."

"You're not Lady Gaga, Lola. You're the girl next door pining for the quarterback, not some sex bomb."

Lola laughed uneasily. "You make it sound like I'm still in high school."

"To many of your fans, you are. Especially when *they're* still in high school."

"My fans have grown up just like I have. A lot of them are queer too."

"Yes, of course—I've seen the hashtags. Those are good points," Gloriana said, and Lola felt buoyed by her praise. "But realistically, it's mid-November. We need to deliver this documentary for Streamy in four months—and that's not negotiable. I'm not convinced the timeframe is right for an announcement. Remember, we're planning for a career that's going to last the rest of your life. I always say, these details are currency. *Who you are* is currency. We need to be careful how we manage that wealth."

"I think this is a good time to spend it," Lola said, but her voice sounded thin.

Gloriana wove her fingers together. Lola's stomach clenched: she was about to hear something unpleasant. "Lola, my job is to do what's right for you. For *you*, not anyone else. I'm surprised to hear you want this movie—which once you had no interest in whatsoever—to expose the most personal and intimate part of your life. I wouldn't be doing my job if I didn't ask if this is really what *you* want. Not just what *she* wants."

Lola's eyes went wide. She felt pinned by Gloriana's stare like a butterfly under glass. "Renee does want this. She came up with this great concept about how being in the closet has affected my creative process. But I think it's a really good idea too."

"It is a really good idea—*for Renee.*" Gloriana grabbed her iPad from her desk, then sat beside Lola on the couch. "You know we're constantly monitoring the online discussion of you. Recently, we've expanded that to include Renee—it would be so helpful if she got representation for herself, by the way. I want to make you aware of what we've been seeing."

Lola sat extremely still as Gloriana swiped through a series of screenshots.

"We have headlines about Renee Feldman."

Who is the woman behind Lola Gray's film?

Lola Gray's childhood BFF to direct Streamy doc

Lola shrugged. "We knew the project put Renee in the public eye. You agreed to that. It's part of the story of the film."

Gloriana swiped on.

More than friends? Fans speculate on a new love for Lola Gray

Lola Gray and "gal pal" Renee Feldman spotted at Hollywood eatery

#LolaGBTQ: Talking to the fans who insist Lola Gray is more than a pop icon—she's a lesbian, too

Gloriana sighed at the final slide. It was a grainy TikTok clip. Lola recognized the mezzanine at once, Renee's suit. She could practically feel the pressure of Renee's hand on her ass, her hot breath in her ear. How she'd brushed off Lola's concerns that they might be seen. The only sound the camera had picked up was an overloud cry: *Oh my god, that's Lola Gray—holy shit, did that girl just kiss her?*

Lola's shoulders folded inward. She wanted to shrink down into nothing. It was one thing to imagine how things would change when she came out. It was another thing entirely to see what it would look like when she'd surrendered the last private thing she had.

"We were only talking, I swear," Lola said, as if that mattered. "There was no kiss."

Gloriana gestured at the screen. "Whatever this is, it worries me, Lola. You know better than this. Now, I don't care what happens behind closed doors between you and Renee. I'm an ally, I support it—did I tell you my nephew came out as non-binary?—but this isn't the Lola I know. I know you're aware that risks like these are how we lose control of the story. So I have to stop and think: Is it really Lola who wants to act like this? Or is someone influencing her? Someone who benefits from this kind of attention, and might not care what it means for you?"

"Renee's not with me to advance her career," Lola said.

Gloriana looked at her like she was pathetically naive. "No, Lola. Renee *is* working with you to advance herself. You plucked her from *graduate school*, of all places, and brought her into a career-defining moment. Let's not pretend otherwise."

It was true. Renee had said as much to her in New York. Lola had used exactly that argument to convince Renee to take on this project.

"Making a good film isn't your job," Gloriana said. "That's Renee's problem. Your job is being Lola Gray. All of us depend on that." She squeezed Lola's shoulder. "But! I know how important this is to you, honey. If you want to explore being bisexual on camera, we can do it. Say the word and I'll call the team together."

Lola hesitated. The way Gloriana had said "bisexual" somehow sounded crass. "This meeting was just to talk it through. I still need to think about it before I make a decision."

28

Renee paced anxiously in Lola's back garden. With slate paving stones set around dramatic succulents and a beautiful pool done in painted Spanish tile, it was so nice, it made it hard to be truly anxious. Still, Renee managed, because her blood felt practically effervescent with anticipation as she waited for Lola to come home from her meeting with Gloriana.

Lola was going to stand up for herself and what she wanted. She was taking control of her story. Once she did that, Lola would truly be unstoppable.

Renee was so damn proud of her.

Renee had a bottle of champagne chilling to celebrate, although they'd probably end up in the bedroom first. Or the couch, if they didn't make it that far.

Renee couldn't wait to get started on the real work of putting the film together. Since New York, her vision for it had sharpened, her anxieties blurring into the background. She could feel their story taking shape—not only on film, but off-screen too. There was something so satisfyingly elegant about how they were intertwined, it was practically cinematic in itself: Lola reclaiming her voice, Renee battling her own creative demons to tell that story, the two of them in love.

Not that they *were* in love. Were they?
Her phone buzzed.

Hello stranger

Renee frowned, disappointed that it was Kadijah. She hadn't answered their texts since before New York.

What is this?

It was a link to another TikTok. Renee clicked through—she had the app downloaded now. *Shit.* Someone had filmed them at the Saint Satin show: her and Lola, pressed together, as Renee murmured into her ear. The creator thought they'd kissed. They used a hashtag referencing Lola's lyrics: #morethanfriends.

Shit, shit, shit. Renee watched it again and again. She'd honestly thought they wouldn't be seen. But of course, there was always someone looking at Lola.

Doesn't look like nothing's going on.

The glare of the sun reflected off the phone's screen and into her eyes. If this had been a normal relationship, Renee would already have gushed to Kadijah about how kind Lola was, how her wry sense of humor only came out when they were alone. How it was so painfully, simply, beautifully *nice* to be in Lola's presence that she never wanted to be anywhere else. How Walk Away Renee was history.

As it was, she hadn't had a real conversation with Kadijah in weeks, since before she realized she had feelings for Lola, after Corkscrew.

> Am I looking at two people who *are* fucking each other or just really, really *want* to be fucking each other?

Renee chewed her lip. Obviously, she couldn't answer Kadijah's question, but she wasn't sure what to say instead.

> I can't believe I'm hearing about your life from TikTok gossip

> Are you seriously not going to reply?

From the front of the house, Renee heard the gate. She'd worry about Kadijah later. She shoved the phone in her pocket and raced to the front hall. She was beaming now, the excitement radiating off her and making her breath quick. She must have looked a little silly, because when Lola opened the door, she seemed startled.

"So?" Renee said.

"So what?"

Renee grabbed Lola by the waist and pulled her in. "Don't tease me, I can't take it," she growled.

But still, Lola didn't answer. Her eyes were searching Renee's, her full lips parted. God, how Renee loved holding her, more than she'd ever loved holding anyone. Renee tightened her arms around Lola and captured her mouth in a kiss. As she drew Lola's lower lip into her mouth, her nose pressed to Lola's cheek, their eyelashes brushing. Lola responded as quickly as she always did, arching her body against Renee—and Renee loved that too, how Lola always kissed her like she was clinging to life.

Lola plunged her hands into Renee's hair, trapping them against each other. Her tongue snaked into Renee's mouth, and Renee accepted it, sucking on it with an eager groan. She slid her hands to Lola's ass and squeezed, making her own hips buck, then lifted Lola against her. With Lola wrapped around her waist, Renee walked them forward until Lola's weight pressed against the door.

Renee took her in for a moment—Lola's flushed cheeks, her swollen lips, her serious eyes now clouded with lust. Renee could feel Lola's heartbeat, and it had to be beating in time to hers.

"I love you." Renee's voice was soft.

Lola's eyes went round, her mouth pulled into an O of surprise. "You do?" she whispered.

Something had broken open in Renee's chest. She hadn't expected to make that confession. She thought about how she loved Lola all the time, but that wasn't the same as *loving* her, was it? Now that she'd said it aloud, the words felt inescapable and honest and true. Tears prickled in her eyes.

"I do. I really do. I love you, Lo."

Lola cradled Renee's face in her hands, then gently kissed the tears from her cheeks. "So why are you crying?"

"I never thought I'd say that to anyone," she admitted.

Renee wanted to remember the look on Lola's face for the rest of her life: the way she seemed to glow, her warmth and her softness. "I love you too," Lola said.

They kissed again, deeply, until Renee's mouth made its way to the sensitive spot on Lola's ear that always made her gasp.

"Are you going to put me down?" Lola asked between breaths.

"No, never," Renee mumbled into her neck. "I love you, Lo. I love you so fucking much. I'm never letting you go. Oh—how was the meeting?"

"The meeting?" Lola tightened her grip on Renee's shoulders. "The meeting was good."

"Really? You told her what you wanted?"

"Yeah, I did. We talked and . . . and everything's good."

Renee's heart felt so full, she wasn't sure her ribs could contain it. She was sure that she'd never been this happy in all her life, that she might never be this happy again.

"That's my girl," Renee said. She lifted Lola off the door and carried her to bed.

29

In the days that followed, Lola was in a state of bliss. There was no other way to describe it. She felt almost woozy, like she was lost in a profoundly good dream. She and Renee couldn't stop saying those three words to each other. They couldn't keep their hands to themselves. They fucked in so many rooms of Lola's house that they spent the afternoon before the housekeepers came doing a thorough pre-cleaning, to be respectful—only to end up on the floor among the cleaning supplies.

But the moment Renee was out of Lola's sight, guilt sucked at her like quicksand. She had lied to Renee. That was unacceptable, but wasn't it an understandable mistake? Renee had just looked so expectant when Lola had walked into the house that day; Lola hadn't wanted to tarnish their perfect moment with disappointment. Anyway, Lola *would* tell Gloriana she'd made her decision—of course she would. Sometimes it felt like she already had! It would only take one little phone call to fix. Renee would never need to know that their wires had gotten crossed.

All the same, she still hadn't managed to correct the mistake. Her sister, Claudia, was coming to visit to do her interview for the film, and then Lola had a short trip to Fiji, where she'd been hired to perform at the birthday party of a daughter of some sheikh, no film crew allowed. Knowing they'd soon be apart, Lola was rightly focused on Renee, not dealing with Gloriana.

And there were songs to finish. Lola insisted that Renee not be present for the last recording sessions.

"I want you to hear the songs for the first time with me," Lola had explained.

"But I've already heard most of them!" Renee protested.

"Not the final versions," Lola said.

"*Lo*," Renee whined. "The film!"

"This is more romantic." Lola had hooked a leg over Renee's hips and straddled her. "What if I want to kiss you but Ackerlund's there?"

Renee's face fell, but they agreed to set up a camera in the studio that would record in Renee's absence.

It made it all the sweeter when Lola came home with the first song, "Starcrossed," completed.

"Seriously? I get to hear it?" Renee asked, eyes bright.

Lola nodded, grinning as she pulled Renee to the couch and cued the song on her phone. "Did you want to film this?"

"Yeah, we should." Renee's brow furrowed. "But maybe just for us, not for the film. We can decide later."

Renee positioned her phone to record, then cuddled against Lola on the couch.

Lola barely breathed as Renee listened, focusing instead on the changes in Renee's expression as she followed the lyrics. Lola already knew this song was a hit, but that didn't matter as much as Renee loving it. The melody built on the notes Lola had picked out on that old guitar at the lake house; the lyrics, a tapestry woven from the fragments of their early relationship, with lines like *We were dancing 'round, screaming out, What's going on?* and *You show up to work, wearing my shirt.* The chorus and bridge, and even the title, were callbacks to Renee's favorite, "Star Sign." More than that, it had amazing energy. The longing of the past barreled into the shocking gratification of *now,* of the first kiss, and the kisses that came after. Lola's voice launched into the bridge, singing,

Too busy watching the stars, I didn't see you watching me.
Now every time you touch me, I get a little more free.

Renee ran her hand up Lola's thigh. "Is that about me?" she whispered.

Lola leaned into Renee's grasp, then cupped her cheek and angled her in for a kiss. It was soft and slow. "The whole thing's about you."

"About *us*," Renee murmured against her. "Thank you for writing it."

Thank you. The words quivered in Lola's chest. No one else had ever thanked her for a song. Kyte had thought it was cool—although later he resented that her songs outperformed his. Lola's songs had delighted Ava, to the point that Lola had found herself screwing Ava with her own voice playing in the background, which was weird. Unsurprisingly, Ava had never appreciated how much care went into it.

But Renee did. Renee saw the effort, the love that went into the song. It meant something to her.

"Do you like it?" Lola asked.

"I love it. It's the greatest love song of all time."

Lola could feel Renee smiling as she kissed her.

They played it a few more times, at Renee's insistence, so she could listen to different parts more closely.

"That line, *Now every time you touch me, I get a little more free*, I hadn't heard that before," Renee said.

Lola grinned. "I changed that after New York."

"It's so good. I'd love it even if it wasn't about us."

"But it is."

"I wonder if anyone else will figure it out," Renee said with a wry smile.

"What do you mean?"

Renee shrugged. "Just like, all the little references that only we know. I mean, Ackerlund didn't get it, did he?"

Lola went still. Whether "Starcrossed" came out before or after she did, this song would launch the Lo-Lites into a frenzy—not to mention the LavaTruthers. They'd treat the lyrics like a mystery to solve—and they *would* solve it. They'd concoct theories based on photos of Renee and even write fan fiction; they'd go through everything Renee had ever posted online and find out what school her mom taught at. There would be stans and haters, and people who'd threaten to kill Renee if she hurt Lola. It had already started—Gloriana had shown her the proof.

Especially when the film came out.

"They'll figure it out," Lola said. "You get that, right? They'll figure *us* out."

"But that's okay now. You'll be out, nothing to hide."

Suddenly she wondered if this wasn't all a mistake. Renee wasn't prepared for what Lola was dragging her into. Lola's heart was racing. *Nothing to hide.* Once she did this, the one thing she'd managed to keep private would be exposed. Her whole life, her past, every song would be under the Lo-Lites' microscope again. Her skin crawled at the thought.

Renee reached for her. "Hey, what's wrong?"

"Nothing," she said. "I just got a little nervous, that's all."

"Nervous is normal. You want to talk about it?"

As Renee circled Lola in her arms, Lola tried to calm her speeding heart. "I'm okay," she said. "Really."

LOLA POURED A glass of rosé and handed it to Claudia, who was basking in the late November sun on Lola's patio. To Lola, it was a little chilly, but Claudia was always complaining about the cold in

Chicago. Lola was happy to brave the L.A. winter under a blanket if it meant making her sister happy. Everything was better with Claudia around. She had flown in for her interview with Renee tomorrow, but the trip would be short—she only had three days off from the hospital, in exchange for working Thanksgiving. They were getting in as much sister time as possible, so Renee was temporarily exiled to her hotel.

"Are Mom and Dad getting on camera for this too?" Claudia asked.

"No, thankfully," Lola sighed. It had been a point of debate in the earliest stages of planning. Micah proposed sending a film crew to Fellows. A visit to the childhood home was conventional for films like this, after all, but Gloriana had vetoed it. Over the course of Lola's career, they had both directed a lot of effort to steering Lola's mother away from the press. Her dad had no interest in that kind of thing, but her mom was unpredictable and craved attention. Lola didn't want to risk getting her in front of a camera.

"That's good," Claudia said. "It would have been funny, though, to see Renee interview Mom."

Lola's blood pressure spiked at the thought. "Why's that?"

"Mom doesn't exactly love Renee. She always complained that she had no respect for authority."

"She still doesn't." Lola laughed. "That's probably why I like her."

"How's it been having her around for the movie?"

"It's been nice." *Nice?* Lola bit the inside of her lip, hard, for a second, then added, "Actually, *nice* isn't the right word for it. There's something I wanted to tell you about that. So, Renee and I have been spending a lot of time together and we, um ... we kind of fell in love?"

Claudia's mouth hung open. "*Shut up*, Lola. Like—*Renee* Renee? Renee *Feldman*?"

"Yes, *that* Renee."

"You could be dating a god-tier celebrity, and you fall for the grumpy weirdo from next door?" Lola's expression went rough, ready to defend Renee, and Claudia burst out laughing. "Oh my god, your face."

"Renee's not the grumpy weirdo next door anymore."

"I saw her this summer—she's still a grumpy weirdo."

"She is, but she's not next door anymore. We basically live together."

"Like, here? In this house?" Claudia's head whipped around, like Renee was going to pop out from behind the box shrub.

"She's at a hotel right now, but most of the time, yeah."

"Wow, so this is serious."

"Claudia! I literally just said we're in love."

"You think you fall in love with everyone you date."

"Renee's different. She's just . . . completely different." A smile spread across Lola's face.

"Okay, okay," Claudia said, now grinning back at her. "It's taking me a minute to process, but I'm happy for you. Dating someone normal will be good for you."

"Why, to keep me grounded?" Lola laughed.

"No, that's your big sister's job. But your last relationship—if you can call it that—wasn't right."

"Renee's not at all like Ava. She looks out for me. You'd love how she handles Gloriana."

"She's hard on Gloriana? Maybe *I'm* in love with Renee Feldman." Claudia lit up. "How's she dealing with all this?"

Lola knew what she meant. The celebrity, the attention. The closet.

"That's the other thing I wanted to tell you. I'm going to come out."

Claudia stared at her for a beat, lost for words. Then suddenly, her eyes were shining, and she said, "Oh, Lola, are you really?"

"Why are you the one crying?" Lola asked, although her own eyes stung now too.

Claudia smeared away a tear. "Because I wasn't sure you'd ever do it."

"I've been talking about it for years," Lola protested.

"I know." Claudia pulled her into a tight hug. "I'm so proud of you."

Lola felt unexpectedly overcome. She hadn't doubted that Claudia would support her—she'd been the only person who encouraged her to go along with coming out even after Ava—but she hadn't realized how much she truly needed to feel that. It was like a knot in her chest had unraveled, and all the anxieties of the last few months—the writer's block, the film, all the reservations she had about coming out, and all the reasons to do it anyway—sprung free. Lola found herself sobbing into Claudia's shoulder, and Claudia petted her hair, like she'd done when they were kids.

When she finally caught her breath and pulled away, Claudia said, "Those didn't seem like happy tears."

Lola dabbed her under-eyes with her sleeve. "It's just a lot. Part of me knows this is what I want, but then when I think about it, I get so *scared*. I haven't really told Gloriana yet. I keep putting it off."

"It's not like you don't know what she'll say. *It's not the right time.*"

"Stop that. Gloriana looks out for me." Lola paused. "How am I supposed to know when it *is* the right time?"

"I can't answer that for you," Claudia said. "But with big changes like this, sometimes a time that's good enough is better than waiting for a time that's perfect. What made you want to do it now?"

"We wanted to do it in the film. I could tell my whole story, myself."

"Who's we?" Claudia asked.

"Me and Renee."

Claudia studied her for a moment. "Have you told her you're having second thoughts?"

Lola thought of Renee's eyes flashing when she talked about this vision for the film. She thought about Nash's blackmailer, and the difference between having your privacy ripped away and surrendering it. She thought about her envy of Saint Satin, and the longing she'd felt at her concert, and the fear that she wasn't queer enough. Beyond this decision lay terrifying uncertainty, like some bizarre interstellar landscape of abysmal trenches and glorious peaks and no oxygen, no safety, no way back.

"This is really important to her," Lola said.

"You didn't answer the question," Claudia said. "If Renee really loves you, she'll understand what you're feeling."

Lola forced herself to smile. "There's nothing *to* understand."

30

Renee was in love with Lola.

She'd said it out loud.

And it was fucking amazing.

Renee didn't know why she'd avoided relationships for so long, when they felt this good. For once, everything was going right. The film was a go—although she needed to put some serious editing hours in before she presented anything else to Dragan. It was already late November. Streamy's March deadline was coming up fast.

Claudia had come to visit. Though she'd known Claudia forever, Renee had felt that same pride she had with Tatiana Jones, like she wanted to prove she'd do right by Lola. She still had to figure out a way to tell her mom, and Kadijah. Kadijah would forgive her for being out of contact when they heard the truth. They'd never say the words *Walk Away Renee* again.

But Renee's happiness was interrupted: Lola was going to Fiji over Thanksgiving, while Renee stayed in L.A. It was as short as a trip to the other side of the world could be—but it would be the longest they'd spent apart since August.

After Lola's car pulled away from the house, Renee allowed herself a few hours of sulking, which felt terribly romantic. She'd never been in the position to miss the woman she loved before. She flung herself onto the bed, to smell Lola's scent on the sheets, then jerked off and fell asleep. The next day was Thanksgiving. It wasn't a holiday Renee cared much for, but she picked up some prepared food at Whole Foods for later and called her mom. Then she wandered into her office. If she was missing Lola anyway, she might as well try to go through some of the hundreds of hours of footage of her.

For once, work came easily. She started by building out an architecture for the plot. It would begin with Lola's writer's block, the sinister sense that she was on a career precipice that only she could see, then flash back to her childhood in Michigan—how Lola realized she was queer and the truth about the inspiration for *Seventeen Candles*. Then they'd jump to Lola's big break on *You're Next!*

She'd skim Lola's relationship with Kyte, to put the spotlight on how Lola had been pressured to stay in the closet and how it had affected her music. That meant spending a lot of time on the relationship with Ava: the oppressive secrecy, the feverish scrutiny from the LavaTruthers, the fear that dating a woman would destroy Lola's image. Then, the breakup, the canceled album, the arranged relationship with Nash. They would, of course, protect Nash's sexuality; he got enough out of dating Lola that it wouldn't need additional explanation. That story alone was nearly enough to make the film work—Renee had never seen a doc that pulled back the curtain on PR relationships.

Renee worked with manic intensity. Her only breaks were texting sessions with Lola. By the end of that first day, she had the core narrative structure and a mile-long to-do list. The next day, Renee played through the footage she'd use for a frame narrative: the writing and production of "Starcrossed." The final segment would hopefully be Lola playing the song live for the first time. The next day, she reviewed the interview footage she'd collected: Claudia, Gloriana, Nash, Jason St. Jude, and Ackerlund, among others. She raced through them at double speed, recording timestamps for anything salvageable. Her inventory was thin. The questions Micah had asked weren't exactly penetrating. She'd prioritize re-interviewing everyone important herself, and talk to everyone Micah had missed: Henry, Lola's head of security, and Cassidy—who saw more than she ever let on—and Tatiana Jones. And of course, they set aside several days for Lola to tell her story in front of the camera.

But the more Renee chewed the concept over, the more she couldn't ignore the other woman at the heart of it all: Ava Andreesen.

Renee devoted several uninterrupted hours to reading interviews with Ava, watching videos of Ava, looking at pictures of Ava until her eyeballs felt like hard-boiled eggs and her stomach roiled with bile and Red Bull.

As much as she resented this woman and the sexy gap in her teeth and the neat palindrome of her name, Renee needed to think like a filmmaker. Ava was central to the story. She was the woman Lola fell head over heels for, the woman she'd put it all on the line for. Ava had sucked Lola dry and broken her heart, plummeting her into a creative drought that nearly devastated her career. Viewers would want to hear from Ava herself.

Renee wasn't sure if Ava would want to expose a relationship they had tried so hard to hide. But on the other hand, would Ava even care? Ava had come out on live TV, casually mentioning her bisexuality while giving red carpet fashion commentary for the Emmys. From Renee's short interaction with Ava at the premiere, she expected Ava would seize any opportunity to put herself in the spotlight. She'd make herself the story's villain with ease, and everyone, not just the LavaTruthers, would understand the pain she'd caused Lola.

By now, it was well after midnight. Renee had consumed an unconscionable amount of caffeine and, over the last three hours, a bottle of rosé. She'd forgotten this feeling, how working could be so exhilarating, her brain energized even when her body was exhausted. She stood and stretched, a little dizzy. She wanted to talk to Lola about Ava—but they'd talked a few hours ago, when her day was starting in Fiji. It was the day of the party, and Lola would be away from her phone. Renee scrolled to the picture Lola had sent her that morning—or was it Lola's night? Renee wasn't sure—a rumpled selfie from the hotel bed, the sheet pulled down to show her gorgeous tits. She had a love bite on the underside of one breast. Lola had insisted on it.

So I can remember you.

Like you'd ever forget me.

Renee sucked in a breath through her teeth.

She wanted this film to be perfect for Lola, to tell her whole story. The parts about Ava would be upsetting for Lola, but it was Renee's responsibility, as a director, to manage that. Lola didn't have to be involved in the interview at all.

Renee stripped and crawled into Lola's bed, exhausted. Her eyelids heavy, she searched for Ava's Instagram page. A DM wasn't the most formal way to set up an interview, but surely it would take weeks of back and forth before Ava got in front of the camera—if she even answered Renee's message at all.

But the next day, when Renee woke and checked her phone, Ava had replied.

I thought you'd never ask.

31

Renee had expected that Ava would direct her to an assistant who'd send her jumping through hoops: advanced review of the interview questions, scheduling hell, an interview with one of Ava's people hovering nearby to cut it off if things got too real.

She had not predicted she'd be parked outside Ava's home on a Venice Beach canal that same afternoon.

She should have told Lola. Renee knew that. But Lola was on the other side of the world, where it was now the dead of night, and things had moved so fast. Ava had insisted that the interview happen that day: she was about to leave for London for two months.

Renee had almost declined. Two months wasn't forever—though it was the bulk of the weeks before Streamy's deadline—and London wasn't inaccessible. But the timing felt *right*. Renee would be underprepared, but so would Ava. It would be real, authentic. Renee scrambled to pull together her questions, check all the gear, make sure her batteries were charged, and get gas so she could sit in traffic out to Venice.

Ava answered the door in a fiery orange kimono with sleeves that swept the ground. Underneath, she wore a white bralette and tiny jean shorts, with a pair of leather ankle boots. Her blonde hair was tousled in the style of Jane Birkin and, aside from her smudgy eyeliner, her skin looked luminous. As she waved Renee into the house, the rings she wore on every finger glinted with the sparkle of real diamonds. Not that Renee had ever *truly* wondered what had attracted Lola to Ava, but five seconds into their meeting it was excruciatingly obvious: Ava was really fucking hot. Beside her, Renee felt trollish.

"Shoes off, please," Ava said in the entryway.

Renee struggled to balance her backpack and camera bag as she took an embarrassingly long time to wrangle off her Docs. It was hard not to see Ava's long, smooth legs, which seemed to go on forever between the boots she had not removed and the hem of her shorts.

While Renee was down there—the seconds stretched like taffy, her heel caught—she said, "Thanks for making time."

Ava watched her through her long eyelashes, her arms folded as she leaned against the wall. When she spoke, she revealed the signature gap in her front teeth. "It's no trouble. I've been hoping you'd get in touch."

At Ava's insistence, they'd film in her studio. She'd taken up painting, Ava explained, and was about to have her first show. Ava perched on a wooden stool, all elbows and angles. Her aloof, sky-blue eyes tracked Renee setting up the camera.

"We're rolling," Renee said. "Do you want a mirror check?"

Ava waved this off. "Let's get started. I'm really looking forward to this. No one knows Lola Gray better than I do."

Renee's eyebrow quirked at that. "Great. Can you explain how you know her?"

"We were best, best friends. As close as girl friends could be." Ava's eyes glinted as the hair at the back of Renee's neck prickled. Girl friends. Girls who were friends. "Although in the last year we've grown apart."

"Let's talk about how you two met."

"Yes, it's such a fun story. I was presenting at an awards show, and of course, all eyes are on you, but I could just feel her staring at me onstage! I had a laugh afterward. I said, 'That hot little pop star in the front row was undressing me with her eyes.' Then she won her little statue and came backstage and wanted to meet me. She had on that smile—you know the one? Where she just wants to make you happy?"

Ava paused, waiting for Renee's acknowledgment.

She cleared her throat. "I know the one."

"I thought so." Ava pursed her lips in satisfaction. "Anyway, Lolly—that's always been my pet name for her—Lolly and I were instantly infatuated with each other. She'd been running around with these silly boys and didn't realize how badly she needed some girl time."

Renee hadn't been sure what to expect of Ava. She hadn't told her that Lola would be coming out in the documentary. Because of that, she'd anticipated that Ava would give a wide berth to the truth of her relationship with Lola, but nearly everything Ava had said was laced with innuendo. Was it catnip for the LavaTruthers or meant for Renee, personally? Ava couldn't know that she and Lola were together now—could she?

"Your relationship—the friendship—got a lot of attention," Renee said.

Ava's eyes flashed. "The attention was the best part! Forgive me for being a little vain, but I loved that the two of us got people talking."

"Why do you think that was?"

"I suppose because we're such opposites. An odd couple. I'm known to be a bit of a wild child, and Lola—she's a good girl, isn't she?"

Heat flared in Renee's cheeks, but she gathered herself. "Sure, Lola's image is America's Sweetheart. That's something we're going to unpack in the film. Where that image doesn't overlap with the real person underneath."

"You think that it doesn't?"

Renee paused a beat, then said, "We both know it doesn't."

"What's your next question?" Ava asked.

"Can you talk about how Lola's changed or grown over the time you've known her?"

"I adore Lolly. I always will." Ava slung her wrists over her knees. "But I don't think she *has* grown all that much. Lola hates to take risks, but if you can't push yourself to try new things, you don't evolve. Lola, underneath it all, is simply so afraid of failing, of upsetting anyone, of being a little bit imperfect."

"No, that's not how Lola is," Renee said, though part of what Ava said resonated. "She's under a lot of pressure to fit this"—Renee tasted bitterness as she formed the words—"this good girl image. But that's not who she is."

Ava's dismissive laugh set off a burst of nausea in Renee's gut. "Who do you think came up with that image? Lola. Who gets out of bed and says yes to that image every morning? Lola. Who makes her money from that image? Lola. Lolly's a girl who knows what's in her interest."

"How can you say that when she was going to come out for you?" Renee blurted out.

"Oh, she told you about that?" Ava sighed. "Think about the terrible position she put me in. Hanging the responsibility for all her hopes and dreams on me, on our relationship. That wasn't fair. I knew enough not to take it seriously. What's that saying? If she'd wanted to, she would have."

"You don't know that."

"Don't I? Or did I miss her big announcement?"

Renee knew she should let it go, that this wasn't her fight, but instead she said, "You left her."

"I didn't have a choice, with what she was asking me to do! Her feelings had always been stronger than mine, and she knew it. I couldn't give her the kind of relationship she thought she needed." Ava fell silent for a moment. When she spoke again, her tone was different—drained. "You have to understand the reality of that relationship. For a whole year, Lola would barely be seen with me. She'd cringe if I looked at her too long in public, always texting her manager in a panic if someone took our picture. How could I have committed myself to something like that? I have to take her actions into account, not just her words. Otherwise, I'm the one who ends up hurt, and I'd rather do the leaving than be left."

"I don't understand how you can say that," said Renee, who understood leaving before you were left with every fiber of her being. "Lola wrote a whole album about you."

"About *me*? No." Ava laughed again, a sound Renee now found as harmonious as a cat vomiting. "Those songs could be about any of her boyfriends. Yes, she left her easter eggs about me in the lyrics, but forgive me if I'm not entirely moved by a consolation prize. Oh, don't look so outraged. Isn't it the same for you?"

Renee's eyes were wide. It was. It was exactly the same for her. "This album is going to be different."

"Let me guess, because she's in love with you and she's written you these songs and she's promised to go public? Tell me, which part sounds different to you?"

32

It was raining in L.A. when Lola landed, and traffic was a nightmare. The flight over the Pacific had been interminable and very dehydrating, no matter how many sheet masks she did. Now, she dozed in the backseat, dreaming of falling into Renee's arms.

Cassidy nudged her awake. The iPad was in her hands and a fearful look on her face. "Um, Lola? You should see this."

Moments later, Lola was on a FaceTime with Gloriana, tears streaming down her cheeks.

"How could you let this happen?" Lola cried.

Lola felt dizzy, like the ground had gone sideways. Staring up at her from Cassidy's iPad was a tabloid article about her and Renee. *Just between them? Lola Gray spotted canoodling with gal pal*, the headline read.

> Days after she ducked out of the premiere for then-boyfriend Nash Walker's box office smash *Fit to Live*, the singer was caught getting handsy with doc director Renee Feldman. In photos taken weeks before Gray and Walker announced their split, the "Just Between Us" songstress got cozy with the short-haired woman at a brewery in her home state of Michigan.
>
> "They were definitely on a date," said a beer lover who witnessed the couple. "Holding hands and everything."

> According to a source close to the star, the pair are just friends: "Lola isn't over Nash. She's been begging him to take her back."
>
> Representatives of Lola Gray did not reply to requests for comment. Renee Feldman could not be reached.

And the *photos*—Lola couldn't look away from the photos. They'd been taken on the street outside that brewery. A real date, with the girl she'd always dreamed of. Lola had felt so happy in that moment. She'd felt *safe*. She'd dared to pull Renee in for a kiss, and that beanie she'd stupidly been using as a disguise had fallen back and let her hair loose. It was undeniably her. The photos were clearly the moment after a kiss: their faces were only inches apart in one.

"I don't control the press," Gloriana said. "We tried to kill this, but we couldn't. I have to tell you that social media is really responding."

"I don't understand," Lola moaned. "They never ran stories this direct while I was with Ava, and she was famous. No one knows who Renee is. And why did they wait so long? The trip was two months ago."

"As I tried to tell you, they know who she is now," Gloriana said, a little sourly. "With Ava, you were careful. You weren't kissing her in the street."

Stupid, stupid, stupid. How had she let herself believe no one was watching? But then again, there really hadn't been any reason to think a pap with a telephoto lens would be tailing them in Petoskey, Michigan—and these were the work of a professional, not grainy phone footage, like the clip from Saint Satin.

The only silver lining, thin as it was, was that the pap had missed the kiss itself. He must have, since the tabloid hadn't released photos of it.

"We prepared a statement denying the whole thing. I'm sending it over now."

"Denying it?"

"It's standard 'nothing to see here': violation of privacy, respecting the breakup with Nash, you and Renee are purely professional."

"I don't want to say that," Lola said.

"Honey, this is the best way to take care of it."

Lola's nails dug into her palms. Gloriana knew the best way out of any mess. But Lola wasn't sure she could do that to Renee—or to herself.

Gloriana read the hesitation on her face. "Lola, this is getting ridiculous."

"Let's say nothing. A statement calls more attention to it. You already got a denial into the article—*a source close to the star* was us, right?"

That unnamed source had denied it by saying that she was desperate to get back with Nash. A few weeks ago, when Nash's scandal threatened to break, his people had asked if they'd consider reuniting the couple. Then, Gloriana had declined, but now it was clear the option was on the table again.

"Fine. But you and Renee need to start keeping a bit of a distance. I don't like the effect she's having on you. Renee has nothing to lose from this and you have everything."

"We're still filming," Lola said. *She practically lives with me. She sleeps in my bed. We're in love.*

"Then keep it strictly to filming. No more slipups, no more little dates. If I see you two together in public, Renee better be holding a camera. If she objects to that, I'd be happy to remind her that her contract allows us to terminate her at any time, and the production company owns her footage."

Lola's heart leapt to her throat. Renee couldn't lose this film.

"No, I'll explain everything to her," Lola said. "We'll be good, I promise."

"And on that point, given this development, I can't sign off on any sort of big announcement about you and your—" Gloriana fumbled for the right word. "About *you*. We don't need to stir things up right now."

Static crackled in Lola's ears. Gloriana was saying no. It wasn't the right time, again. But she'd already told Renee that everything had been approved! Renee was counting on this.

Lola was counting on this. She wanted to be able to kiss her girlfriend in the street and take her to an awards show and dance with her at Tatiana's next wedding.

Then again, Gloriana wanted the best for her. She had been there for her since the very beginning and Lola had always been able to trust her.

The truth was, a part of her felt relieved. Coming out was so overwhelming, so riddled with uncertainty. It would be so simple to avoid all that.

But Lola had promised Renee. She wanted to be the person Renee believed she was. She had to try being brave.

When she spoke, her voice sounded so small. "Coming out would do the opposite of stirring things up, wouldn't it? I mean, it would clarify things. It looks like I'm doing something queer because I am. I'm queer."

"I think 'bisexual' would be an easier phrasing," Gloriana said. "But we can decide on that when we work through the messaging— after the film's done, after the album. And hopefully after the world tour, because we don't want to limit ourselves there." Gloriana's tone softened. "Honey, you've been through so much recently. You're still fragile—maybe you can't see it, but I can. This isn't the time to make things harder than they need to be."

Okay but where are the photos of the actual kissing? ♡ 48.5K
Reply

↳ Came here to say this. ♡ 199

↳ this photographer missed the money shot? ♡ 154

↳ You all are disgusting ♡ 21

↳ Two women kissing disgusts you? ♡ 109

↳ Maybe the pap is gonna sell them for more $$ ♡ 1

↳ No photos of them kissing because they probably weren't kissing ♡ 89

↳ for real I'm so tired of Lola pretending to be queer ♡ 71

↳ Why would anyone pretend to be gay? ♡ 0

Lola's windbreaker tho 😭 ♡ 201
Reply

↳ Nooo the windbreaker is a total slay ♡ 20

↳ Vintage windbreaker is the queerest thing in these photos ♡ 99

She CHEATED ON NASH what a bitch ♡ 191
Reply

↳ I can't believe lola would do that ♡ 9

I just love seeing Lola so happy ♡ 2641
Reply

↳ her SMILE 🥹 ♡ 158

33

"Is that my girl?" Renee said as Lola entered the house. Lola's body flooded with hot, exhausted relief. She launched herself into Renee's arms and hugged her tight.

"I missed you," Lola said into Renee's shoulder. She was blinking back tears, still. She hadn't entirely stopped crying since Gloriana's call.

"It felt like forever," Renee said. "Kiss me?"

Lola rose up on her toes and kissed her, her lips firm and insistent against Renee's mouth. She needed it to mean something. It was the last kiss they'd share before she told Renee that everything had to change.

Renee broke the kiss and grinned. "You want to go upstairs?"

"I have to talk to you."

Renee's face fell at the wavering in Lola's voice. "What's wrong?"

Just then, Renee's phone buzzed on the hall table. Reflexively, both Renee's and Lola's attention snapped to the screen.

> You gonna ignore this too?

Renee had the pictures up in seconds. "Whoa."

"I know, I just saw it," Lola said. Panic thinned her voice. "My team got a denial in the article. Actually, they offered to put out a statement denying the whole thing, but we agreed that ignoring it is best—unless you want me to say something."

Renee looked up from her phone. "What are you talking about?"

"Like it's a violation of privacy or the photos were taken out of context or something. I know what you're thinking, but these things always blow over and everyone will forget about it eventually."

"You think *that's* what I'm thinking?"

Lola stared at Renee, her tired brain racing. She'd been certain Renee would be upset that their private moment had been thrust into the spotlight. She'd been trying to reassure her, but Renee just looked confused.

"I don't need people to forget about this, Lo," Renee said. "Yes, it's messed up. This isn't how I wanted everyone to find out we're together, but I don't want to keep hiding. People are going to find out soon anyway, with the film and everything." Renee thumbed through the photos again. "Honestly, we look really cute—although it's weird they didn't publish the actual kiss. What was a pap doing in Petoskey anyway? Maybe it was, like, a nature photographer in the wrong place at the right time."

Lola didn't know what to say. How could Renee talk about the photos like she might post them on Instagram, when that paparazzo could easily have blackmailed Lola, like someone just did to Nash? Not that Lola had told Renee about Nash's situation, but Renee had to know those things happened. The pap had obviously sat on the photos for so many weeks to sell them when it would really hurt. But of course Renee didn't understand. She didn't have Lola's status. She was, like Gloriana had said, a graduate student.

"It's better not to fan the flames of this kind of thing," Lola said. "Gloriana asked that for the time being, when we're in public, we keep it strictly to filming."

Renee started. "What the hell?"

"She doesn't want us to be seen out together unless you're with the camera, that's all."

"Oh, *that's all*?" Renee rolled her eyes. "Did you tell her to go fuck herself or should I? Oh—Lo, you *didn't*."

"Only until this blows over!"

"I don't want to wait to be seen in public with you until 'this blows over.' Can't your team build this into their twenty-step coming-out strategy?"

Lola's breath caught in her throat. She shrank under Renee's insistent gaze.

"They can, right?" Renee asked slowly. "They're on board. Right?"

Lola felt very far away from her body, like she was a balloon barely tethered to a weight on the ground. She heard herself say, "We decided to put the plan on pause."

Renee's whole body seemed to flare with outrage. "On pause? The hell does that mean?"

"We're not sure this is the right time."

"God, Lo, after everything, how can you still let her run you over like this?"

"I'm not! Gloriana looks out for me!" Lola said, bristling. "I don't think you realize how complicated this is for me."

"And I don't think that you realize that you've got a whole team of people who are making it as complicated as possible, to keep you in the closet, because they think it's better for your career."

"That's not true!"

"Then what is it? Is it you? Because you've told me a thousand times that you wanted to come out, and I believed you." Alarm flashed over Renee's face at Lola's cowering. "You did tell Gloriana that this is what you wanted. Coming out, the film. You told her like you said you did. Right?"

Lola couldn't think, couldn't figure out what to say. She couldn't lie, but the truth felt like a sword hanging over her neck.

"I should have fucking known," Renee moaned. She shoved a frustrated hand into her hair. "But it's exactly like she said: if you really wanted to, you would."

"Like who said?" Icy cold washed over Lola. "Who said that, Renee?"

"I was going to tell you about it today—"

"Did you talk to Ava about me?"

Renee's shoulders were immediately at her ears. Her gaze darted to the door, then the ceiling, then she said, "I should have discussed it with you first, but it came together so fast, and you were traveling. And I was going to have to interview her eventually."

"No. No, you weren't." Lola's chin was trembling, her words uneven.

"Right, *now* I won't have to, but this happened before I knew you would do a complete one-eighty on the project."

"This is my life!" Lola cried. "It's not some school project."

"The film is more than a school project!" Renee shouted back.

"I've seen what you've been doing, all the attention you've been getting. That's why you put so much pressure on me, isn't it?"

Renee's face had gone bright red. Angry—Renee was angry, which felt ferociously unfair when Lola was *hurt*. How could Renee expect Lola to shove her own pain aside just because Renee was bigger and louder and more demanding than Lola ever allowed herself to be?

"No," Renee said. "You don't get to act like I was using you when you told me this is what you wanted. But you were never going to come out, were you?"

Tears were streaming down Lola's face now. She didn't bother to wipe them away. "I would have done it for you."

"I don't want you to do it for me!" Renee roared. Lola flinched, but

Renee didn't stop. "Don't you get that? You're supposed to do it for yourself. How am I supposed to know what you actually want, when you only ever say what you think I want to hear?"

"*Renee.*"

"Were you faking all your orgasms with me too?"

"*Renee!*" Lola sobbed.

Renee folded her arms. Her eyes were dry.

"I've done nothing but try to make you happy," Lola cried. "What else do you want from me?"

"Nothing." Renee's voice was suddenly flat. "Look, I'm going to stay at the hotel tonight."

"Renee, no—stay, please. We can work this out."

"I need to clear my head." But Renee's face was still and calm. There was a distance in her that Lola had never felt before, like she barely saw Lola standing right in front of her. It terrified her. "I'll just grab some stuff so I can try to get some work done. See what I can salvage."

Lola stood frozen at the bottom of the stairs while Renee went up, then came back down with her stuffed backpack. Lola grabbed for her. "Don't go, please. I'll do anything you want, absolutely anything."

But Renee pulled her arm free. Her green eyes were cold. "What I want is for you to stop saying things like that."

When Renee was gone, Lola sank to her knees on the marble floor and cried.

34

Deborah stood in the kitchen, staring at Renee with her mouth hanging open. Renee was fresh from the airport, her bags dropped in the living room.

"You quit the movie?" Deborah said.

"I *resigned from the film*, Mom."

"You only gave it four months."

"It wasn't the right project for me."

Yesterday, Renee had left Lola's, gone back to her hotel, and packed. Anything that belonged to production, she left behind. Whatever was still at Lola's house, well, that was a loss, the rust-colored suit especially. Then she booked a flight home and spent her final hours in L.A. getting drunk in her room. She ignored her phone in favor of whatever was on TV until she fell asleep. The next morning, she cleared her notifications without even looking at them. At the airport, she'd fired off an email to Micah, Gloriana, and Lola officially resigning, and letting them know that everything she'd shot for them had been uploaded to production's server. As her plane took off, it was like drifting away from a dream that had gotten tedious. She was ready to wake up now.

Unfortunately, when that dream did end, Renee found herself in her mother's house in Fellows, Michigan.

"Oh, Renee," Deborah said in a freighted tone that managed to feel worse than her usual prodding. "Okay."

Where was the encouraging lecture, the well-meant but vaguely insulting professional advice?

"*Okay?* What does that mean?"

Deborah dried her hands on a Hanukkah dish towel. "It means, okay! If that's what you want to do, okay. It's your life, sweetie."

Now it was Renee's turn to stare.

Deborah continued, "If it's not going to be film, something else needs to get you on your feet. I don't want you living in my Airbnb for the rest of your life."

"I don't want that either!"

"Then we agree! Let's give it one month, till New Year's."

"Give what one month?"

"Finding your own place to live. I love you like crazy, Ree-Ree, but I don't want that love to hold you back. Free to fly means free to fall."

AT PRINCE'S, THE winter seasonal drinks were on the menu. Renee packed the grounds for an espresso shot with a little extra force. Kadijah had been promoted to Renee's old position as shift manager, which meant that when Renee had begged for her job back, Kadijah had been the one hiring.

The machine spewed out a frothy espresso shot. Renee sloshed it into a cup, topped it off with steamed milk, then dropped it on the counter.

The customer looked at it skeptically. "Is this cow milk? I ordered oat."

Kadijah slid down the bar from the register, a big customer-service smile on their face. "We'll remake that right away."

They grabbed a carton of oat milk and practically shoved it into

Renee's chest. "That's the fourth time this week, and it's only Wednesday! What's wrong with you?"

"Nothing's wrong with me," said Renee, who was pretty sure something was wrong with her.

"Then stop screwing up, because it would suck to have to fire you."

Zane glared at her from behind his stack of poetry books.

Renee's friendship with Kadijah still hadn't settled back into its old rhythm. Although they were working together again, they hadn't really caught up. Renee kept meaning to invite Kadijah for drinks, but moving home *again* hit her harder than she'd anticipated. She was never in the mood to do anything anymore. She struggled to get out of bed, felt sluggish no matter how many red eyes she drank. Maybe she just needed to reacclimate to Michigan's brutally cold and dismal December days, or for Kadijah to give her a break, so she wasn't on eggshells at work, or to finally find a room to rent.

Though maybe moving out would help. She wouldn't have to see the old Grigorian place every day. More than once, she found herself staring out the window at the patchy snow in the backyard and thinking of the meteor shower. Renee couldn't remember now what the memory used to be, before Lola's fantasy of it wormed its way into her brain.

She wasn't upset that Lola wasn't ready to come out. Renee would never have manipulated Lola into that for her own sake. But Lola had assured her, again and again, that it was what she really wanted to do. Renee, fool that she was, believed her. Now, Lola was convinced Renee had bullied her into it. Chronic people pleasers were like that. They thought they were putting everyone else first, but Lola had never understood how much energy Renee spent making sure that Lola was okay, because she could barely do it herself. It had been exhausting, and Renee had done it at the cost of ignoring her own feelings. If she hadn't, things probably never would have gotten to this point.

Renee couldn't believe she'd let herself fall so hard for Lola Gray.

RENEE IGNORED DRAGAN'S emails.

SHE FOUND A room to rent through one of Zane's friends. It was affordable on her wage from Prince's, but Renee knew the clock was ticking on her barista career. Deborah was right about that: if Renee wasn't going back to school, she'd have to find another job. But the prospect of making a LinkedIn profile and sending out cover letters made Renee cry. The tears seemed to spring straight from the doomful pit in her stomach. Actually, she'd been crying a lot since she got back from L.A. The tiniest things would set her off, like the way Dave looked at her mother or how the contestants on *The Great British Bake Off* were so brave about making their cakes.

The night before she moved, Deborah checked on Renee while she was packing, only to find her clutching a very high-end button-up shirt.

"That looks fancy," Deborah said. "Did you get that out in L.A.?"

"It's Lola's," Renee said weakly. "She loaned it to me, the first day of shooting."

"I don't want to pry but, Ree-Ree, is something wrong?"

Renee burst into tears.

She told her mom everything. Even though there was nothing Deborah could do to make it better—and Renee wasn't sure she understood all the nuances of the story—she made Renee feel steadier. Listening to her mom's gentle *mm-hmm*s and *Oh, Ree-Ree*s as she talked, Renee realized with a pang that Lola didn't have this, and never had. The idea of Lola going to someone like Gloriana for reassurance made Renee's heart ache, and she cried all over again.

"Am I—Am I like Dad?" Renee managed to ask.

"What does this have to do with him?" Deborah asked.

Renee scrubbed at her eyes. "I walked out, just like he did."

"Oh, Ree-Ree, no! Your father didn't just walk out." Her mother squeezed her hand. "Your father and I hadn't been in a good place for a long, long time. Don't you remember all the fighting?"

Renee stared at her mother. "No."

"Well, maybe you wouldn't. We tried to hide it from you, because you were a kid. Your father and I tried everything to make it work—two years of couples therapy!—and we just couldn't. I wasn't surprised that he left."

"You cut him out of all those pictures."

Deborah looked like Renee had pressed an old bruise. "Yes. I did, and maybe I shouldn't have. We'd been together for twenty years and I needed to be able to see my life without him."

Renee's eyes stung all over again. All this time, she'd believed there was some core part of her that was built to walk away. But if what her mom was saying was true, her father had made an effort that she'd never allowed herself.

She'd been doing to others the thing that had hurt her most.

"Leaving so abruptly was his decision. He insisted it would be easier on you that way. I knew better, but we weren't agreeing on anything back then. I know he hurt you, and I'm so sorry." Deborah leaned in and brushed a tear from Renee's cheek. "I can't even count how many times I've told him that he should reach out to you."

Renee's head jerked up. "You talk to him?"

"Only about you. You're his daughter, after all. I'm not going to excuse this whatsoever, because I don't agree with it, but he says he doesn't think you want to hear from him."

"I do," Renee said immediately. She'd spent years being angry with him, forcing herself not to care about a man who didn't care about her. Now, all at once, the need for him broke painfully to the surface, all the aching hurt of his absence. The anger was still there, but it was so clear now that it came from sadness.

Renee buried her face in her mother's shoulder. Deborah's arms were warm and heavy around her as she cried.

"I still think he's a dick," Renee choked out.

"That's fair," Deborah said as she rubbed Renee's back in soothing circles. "I'll tell him that you'd like it if he called."

RENEE ASKED KADIJAH to drinks right before Christmas.

"I want to apologize to you," she said.

Over their teal eye shadow, Kadijah's eyebrows arched deeply. "Do you now?"

"I know you're mad at me for ignoring you when I was in L.A. I wasn't trying to do that. Things got really complicated, and I was so busy filming, and there were the NDAs and Lola's privacy—"

Kadijah stopped Renee with a hand. "I was told this would be an *apology*. All I'm hearing is rationalization."

The impulse to argue woke like a beast in Renee's brain, but she forced herself to ignore it. "You're right. Can I start again?"

Kadijah, still dubious, nodded.

"I was ignoring you. It wasn't an accident. Things were complicated and hectic, and that stuff about the NDAs and privacy is true, but those are excuses. A lot was happening that I didn't know how to talk about. But instead of trying, I avoided it. That was wrong."

Kadijah fiddled with the garnish of their cocktail. "And stupid too, because I give really good advice."

Renee laughed, but a lump had formed in her throat. "You do. I'm kind of realizing that I tend to run away when things get uncomfortable. I'm sorry, Kadijah. You're one of my favorite people, and I hate that I hurt you."

"You did hurt me," Kadijah said. "You know I went through stuff too after you left? Zane caused all this drama in the polycule. He tried to bring in this girl who didn't want to get STD tested."

Renee mimed a gag. "Who has a problem with getting tested?"

"People who probably have STDs! But I had no one to bitch to about it, because you're the only one I can bitch to about the polycule, because you're not in it!"

"Do you want to bitch to me now?"

Kadijah waved this off. "We vetoed her polycule membership, but Zane sulked for weeks. And you know, being a manager at Prince's is actually really hard. I had to fire the guy I hired to replace you, and I felt terrible. And everyone complained about the shifts I gave them."

"I'm so sorry. I should have been there for you."

Kadijah let out a heavy breath. "Actually, I hate managing so much that it made me realize I can't spend my life slinging coffee. I've been talking to your mom about getting into teaching. She got me started doing some substitute jobs and I'm applying to programs."

"That's amazing—you'd be a great teacher. I can't believe I got so wrapped up in my own drama that I missed all that. The only thing I can do is promise to do better in the future."

"I appreciate that," Kadijah said.

"Are we good?" Renee asked, hopeful.

"We're good."

They hugged. Renee squeezed Kadijah hard, thankful to have them in her life—and that she'd put in the effort to keep them there.

As they settled back into their seats, Kadijah said, "Look, the apology's great and all, but you better be planning to spill the tea about Lola. I know something was going on with you two."

"Yeah, you and the whole fucking internet," Renee grumbled. "I'll tell you, but honest to god, you can't tell anyone. I wasn't kidding about the NDAs."

"I'll take your secrets to the grave," Kadijah said, with a hand laid honorably on their chest.

Renee took a fortifying swallow of bourbon, then glanced around the bar, like she'd seen Lola do so many times. "Lola and I, um, fell in love."

"You *what*?" Kadijah sputtered. "But then why are you—and she's in—"

"Everything got ruined." Renee was already blinking back tears.

"Tell me the whole story, from the beginning."

And Renee did, as honestly as she could. She told them about the one-night stand—to which Kadijah gasped, "I *knew* you got some at that wedding!"—and how they struggled to ignore their chemistry on set. She told them about the PR relationship with Nash, because the story wouldn't make sense to Kadijah without him, and the truth about #Lava. Kadijah said it was very romantic of Renee to sweep Lola away up to Michigan, even though Renee protested that she'd only had platonic expectations at the time.

"Didn't look platonic in those pictures," Kadijah said. "I still can't believe you got papped in Petoskey."

Renee grimaced. "I don't know how they found us. Only like three people even knew where we were, and one of them was my mom."

The next part was hardest to tell, because it had felt so good at the time that now the memories were painfully tender.

"When we got back, everything fell into place. Lola was writing songs again—really, really good stuff."

"Good stuff about *you*?" Kadijah said.

When Renee blushed, Kadijah hooted with glee.

"I know she was happier with me, but it was obvious that staying in the closet was holding her back. She'd told me a dozen times that she was ready to come out but had never found the right moment. So, I suggested she do it in the film."

Kadijah clicked their tongue. "I don't think you're supposed to suggest that kind of thing to people."

"I thought I was giving her the encouragement she needed. Her management was always against it, and she never stands up for herself. She seemed excited, but then put off talking to her manager for weeks." Renee pressed her lips together and took a deep breath. "But I was under pressure too. I was really counting on that angle for my thesis. Instead of telling me she was having second thoughts, she said her manager had approved it when she hadn't."

"Yikes," Kadijah said. "That's really shitty of her, but honestly? It sounds like neither of you did a great job communicating."

"I tried! What can I do if she's lying to me about how she feels? I just wanted to make her happy, and I really thought this would."

"Sometimes it's not about making your partner happy. It's about being there for them when they aren't."

As wise as that sounded, Lola had needed someone to tell her it was okay to choose herself. Renee couldn't bring herself to regret doing that.

"When those pictures came out, her manager talked her out of coming out, so the film was screwed."

"Which you got mad about."

"I was already mad." Renee downed the rest of her drink. "She'd just told me that she'd agreed not to be seen in public with me."

Kadijah's eyes went round. "She *what*?"

"It was her manager's idea, but she said yes to it. It really—it just really fucking hurt." Renee's voice broke. Kadijah reached across the table and squeezed her hand. After a moment, Renee said, "But I hurt her too."

She told Kadijah about interviewing Ava.

"It was a huge mistake. I was going to apologize, but I didn't get the chance. I mean—I walked out before I apologized." She glared at Kadijah. "*Don't* say it."

Kadijah's jaw was set, but Renee could still hear them, loud and clear, calling her Walk Away Renee.

"To summarize," Kadijah said, "Lola thinks you put her up to coming out for your film career, and even though that's not what you were doing, you basically proved her right by sneaking around with Ava and leaving her the minute the film hit a speed bump."

"It sounds pretty bad when you put it like that."

"That it does." Kadijah flagged down the waiter. "We're going to need another round."

35

Lola lay in bed. The room was dim. She didn't know what time it was—she'd flung her phone somewhere. Lola knew Renee wouldn't contact her, not after that blank look had fallen over her face. Lola had texted her frantically after she'd left, but then Gloriana called to say that Renee had resigned from the project. After that, it felt pointless.

That was three days ago.

Three days Lola had spent replaying their terrible fight. Even in her imagination, she couldn't convince Renee to stay. Lola had put Renee first, always. Done everything she could to make her happy: encouraged her talent, written her songs, satisfied her in bed. Done everything she could to make herself easier to love. But ultimately, Renee had asked for more than Lola could give.

She should have listened to Gloriana.

At least one person would be pleased that Renee was out of Lola's life, she thought ruefully. Gloriana never liked Renee and she had been right, as she so often was. Renee hadn't approved of the film she'd been hired to make—which Gloriana had known was absurd and entitled—so she'd convinced Lola to expose her secrets on camera instead. Now Lola was back exactly where she'd been a year ago: heartbroken, betrayed, and with an album full of songs she would never again bear to play. Her ever-after had been dangled before her, then snatched away, again.

At least she hadn't shared her new songs with the label yet. They knew she'd been in the studio, but the songs still lived on the drive she and Ackerlund shared, waiting for their final polish. Lola would be in deep shit for all the studio time she'd wasted, in addition to the canceled sessions. But at this point, who cared? It was only a matter of time before they sent her the ghostwritten roster of hits for her next album. All she'd have to do was record the vocals.

She pulled the blanket over her head and tried to sleep.

LOLA HEARD THE bedroom door open.

"I'm fine, Cassidy," Lola croaked.

"You're clearly not." That wasn't Cassidy's voice. Lola poked her head out of the covers and startled. The imposing figure of Tatiana Jones stood in the doorway. Lola pushed herself up in bed, suddenly conscious that she didn't know how long it had been since she'd washed her hair.

"What are you doing here?"

"What are *you* doing here?" Tatiana said, coming to sit on the edge of the bed. "Cassidy said you've been holed up in here for a week. She's worried. And so am I."

"Renee's gone." Lola fell back against the crumpled pillow. Her eyes welled with tears again at saying the words out loud.

"I know, babe." Tatiana kicked off her shoes and lay down beside Lola. "I'm so sorry."

Lola cried for a while, taking comfort in Tatiana's presence. It was nice to have someone there beside her. Cassidy had been sneaking nervously into the room to set pretzels and Gatorade at her bedside, as if Lola were a sick child, but Cassidy was employed as an assistant, not a therapist. Lola was grateful that Cassidy had reached out to Tatiana.

"Here's the plan," Tatiana said when Lola's tears tapered off. "I have four hours until I have a flight to catch. You're going to shower and I'm going to order pizza and milkshakes. And then you're going to tell me what happened. Okay?"

"Okay."

LOLA FELT A little more like herself for following Tatiana's instructions. They sat in the kitchen, and Lola managed to eat two slices of pizza, washed down with a milkshake. Then she told Tatiana the whole story: how Renee had played her for fame, convincing her to come out, and when Gloriana had asked Lola to walk it back, Renee had left.

"She didn't seem like a famewhore," Tatiana said with a shake of her head. "And I've seen my share. I'm a pretty good judge."

"I didn't think so either," Lola said. "But Gloriana saw it all along. She told me, and I ignored it."

Tatiana thought for a second. "If she was after fame, she did a shit job of it."

"What do you mean?"

"You were together for months and there's really only one article about the relationship. Usually people like that will milk their moment for all it's worth. It's like she didn't even have her own publicist."

"She didn't."

"A manager?"

"No. She had a thesis advisor. She's finishing grad school."

"Doesn't really sound like it was about fame." Tatiana's mouth puckered to one side. "Tell me again why you had that fight?"

"Gloriana saw those tabloid photos. We talked about issuing a denial. I convinced her not to, but we decided to put coming out on hold. She asked that Renee and I stick to filming in public, until the rumors blew over. I told Renee that and she lost it."

"But you think she was upset about the *movie*?" Tatiana pressed her hands flat to the counter and blew out a breath. "Look, I know you're not in the best place to take criticism right now, but you can be so oblivious, Lola. Of course she got upset—you basically told her you'd decided to hide your relationship indefinitely!"

"I guess that's true, but we'd already *been* hiding it."

"And she was happy with that?"

"She never *complained*," Lola said lamely. "She thought it was temporary. The plan was for me to come out in the documentary."

"Wow. Okay. That's a big step."

"I know. But it felt like the right time. And Renee was really excited about it."

"What happened? Gloriana changed your mind?" Tatiana asked.

Lola picked at her pizza crust. She was disappointed in herself that she'd agreed to Gloriana's suggestion to wait, but in that moment, the feeling of safety had been more powerful. "It was more like Gloriana saw I had some doubts, and she made it okay to lean into them."

"And you'd told Renee about those doubts?"

Lola thought back through their conversations. All the times she'd told Renee things were good, all the times she'd swept aside her anxieties in favor of bringing that smile to Renee's face.

"I didn't want to upset her," Lola admitted. "The film meant a lot to her."

"*Lola*." Tatiana's voice was stern. "I love you, but I'm dead tired of watching you do this. You get into these relationships and you slowly, slowly annihilate everything about yourself. It's like you'd give up everything to make the other person happy."

"That's what you *do* in a relationship," Lola said, feeling wretched again. "You're supposed to give everything, and I do—I did—and it wasn't enough. Why is it never enough?"

"Have you ever considered that *everything* might be too much? Maybe Renee didn't want you to put her first like that. Maybe she wanted you to be partners. That can't happen when you're trying to control how she feels."

"I wasn't trying to control how she felt," Lola sputtered.

"You just said you were trying to make sure she was happy all the time. That's impossible, and it isn't healthy. You can't keep putting everyone else first and then blaming them when you don't get what you want."

"Was that supposed to be encouraging?"

"If there's one thing I've learned in, like, hundreds of hours of therapy, it's that if you don't own it, you can't learn from it. I want you to learn from this. You worked so hard to get out of that hole you fell into after Ava. Do you really want to keep going back to that place?"

"No."

"Then don't. You're incredibly strong, Lola. You can do whatever you set your mind to. If that's lying in bed, fine. But it doesn't have to be."

LOLA HUGGED TATIANA tight, fully expecting to crawl back into bed once her car pulled out. But when she got to the top of the stairs, somehow she didn't want to.

Lola wandered into her studio, bright with the late-day sun. The light felt good.

Maybe Tatiana had a point. Had she been repeating the same mistake?

As crushed as she was, Lola wasn't about to rewrite history: more than anyone she'd been with, Renee had been invested in her happiness, and her comfort, and her pleasure, and she'd wanted Lola to be invested in those things too. With Kyte, she'd been too immature, and with Ava, too scared to ask for more. Renee had been different.

Had *Lola* been different?

In some ways, yes. She'd been more at ease with Renee, more open and trusting. But she'd hidden things from her too: how out of place she'd felt at the Saint Satin show, or the nagging worry that she didn't qualify as queer. She hadn't explained why Gloriana's arguments against coming out always somehow resonated with her.

Even if Tatiana was right that Lola should have shared her doubts with Renee, that wasn't the only problem. Renee had gone behind her back to talk to Ava, which Lola should never have needed to forbid.

And Renee had left.

The iPad on the coffee table lit up with a notification. Lola's heart lurched, then she chided herself. The text was from Ackerlund.

> Where you been?

Below his text were several notifications from their shared server. He'd uploaded new versions of four songs.

All her work, wasted, because she made the wrong choices again and again.

In case indulging her pain would lessen it, Lola played "Starcrossed" for herself. It was like watching a carousel of memories of Renee, each lyric bringing to mind a moment, a touch, a shared glance. She played it again, just to see if that helped or made things worse, then again. On the fifth or sixth listen, the lyrics started to lose their meaning, and she focused on the song itself. It was good—great, even. It had number one potential for sure. Now no one would hear it.

Lola played it again. What if she wanted people to hear it?

Maybe it hurt to listen to it now, but it would only ever hurt unless she turned that pain into something more.

Into something she needed for herself.

Lola looked around her studio at the relics of her life in music. Songwriting was who she was at her core. She wasn't going to give that up.

She listened to "Starcrossed" again, setting sentiment aside to concentrate on what others would hear. She could change the lyrics, remove all the sapphic easter eggs—but no. The song was right as it was. So what if it sounded a little gay? Lola *was* a little gay.

She replied to Ackerlund: Sorry I've been MIA. Personal stuff. But I'm back now. I'm sending Starcrossed to the label.

When Lola was starting out, her label had assigned her an A&R person to give direction on her sound and what songs to record and release, then he ran her music up the chain for approval. Now that Lola was a global star and one of the label's top artists, Lola developed her songs herself. When tracks were ready to go, Gloriana sent them directly to Jamie Alexander, the label's exec, for sign-off. Lola and Jamie had a good relationship—he usually let her do what she wanted, and she made him tons of money and hired his niece, Cassidy, as her assistant.

Before she could change her mind, Lola texted Gloriana on the iPad: Can you send the final version of Starcrossed to Jamie? She added a link to the file and hit send.

Immediately, an incoming call appeared on the iPad.

"Hi, honey, how are you feeling?" Gloriana trilled. Lola could hear sounds of the highway in the background. "Let me send a facialist over for a little pampering."

"No, thank you. I'm doing a little better. Tatiana was just here and—"

"That's fantastic," Gloriana cut in. "Listen, about the song. I can buy you more time, you don't have to rush into anything."

"I haven't released new music in almost two years. It's hardly rushing."

"I'm looking out for you, honey. You're so fragile and I know this song is about Renee."

"I'm not that fragile," Lola said, a little annoyed. "It's just a song. A great song. And I want to play it for Jamie, okay?"

"Absolutely. Will do. While I have you, there is some business about the film. I've reached out to Chess Waterston's people and he's willing to step in."

Lola's stomach turned at the thought of a camera tailing her again, this time with Chess Waterston's fedora behind it. Gloriana and the rest of the team wanted this film to happen so badly, but what had Tatiana said? To get what she wanted, Lola had to stop putting everyone else first.

"No," she heard herself say.

"No?"

"I was clear that I don't want to work with him—"

Gloriana huffed. "Is there another childhood acquaintance you'd like to dig up to make the film? This is urgent. We need—"

"I said no," Lola said decisively. "You know what? I think it's best to put the film on hold."

"On *hold*?"

"Like you said, I'm so fragile," Lola said.

"We've gone over this, Lola. We have an obligation to Streamy."

"Either the film's on hold, or I'll pay to break the contract."

"You'll *what*?"

"If they want me, they'll wait. That's the only way I'm doing it."

"Let me remind you that our objective here is to make sure that America remembers who Lola Gray is."

Lola frowned, though Gloriana couldn't see it. "When we release this song, they'll remember."

THE NEXT DAY, Lola padded into the kitchen while Cassidy was unloading groceries. At first, Cassidy went cautiously still, like Lola was a bird that might startle and fly away, then she held up a bag of fruit.

"I was going to bring you a smoothie, in case you're low on micronutrients."

Lola's heart swelled with affection at how Cassidy had cared for her the last few days. "I think I am low on micronutrients. Thanks, Cassidy."

"How are you feeling?"

"A little rough, but better. Could you ask the housekeeper to do my room? I'm going to be . . . getting back to normal."

Only when Cassidy perked up did Lola realize how worried she had looked. "I hate seeing you sad like that again."

"Me too," Lola said. "Thank you for checking in on me. And for calling Tatiana."

Cassidy ducked her head, smiling to herself, and focused on deseeding a papaya. Lola had always kept Cassidy at arm's length. But Cassidy had already seen Lola at her worst. Maybe Lola could let her in.

She leaned a hip against the counter. "Listen, I've been thinking—maybe I should release the album anyway? The songs are all about Renee, but they're good, right? I don't want to waste them. What do you think?"

"What do *I* think?" Cassidy's cheeks pinked. She stopped fussing with the fruit. "I think that would be great! I know those songs mean a lot to you. The ones I've heard are really good—I've been getting them stuck in my head all the time. But isn't the album shelved?"

Lola popped a strawberry into her mouth, the flavor bright on her tongue. "No, that's the Ava album," she said as she chewed. "But who knows, maybe I'll put some of the Ava songs on there too and write a break-up anthem or two."

"No, I meant, isn't *this* album shelved?"

Lola shook her head. "No, this time is different."

Cassidy's face had gone pale above the partly sliced papaya. "Lola, Gloriana told Jamie it was shelved."

Gloriana hadn't mentioned that. Maybe she'd assumed that's what Lola would want. She was probably trying to make things easier on Lola. But there was a doubtful pit in Lola's stomach.

"When did she do that?"

"Yesterday. He texted me because Gloriana told him there was going to be a new direction for the album, and he wanted to check if everything was okay with you—but I told him it was!"

"That's weird," Lola said uneasily. "I had just talked to her about playing 'Starcrossed' for Jamie. I was clear that I wanted to move forward."

Even if half of Lola's brain was churning out excuses for Gloriana, the rest of it recognized the simplest explanation. She needed to have a serious talk with her manager.

But Cassidy was looking wan. "I'm not mad that you talked to your uncle about me," Lola said. "I trust you, Cassidy."

Cassidy burst into tears. "You shouldn't! I'm so sorry, Lola. I feel terrible—"

Lola gently took the knife from her hand and sat her down on a stool. It took Cassidy a minute to calm down before she could speak.

"You know those pictures, from Michigan?" Cassidy hiccupped.

Lola stilled. "What about them?"

"It's all my fault—I think she sent that photographer after you."

"Who did?"

"Gloriana."

Lola's insides went ice cold. Gloriana had treated those pictures like a scandal—and the only way to clean it up was to do exactly what Gloriana said. To stop being seen in public with Renee. To put off coming out. To get back together with Nash. Lola pressed her lips together hard, then asked, "Why do you think it was her?"

"Gloriana called when you left and said she was worried, that it wasn't like you to run off, and—and she wasn't wrong, you never do stuff like that! She knew you had shared your location with me, and she asked me to watch it and to tell her if you went anywhere."

It all made sense. The paparazzo had no reason to be in a small town in Michigan, camped out at that exact brewery. And why expose the moments before and after the kiss, but skip the money shot? Lola Gray kissing a woman was a much bigger story than Lola Gray "getting cozy" with one. But now she understood: Gloriana had made sure they didn't have photos of the kiss. She'd only sold them the photos she could spin—as long as Lola fell back into line.

For years, Claudia had been telling her that Gloriana was manipulative and controlling, and Lola had defended her. Lola had thought Gloriana cared about her—Lola Grigorian, not Lola Gray. Worse, she thought Gloriana loved her. After all, Gloriana had been like the mother she'd always wanted. Lola had trusted Gloriana's guidance over her own opinions, because Gloriana had made a million good decisions that had built Lola's career. But now Lola could see that there was one issue they would never agree on. Gloriana would never be convinced that Lola should come out. Those paparazzi photos were proof. Yet as mad as Lola was over that, the fact that Gloriana had tried to block "Starcrossed" made her furious.

Gloriana could try to control Lola's personal life, but she could not fuck with her music.

Fresh tears spilled down Cassidy's cheeks. "I'm so sorry. I shouldn't have done it, but she said you could be in trouble."

"It's okay," Lola said. She hugged Cassidy tight. "This isn't your fault."

"Am I fired?" Cassidy sniffed.

"No. You're not."

LOLA BIDED HER time, though not because she expected Gloriana to correct her mistake and send the song to Jamie.

Lola had known immediately what she wanted to do, like a lump of lead in her belly. That certainty felt unfamiliar. She called Claudia to talk it all through, though as usual, her sister only ever encouraged her to follow her own heart. She talked to Tatiana, who had professional insight to share, and a satisfying string of profanity. Still, Lola had never made a decision this huge without talking to Gloriana first. It felt strange and scary to act on her own—but that didn't mean it wasn't right.

Lola also waited because she had a lot of planning to do. Cassidy, who knew a lot about the music industry and had apparently been underutilized coordinating the dry cleaning, helped. Lola made calls to her accountant and her lawyers, people she hadn't spoken with directly in years. She even wrote the start of a new song—her first female empowerment anthem.

Part of Lola wished Renee could see her now. Those final words—that she wanted her to stop saying she'd do anything that Renee wanted—still scalded like a fresh burn. But Renee had been right.

As Lola's car pulled up to Gloriana's office, Cassidy—clutching her phone with her usual intensity, but with an added dose of impish excitement—said, "Ready?"

Lola nodded.

Cassidy's fingers flew over the screen as she changed the password and email contact for Lola's Instagram account. "Done. The comms team won't have access now, but the account might get locked. Here, you should do it."

Cassidy held out the phone to Lola. The post was queued up. All Lola had to do was hit share.

A satisfied grin spread over Lola's face. She tapped the button, then stepped out of the car and into the hardest conversation of her life.

THE ELEVATOR DOORS opened onto a large silver Christmas tree decorated with ornaments representing the agency's clients. Lola spotted her face bobbing on a branch and, on impulse, yanked it off.

"Ms. Gray!" The receptionist choked a little on his iced coffee. "I didn't know you were coming in—"

Lola didn't force herself to smile. It felt good. "I need to see Gloriana. Now."

The receptionist clicked frantically around his screen. "She's in a meeting—"

"I'll wait in her office while you pull her out. I know the way."

Lola headed down the hall, half expecting the receptionist to stop her. But of course he didn't. She was Lola fucking Gray.

A few minutes later, Gloriana strode through the glass door of her office. "Lola, what a nice surprise!"

Lola had seated herself on the couch and didn't rise to cheek kiss Gloriana as she normally would have. Gloriana stood awkwardly for a second, then sat opposite Lola.

Lola gave Gloriana a tight smile. "What did Jamie say about the song?"

"Lola, honey, you didn't have to come down here for that. I know you've been having a hard time." Gloriana's tone was laden with the affected sympathy that Lola had always misconstrued for the real thing.

"That's true," Lola said. "Yet here I am."

Gloriana pressed her hands together thoughtfully. "Jamie liked the song. Anyone would—it's fantastic. But he had reservations about some of the lyrics and how they'd be interpreted, and whether that interpretation is consistent with the Lola Gray image."

"How so?"

"Well, we were hoping the fans would understand that these songs are about Nash, and some of these lyrics don't make sense for him. Like this line about your *love interest* wearing your shirt."

"The song's not about Nash."

"Exactly," Gloriana said as if Lola had agreed with her. "With a few tweaks to the lyrics, they'll really love it. I have a list somewhere here of the lines to change. The label is fine with you taking more time. I have that sorted already."

"Gloriana," Lola said heavily. "I'm not changing my lyrics because you don't like them."

"It's not me, honey. I support your vision, I always have, but the label—"

"I don't pay you to lie to me." Lola barked a laugh. "Actually, I guess I have been. But I won't anymore. I know you didn't send the song to Jamie. I know you told them the album was on hold."

The barest flash of surprise crossed Gloriana's expression, which, given how immobile her facial muscles were, Lola counted as a victory. "I did ask them for more time, that's true. But I did that for you, so you could heal. I'm looking out for you."

"Were you looking out for me when you sent that photographer after me in Michigan, then sold the photos to a tabloid?"

Gloriana flinched, but quickly smoothed it over. "I—well, yes, I was."

Anger gathered hot and hard in Lola's belly. "Explain that to me."

"I saw through that girl the minute I met her. Renee was using you. You're a star, Lola, and she was nothing. She got her claws into you at that wedding, then she wormed her way into your life. You couldn't see it, but you started acting different. I tried to warn you, but you were under her spell. I thought if you got a taste of the future that Renee wanted for you, you'd see." Gloriana's eyes were shining, and her hands spread, looking like some blameless saint. "You're family to me, Lola. I know you're hurt and I'm sorry, but I'd do anything to protect you, and I won't apologize for that."

Lola paused a moment. It was strange, how plain it now was that Gloriana manipulated her. She could feel it working, like a psychological trip wire, triggering the relief of receiving help from someone who loved you. Now she knew it wasn't real.

Gloriana was still looking at her with those righteous, loving eyes. She truly expected Lola to forgive her.

"That's not how it happened," Lola said.

"Of course it is." Gloriana's face softened into gentle confusion.

"No. There was nothing going on between me and Renee when we went to Michigan. We'd fucked once, that's all." Lola relished the edge of rough language on her tongue. "She took me out of town, as a friend, because I needed to get away. There was no reason to worry that she had her *claws* in me, but you still had us followed. You knew I didn't have any security with me, and you sent a pap after me. And then you waited two months to leak the photos, for a time when it made sense for you."

"For *me*?"

"Stop making that face!" Lola snapped. "Take responsibility for what you did. I told you I wanted to come out. It was out of your hands, and you knew that, so you used those pictures to stop me."

Gloriana stood and smoothed her skirt. "Lola, you're going through a lot right now, so I'll do you the courtesy of forgetting this conversation. Head home and get some rest. We can speak again in a few days."

There was a lot Lola wanted to say. She wanted to explain to Gloriana the yearslong pain she had been in—a pain she had accepted—of denying herself. How wounding this betrayal was, how she wasn't ungrateful, how Gloriana needed to let her grow up. But explaining it would only create the impression that her experiences were open for debate, and they weren't. Gloriana wasn't her mother. She was her manager, and the clock on that relationship was quickly running down.

Lola stood as well. "I will head home. But before I do, I should let you know that I'm terminating my contract with you, effective immediately. My lawyers will be in touch. Let's run all communication through them. It'll be simpler."

Gloriana started. "Lola, no, that's—what are you saying? Let's talk about this—"

"We just did. But I want you to know that you were family to me too. I guess that doesn't always mean as much as we'd like."

Lola paused with her hand on the door. Even now, Gloriana didn't quite look upset. That figured. In all the years they'd known each other, Gloriana had so rarely seen Lola resolved.

"I was really happy with her. That's why I was acting different," Lola said. "Goodbye, Gloriana."

In the elevator down, the emotion hit her all at once. Heart racing, sweating, vision blurring, nervous system shrieking. She made it to the car. Cassidy was waiting, staring into her phone.

"Did it go okay?" she asked.

Lola released a deep breath.

"Not really. But it's done." Lola gestured to the phone, eager for a distraction. "Is *that* going okay?"

A grin lit up Cassidy's face. "Oh, yeah. More than okay."

🚨💥 NEW LOLA MUSIC 🚨💥 this is not a drill!!   ♡ 92.2K
Reply

↳ Where? There's nothing on Spotify   ♡ 172

   ↳ She posted a clip on her Instagram   ♡ 74

↳ merry Christmas to us!   ♡ 152

When's the full song dropping   ♡ 45.6k
Reply

↳ In January, it says in the insta post   ♡ 36.0K

↳ This chorus is killing me!!!   ♡ 151

Who is she singing about? Nash?   ♡ 2704
Reply

↳ Ava!!   ♡ 500

↳ me lol   ♡ 2

↳ This doesn't have nash vibes   ♡ 9

I am crying you guys I'm so happy she's back she's been through so much   ♡ 21.8K
Reply

↳ Except she literally hasn't. What has she been through?   ♡ 103

   ↳ The breakup with Nash!   ♡ 51

I'm getting married in may and if the full song isn't released by then I'm going to actually die   ♡ 4
Reply

36

When the song came on, Renee was shoveling ice into a cup. The opening notes hit her so hard, she flung ice cubes all over the floor.

"Excuse me?" Kadijah said from the register.

But Renee didn't hear them. She knew that building melody—then Lola's voice came in.

Too busy watching the stars, I didn't see you watching me.

"Holy shit," Renee breathed.

Kadijah turned to her. "Oh my god, is this . . . ?"

Renee nodded. Her eyes felt round as dinner plates. Her hand still gripped the ice scoop.

"Uh, is that my iced coffee?" the customer said. Kadijah grabbed the half-finished drink from Renee so she could listen.

It was hard to explain the feeling in her chest. It was like a bird with a half-broken wing had taken flight anyway, swooping around with painful joy. Maybe Lola had changed the lyrics—but no, she hadn't. Every reference she'd woven in was still there.

How long have we been in the middle of our love story?

All at once, Renee was transported back to Lola's studio, dancing while Lola played guitar. To that night in the hammock, when Renee had realized she was falling for her. To their first true kiss under the stars, then the swell of happiness first thing in the morning at waking up beside her.

Now every time you touch me, I get a little more free.

When Lola had played her the finished song, Renee had wondered if people would know it was about the two of them. Hearing it now, the question felt inconsequential. Her name was buried in its DNA.

Also, it was still a banger, the kind of song that wouldn't just be a hit this year, but that she'd be hearing in grocery stores in two decades.

"Are you okay?" Kadijah asked as it ended.

Renee tried to breathe normally. "I think so."

"Some of those lyrics were—wow. The LolaGBTQ girlies better strap in."

"I can't believe she released it." The way they left things, Renee had assumed that Lola would do what she had with the Ava songs. She never imagined that Lola would move ahead with the most queer-coded song she'd ever written. She *really* couldn't imagine Gloriana being okay with that.

"New Lola Gray album announced for later this year!" Kadijah read from their phone.

Renee grabbed Kadijah's phone and read the article. Surprise single dropped on January 8 . . . full album coming . . . tour to follow . . . Gray parted from her longtime manager Gloriana Catalano in mid-December.

"She left her manager," Renee breathed.

"The evil one? Yes! Oh my god, Renee, do you think she released this song as, like, a secret message for you, because she wants you back? Like a declaration of love?"

Renee only needed a second to think about this. "It's a cute idea, but definitely not. She released this song because it's amazing, and she worked her ass off on it. If Lola wants to say something to me, she has my number."

Alejandro called a few days later.

"What's good, Renee?" he said. "How's Michigan? I bet you miss the sun."

They chatted about the Lola doc—it was on indefinite hiatus last Alejandro had heard—and the work he was picking up. He took it in stride when Renee admitted she wasn't on another film, and getting back on her feet as a barista.

"Hit me up if you head back to Cali. I'll put out feelers for camera operator gigs."

"Camera operator?"

"I know you're into the directing, but you're a boss behind the camera too. I'd vouch for you anytime."

"That's not really—" Renee began, but stopped herself. She'd meant to say that she was interested in serious directing, and her priority was completing her MFA. But if Renee was honest with herself, that wasn't true. Her thesis simply did not exist. It never really had. She couldn't rightfully claim that it was a priority when she'd spent the last month ignoring Dragan's messages.

The truth was, Renee hated her MFA program. The atmosphere of hypercritical destruction, the pressure to produce unwatchable art films, the toxic trauma-bonding among her cohort. In three years, she'd barely created anything that she actually liked. She'd barely created anything *at all*. Alejandro had taught her more about the actual practice of filmmaking in a few months than Dragan ever had, and Alejandro had learned it all on the job.

"Actually, I might be into that," Renee said.

They talked it through for an hour: what roles would fit Renee's skills and interests, how to get jobs and join the union. Alejandro promised to connect her with some buddies who were working on their own projects on the side.

It wasn't a plan, but it was a path she could take, if she wanted it.

Three days later, Renee withdrew from her MFA before the spring semester deadline. She'd talked it through with her mom and Dave. They agreed there was no shame in not finishing the degree if it wasn't the right fit for her. Renee was aware that it was only possible to have this conversation at a sane emotional level because the money she'd made on Lola's film had made a considerable dent in her debt, even without finishing out the contract. Still, the loans for her tuition were a mistake she'd bear the costs of for a very long time.

Her plan was to take a few months to save money, then head to L.A. and build up her industry experience. Her income from Prince's wouldn't be enough, so she put together a website for her own videography business. It would be temporary, but her rates were the lowest in the area, so she hoped to stay busy. Deborah had already set her up with a first gig at a bat mitzvah.

She forced herself to email Dragan. His reply was terse, mainly about administrative processes, and concluded with the very polite fuck-you of *I wish you the best*. That was fair, Renee supposed. She really had wasted a lot of his time.

37

"So let's talk about concepts for the 'Starcrossed' music video," said Eli, Lola's new manager. It was mid-January, and they were in his office. With its exposed brick and extremely large number of well-tended plants, it could not have been more different from Gloriana's glass box. "The song is doing fantastic. The leak created phenomenal buzz, and now that it's officially released, the fans are living for it."

Before firing Gloriana, she'd posted a clip from the "Starcrossed" demo on her social media as a bit of insurance: Jamie Alexander, or anyone else, couldn't force her to change the lyrics once they were out in the world. She'd called Jamie a few hours later—the song was already viral on every app—and braced herself for his reaction, since leaking her own music was definitely crossing a line. To her surprise, he'd loved her "stunt" and her evolved sound, saying, in his unvarnished way, "It's a little sexy. That's good. You've been writing these love songs for virgins for too long." He wanted it up on all the streaming services and a music video ASAP.

But first, Lola needed a new manager, fast. Eli had come on the recommendation of a few of her industry friends. She'd signed a contract with him not as a green seventeen-year-old, desperate for her break, but as a superstar. She'd paid Gloriana a grotesque sum to walk away from everything, including the ventures in which she'd had partner status, like the production company. She'd lost everyone who had worked under Gloriana: her publicists, social media, creative consultants. Everyone except Cassidy, who'd stepped into a chief-of-staff role with aplomb.

"Do you have anything in mind for the music video?" Eli asked her now.

"Only that I don't want to play one of the love interests," Lola said. She'd done that in most of her videos—acting as herself falling in and out of love, with actors cast as her exes. She had never minded it before. But pretending to be in love with anyone who wasn't Renee, especially for "Starcrossed," was beyond her.

Lola missed a million things about Renee. Anything could set it off—having cold toes that she wanted to worm under Renee's leg on the couch, expecting to share a knowing glance with her across the room and finding no one there. Lola missed being dragged from her work when she hadn't realized it was already the middle of the night. She missed Renee's fingers slipping into her, the way she had only ever looked starstruck when Lola had just made her come.

"Great, that makes things simpler," Eli said.

Lola's eyes narrowed. She'd disclosed her sexuality and the story behind this album in the final stage of their NDA-clad interview process. Eli was gay himself and had managed the coming out of a few other clients. He'd assured her that he would support whatever she wanted. But he still had to earn her trust. "What do you mean?"

"Well, assuming you'd want a female love interest, we'd need to move more quickly on a coming-out announcement, so we beat the music video release. To be clear, I am more than happy to do that, but I don't want you to feel pressured to take things too fast, simply because of the music video timeline.

"Unless that *is* what you want," Eli added. "If it is, say the word. Like I told you, this decision is fully yours, and I respect whatever you want to do."

Lola's heart was beating in her ears. She could tell that if she wanted to go public that same afternoon, Eli would leap into action, no questions asked. That was supposed to feel good.

But it didn't. Her pulse was racing and her breathing was getting shallow.

She'd imagined that firing Gloriana would magically simplify everything, like her homophobic manager was the only thing standing between herself and freedom. But in the last few weeks, without Gloriana's interference, she'd found herself freezing up whenever she thought about coming out. The reality was, the obstacles that Gloriana had given a voice to were still there: the label's reaction, the risk of rejection by her fan base, the pressure from the media, the effect on her business. Eli assured her that they'd worry about all that after the fact, that the most important thing was what Lola wanted. He didn't understand that what Lola wanted was to find the perfect moment, when all those problems would be minimized.

Lola missed Renee in moments like these most of all—when her emotions were messy and conflicting, and she wasn't sure how to navigate them. The irony wasn't lost on Lola that this was exactly what had driven Renee away.

Alone the night she'd fired Gloriana, she'd been elated, proud of herself, a little terrified, tremendously sad, and guilty. She had celebratory calls with Claudia and Tatiana, but she hadn't explained everything she was feeling. It wasn't that they wouldn't understand. It was that the person she wanted to share it with was Renee. Renee would have rubbed her back while she cried over firing the woman who had screwed her over. Renee would have reminded her to breathe. Renee would have flashed that crooked smile and told her she was proud of her.

Lola had almost called her then. She'd even pulled up Renee's number on her phone. But she didn't. Her realization had come too late. Now, she was on her own.

"No, you're right," Lola said. "I don't want to rush anything just to make the music video work."

"Great," Eli said, pulling up a slide deck on his laptop. "I have a concept sketched out here. You're a celestial goddess of love—very pretty and romantic, and you're in this beautiful temple looking at these star-crossed lovers down on earth. We'll do mainly queer couples, to emphasize that aspect of the song without bringing the focus on you personally."

Lola stared at the rendering of herself in a Grecian temple on the moon with a growing knot in her chest. It was dreamy and would make a lovely video. She couldn't help but think that if Renee was here—if Lola hadn't done what she did—she wouldn't be left watching other people's love stories from afar; she'd be living her own.

"I don't know," Lola sighed. "I need to think about it."

"Sure, it's up to you."

Just like everything else.

Is this new Lola song queer-coded or just queer? ♡ 22.7K
Reply

> You CANNOT tell me she's singing about Nash ♡ 179

> lesbo written all over these lyrics ♡ 375

> This song inspired me to confess to my crush and now she's my girlfriend 🖤 ♡ 2614

>> Omg so proud of you! 🥹🏳️‍🌈 ♡ 64

>> So jealous I wish I could do that ♡ 2411

I am dead tired of this queerbaiting from LG. ♡ 3629
Reply

> Thank you for saying this! The queer community has supported Lola SO MUCH and at this point I just feel used ♡ 252

>> She doesn't owe "the queer community" anything ♡ 89

>>> Except she literally does since she makes money off us ♡ 107

> A person can't queer bait. She's not a shitty TV show. ♡ 36

>> She's making us think she's queer when she's not, that's the definition of queerbaiting ♡ 6

> This is really hurtful. Maybe she can't come out ♡ 569

>> She's lola fucking gray? Why can't she? ♡ 68

>> Literally one of the most powerful women in the music industry. She can do what she wants. ♡ 378

I'm dying over this song, Lola sounds sexy as hell ♡ 18.6K
Reply

> lola hit me with your car! ♡ 5420

This woman needs to stop. Don't put a queer identity on like a costume then take it off when it's convenient ♡ 13.2K
Reply

> For real if you care about queer artists, then support artists who are actually queer ♡ 4813

> I'm done assuming this woman is in the closet when she's barely an ally ♡ 619

I will die on this hill, Lola Gray is queer ♡ 7257
Reply

> hope u made ur peace because she's never coming out ♡ 5624

> I don't get it if she was queer why not just say that? ♡ 43

>> Bc she's not really queer, that's what we're trying to say ♡ 10

> She's straight until the Personal Life section of her wiki page says otherwise ♡ 183

this whole conversation is so toxic and homophobic ♡ 1985
Reply

> THIS! ♡ 12

38

Huddled under a faux-fur throw on a flight to New York, Lola scrolled through video after video by creators with pride flags in their usernames. She wanted to watch them herself, even though Cassidy and Eli strongly discouraged it. It was a small number of queer fans, Eli argued, who were up in arms about "Starcrossed"—though, in the two weeks since the song dropped, they'd only gotten more outraged.

Lola dug a nail into an already-inflamed cuticle as she watched another critique. Lola Gray had been leading queer fans on for years, the creator argued, hinting at queerness just enough to stir her fans into a frenzy for her own clout. But she didn't see herself as part of the queer community. If she was one of them, wouldn't she come out and say it? Her queer fans didn't want more hollow, queerbaiting songs like "Starcrossed." The commenters agreed.

Tears stung her eyes, but she couldn't stop. Lola had taken a lot of criticism in her career. She had legions of haters who acted like despising her was a personality trait. She'd gotten death threats. She had critics who treated reviews of her albums like an exercise in creative insults.

This felt worse than all of it: a rejection from the community she so wanted to join, but hadn't allowed herself to approach.

It was wrong, obviously, to pressure anyone to come out. These same fans had done just that for years, and Lola had resisted. They'd said that it would mean something to them for Lola to come out. She couldn't blame them now for accepting as truth what she'd always projected in her image.

Cassidy fell into the seat opposite Lola and passed her a tissue. Lola blew her nose loudly.

"Some of them are defending you," she said, and handed Lola her phone.

In the video, a young woman argued passionately that Lola had the right to be closeted, that she was doing her best, and everyone's coming-out story was different. Her own story, the creator said, had been hard. She was eighteen, from Missouri, and her parents had kicked her out when she came out as trans; now she was starting community college living with friends.

Lola's tears stopped. Suddenly, she felt too hot under her throw, in her label's jet.

She looked Cassidy in the eye and said, "This is *ridiculous*."

"What?"

Lola thrust the phone back at Cassidy, the throw falling to the floor. "This is a *teenager* who's practically *homeless* because her parents can't deal with the fact that she's trans, and she's spending her time and energy defending me? I'm *Lola fucking Gray*! I should be defending her."

A wave of self-disgust crashed over her. For years, she'd been so obsessed over what coming out would mean for herself and her career that its significance for anyone else was an afterthought. She was terrified that the queer community would reject her and, now that they had, she had to admit they were right. She'd never done anything for them. It was just like Chloe had said, when Lola was meant to be the one doling out advice: queer women in the public eye had a responsibility to be visible. Lola convinced herself that giving to charities and posting pride-month messages was enough. That had been naive—no, worse, privileged and ignorant. She'd never allowed herself to connect to the problems of the queer community, because she could hold herself separate from it. She'd had the audacity to sulk when she didn't feel accepted, when she'd only been brave enough to call herself queer for a few weeks. And through all that, her queer fans stood by her. Those fans deserved more. They deserved to find solace and joy in her music, and to save their energy for fights that mattered.

"DM that creator and ask what she needs. Rent money, tuition. Anything," Lola told Cassidy.

"For real?" Cassidy said. "Cool."

If she wanted to be part of that community, to be accepted by it, she had to stand up for it. She had to give them something in return.

"I want a meeting with my accountant," Lola said. "Today."

39

Renee booked a glitzy Sweet Sixteen for mid-February on a word-of-mouth recommendation after her first bat mitzvah. It felt good to be filming again, now that she wasn't racked with guilt and stress. Sure, the videography of this party wasn't making it to the Criterion Collection, but it *mattered* to these people. The birthday girl cried with happiness, her friends showered her with hugs, and her dad gave a speech about how proud he was of the young woman she was becoming, which brought a tear to Renee's eye too.

Once the dancing started, the DJ played a lot of Lola's songs. Renee just clenched her jaw.

When "Star Sign" came on, the girls went bananas.

Renee willed herself not to avoid the pain of hearing it. She trained her camera on the birthday girl, capturing how she and her friends sang every word.

Then "Starcrossed" played. Of course it did.

For a moment, Renee was lost in memories. This song was precious, and like most precious things, Renee's love for it threatened to overwhelm her.

But when she forced her attention back to the action on the dance floor, Renee found herself grinning. The girls were really losing it now, the boys forgotten. They were grabbing each other's hands and spinning in circles and clutching their chests as they belted out their own hopes of finding love like Lola had.

The song brought them so much *joy*. They didn't care who it was about, or that its love story had ultimately fallen apart, or even that it was pretty queer, if you knew what to listen for. Renee could tell that the girls would love this song forever. They'd listen to it when they ached over a crush or fell in love or got their hearts broken. They'd remember the ecstatic belonging they felt right now, dancing in their party dresses with their best friends. They might even play it for their own little girls one day.

The song would always be Renee's—after all, she could play back memories of almost every scene Lola referenced in her lyrics—but it was *theirs* now too.

As "Starcrossed" wound down, Renee realized she really did have those recordings. She'd filmed almost all the moments that Lola had included in the lyrics.

Once Renee had imagined it, she couldn't get it out of her mind. She knew exactly how the fragments of footage would piece together. She'd surrendered the hard drives with the film's official footage back in L.A., but she'd backed up a lot of it on her own drive as a precaution, plus she had everything she'd shot on her phone or her own camera.

In her car after the party, Renee checked if there was a music video for "Starcrossed" with a knot of dread in her stomach. Thankfully, there wasn't. Renee couldn't handle seeing their love story played out by anyone else. But her search turned up a few results she didn't expect, from Lo-Lites up in arms about the song.

Queer Lo-Lites.

Renee felt hot all over as she read the posts. The song's lyrics were too queer-coded to have registered with mainstream homophobes, but the sapphics had caught every reference. One person said it sounded like a Mad Libs of lesbian stereotypes. But instead of embracing the song, these same fans despised it as gay pandering from a straight artist. If Lola wanted to make queer music, she had to come out, otherwise it was cultural appropriation. Renee didn't think that was how cultural appropriation worked, but the public's lack of media literacy was the least of her concerns.

Renee drove home intoxicated by an emotional cocktail of genuine rage mixed with the burning desire to take Lola in her arms and hold her. After all the speculation and conspiracy theories, Lola's queer fans were rejecting her? Everyone had their own challenges to face when they came out. Queer people *knew* that, yet they dared to act like they were experts on her situation. *They'd* never had to deal with millions of people publicly debating their sexual orientation!

Although, Renee realized as she parked her car, hadn't she herself been guilty of the same thing? She'd dismissed what coming out meant for Lola's business. Seeing the reaction of Lola's queer fans made Renee sick, but she felt sure that Lola had considered this. Lola considered everything. If she hadn't felt comfortable enough to share it with Renee, that was Renee's fault too.

She made it to her room and dropped her gear, morose again. How could she have not understood? She was about to throw herself on her bed and cry, again, but wallowing in self-pity wouldn't make things right with Lola.

At least she could let Lola know she still cared.

Renee dried her eyes and opened her computer.

AT 5 A.M., she attached the finished video to an email and wrote out a brief message, but didn't send it. Lola probably didn't want to hear from her, let alone watch her music video, and if she did, she'd probably think Renee was still trying to pressure her into making the film.

She closed the computer and went to sleep.

When she woke up, it was early afternoon. She watched last night's work. In daylight, it was a little ridiculous. So sweet and sincere and romantic, it was the kind of thing that might play at a wedding while Renee rolled her eyes through the whole thing.

It was the kind of thing Lola loved.

Still, she hesitated. Then her eyes caught on the top right of her screen, on the date.

It was Valentine's Day.

Renee hit send.

40

Lola adjusted her glasses in the Zoom video of herself. There were still a few minutes before Zoe Mitchell joined for her interview, and Lola was nervous.

She realized she'd misplaced her copy of Zoe's resume. Her desk was a mess. The overly designed office she'd once hated had become a command center in the frenetic last few weeks. An extra workstation had been added for Cassidy, and a whiteboard, scribbled with multicolored to-do lists. The designer chairs were stacked with books on queer liberation and nonprofit management and community organizing, with dog-eared pages and sticky notes marking important passages. A Progress Pride flag was tacked up on the wall.

Lola dug through a folder, yanked out the highlighter-covered resume, and reviewed it, as if she hadn't already memorized it. Zoe Mitchell had a master of public administration and ten years of experience at the Houston LGBTQ+ Center. She'd testified before government commissions and organized marches and lobbied against anti-trans bills. On top of all her qualifications, as a trans woman of color, she'd bring perspective and experience to the Star Sign Foundation that Lola could not.

The Star Sign Foundation.

The project was still so new that even thinking the name sent Lola's stomach fluttering. That moment on the plane a few weeks ago had galvanized something in Lola. It was suddenly crystal clear that she had the means to make a difference in people's lives—she'd just been blinded by her own problems. She threw herself into learning—meeting with experts and activists, reading more than she ever had—to figure out how she could best serve the queer community, what was most needed, what voices to listen to and elevate. She'd known the contours of major issues, like violence against trans women, the specific issues faced by queer people of color, the continued lack of legal protections, and the fight to protect trans kids, but now she couldn't believe how superficial she'd allowed her concern to be. This time, she wouldn't be satisfied by writing a check and attending a gala.

Still, she couldn't do it all on her own—and it wouldn't have been right to. Lola knew she was a wealthy, white cis woman who passed for straight so easily she'd done it with the eyes of the world on her for a decade. Also, she was a professional pop star who might know the first thing about running a foundation, but not the second or third. She needed help.

A Black woman with honey-colored hair in glossy waves appeared on the screen.

Lola's face lit up. "Zoe! I'm Lola. Thank you so much for meeting with me."

"I'm excited to hear more about this undertaking." Zoe smiled politely, but she didn't look starstruck or overeager. If anything, she looked skeptical. That was good.

"It's still in the early stages, but I'll take you through what I've planned so far."

Lola explained that she'd earmarked $15 million of her own money and a percentage of her income off the next album in perpetuity for Star Sign. The goal was to supplement those funds with donations from her famous connections. She'd tie Star Sign into every promotion she did for her own work, giving it the kind of attention nonprofits dreamed of. While Lola handled fundraising, Zoe—if she took the job—would oversee programming. So far, Lola decided that the foundation would take a three-pronged approach to supporting the queer community: micro-grants for things like name changes, medical expenses, and emergencies; a legal defense fund; and political lobbying to advocate for legal protections. There was so much still to do, Lola warned. They needed a board and a charter, real office space, employees. Right now, all they had was a web domain. But Lola would do anything to make this work.

"It's ambitious," Zoe said. "I'll admit, I'm intrigued. You don't often get the chance to build something from the ground up. But I have to ask why you're doing this."

Lola hesitated. She hadn't asked Zoe to sign an NDA. If Lola wanted to work with Zoe, she would have to trust her. And if she wanted to come out, she'd have to get used to, well, coming out.

"I'm queer myself," she said. "That's not public knowledge at the moment. Recently, it really clicked for me that I'd been so focused on what coming out means for me personally that I never really considered what it could mean to others. What I could *do* for others."

"Coming out is personal," Zoe offered. "Everyone handles it differently."

Lola smiled graciously. "Thank you for saying that, but for someone in my position, it's not just personal. I have the power to make a difference. I know that representation matters, but I want to do more than, you know, prove that a pop star can be bisexual. I want to actually help people." She adjusted her glasses again, trying to ignore her nerves. "I'm planning to come out soon. I'm trying to find the perfect time. Coordinating it with the launch of the foundation and my new album would really maximize the impact."

Zoe's brow dipped. "People might say you're doing it for attention. For profit."

"To some extent, they'd be right," Lola conceded. "But the money and attention are going to a good cause. Look, I've taken a lot of criticism in my career. I've realized that I simply can't please everyone. People will complain that I didn't come out sooner, and some will be upset that I came out at all. They'll criticize me for having too much privilege, even when I'm trying to use it to make a difference, or say that it's too little too late. But I'd rather try too hard to help my community than not try at all."

Zoe regarded her, unsmiling. Lola's shoulders drooped as the adrenaline of her little speech ebbed. If Zoe didn't want to join her, she'd find someone else. She wouldn't stop. She'd find a way.

Then Zoe nodded, her hair bouncing. "Okay, let's see what we can do together."

Lola found herself babbling with excitement but promised to send over the offer letter that same day.

When she closed Zoom, her email was open behind it.

Lola's breath caught. There was a message from Renee.

The text was short enough that she could read the whole thing in the preview.

> Lo, This is just for us. I couldn't help myself. x Renee

She didn't know what to make of that, but then she saw there was an attachment.

A video.

She opened it. The screen was black at first and then filled with the opening notes of "Starcrossed." Lola held her breath, her teeth tight against her lip as an image of herself appeared on the screen. She was on the beach on Lake Michigan, with her glasses and that windbreaker on, her hair tangling in the wind. The song played as she reached for the camera and then there was Renee—Lola's stomach lurched. Renee looked beautiful, her strong jaw, her messy bleached hair wild in the wind too, her eyes not on the camera, but fixed on Lola behind it. Lola had missed the effect Renee's face had on her—a kind of hunger, insatiable, like Renee was always exactly what she needed. Renee stepped out of frame, and Lola remembered what was coming before she saw it. She flipped the camera around to film them both, Renee's cheek pressed to Lola's temple, her arms circling Lola's middle and holding her tight. They'd been together for two days at that point, and Lola had never seen two people who looked more in love.

Renee had found actual footage of the moments Lola sang about. Renee wearing Lola's shirt on set as she rubbed her shoulders that first day. The pair of them goofy and laughing in her studio, belting out the 4 Non Blondes. Kissing on the couch after Lola had played "Starcrossed" for her.

It was a collection of perfect, private moments, set to the music written for them.

Lola smiled to herself at the second half of Renee's message: *I couldn't help myself.*

Of course she couldn't. Renee couldn't stop making films any more than Lola could leave behind songwriting. Watching Renee's work, now, Lola wished not only that Renee had stayed, but that she'd never stopped filming. In some ways, over these last few weeks, she'd been living out the story that Renee had always wanted to tell. A story Renee had believed Lola was capable of living.

Something locked into place—Lola did know what was right for herself, that she deserved to be happy. She understood now that it wasn't Gloriana, or Ava, or anyone else preventing her from having that. Lola had to be brave enough to make those choices for herself.

She was ready to do that.

Renee had a lot of reasons to be angry at Lola. Lola had lied to her repeatedly about talking to Gloriana. She'd repressed her own fears about coming out, until she'd caved when Gloriana applied the right pressure, although she knew it would hurt the person she loved most. Renee *had* gotten too invested in making Lola's story her thesis, and she'd made a serious error in judgment when she'd gone to talk to Ava—but none of it felt malicious now.

Lola wanted to apologize.

More than that, she wanted Renee back.

* * *

Renee was alone for closing at Prince's, wiping down the counter, when she spotted the Lo-Lite on the sidewalk. Who else would film themselves outside a not-particularly-charming coffee shop during a February cold snap? The weather had scared off all the customers, and Renee had been hoping to get away early. She didn't look up as the door swung open, but instead concentrated on praying this person did not ask about Lola Gray.

"Heads up, we're closing in five," Renee said.

"Okay."

At the sound of that voice, Renee's heart shot to her throat, her fist clenching up on the wet rag in her hand.

"Hi," Lola said. She was wrapped in a puffy coat, her cheeks stung red by the frigid evening.

"What are you doing here?" Renee breathed.

"I was in the mood for a coffee." Then she blushed violently—*god*, Renee loved when she blushed. "Sorry, this probably isn't the moment for a joke."

"I don't know, I've always liked your terrible jokes."

Lola's sheepish smile lit Renee up. "Can we talk?"

"Sure." Renee hurried to lock the door as her internal systems moved to high alert. "Wouldn't want one of your fans to interrupt us, ha ha." She actually said *ha ha*. "We get them in here all the time."

This was her chance to say all the things she'd been imagining she'd say to Lola—the apologies, the confessions of everlasting love—and she was talking about Lo-Lites?

"You don't have to be nervous," Lola said.

"I'm not nervous," said Renee, who was screamingly nervous. She took a few steps toward Lola, that stupid wet rag still in her hands. She flung it behind the counter, where it landed with a smack on the floor. "Okay, I'm a little nervous."

"I got your video."

Renee's stomach twisted. She'd sent the video two days ago, and Lola hadn't responded. "I'm sorry if that was too much. It felt like what the song needed, you know? It wasn't meant to be the official music video or anything. It was just for you. For us."

"It was perfect. It was everything I wanted."

Lola's big brown eyes were round and shining. *She* was everything Renee wanted, and so close. Renee could have reached out and touched her, but the space between them felt as huge as the last three months.

"God, Lo, I'm so sorry." Her voice had already broken. "I did so many things wrong. I never should have pressured you on the—on your privacy and putting it in the film. I really thought I was being supportive, but I can see now that it didn't feel that way. I was so stressed about my thesis, which is completely stupid because I actually dropped out of school and I'm a lot happier now. I should never have talked to Ava without your permission. That was so fucking stupid. I've been *so fucking stupid*.

"But the stupidest thing, the thing I regret the most, is walking out on you. I was really hurt and I didn't know how to handle it, so I just left. That wasn't fair. I'm not asking you to forgive me, Lo. Well, I kind of am, because this is an apology—but I understand if you can't."

Renee's heart raced from so much blathering, but Lola was staring at her with her eyes wide. "Fuck, that was a terrible apology. I've been thinking about that for weeks, and it came out *awful*."

"I'm the one who should be apologizing. I wasn't sure if you'd want to talk to me."

Renee didn't mean to laugh again, but that was just ridiculous. "Lo, you're the only person I want to talk to."

"Me too," Lola said, her voice soft. She took a few steps closer to Renee. "The last few months, so much has happened—good things—but it all feels hollow without you. I have a lot of regrets too. I didn't trust you when I should have. I was having second thoughts about coming out. I see now that that's normal, but at the time, I thought I'd be disappointing you if I was honest—"

Renee's feet moved without her thinking, closing the rest of the space between them. "No! Lo, never. That's your decision."

"You were right! I wasn't happy and you saw that. You told me I could change, but I wasn't ready to accept that advice. And I had people in my life who I trusted, who wanted things to stay how they were."

"Gloriana."

"I let her convince me that you were the problem, when you were so far from it. I should never have told her we wouldn't be seen together."

"You were trying to protect us," Renee said.

Lola shook her head. "Don't make it sound kinder than it was. I was trying to protect myself. After you left, I thought about shelving the album, but I couldn't bring myself to do it."

"Yeah, because those songs are fucking *good*."

Lola's eyes flashed. "I know. I wanted to release 'Starcrossed' anyway, but Gloriana wouldn't let that happen. She told me the label needed me to rewrite the lyrics."

Renee's chest swelled. "She came for your *music*?"

"That's not all. Gloriana admitted to sending that photographer after us in Petoskey. She didn't like *who I was becoming with you*."

Renee felt sick for Lola. Gloriana was like a second mother to her. That kind of betrayal *hurt*. She wanted to take Lola in her arms and hold her close, but instead she said, "Do you want me to murder her? I've never done that before, but I think I could pull it off."

Lola laughed. "I fired her, which is the next best thing. My new management supports me coming out whenever I decide to."

As Lola said this, Renee's phone rattled against the counter. Renee ignored it, but a little smirk appeared on Lola's face.

"I saw the reaction to 'Starcrossed,'" Renee said. "I know the gays can eat their own, but I never thought they'd be so cruel. Like, I thought the conservatives would hate it—"

"Oh, they do," Lola said. "You're just not on that part of the internet."

"But the queers should have loved it and they're dragging you like their lives depend on it. You don't owe them anything, you know that, right?"

"I don't know," Lola said. "They're right to be mad that I've been having it both ways. I haven't even been a good ally, let alone a good queer person."

"You don't have to be a *good queer person*," Renee snorted. "It's enough just to be yourself."

Renee's phone buzzed again. Renee grabbed for it. "Sorry, that's so annoying."

But then she looked at the screen. It was filled with texts from Kadijah.

Did you see lola came out?

Omg I think she's At PRINCES????

Omg are you there?

This is so romantic I'm literally dying!!!

Renee gazed up at Lola, her mouth hanging open. "Lo, what did you do?"

Lola was beaming back at her, a huge, satisfied smile. "I just made a post from outside."

Renee's thumb was trembling as she navigated to Lola's Instagram. There was a video there of Lola standing outside Prince's, her breath steaming in the bitter cold.

"*I'm back in my hometown for a few days and there's something I want to tell you. I've been keeping this to myself for a long time, because it felt like there was never the perfect time to share it. But I've realized that the perfect time is one you choose for yourself. The big secret is that I'm queer. I'm bisexual, and I always have been.*" In the video, Lola paused and looked away from the camera as emotion passed over her face and resolved into a smile. "*It feels so, so good to finally say that. So, yeah, that's it. Love you all.*"

Renee stared at her phone, slack-jawed with shock, as the video looped.

"Can you stop playing that?" Lola said. "I love listening to myself talk too, but..."

"Wait, so you just—" Renee asked, baffled, as she silenced the video. "Like just now—outside? No parade?"

"I got tired of waiting for the parade planners to get their act together," Lola said, grinning.

This time, Renee didn't stop herself. She circled her arms around Lola's waist and drew her in. Even in her huge parka, Lola's body still fit against hers like it belonged there.

"How do you feel?" she asked.

The look on Lola's face was something like happiness, but she wasn't smiling. Her eyes were shining, her lips parted. She looked, Renee realized, relieved.

"Incredible. Terrified. I waited too long to do that."

"You didn't have to do this for me—" Renee moved to step back but Lola clung to her apron.

"I didn't do it for you! I did it because this is what *I want*. I've spent years trying to find the right time and what I want has only ever been an afterthought. It's not only Gloriana, or my career. *I* let that happen. I'm not doing it anymore. This is the right time for me, Renee, because I want to walk out of here holding your hand. *I* want that."

"Lo, I don't know what to say," Renee said softly.

Lola released Renee, straightened her parka, and adopted a serious expression.

"I love you, Renee. You saw something in me that I had stopped seeing in myself. Before this summer, it was like I'd forgotten who I was. You helped me remember. I know I'll have to work to be the best partner for you. I wish I could say I have it all figured out, but I don't. But I promise to be honest, even when it's hard, and that I'll put us first, if you give me a chance."

Renee looked down at Lola, her warm, hopeful eyes and the smile playing on those Cupid's bow lips. She had known that face her whole life, and yet never wanted to stop rediscovering Lola. No matter how long they were together, she knew she never would.

"Do you remember when I told you I loved you, I said I'd never expected to say that to anyone?" Renee said, her voice thick. "At the time, I didn't realize why. I couldn't see how scared I was. I was trying so hard to avoid being hurt that I closed myself off from a lot of things. But I was hurting the people I cared about. I hurt you. You made me realize that risking my heart is worth it. As hard as the last few months have been, as scary as it was to let you in, I would do all of it again for the chance to love you."

Tears were shining in Lola's eyes. "If you don't take me back now, I'm going to be really disappointed."

Renee grabbed for her, pulling Lola in so close their foreheads rested together. "Of course I do. I love you, Lo. And I'm so fucking proud of you."

Lola kissed her. Renee's eyes closed as she slipped into the softness of Lola's lips, the easy opening of her mouth, the warm press of her cheek. It felt like coming home, like forever, like the fluttering in her chest when Lola sang to her.

Still, after a moment, Renee broke the kiss. "We're right in front of the window."

"It doesn't matter now." She could feel Lola smiling against her lips.

"Well, you just posted your location to the entire world, so maybe we could go somewhere private."

Renee kept her arms around Lola as they waited for her driver, alarmed that Lo-Lites would swarm Prince's. They'd probably be packed for months with Lo-Lites on pilgrimage.

Henry greeted Renee with a warm smile as they hopped into the car.

As they pulled away, Lola asked abruptly, "Wait, did you say you quit your MFA?"

"I did. I can't believe I didn't realize sooner that it was killing my love for film. But I'm going to get it back. It's not something I can just stop doing, like you said. I'm planning to move to L.A. and look for gigs once I save up some money."

Lola's face fell. "Does that mean you're not directing anymore? Because I'm looking for someone to finish my documentary."

Renee gaped at her. "I heard it was canceled. The Streamy deadline is in three weeks."

"Gloriana acted like Streamy was going to bankrupt me if we missed the March deadline, but they gave me an extension as soon as I asked. Although it helped that I promised the film would tie in to a major announcement."

"Which you just made," Renee said.

"Actually no." Lola's eyes were sparkling. "There's something else. I'm starting a foundation to support LGBTQ+ people and fight for our rights."

"You are?"

"I figured, I have the money, and I have the star power. I could really make a difference. I'm going to launch all three at once—the foundation, the album, the film. A story with a purpose. What do you think?"

It was like everything had fallen into place. Somehow the universe had set up all the dominos when Renee wasn't looking. The girl she loved, the film she wanted to make, and even more. Renee would have found her way alone. She knew that. But it was so much better to have Lola with her.

She grabbed Lola's hand and planted a soft kiss on her knuckles.

"I think it's perfect."

Epilogue

Five Months Later

Lola and Renee waited in the dark wings of the theater. On the screen, the final moments of *Lola Gray: Starcrossed* played, over a song Lola had written for the film.

But Lola and Renee weren't watching. Instead, Lola's arms were looped around Renee's neck and their eyes were fixed on each other. She pressed her palms to the nape of Renee's neck. It was damp with sweat.

"Can you believe it?" Lola whispered. "We're at your premiere."

Renee was chewing her lip nervously. Even though Lola was filled with effervescent excitement, this was Renee's first premiere, and Lola knew it would feel different, scarier, bigger than everything that came after.

"What if they don't like it?"

"Then they have bad taste," Lola said.

"There are literally professional critics in the audience, Lo, they can't all have bad taste." Renee's eyes wandered toward the screen. The film was in its final moments. It was a shot of her benefit concert at Pride last month. It was the culminating, victorious shot of the film, intercut with flashbacks to the tough moments that came before and shots that promised a brighter, freer future. They had less than a minute before the credits rolled.

"Look at me, Renee."

She did, her green eyes gray in the dark.

Lola slid her hand down to rest against Renee's breastbone. "Take a breath."

Renee's chest expanded against her hand.

"No matter what anyone says, this film is good, and you know it. It's everything we set out to do. Right?"

"Right," Renee said.

"I'm proud as hell of it. Are you?"

"Yeah," she said.

"So if they don't like it, fuck them," Lola said.

"Lo!" Renee was still delighted whenever Lola swore, although she was doing it more often recently—specifically for that reaction. Behind them, the screen went black, and Lola pulled Renee down into a kiss. Her lips were insistent, forceful, and Renee leaned into her, needful of her reassurance. That kiss bore the weight of everything Lola didn't have time to say—I love you, I'm proud of you, be brave—because the applause had started. Lola broke away as the lights came up, and whispered, "If you're nervous, just remember, I'm going to fuck you so good tonight, you probably won't remember this anyway."

Renee gaped at her, disarmed. "The mouth on you now, Jesus."

Lola grinned deviously at Renee, then took her girlfriend's hand and led her out onto the stage.

***

As Renee stepped out before the massive audience, she searched the front rows for Kadijah and Zane, who were screaming their heads off, and for her mom and Dave, clapping like their lives depended on it. A few rows back, her dad was on his feet, but he wasn't clapping. He was crying so hard his girlfriend was trying to force a tissue on him. The applause from up here was deafening.

Renee spotted Nash and his new "girlfriend," Claudia and her husband, Josh—who were celebrating their anniversary that weekend—as well as Tatiana, Cassidy, Alejandro, and other members of the crew. Even Micah was there, and Dragan, who had accepted Renee's invitation despite her no longer being his responsibility, and Zoe, from the foundation, with her partner and child. There were so many people there, so much star power, and they were cheering for them, for Renee and Lola.

Her stomach was starting to go, her palms getting clammy and her throat tight—but Lola was there, right there beside her. She gave Renee a steadying look and squeezed her hand hard, and said into the microphone, "I'm Lola Gray, as I think most of you know."

In spite of everyone else in the theater, Renee didn't want to take her eyes off her. Lola was radiant tonight, and not only from the spotlight. She'd been glowing all day. Being part of Lola's happiness made Renee's heart feel too big for her chest.

"I have the pleasure of introducing the director of *Starcrossed*, Renee Feldman."

Applause surged again as Lola turned and met Renee's gaze. No matter what Lola had promised backstage, Renee was always going to remember exactly how Lola looked at her in that moment.

THE NIGHT WAS a whirlwind. She and Lola both did press—a new experience for Renee, but she could see Lola from the corner of her eye, confident and poised, and tried to embody that. Then Renee joined her while she spoke with some prospective donors to the foundation, and a representative of the City of New York's LGBTQ+ task force about a potential partnership.

The after-party was in full swing by the time they arrived. The plan had been to combine the premiere with the New York City launch for the Star Sign Foundation, which made for an epic party that Streamy had paid for. The donations were rolling in.

Renee spotted Dragan talking with Tatiana and Nash, whose date had wandered off. She could tell from Dragan's body language that he was discoursing. Tatiana and Nash needed rescuing.

"Dragan was giving us some analysis of the movie," Tatiana said in a tone of someone whose patience had been tested by academic pretension. "I loved it, by the way."

"I cried, like, three times," Nash said.

"Only three?" Renee said. Nash had already seen the film. Renee and Lola had given him a private screening to make sure he was okay with how he was represented, which was as Lola's 100 percent heterosexual beard. He'd cried so much Renee had been concerned about dehydration.

"Renee, what you've achieved is very special," Dragan said. "You've taken what could have been a trivial enterprise and found a way to elevate it."

"Lola's story was never trivial," Tatiana said. "It was only a matter of time before she was ready to tell it."

"You're both right," Renee said. "That's why Lola and I say we made this film together. It couldn't have happened without both of us."

"Ugh, that is so *sweet*!" Nash sighed.

Behind him, Renee spotted Kadijah and Lola locked in a very intense hug. Kadijah, champagne flute in their claws, was apologizing for having shipped Lola and Ava. Renee excused herself to intervene.

"That's so sweet of you, Kadijah, but you don't need to do this every time we see each other," Lola was saying as Renee swept in.

"I need you to know that I was wrong!" Kadijah cried, not entirely sober.

Renee patted Kadijah's shoulder. "She gets it, babe."

"I'm not going to apologize for being emotional!" Kadijah insisted. "My best friend just premiered her amazing film!"

"Thanks, Kadijah," Renee said. "I'm going to steal Lo to say hi to my mom."

Deborah nearly suffocated Renee in a hug and showered them both in praise. When Renee had told Deborah that she and Lola were going to make it work, Deborah had been, in her own words, over the moon. Months later, she still hadn't come down to earth. She was as invested in their relationship as any of the obsessive #Rola fans.

"Are your mom and dad here, sweetie?" Deborah asked Lola.

Lola winced. "I actually prefer my parents not come to things like this. It's a lot for them—and me."

Deborah gave a sympathetic look. "Well, can I give you a hug, since your mom's not here to do it?"

Lola nodded, and Deborah squeezed her tight. "I'm so proud of you, Lola. You were already so accomplished, but gosh, look at how you've grown!" She released Lola, but held tight to her hands. "You've always been part of our family. You know that, don't you?"

"Mom, you can't say that now that we're dating," Renee groaned, although it was exceptionally sweet.

"I would say this to her even if you weren't! I watched you and Claudia grow up. If you ever need anything, you can always call me. No matter what."

At the night's end, they were too tired for Lola to make good on her earlier promise. It was all they could do to undress, then crawl into bed in each other's arms.

***

"Lo, wake up," Renee was saying.

Renee was gazing down at her, her hair rumpled. Lola stretched and smiled. "Do we have to get up? I thought we didn't have anything this morning."

"I have a surprise for you."

"You do? Why?"

"It's our anniversary," Renee said.

Lola pushed herself up against the pillows. "No it isn't. It's July. It's Claudia's anniversary—Oh."

Renee leaned into her, pressing Lola back into the down as she kissed along her neck.

"Mmm, is this my surprise?"

"No, we have to get out of bed for that," Renee murmured against her ear.

Lola twisted around to check the time. "But we didn't get home until three last night."

"You can sleep on the plane," Renee said.

Now Lola sat up for real. "The plane? Where are we going?"

"Telling you would ruin the surprise," Renee said. "I packed everything you need. You just have to get dressed."

As LOLA RAN up onto the deck of the lake house, the sky was brilliantly blue, the sun heavy overhead and glittering off the lake. When Lola had last been here, it was nearly winter, everything muted brown and ochre. It looked so alive in the summertime. She'd forgotten how Michigan's northern climate exploded ferociously into vibrant green once the weather turned, desperate for sunshine. The air was thick with humidity and the click and snap of bugs, but still fresh and clean as Lola pulled in a deep breath.

Behind her, she heard Renee on the steps setting their bags down. Lola remembered their first night on this deck; it had felt like the whole universe had aligned to bring them to that kiss—to bring them to all the moments in their story, from the earliest ones, to the years they spent apart, to the night a year ago at Claudia's wedding, to all their stolen glances on the film set. But Lola didn't actually believe in fate—she believed in hard work. She believed in herself, and Renee.

She believed in their love story.

Renee gazed at her, a smile playing on her lips. "It feels good to be back, right?"

Lola pulled Renee toward her and kissed her in the bright, streaming sunlight.

Acknowledgments

The year before I started this project was the worst of my life, and I swore off writing novels for ever and ever. But then, in the midst of a melodramatic bus ride, an idea sprang into my head that seemed like it might be kind of fun. I started outlining it between bouts of tears on the bus, and then between bouts of tears at the airport, where the melodramatic bus ride ended. Things continued to be shitty for a while after that, but writing was indeed fun again. (Also it took me six months to realize there might be a vague parallel between this and Renee's and Lola's creative struggles.) All this to say, a lot of people helped get this thing to publication.

I feel so fortunate to be working with Ariana Sinclair, who has been a great ally for this project and whose suggestions have made it stronger in every way. I'm very grateful to be represented by Allison Hunter, and to have everyone at Trellis on my team, including Natalie Edwards and Allison Malecha. Thank you for your faith in this story and in me. Many thanks as well to Maddalena Cavaciuti, Hannah Smith, and Michael Joseph/Penguin UK, and my other foreign co-agents, publishers, and especially translators. I would not still be in this business were it not for Patrice Caldwell, Trinica Sampson, and Joanna Volpe.

I am grateful to everyone involved in the production of this book, particularly production editor Jessica Rozler; Diahann Sturge-Campbell, who handled the fiddly interior design; and Paul Miele-Herndon, who designed the cover. I am beyond excited to get to work with Kevin Wada on the cover—no one could make my girls look better. Thank you to the team behind the audiobook, especially Hillary Huber and Lauren Fortgang for bringing these characters to life. I'm thankful to be in the capable hands of Jen McGuire and Kelly Cronin for marketing and publicity. I am writing this many months in advance of publication, so I am inevitably missing people, but if you contributed to this book, please know that I appreciate you.

I greatly benefited from phenomenal early readers, including Jordyn Taylor, Jennifer Iacopelli and jek. I'm also very thankful to my sensitivity readers for lending their insights and experience to improve this story.

Numerous people generously shared their knowledge of the entertainment, music, and filmmaking industries with me. I am especially grateful to Thomas Paredes and Maria Luisa Gambale. Thank you to all the friends who ever let me backstage. I know I have taken some liberties with reality, but I did so in the service of making things cute, okay? The opening to the song "Star Sign" is inspired by "80 Windows" by Nada Surf, although it sounds entirely unlike anything Lola would write.

Thank you to the boys for providing me with very specific information about the vegetation of Michigan (sorry that I didn't use any of it—Lola and Renee had bigger things to do than describe local flora), and to Jeff and Nel for taking me to visit areas adjacent to the Traverse City micropolitan area.

Thank you to the hotties at Ginger's for making me feel at home. Everyone should be lucky enough to have a lesbian bar as their local.

Thank you to everyone who welcomed me to North Carolina when I took up residence somewhat against my will and knowing nothing about anything. A&D, I love you. Thank you to my powerlifting family, most of all, Allison, for introducing me to so many new kinds of candy and strength.

My brain would have fallen out of my head completely without Ashraya, Kylie Schachte, and Hillary; thank you for being the best cheerleaders/literary critics/therapists. I am also forever grateful for the support of Erin, Devi, Stephanie, Laura, Amanda, Caroline, Mariel, Jennifer Udden, Bridget Flannery-McCoy, and Andi Bartz.

To my parents and Alissa, I am so glad I have the chance to thank you in one of these things again. Thank you for always believing in me.

Sasha Laurens is the author of *When I Picture You* and the young adult novels *A Wicked Magic* and *Youngblood*. She has a PhD in political science, and she spends her time doing research on authoritarianism, training for powerlifting competitions, and hanging out with her mini dachshund, Kiki.